1 MONTH OF
FREE
READING

at

www.ForgottenBooks.com

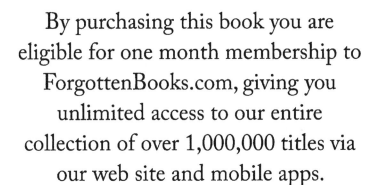

By purchasing this book you are eligible for one month membership to ForgottenBooks.com, giving you unlimited access to our entire collection of over 1,000,000 titles via our web site and mobile apps.

To claim your free month visit:
www.forgottenbooks.com/free79440

ISBN 978-0-483-13723-3
PIBN 10079440

FROM THE EAST UNTO THE WEST

BY

JANE BARLOW

METHUEN & CO.
36 ESSEX STREET, W.C.
LONDON
1898

2142 3,23,16

TO

KATHARINE

CONTENTS

THE EVIL ABENOOYAHS:

A TALE OF THE GREAT RED DESERT

CHAPTER I

THE Eymorrahs lived on the eastern edge of the Dahna, or Great Red Desert, whose hot sands drift over southern Arabia. Their dwelling-place was almost an isolated oasis, but not quite, the tract that stretched behind them to the northward being not absolutely barren, though, for want of cultivation, it could offer the infrequent passer-by nothing better than an occasional draught of brackish water, and a handful of gritty samh-seed or acid musa'a berries. The nearest hamlet was distant three days' journey, the nearest town far more vaguely remote, and before them lay the illimitable desert spread out like a sealess shore.

The little valley which they inhabited was in con-formation a loop, banked in by low sandhills, and narrowing where the curve became sharpest, to a width of a few hundred feet, and this loop encircled a sandy, stony, thorny space, available only for one melancholy purpose—it was the Eymorrahs' burial-ground.

But the valley itself contained accessible earth and water; and, in Arabia, wheresoever nature yields that tribute, there man can generally make good his

A

claim to existence at least, if not dominion. The Eymorrahs sustained theirs successfully enough by means of sundry small patches of maize and millet, grown stuntedly in the shallow soil, some score of date palms, a flock of lop-eared goats, and a few dishevelled-looking fowls. These formed their sole barrier against sheer starvation, and together with their ragged clothes and tents, and primitive domestic paraphernalia, constituted all their worldly wealth. If that animal and vegetable barrier had at any time fortuitously broken down, the ensuing calamity would have been on a quite unpretentious scale, for the Eymorrahs of Wadi Talfook were but an insignificant clan-fragment, numbering not much over forty souls all told. Several generations had passed since they first pitched their camp in its hollow, and definitely abandoned a nomadic life. Evolution, however, is a particularly slow process in and about the desert, and they had not yet substituted more solidly constructed dwellings for their black goat-hair tents.

Only one short step had been taken towards that change in the case of Youssoof, who had at the time we speak of improved upon the general practice of weighing down flapping folds with large stones, by erecting a rough wall on the side of his tent most exposed to the south wind. But the innovation was not viewed with favour; no imitation flattered it, and old Alee was even disposed to trace a connection between it and an unusually high death-rate among that season's chickens.

Old Alee the Conservative and Youssoof the

Radical were both members of a group into which a majority of the Eymorrahs had formed themselves one glowing summer afternoon, their assembly-place being the foot of a charred-looking basaltic rock that rose singly at the north-western end of the valley, its most fertile part, and hence selected for habitation and tillage.

Here the sharply outlined blue shadow had slidden over the slippery parched sod far enough to afford within its precincts ample squatting ground for all probable comers, and during the hours of *Asr*, or late afternoon, it was always a fashionable resort. It must be owned that at a little distance these lords of Wadi Talfook looked uncommonly like a cluster of old beggar-women. The Bedouin garb is rather apt to produce such an impression, soon dispelled, however, on a nearer view of the lithe, sinewy forms and swarthy, keen-eyed visages enveloped and surmounted by the tattered, striped cloaks and wildly wisped-on kerchiefs.

The most outlandish and uncouth figure among them happened to be the only one of the party who had ever come into contact with civilisation. This was Zaif, a man about forty-five, who, born at Wadi Talfook, had roved away from it while still a youth, and had spent twenty years in promiscuous wandering. His adventures were long to tell, and had led him among folk who never saw a grain of desert sand. Once, indeed, he had penetrated as far westward as Constantinople, and had actually twirled in the Derwish *Tekké* of the Grand Rue de Pera, before the gaze of the Personally Conducted. This stage of his career, however, had been of but short duration, and he had eventually strayed back to his birthplace, bringing with him no tangible signs of his intercourse with strange peoples save only his brown Derwish garb.

Changes of raiment being scarce in Wadi Talfook, this was still his wear, and the high, flower-pot-shaped felt cap, now grotesquely distorted and battered, and the flowing mantle, which draped itself in fantastic folds, never contemplated by its fabricator, lent even in that unconventional society a singularly wild aspect to his tall, gaunt form and harshly-hewn features.

But Zaif's absence had wrought in him some mental alterations, the development, probably, of an innate tendency, accelerated by an attack of brain fever with which he had once been visited. Zaif certainly was crazy; certainly, also, he—to paraphrase Chaucer — "seemëd crazier than he was"; the only doubtful point being the limits of this seeming.

For it could not easily be determined how far he belonged to the class of persons who, lured by the respect which ignorance accords to insanity, have more or less deliberately put an antic disposition on, and, finding themselves unable voluntarily to restore the balance of mind which they have voluntarily helped to overthrow, become entangled in their own toils, somewhat after the manner of a Hamlet—with the "parts" left out.

Zaif, it is true, had hitherto met with no great success in this *rôle*. The little community upon which he had quartered himself was too small to furnish materials for any satisfactory flare-up of enthusiastic fanaticism; that needs numbers for kindling as a spark needs tinder. His attempted manifestations of prophetic and other miscellaneous occult powers very commonly proved failures, and though luck and rude jugglery did occasionally secure him a triumph, the Eymorrahs were upon the whole inclined to agree with Youssoof, his sole surviving relative, when he said, "Of a truth it seems to me that you and I see things to come well-nigh as clearly as my nephew Zaif—and without rolling our eyeballs round in their sockets like a live beetle in a bowl of curd."

Be that as it may, Zaif on this afternoon was seated silently, a dumb oracle, among his drowsy neighbours, when down from the opposite sandhills strode Khifaz, a lad who, lad-like, had been there engaged in setting snares for wily sand-foxes and munching musa'a berries, and who now, checking his stately Arab stalk in front of the apathetic group, extended both his arms dramatically and announced, "By the beard of the Prophet—the Evil Abenooyahs!"

In an instant every eye twinkled widely awake, and the news was received with a general groan. The Eymorrahs' feelings may perhaps be best defined as an exaltation of the dismay experienced by the peaceable inhabitants of some secluded British hamlet upon the advent of a large troop of vagrant tinsmiths, with their tottering donkey-carts, and fires under the hedgerow, and ragged children begging along the lane; a dismay, moreover, unmitigated by any reassuring consciousness of a last resort to rural police, and magistrates, and prosecutions at petty sessions.

For the Abenooyahs—dispassionately to drop the adjective — were a small band of nomads, whose temporary sojournings in the vicinity of more settled folk always proved conducive to mysterious disappearances of fowls and kids, unaccountable depletion of date and meal-bags, and general insecurity of all portable property.

They had already made several calls at Wadi Talfook, invariably establishing themselves at the north - eastern extremity of the valley, where the waste cemetery patch intervened between them and the fixed encampment; and although more than two years had elapsed since their last visit, its incidents were still vivid, not to say lurid, in the Eymorrahs' memories.

"Verily, I was about to have foretold you this," averred Zaif, resolving with commendable presence of mind to score something off the untoward hap, "for when I left my tent this morning at daybreak, three straws came fluttering to my feet from the eastward, and never a breath stirring; wherefore I well knew somewhat was on the road hither. And what should come from thence save the Evil Abenooyahs?"

But nobody had leisure, amid hurried question and answer, to heed his belated auguries.

"Where are they?"

"Just now crossing the ridge yonder."

" How many might they be ? "

" There are with them, O Youssoof, ten camels and four horses."

" May the Evil One tarry among them," said Mooscheed bitterly, " I had thought to drive the goats across for pasture this same night, but now the browsings of their accursed beasts will leave neither blade nor shoot."

" One of the camel-beasts," continued Khifaz, " was laden with a great burden of that big yellow fruit, which hath husks like to smooth bowls, and is full of sour water and I know not what besides — such as grew. long ago in Youssoof's field-corner, and crawled upon the ground with stalks and round leaves, till the jerboas gnawed through the stem——"

" Gourds, gourds," someone interrupted impatiently. " And would that they and their gourds were a hundred days' journey hence," everyone else said in a sort of liturgical response, as the assembly rapidly dispersed, some to watch the approach of their unwelcome visitors, and some to afflict with the tidings the womankind in their tents.

The second day after the arrival of the Abenooyahs found the Eymorrahs still deploring that event, albeit the new-comers had as yet done nothing to sustain their evil reputation. An ugly toad of adversity had crept into Wadi Talfook, where only one person inclined to think that he had caught a glimmer of its head-jewel; and this person was old Alee.

" Yes, O Salim," he said to a contemporary crony, as they sat at the tent door towards sundown, " I would give the girl Arelzah to any one of them for the price of two milch camels—not for less. She is useless; I can make my daughters-in-law do all my work; but I am in no wise compelled to any bargaining. Long have I desired to be a possessor of camels. The ghada bushes yonder, where the strangers' infidel brutes are feeding, would pasture them right well; and fain would I be to see their shadows move upon the sand, and to taste of the cheese of their milk, before I depart hence."

"When we were boys," said old Salim, "I remember my father's father gave his sister to a Sherarat for but three goats, and the brazen pan that is in our tent this day. Where should the Evil Abenooyahs, O Alee, acquire wealth to purchase in such a fashion?"

"Wanderers hither and thither find ways to gain that fall not to our lot. But it is true that many of them have already what wives they need. The young man called Feyzal, however, is still unwed."

"A goodly youth, and walks with the step of a sheikh," observed Salim.

Feyzal, the son of Astar, had within the past twelve months succeeded his father in a quasi-chieftainship over the half-score or so of turbulent spirits who, with their submissive wives and sedate children—an Arab baby is a very solemn thing—were, collectively, the Abenooyahs. Despite his youth, he had been able to retain, and even strengthen, his predecessor's ascendency, aided therein by the advantages of much courage and intelligence, and a remarkably fine physique.

Feyzal, indeed, was stalwart and handsome in a measure seldom co-existent with a purely Bedouin pedigree, and as a matter of fact—though one that he would have indignantly denied—a great-great-grandmother of his had come of Greek ancestors.

"The maiden, too, your granddaughter," old Salim continued meditatively, "is growing up not amiss, as such things are ; straight as an ithel-stem, and hath eyes like a gazelle."

The old man was quite unconscious that while he spoke those gazelle-like eyes were darkening and dilating with terror and trouble ; nor would knowledge of the fact have caused him much concern. For the useless Arelzah, listening there in her grandfather's tent, had never been a person of any consequence from the time when her parents had died of fever in the same week and found a resting-place among the thorny sand-hillocks, and when a general council of elders had debated the expediency of providing the one-month-old girl-child with a similar lodging.

It was Saideekha, Alee's half-sister, who had then given the casting vote against that simple plan by undertaking to bring up the inconvenient orphan, thus conferring a doubtful boon, which its recipient, however, had, when sufficiently brought up, requited with a very unqualified and constant devotion. But in the course of the fifteen years which had since then gone by, Saideekha, widowed, childless, and blind, had herself become fully as superfluous as her *protégée*, so the fact that the latter waited upon her foot and hand, serving as messenger between her dimmed eyes and the shut-out day, is not logically inconsistent with Alee's depreciatory mention of his granddaughter as "useless."

In a society compelled by force of circumstances to look at things from a crudely practical standpoint, indispensableness to a superfluity can bestow no utilitarian status ; and Arelzah, though she could not have expressed herself in such choice philosophical terms, felt ruefully aware of her own social insignificance as she sat glancing uneasily towards the bundle of complicated rags and wrinkles which represented old Saideekha, who was fortunately too hard of hearing to share that discomfortable eavesdropping.

Arelzah had long been familiar with the idea that one of those days her grandfather might, for a consideration, transfer her to the keeping of Ahmet, or Mooscheed, or Suleiman; such a transaction would be a mere matter of course.

But she had never contemplated the possibility of being carried off by a stranger, away from the old life and home, and, worse than all, from poor Saideekha, poor groping Saideekha, to whom nobody spoke kindly, and who was found in the way even in her dark corner.

This prospect was heart-breaking, and Arelzah brooded miserably over it ; her apprehensions gaining strength as during the next day or two she heard a word dropped now and then which seemed to betoken that some negotiations were in progress between her grandparent and the young Evil Abenooyah.

And she was withal utterly helpless and hopeless ;

so much so, that she never even dreamed of protest or entreaty, and only manifested her sentiments by shrinking silently away, like a scared dumb creature, when, as happened twice or thrice, Feyzal met her and spoke a word to her going or coming with her water pitchers; and, as conversational brilliancy is not deemed by any means an essential accomplishment for a Bedouin maiden, the little demonstration was, it may be feared, wholly ineffective.

Her dejection, however, drew no comments from her neighbours, being, indeed, unnoticed by anybody except Zaif, whose wits were sometimes not less alert than erratic. But during the days immediately following the arrival of the Abenooyahs, his attention was mainly engrossed by a matter apparently not at all connected with Arelzah's affairs.

From the first moment when he had watched the ill-favoured, splay-footed camel lurching along between festooned clusters of golden-hued gourds, which were afterwards carefully stowed away in the young Feyzal's tent, Zaif had been busily speculating upon the import of that unusual load. He had at once taken it into his head that some mystery attached thereto.

"The evil folk must have carried them from beyond Bir-el-Sila," he argued, "for the like grow not nearer our Wadi; and, I ask, with what purpose? They are of a kind that would yield but sorry eating, even if the sun-blaze burning so long upon them should not have shrivelled the pulp within them into nought else than unsavoury seeds. By the moon of Ramazan they had to me an aspect of overripeness. Moreover, the Abenooyahs—ill be their lot —have eaten not of them, else would the rind lie strewn around. Then to what end be they stored in the young man's dwelling?"

As he secretly pondered upon the subject, Zaif's curiosity became hourly more poignant, while his suspicion of some marvellous mystery hardened into an *idée fixe*; and, in hopes of assuaging the one by justifying the other, he availed himself of his recognised character for eccentricity often to visit the Abenooyah encampment, which his tribesmen scrupulously avoided.

CHAPTER II

ONE morning, about a week after the invasion of Wadi Talfook, Zaif met Arelzah at the well, and entered into conversation with her. Arelzah had always found the unkempt-looking ex-Derwish friendlily disposed towards her, and in her forlorn childhood he had shown her some small kindnesses which she still gratefully remembered, and which led her to take the most favourable view of his disputed claims to supernatural gifts. So she now listened respectfully for what he might have to say.

"Arelzah," he began abruptly, "you have not laughed once in these five days, and you speak no word to the other women, and every morning I see your great eyes grown sadder and deeper, as if they looked out into darkness beyond the daylight. And," he added, after a short pause, during which Arelzah merely hung her head, and twirled her pitcher nervously, "I know well why you are thus troubled in your mind."

"How can that be, O Zaif?" said the girl in a low tone.

"You are grieved," quoth Zaif authoritatively, "because old Alee gives you in marriage to the young man Feyzal, and you list not to leave Wadi Talfook for ever, and dwell among the Evil Abenooyahs."

13

"Ah, Zaif," Arelzah cried aghast, "who has told you?   Is it surely so to be?"

"By the nine Fountains of the Sagacious, most assuredly so," asseverated Zaif, drawing more upon his imagination than his knowledge of the facts. "The whole matter was agreed on last night.   The young man pays down for you more coins than you can count.   The blessing of the Merciful must of late have rested upon his robberies.   And when the Evil Abenooyahs presently depart from hence— misfortune be in their road—you likewise shall go with them."

"What shall I do?   Oh, what shall I do?" exclaimed Arelzah, dropping her pitcher and glancing fearfully around into the unsympathetic sunshine as if with some wild idea of immediate flight, abandoning which, no more rational resource presented itself to her than to begin to cry very bitterly.

"Nay, now, Arelzah," Zaif said encouragingly, "do you forget that where Zaif is, strange things are apt to happen?   I tell you, girl, that if I pleased I could turn this wealthy Feyzal into a poor, pitiable man, owning not the price of a lame kid, much less of a wife, and then there need be little fear but that you should tarry on in Wadi Talfook."

Arelzah looked up with a hopeful gleam from beneath long wet lashes, and he continued—

"But if that is to be so, you must be most heedful to keep silence when I bid you, and to do what I bid you—must obey me in word and deed, lest I know not what untold wrath and destruction should light upon you.   For your help will be needed in the affair. The lion may learn from the carrion crow when the caravan is on its way."

Arelzah remained silent for a few moments, not, however, in the least affronted by this uncomplimentary little apologue. Then she said earnestly: " I will do whatever you bid me, O Zaif, if you will not let me be taken away. That I cannot bear to think of. It is not that the young man is hateful to me; he speaks softly and looks kindly. But I can never leave the old Saideekha. What good would her life do her if I were gone? They would give her the burnt crusts and the withered dates, and I would not be at hand to steal for her. Who would lead her out to sit in the breeze at sundown? She would speak in the darkness, and no one would answer her. Nay, how can I tell what might befal her? For I have heard Alee's daughters-in-law say that it is time she learned the road to her grave. Zaif, I will verily do whatsoever you bid me, even if it be to visit the Well of Ghouls by night."

" Good," said Zaif, well satisfied, " then hold your peace now, and before noon you shall hear what you must do. It is a plan that can by no means fail."

But who can tell what a day shall bring forth? Even a seer may meet something to upset all his calculations.

Wadi Talfook was to be upon the morrow the scene of a sumptuous banquet, at which the residents were to entertain their interloping visitors. For although relations between them were undeniably strained, an amicable semblance was to some extent kept up, while the rarely occurring pretext for a feast proved a powerful peacemaker. On this occasion the Eymorrahs' standing dish of goat's flesh had been supplemented by the Abenooyahs with a sack of wheat flour, so that the bill of fare assumed a peculiarly *recherché* aspect, and the preparations began over-night amid much enthusiasm.

But a gloom was all at once cast upon the proceedings by an unlooked-for fatality. The sun had scarcely risen upon the morning of the feast day, when Youssoof, whose tent Zaif shared, electrified the community by rushing out with the news that his nephew was lying stone dead on his camel-hair mat. The truth of the statement was forthwith verified by an in-crowding of eager eye-witnesses. There could be no doubt of it; Zaif lay stiff and stark, and since sudden natural deaths are very infrequent among these nomads, this one was regarded as a tardy and ill-timed attestation of the dead man's abnormal character.

Still, however melancholy the event, it could by no means be permitted to interfere with the imminent festivities, the main materials for which were already awaiting the seething-pots. The Eymorrahs' funeral ceremonies were, luckily, at all times curt and inelaborate, so that poor Zaif's obsequies could now be got through very expeditiously without seriously maimed rites.

A shallow scooping out of hot sand, a scanty oversprinkling of the same—why throw unnecessary difficulties in the way of the great white expectant vulture?—were all that was needed for the disposal of his corpse, clad in his wonted garb, minus the high felt cap, which, Mrs Youssoof thriftily remarked, would be handy for holding spare tent pegs.

A few of the women, it is true, thought fit to mark the completion of the interment by setting up a forced and perfunctory howl; but one of them being roughly cut short by her lord with an injunction to hurry home and finish her baking, the others took the hint, and the dreary patch was soon left to solitude.

It remained so for a considerable time, and the scorching sun was nearly two hours past his zenith, when a figure came over the western sand-ridge with its crest of three thorny talh-trees; it was the girl Arelzah. By this time the banquet was in full swing at the Eymorrah settlement, whither all the Abenooyahs, babies in arms not omitted, had repaired, and where squatting groups were gathered round the steaming pots, in which somebody ever and anon too precipitately scalded the tips of his fingers, and notified the accident by a limber-wristed flapping of long brown hands, slightly suggesting the wing-beats of some hovering bird of prey.

Arelzah was quite aware of this, having a few minutes before surreptitiously conveyed to old Saideekha's corner a tolerably intact joint of stewed kid; yet she paused, and gazed cautiously in every direction ere venturing on further progress. Nothing, however, was astir, except two or three shrivelled-looking lizards slipping in and out among the rock-chinks, and a scared jerboa jumping away with the gait of a fairified kangaroo; so she quickly crossed the waste ground towards Zaif's newly-made grave.

Standing beside it she once more glanced furtively

B

around, and then gave a low call, which was immediately followed by a sort of working below the surface, such as might have betokened the burrowing up of a concealed scorpion, but which very soon resulted in the emergence of a dark, lean, wildly-clutching hand, and in another moment the tall form of Zaif, successful feigner of cataleptic trance, had risen to its feet, and he stood in the sunshine blinking his dazzled eyes, and shaking the sand out of his matted locks.

"Truly, girl, I thought some folly had hindered you from coming at all," he said grumblingly. "Oof, woof—my tongue is like dressed leather for thirst. But now, since all are away, we have no time to lose," and he began to stride towards the Abenooyahs' quarters with long steps that made Arelzah run.

In the deserted camp, where no sounds were heard save the uncouth grunting of the camels tethered close by, Zaif made at once for Feyzal's tent, and there his first act was to gulp down a great draught from a convenient water-skin; his next to pull off a dingy blackish rug, which covered a symmetrical pile of yellow gourds.

"Listen, Arelzah, listen," he said in an excited whisper, taking up the topmost gourd and shaking it gently. "Do you hear aught?" As he shook it a faint jingle was distinctly audible. "Ay, by the Prophet, girl," he went on breathlessly, "ever since the day when I contrived to slip in here and move one of these, and heard it go tinkle, tinkle, like the bells on a dancer's ankles, I vowed that I would see, too, and handle, come what might of it—and now look—look Arelzah." He ran the point of his dagger-like knife along the suture of the gourd, which presently parted in two, showing that its hollowed-out rind enclosed several finely wrought armlets and a filigree chain—all of shining gold. "There, Arelzah," gasped Zaif, whose eyes were begining to roll very fast. "This is the treasure of the Evil Abenooyahs. These are the wherewithal young Feyzal purposes to buy you of old Alee, and bear you away into the wilderness. But trust Zaif, they shall be far enough beyond his reach before he has made an end of gorging himself yonder. Give me two days' start, and he need never think to overtake me, not if his accursed mare were thrice as fleet." Several other gourds being opened, disclosed similar, or even more valuable contents. For besides jewels of silver and jewels of gold, there were bubbles of moonlit foam from the pearl fisheries of Bedaa, and many precious stones, which, though still rough and unpolished, emitted rich and wondrous gleams. It was, in truth, a very compactly opulent hoard, the history of its amassment long, intricate, and often grim, though the tragical circumstances under which it had come into the possession of the Abenooyahs can be related briefly enough. The small party of traders, who were convoying it from Bahhola to Soor, had perished in an overwhelming simoom at no great distance from the former place, and the Abenooyahs, shortly afterwards roaming by, had reaped the harvest of that ill wind.

To Feyzal's invention, mothered by the necessity of crossing a desert tract much infested with predatory bands on the lookout for passing pilgrims and merchants, was due the device of concealing their booty in the innocent-seeming gourds, deftly split, hollowed and joined again with strong tragacanth gum.

This stratagem had hitherto answered so well that they had determined upon using it until their arrival at Hofhoof, their ultimate destination ; but now, at an apparently unperilous halting-place, it had been seen through by the unsuspected acuteness of the half-crazy Eymorrah.

He, meanwhile, was gathering up his spoil with tremulously eager hands.

"Go, Arelzah," he said, "look warily around, and bring me hither the most tractable of their camels ; the grey one, mind you, with the jagged ears and red saddle-cloth—however, in sooth, any of the others will but bite you if you go within reach."

During her absence he rapidly stowed away his treasures, coiling long chains round his neck and far up his lean arms, lapping up bracelets and anklets and jewelled clasps in the many folds of his voluminous mantle, and putting most of the precious stones into a half-empty meal-bag, which lay opportunely to hand.

Then he replaced the rug over the plundered gourds, and his preparations were complete when Arelzah returned leading the reluctant, vindictive-visaged Father of Job. Zaif attached meal-bag and water-skin to the saddle, and clambered into his seat.

"Farewell, girl," he said, as he endeavoured with prods and thumps to stir up his kneeling beast. "Make your mind easy; I have left the young man nought but empty rinds, which, be sure, old Alee knows better than to take in payment for aught he seeks to sell."

"And you, O Zaif," said Arelzah, rather wistfully, for she had but few friends, "will you never return to us again?"

"Not I, assuredly. What forsooth should I be doing with these riches in little Wadi Talfook? Why, I shall be as a prince even among the wealthy merchants of the great cities. Nay, nay, farewell, Arelzah, you will behold Zaif no more."

As the sullen camel reared itself up with dislocating heaves and jerks, a small silver bangle was shaken out of the richly-fraught cloak, and fell at Arelzah's feet—a pretty trinket of trivial value.

"Keep it, girl, keep it, in the name of Good Luck," exclaimed Zaif, whose glittering eyes were by this time rolling as they used to do when he span in the Derwish *Tekké*. "But let no one see it—for your own sake. As for me, I shall have passed the Well of Ghouls—Inshallah—before nightfall, and on the morrow I may be at Wadi Skirh. Hold your peace for three days, Arelzah, and then you may say what you will, for all it concerns me; but if you are wise, you will tell them nought. Farewell, dark-eyed one."

His camel shuffled off at a shambling trot, and Arelzah stood to watch the strange figure ride away eastward, with a grotesque shadow gliding before, the long cloak bulging against the breeze, and the fierce sunbeams beating on the bare, elf-locked head. Then she turned and stole noiselessly back to the Eymorrahs' tents.

CHAPTER III

O N the morning after the feast, which had been prolonged far into the full moonlight, neither Eymorrahs nor Abenooyahs were very early astir. The first to leave his tent was Feyzal, whose slumbers were abridged by his desire to follow up some gazelle tracks, which had been observed at a low rock-ridge about an hour's camel-march into the desert. He intended to ride thither on his beloved grey mare, whom he found grazing among the ghada-bushes at a little distance, and began to groom *con amore* as a preliminary to the expedition, which he had not spoken of to his comrades, knowing well that his shy quarry might best be hunted single-handed.

His movements, however, did not elude notice. On the contrary, they were watched by two pair of sharp eyes, made wakeful through a passion more potent than love—even of sport. Mesharee and Jad, father and son, had viewed with deep-rooted, though undivulged, jealousy the assumption by young Feyzal of the deceased Astar's predominance among the Abenooyahs, and their jealousy had reached the not uncommon phase of a firm belief in the moral deformity of its object, accompanied by an ardent desire to unearth and set in the clearest light the sins which, so unblessed being his disposition, he must inevitably have committed.

22

Ever since the finding of the treasure, Feyzal's custodianship of it had formed an obvious centre round which suspicions could freely revolve. Who could tell but that he might some night give them the slip, and gallop off with it all to where they should never hear more of so much as a pearl or an earring?

And now at Wadi Talfook, the matrimonial negotiations which were known to be proceeding between Feyzal and the old Eymorrah Alee, opened a new channel for sinister surmises. For, again, who could tell but that Feyzal might secretly hand over to the old man valuables to the amount of the stipulated purchase - money, and yet afterwards, when it came to the final decision, claim his full share, as if he had made away with nothing?

In short, it certainly behoved them to keep a strict lookout, assuring themselves from time to time by ocular demonstration that the gourds were still untampered with; and here Feyzal's early exit seemed to offer a favourable opportunity for taking this precaution. As soon, therefore, as he was safely round the corner, Mesharee and Jad walked boldly into his tent, and in another moment became aware that their suspicions had been only too well grounded.

Zaif in his headlong haste had merely paused to fling the rug back over the tumbled heap, without attempting to rearrange the sundered rinds, so that the first glance revealed the condition of the rifled gourds; and the alarm raised by father and

son brought forth in confusion the sleepy occupants
of the surrounding tents, who promptly shook off
dull sloth as they listened while the discoverers of
the crime declared with authority, as beseemed them,
their views upon the situation.

Doubtless the perfidious Feyzal had hidden away
the treasure in some secret place, whither he had
now repaired with the purpose of securing it and
taking flight, while he believed his defrauded tribesmen to be still lapt in unsuspecting slumber. But,
if so, he could not yet have got off; his design
might even now be frustrated, the theft recovered,
and vengeance wreaked.

Whereupon, helter-skelter went everybody in the
direction which the miscreant had taken, only two
or three hastening towards the Eymorrahs' camp
to ascertain whether anyone had haply departed
thence, and to look out for traces of possible con-
federates.

Thus it came to pass that just as Feyzal, ready to
mount in very good spirits, had put a hand on his
Hamdanee's satin-glossed shoulder, he suddenly
found himself encompassed by a troop of what
a few hours earlier had been friends, or at least
inoffensive familiars, but who now shouted almost
inarticulate abuse at him, glared with bale-flashing
eyes upon him, and gesticulated towards him with
a violence which seemed likely soon to overstep the
bounds of menace.

Their wrathful railing was so incoherent, that he
gained no clear apprehension of what had occurred
until he had been hustled back into his tent, where

the sight of the scattered gourds at once explained the nature of the case.

Nor was he slow in perceiving that it bid fair to prove an extremely serious one for him. The Abenooyahs' moral code was, no doubt, not free from what some ethical systems would regard as grave defects; but upon many points its rulings had the merit of a most rigid inflexibility; and the penal code therein followed suit. One of these points concerned the offence of *theft from comrades*. This violation of an old principle of honour was an act of high treason, an unpardonable sin; and its penalty was death without benefit of anything whatever — not even of a preliminary month in the condemned cell. But their mode of conducting trials also left, according to our ideas, much to be desired; for our beautifully simple law of evidence was persistently ignored, while the functions of judge, counsel, witness, and executioner were jumbled up in a manner well calculated to make the bench's hair bristle beneath its most ponderous wig.

Feyzal saw plainly that on the present occasion the opinion of all these officials was strongly adverse to him. Appearances were certainly against him, and in the case of another person he would probably have himself demanded, or at any rate — for Feyzal's disposition was not bloodthirsty — have acquiesced in, a summary conviction.

His indignant repudiation of the charge evidently made no impression, and, upon the whole, he thought he had better prepare to meet the worst. He was

therefore considering, with his fingers on the hilt of
his finely-engraved short sword, that if he had any
luck he might be able to despatch the malicious Jad,
and possibly Mesharee likewise, before his own
quietus was made for him, when a small tumult
began about the doorway, through which came the
two scouts, dragging between them Arelzah, and
followed by Alee, Youssoof, and a few other
Eymorrahs.

Arelzah's bangle had betrayed her—her bangle,
unintentionally aided by old Saideekha, who was
at this moment huddled miserably in her dark corner,
aquake with dimly understood dread. For Arelzah,
whose possessions were but scanty, had been quite
unable to resist her longing to take another look
at her newly-acquired ornament by the light of the
first beams that slanted in through the tent chinks;
and she had even ventured to slip the trinket round
her slender brown wrist, secure in the knowledge
that only Saideekha was by—not to see.

Nobody could have foretold that the old woman
would suddenly lay a hand upon the girl's arm,
and with her blind touch discerning the unfami-
liar embossment of the bangle's ends, exclaim,
"Eh, eh, Arelzah, where got you this fine new
bracelet?"

But this is exactly what did happen, and although
Arelzah hushed her at once, the exclamation had
caught the adjacent ears of Alee's daughter-in-law,
who pounced upon the unlucky ornament, and was
exhibiting it to all the other inmates of the tent,
at the very juncture when it was entered by the

Abenooyahs' emissaries, come thither straight as to the abode of the most venerable Eymorrah.

Naturally there ensued a scene of stern questioning and furious objurgations on the one hand, met by terrified silence and futile denial on the other, which ended in Arelzah's being haled to the other camp, amid only faint protests from her tribe, willing enough that she should become a scapegoat, were such needed, to avert the wrath of these Evil Abenooyahs, fewer, indeed, but fiercer and better armed than themselves.

In Feyzal's tent poor Arelzah found herself confronted with more darkly scowling brows, assailed by more angry demands and accusations; and, amid her dismayed bewilderment, could cling fast to but one clear fact—that she had promised Zaif not to tell.

"Courage, maiden, courage!" said a kindly-sounding voice, as she stood forlornly trembling. "Inshallah, it will be seen that you know as little about the matter as I do myself." She looked with a thrill of comfort towards the speaker, and saw that it was no other than Feyzal, the first cause of all her trouble, yet who in his unique friendliness seemed to her like a sort of splendid guardian angel—one, it must be owned, who wore upon his head a rather dirty white handkerchief, tied on with a black string, and just now accidentally twitched somewhat awry; but circumstances did not favour hypercriticism.

Feyzal's speech was greeted with a derisive howl. "Nay, forsooth, as little as *you* know, and yet, by the stones of Mecca, O Thievish One, she may know all that we seek to hear; as hear we shall, and that speedily."

"As little, then, as the dead who was buried yesternoon," said Feyzal, amending his phrase with an unconscious irony worthy of a Greek play. Thereupon Arelzah's heart sunk again lower than ever. So this Feyzal, who alone seemed disposed to befriend her, was himself deemed guilty—how unjustly she best knew—and stood, like her, in danger of those terrible, swiftly-sliding daggers and knives.

Then she had not only refused him a civil word, and afterwards helped to rob him, but was also to be the means of encompassing his death. Here was a reason, over and above the chance of saving herself, for breaking her promise and speaking out. The empty grave would sufficiently attest the truth of her strange story; and, after all, Zaif might have had start enough to escape in spite of her betrayal.

A desperate and truly tragical conflict went on in the girl's mind before she resolved to keep silence, come what might. Zaif had assured her that he essayed the enterprise solely on her behalf, and albeit his subsequent gloating over the treasure had thrown some doubts upon the disinterestedness of his motives, her promise remained an unalterable truth, which rendered it impossible for her to set his enemies upon his track.

Feyzal, Saideekha, her own life, could not so far outweigh her sense of honour.

"Nay," she said, speaking more boldly than she had yet done, though it was in answer to a peremptory command from Mesharee, who, with a hard grip on her shoulder, and three inches of his dagger-blade out of his sheath, looked a very ugly customer. "The young man gave it not to me: he never gave me aught, and he knows nought about the matter. Of a truth, I picked it up off the sand."

A few contemptuous *Ho-ho's* was all the notice vouchsafed to this statement, and Mesharee's fingers twitched ominously.

"And if I did give the trinket to the maiden," interposed Feyzal, anxious at all costs to create a diversion in her favour, "why should she be held to blame? Whence should she learn how I came by it?"

But Arelzah would not permit this self-sacrifice. "You know right well, young man, that you had no concern in it;" she said, "why, then, would you make it seem to be otherwise before these?"

"Hearken to them!" yelled Jad, assuming a mien of ungovernable rage. "Is it not plain that Soth, the spirit of lying, has entered into each of them? It was but yesterday I saw them talking together at the well. Why spend more time in entreating them? Slay them both straightway for the villainous robbers they are; or, at least, slay one of them, that we may have the fewer lies between us and the truth about our unhappy possessions." His proposal was followed by a grim murmur and movement of assent.

"Stay, stay, in the name of the Merciful!" cried Arelzah, in this extremity suddenly bethinking her of Zaif's conditional permission, "If you will but wait awhile I will tell you. I will tell you all—in three days."

"In three days!" shouted Mesharee. "By the beard of the Prophet, she said in three days. Nay, girl, but you shall tell us all in three winks of an eye, or——" He raised his armed hand threateningly, and Arelzah cowered away with a shriek from the poised steely gleam.

At the same instant Feyzal started forward with a quick movement, and was just in time to catch the thrust on his arm; but as he did so, Jad, from behind, stabbed him under the shoulder with his dagger, and there was a heavy fall and a smothered groan.

While these things were happening within the tent, strange sounds, which nobody was at leisure to heed, had begun to be audible without. Now, however, just as Feyzal fell, they waxed so loud and near that they perforce attracted attention.

Someone appeared to be coming rapidly up the valley, uttering wild and terrible cries, which, as they approached, resolved themselves distinctly into shouts of "Sheitan, Sheitan—the Ghouls, the Ghouls, the Ghouls—Sheitan, Sheitan—the Ghouls!"

So fearful was the maniacal voice that three-year-old children who heard it remembered it when their heads were grey, and the womenkind, whom any ordinary disturbance would have brought all agog to their doors, crowded horror-stricken in the innermost recesses of their dwellings, greeting each renewal of the outcry with deprecatory ejaculations.

But the men in Feyzal's tent were not deterred from rushing forth to behold, not many yards distant, a tall grey camel reeling and staggering along, urged on by the frenzied yells of its rider, whose glaring eyes, streaming locks, and fluttering garments, made his aspect harmonise with the wildness of the clamour.

The wearied beast shuffled a few paces farther towards the group, and then abruptly swaying to one side, like a cutter in a squall, collapsed into an amorphous heap upon the ground, flinging down Zaif—for Zaif it was—with a thud which rattled all the chains wound about his arms, while the violence of the concussion shook out of a fold in his sleeve a little pile of wrought gold, that lay glittering in the long rays, and was at once espied by the amazed Abenooyahs as they sped to the rescue.

Amazement, indeed, continued to have a very absolute reign among them, as they gathered, gabbling, around the prostrate form of this most unexpectedly returned traveller, from whom it was very bootless to seek any explanation of his unaccountable proceedings; since motionless, mute, and with an appalling look of terror frozen upon his rigid face, Zaif was lying, and so lay until at sunset he was once more, and finally, deposited in that shallow grave among the sand-hills and thorn-bushes.

For there was no feigning this time about the

seer's demise; and although, as was natural under the circumstances, he was long suspected of "walking" in the vicinity, he did never reappear above the surface.

As touching the events which had led to this failure of his boldly-conceived plot, many wonderful stories became rife among both tribes; but the facts are somewhat as follow.

Zaif had started in a flurry of perilous excitement, which was aggravated by the prolonged glare on his undefended head of the scorching afternoon sunbeams; so that when he reached the ill-reputed Well of Ghouls, his wits, at no time over-steady, were in a state of unusually unstable equilibrium. And here, as the abruptly closing-in dusk overtook him, he was seized by an access of the superstitious fear which always haunts such desolate legend-shadowed spots, but which in his case swelled into an uncontrollable panic, throwing his mind completely off its balance.

Turning his camel's head, he rode, raving, back by the way he had come, firmly believing himself pursued by hosts of djinns and demons, and ever and anon giving vent to his agony in frantic shouts, such as had announced his entrance of Wadi Talfook.

There, as we have seen, his career summarily terminated, whether through heat-apoplexy, sunstroke, or concussion of the brain, it little behoves us to inquire. Certain it was that all his busy, and sometimes injurious, plotting and scheming were ended for ever, and that even-handed Justice had constrained him by his own involuntary action to frustrate his nearly-accomplished design of carrying off the Abenooyahs' hoard.

The truth, as far as she knew it, Arelzah confessed only to Feyzal, who kept her counsel for her; but that was not until after several days, during which it remained doubtful whether the young man would not also require accommodation in the dreary little cemetery.

And when his more serious hurt had ceased to threaten any evil consequences, he still failed to make a complete recovery. For the stab which he had received in the wrist had so disarranged an intricate network of important muscles and nerves that his left hand remained grievously and, as it seemed, permanently crippled. The plan which he now formed during his convalescence was probably suggested to him by this circumstance, life among the Abenooyahs being a mode of existence wherein a man could ill afford to dispense with the use of any of his limbs.

Probably, too, he was in a measure influenced by resentment at his comrades' readiness to hold him guilty of a most disgraceful charge, a bitter feeling not to be entirely allayed by their subsequent manifestations of compunction towards him, and hostile demonstrations against Mesharee and Jad. And it is possible that Arelzah's piteous little story may have had something to do with his resolve.

His plan was that he should take up his abode for good in Wadi Talfook, retaining his tent and his mare, and receiving as his share of the recovered

c

treasure the amount demanded by Alee for his granddaughter's hand, with a little over and above for the purchase of a few agricultural requisites, Feyzal's observations having led him to conclude that the sinking of more wells and industrious tillage would soon render the north-eastern end of the valley as productive as that occupied by the Eymorrahs.

It was a moderate claim on Feyzal's part, as of the rich spoil nothing was now missing, except the precious stones, which Zaif had bestowed in the meal-bag, where nobody thought of looking for them, and where for the present they lay unheeded; and it was conceded with little demur by the Abenooyahs, not altogether loth, perhaps, to be rid of so masterful a comrade.

More objections were raised by the Eymorrahs, who were at first inclined to view with strong disfavour the proposed settlement among them of an Evil Abenooyah. But the prospect of camel's milk cheese, and of a new plantation of date palms, gradually grew attractive enough to shut out their doubts and scruples, and at last even Alee the unenterprising withdrew his opposition.

"It may be," he said, "that the young man purposes to dwell peaceably among us, and in any case he will be but single against a many, and, furthermore, one - handed," added the old Bedouin with a hardly chivalrous chuckle.

In this way it came about that a few days later, Arelzah, feeling as if everything were much too good to be true, stood by Feyzal's side, and watched the slow exodus from Wadi Talfook of the Evil Abenooyahs.

About two years afterwards, old Alee and Youssoof were sitting one fine evening under the shade of a talh tree near Feyzal's tent, which, though still pitched on the site of the Abenooyah's temporary encampment, was encircled with flourishing grain and pasture patches. At the door sat blind Saideekha, placidly plaiting straw, with contentment in every wrinkle; and Feyzal himself leaned against the post, alternately looking out upon his crops, and looking in with a remark to Arelzah, who was mixing flat cakes for supper close by.

Three notable pieces of good luck had befallen him since his domicilement with the Eymorrahs. Of these, the first, chronologically, had been the discovery, soon after the departure of the Abenooyahs, of the precious stones secreted in the meal-bag; a find whereby his wealth was more than trebled. Then, having taken an arduous journey to Bereydah for the purpose of purchasing camels, he accidentally fell in with a travelling Hakeem from Europe, whose curious treatment of his disabled hand had the pleasing effect of restoring it to almost its former serviceableness. Lastly, and most marvellous chance of all, the merchant to whom he disposed of his jewellery and gems was a man of such abnormally tender conscience that he contented himself with a profit upon the transaction of not much more than three hundred per cent., an exercise of forbearance through which Feyzal was enabled to invest not only in four

she-camels, and certain plants and seeds, but also in
sundry agricultural implements, simple and ordinary
enough from a high farmer's point of view, yet
deemed well-nigh uncannily ingenious and effective
by the unsophisticated tillers of Wadi Talfook.

"Good luck alight upon us!" said Youssoof, looking
around him with complacency; "it was a happy day
for the Eymorrahs when Feyzal took up his abode in
Wadi Talfook. Behold the camels, behold the goats,
behold the thickset corn-ears! And all where time
was you might have stepped threescore paces without treading on a single blade!"

But Alee, who was subject to reactionary fits,
under the influence of which he regretted all in-
novations, and took a despondent view of every
form of progress, merely grunted discontentedly in
response.

"And pleasant it is to see young date-palms
springing up," Youssoof continued, noways dis-
couraged; "Khalas, too, every one of them, fruit
wherein, ere the skin be split, you mark the stone
appearing, as if afloat in pure honey."

"They will not come into bearing in my time,"
said Alee with a gloom that argued him devoid of
altruistic sentiment; and indeed the infant plantation towards which Youssoof had pointed, left much
to the eye of faith.

"And hark you to that!" the old man went on
with increasing acerbity, as a faint squeak sounded
from the recesses of Feyzal's tent. "It will not be
long, at this rate, before we shall have as many little
Evil ones as Eymorrahs running about the place;

and that, O Youssoof, say what you may, will be a strange thing in Wadi Talfook."

"But of a truth, O Alee, that also will not come to pass in your day,"—a *consolatio ad hominem*, was Youssoof's reply—"and if it did, it were perchance no such sore misfortune. There be folks ill to deal with in every tribe. What else than an Eymorrah was he who—the Merciful shield us—had well-nigh brought the whole host of djinns and ghouls upon us, save that his soul departed hence suddenly, and set them on another track? Nay, verily, I hold that you did well enough when you wed your granddaughter to young Feyzal, and, furthermore, that we might find in this world—consider, O Alee, the comeliness of those your three camels—worse neighbours than some among the Evil Abenooyahs."

THE PUZZLE OF JARBEK

L IFE seems, as a rule, simple and easy enough
from year's end to year's end, for the few inhabitants of Jarbek, a little valley which, by some
caprice of Nature is covered, not like the surrounding
vast plains with drifts of red sand, but with a deep
black loam, wherein vegetation thrives exceedingly
beneath a fervid sun. The Jarbekians shelter
themselves from its beams in half-a-score of mud-
walled huts, sleekly thatched with dried grass. If
an Irish cabin had its angles all rounded off into
curves, and its eaves drawn down to within a foot
or so of the ground, it would look very like a
Jarbekian dwelling.

In Jarbek fruit may chance to be rather more
plentiful at one season than another, so that
mothers of families sometimes let the children
play at ball with the biggest oranges, and pod
fresh bananas, and smash up fine melons by
the dozen, just for diversion, but sometimes restrict
them to the use of inferior qualities for their
games. This is almost the only measure of economy
ever taken in Jarbek. Why, indeed, should anybody be over-careful? There stand the slender-
shafted date-palms all laden with ponderous clusters
of clear-amber sacs, filled with sheer syrup of
sunshine; there the dark green and purple figs

swell and crack their skins in a profusion scarcely screened by their ample leaves; and the trellis-work of grapes and gourds climbs and creeps in endless intricacy about fields where maize and millet flourish, or where browse long-haired white goats and dust-coloured camels; while, surest pledge of plenty, never-failing springs of cold, delicious water well up among the rocks, with perpetual sobbing and murmuring, as if it fretted for liberty to rush forth and lose itself among the leagues of burning sand. The air that wafts over them to Jarbek is the pure breath of a desert, and keeps this small oasis clear of those miasmatic poison-mists which are often the fine attached to a bountiful soil. So the Jarbekians have little sick-ness to complain of, and seldom require the services of old Quanni, who knows many curious remedies.

Still, trouble does find its way thither now and again, and once it came to the widowed Zella in this wise. Her only son Breð had gone out early with his friend Oldaz, pheasant-shooting. Their shooting was done with slings, and the birds were much less confiding than those that are reared in coops; but it is a favourite and fashionable pastime at Jarbek. And at evening Oldaz returned alone with bad news. Breð had been taken suddenly ill, while a long league from home, and was quite unable to get any farther. "It was the sun knocked him down, good Zella," Oldaz said, "and when he got up, he seemed senseless and erring in his mind. Luckily, this happened just at the Split Rock, and I persuaded him to squeeze himself in at the opening, and lie down in the cool of it, where he would be out of harm's way, till I brought you word. I'd never dare try to get inside it myself, for fear of sticking fast. You know I take up a good bit more room than Breð" —dusky-faced Oldaz was in figure stout and squat —"but you and he that are lean, can slip in flatwise like a couple of melon-seeds. And you might find him a trifle better, or he may by this time be cold and stiff. They that know, know."

Zella said: "Woe's me. And may evil light on everything that flies in feathers," and began to make hasty preparations for setting out.

The place Oldaz spoke of lies perhaps a league to the east of Jarbek, and is marked by a long wedge of red sandstone, which points its thin end towards the sunset. Its southern face is all weathered into hollows and mounded up with sand by the sweep of the prevailing winds. On the northern face, not many paces from the tapering point, there is a narrow, black-looking crevice in the rock, like an enlarged arrow-slit, which forms the straitened entrance to a spacious cavern. So very strait is it, indeed, that a person of Oldaz's proportions might well hesitate to attempt the passage. But Breð, being a spare, long-limbed youth, made it without hindrance.

Having stumbled into the dark, he lay there for what were to him limitless tracts of time; for the fever-demon had seized hold upon him. Raging thirst possessed him, and he had mirage visions of water in a great glimmering pool, with its silvery

rim sliding nearer and nearer to him, but never
coming quite within reach, though he tore his hands
on the stones in grasping after it. At last it did
actually touch his lips, and he drank rapturously,
but it vanished away all too soon, leaving him to
grope and toss and rave as before. However,
at long intervals, it would come back again, cold
and delectable always, whether it tasted sharp, as
if mingled with fruit-juice, or had the bland soft-
ness of milk. Then, all at once, he discovered that
the rim was only the rim of a wooden bowl, which
somebody was holding for him ; and soon after
that the sound of a voice came from far-off through
a mist. And presently he saw a lovely sight—his
mother's face of flexible terra-cotta, full of anxious
wrinkles. So the fever passed away from him, and
he had only to regain his dwindled strength. Zella
plodded to and fro as often as ever she could, with
fresh food and drink for him, her neighbours sometimes lending her a hand. On such occasions,
Oldaz would warn her jestingly against feeding her
son so fat that he would no longer fit the narrow
doorway. Before many days he was so far recovered that it seemed he would be well able to ride
home to Jarbek, and Moum-mando, who owned a
tractable camel, offered the loan of the beast for
that purpose.

They had arranged that Breð should be fetched
in this way on a certain morning ; but when it
came, Moum-mando disappointed them, declining
to send the camel, by reason, he alleged, of some
defects in the trappings, though in reality because

he did not like the feel of the weather. Therefore Zella set off alone to the Split Rock on foot,
bearing as consolation for the detained prisoner,
Breð, an extra fine bunch of grapes, wrapped up in
a couple of large flapping leaves like elephants'
ears, and also Moum-mando's promise to come for
them without fail in the course of the following day.

The Lion moaned softly to himself and grinned
a little, as he padded along under the southern façade
of the Split Rock.   He had come a far journey
across desert from the edge of an outlying jungly
tract, travelling latterly both by daylight and dark,
because he was too hungry to sleep, even at noon-
tide.   Four times had the sun and moon swung
up and down again like fiery gold and frosty silver
balances, since he had dutifully carried home a
gazelle, with its swift feet dangling limp, and the
terror filmed over in its wild eyes.   But then the
eyes of his Lioness had blazed into such a fierce
topaz brilliance of wrath and scorn, when he seemed
disposed to encroach upon the portions of their two
fat cubs, that he really secured only a meagre share
for himself.   And not a living thing had he met
with on his solitary prowl, unless you count a black
speck quivering high up in the skies, like a spider
vibrating at the end of his thread, which represented
a pair of vultures.   So that by this morning he was
a very desperate vagrant.
Just about the time that he reached the Split
Rock, however, something had begun to divert his
attention from his own ravenous famine.   What it

was he did not know; a peculiar sensation of uneasiness, indefinable, yet certainly quite distinct from hunger. Much the same, probably, as the feeling which had made Moum-mando refuse to let his good-tempered Fariet go abroad that morning. It was remarkably sultry and still. An unnatural hush reigned all around, as in the vicinity of a naughty child engaged at surreptitious mischief. Not a breeze stirred, not a cloud crept by; the sun-fire blazed without a flicker in the hard moteless azure. Only low down on the western horizon lay a band of orange light, faded and dim, like a belated remnant of the last sunset.

Yet when the Lion, stepping past a flying buttress of sandstone, came in view of this discoloured margin, he stopped short with one forepaw lifted as suddenly as if a violent blast had met and staggered him. Then he dropped his paw, and stood for a while fixedly gazing. There was nothing apparent to watch except a blur of slate-grey shadow that came rolling up over the edge of the world, and held on an easterly course. One might have supposed it merely a heavily trailing rain-cloud, but not so the Lion, who whined disconcertedly, and swung his tail in agitation. And the Lion was right. Again, one might have considered that whatever menace this gliding shadow did contain, was at any rate still so far distant as to call for no immediate precautions; yet the Lion held himself poised in readiness for taking some instantly active step. And he was right here too. For the vague, dark mass was as incredibly swift in its

motion as a stream of spilt ink shooting across a
white page. Moment by moment it engulfed the
glowing tawny leagues that spread before it, and
it gathered blackness on the way. Its path grew
lurid with mingled mirk and glare, as the fierce
sunshine beat down on it, and showed that it was
no simple aggregation of vapour, but a vast hollow
of gloom with a weltering whirl at its core. And
now could be seen how the smooth floor over which
it slid was flying up at its approach into spinning
spiral swirls, free and fantastic in their motions as if
the solid earth had become possessed by the spirits
of the air. The wild red turmoil, continually pursued
and swallowed up by that sliding tunnel of black
shadow, seemed Day re-creating a fragment of
chaos, with Night hurrying on to muffle it away
out of sight.

Still, the Split Rock had been lying steeped in
unwavering rays, and a feathery grass-plume sprung
from a crevice close beside the Lion had not trembled.
Presently it shook very slightly, and at the same
moment, as if at a signal, the sun ceased to shine
upon it, changing more rapidly than can be told
from a dull scarlet wafer to a spectral green one,
which receded into blank space. The Lion made a
single bound sideways, and crouched behind a pro-
jecting rock. He gathered himself into wonderfully
small compass, and set his face into the angle not
a second too soon. For he had scarcely breathed
again, when he was on an island amid a deadly sea.
Billows of stifling sand hissed over and over the ridge
of rock; hurricane gusts battled with its impassive

bulk, tearing up by their knotted roots the wild
fig-trees and thorn-bushes which crowned it, and
dragging down clattering crashes of loosened stones.
The rage, the roar, seemed irresistible and inter-
minable, but was in fact of very brief duration, and
ended as abruptly as it had begun. Some monstrous
power had clutched at the Split Rock in passing,
and failing at first, did not tarry to renew the attempt.
Calm sunshine was settling down over the place in a
noon-tide hush two minutes after the maddest storm
that had come thither for many a long year had gone
raving by. The Lion uncoiled, and shook himself
like a dog coming out of the water. Then he moaned
again, and grinned a little, and resumed his walk.

Meanwhile Breθ in the sunless cavern had been
spending a long tedious morning without much
inkling of what went on around him. The oppres-
sive atmosphere of the day weighed upon his spirits,
making him languid and incurious: and he was,
moreover, listlessly disappointed at the non-arrival
of the promised camel. The opening into his
chamber was so narrow and beetle-browed that light
and sound made small way in; it looked northward,
too, whereas the brunt of the storm was borne by the
south-western face of the rock. Nevertheless, blasts
howling by, hyena-like, and a movement in the
shadows, as it were the flapping of a sable cloak,
did impress him with a dull sense that something
unusual was in progress, and he said to himself as
he lay half-dozing in his dusky corner, that there
must be wildish weather outside.

He had fallen quite asleep for some little time, when he was suddenly aroused. What awakened him was a burst of strong light flashing into the cave, and he sat up to stare at it in great bewilderment. At the side opposite to the narrow door-slit, there appeared, to his amaze, a large opening in the rock, wide enough to admit an ox, ay, or for that matter a pair of them abreast. It let in a spacious view over the basking desert, and a little flood of sunshine, which streamed to his feet. The fact was, that in this wall of the cavern, a natural gothic archway had time out of mind been filled up and hidden by a mask of wind-driven sand, clotted and compressed, which, stricken by the full fury of the tempest, had cracked across and across, and now flopped down all of a piece, like a flake of ill-blended plaster peeled off a house-front, or of icing off a cake.

But neither this nor any other explanation had yet occurred to Breð, and he sat still astoundedly blinking, when the new doorway was darkened by somebody who stepped in at it. To Breð's confused vision it at first appeared as if a man were standing there brandishing a camel-rope in his hand, and he said to himself that Moum-mando had sent after all. But very speedily did he discern how completely his eyes had deceived him, and the flowing robe became a shaggy mane, and the swinging cord was resolved into the lashing of a tufted tail.

As the Lion came softly pacing forward he lowed rather like a cow, but the low ended in a snarl. It struck Breð as the most unpleasant sound he had

ever heard, and he did not stay to listen. Out at
the little opening he squeezed himself in headlong
haste, and immediately tripping over some loose
stones, came down prone on the sand. His mother
had piled them up in the entrance to keep out foxes
and lizards, the only probable intruders, and the
wind had blown down and scattered them. He had
just regained his footing, with a relieved sense that
he could not possibly be followed, when round the
left-hand corner, a few paces distant, the Lion came
springing upon him, and he had barely time to bolt
in once more by the way he had so hastily come.
The cave indeed, was situated so near the end of
the rock-edge that three bounds would bring the
beast from one entrance to the other, a fact once
more clearly impressed upon Breô, as a few moments
later a tawny flash in through the wider opening sent
him fleeing forth again through the narrower one.
This time the pounce actually tore his sleeve as he
shoved himself out.

Then a horrible fear seized upon Breô. For he
reflected that no end to this perilous dodging, this
mirthless game of hide and seek, could by any
means be seen except the wearying out of one of
the two who were taking part therein; and which
one that would be seemed all too easily foreknow-
able. Weak as he was, what chance had he in a
competition with those iron sinews and agile limbs?
But it was forced peremptorily upon him. Flight
in the open would be a very brief madness. All he
could do was to keep close by the lion-proof entrance
and elude capture by slipping in and out. And a

few recurrences of the manœuvre warned him that even this exertion would soon exhaust his stock of strength. His heavy feet would fail, his light head would betray him, and he would collapse helplessly on one side or the other, on which it mattered nothing, as it would be in either case practically a fall sheer into savage jaws.

That fate had begun to hang most imminently over him, for his heart was stumbling, and his hair clung to his temples, and his tongue clave to the roof of his mouth, and the world spun unsteadily round, when as he staggered desperately out once again, the leap and growl before which he had fled were instantly succeeded from the same direction by a strange rushing thudding sound. It swelled for a moment into a clattering roar, and then abruptly ceased, while at the same time Breð, glancing nervously behind him, saw that the cave, which had been vivid with sunlight had grown dark and black again. Evidently something had entirely blocked up the new bright outlet, and reduced the interior to its ancient gloom.

Did it still contain its latest visitor? That was the question which forthwith occurred to Breð, and he had not to wait long in suspense for the answer —an angry booming bellow sounding from within. Next came noises of scampering and snuffing round and round; the Lion was seeking the vanished exit, and to them Breð listened with an intense interest, feeling that much, very much, depended upon the result of the quest. Then a great paw was thrust out at the baffling slit, and made futile scrawms in the sand. At this sign of failure Breð joyfully reflected how by no possibility could the shaggy growling head follow suit. As well might a portly round melon attempt to get into the rind of a lanky green cucumber. Beyond a doubt the Lion was fairly trapped. With the large aperture closed behind him, and the small one mocking him in front, in the cave he might abide, unless some unlikely convulsion of nature came to effect his release.

Being happily assured on this point, Breð fell to wondering how the thing had happened, and his conjectures were not very wide of the mark. The fact simply was that a mass of sand, which had been left overhanging the archway like a portcullis, and come sliding down just as the beast leaped in, had closed it with an impenetrable curtain. When Breð stole warily round to the south side to investigate, he saw in the place where the opening must have been, a smooth, steep glacis of sand, freshly fallen from the long-laden rock-ledges above. A hundred bullock-loads, he said to himself, would hardly clear it all away. No thoroughfare had been very safely established.

Breð sat down for a while on a boulder to rest, and then thought he had better be making his way back to Jarbek. The apartment at the Split Rock could no longer afford him suitable accommodation, now that it had received and harboured a tramp of such more than suspicious character. He would be glad to find himself beneath the shelter of their own roof before nightfall, and though he could not

D

go fast, he might accomplish that much. A muffled howl arising hard by seemed to clinch his purpose.

So he got up and began to saunter slowly along, a somewhat ghostly-looking person, tall, gaunt, and glittering-eyed, in pale grey draperies, which the strong light bleached white. Hot though it was, the mellow afternoon sunshine and pure air, winnowed by the flown storm-wings, were pleasant to his senses, the sharper for their late abeyance. He noticed a little ash-coloured bird with slender black legs and a pink crest, hopping on the sand, and a white cup - shaped blossom, that had one petal splashed with dark violet, and he liked the look of both. He gazed far away across the red desert, where the distance now was softened with a faint lilac haze, and hoped that he would soon be roving on it again with his friend Oldaz. And he thought it was a good thing that he had been just too quick for the lion's pounce. Then he looked forward with eagerness to telling his mother and the neighbours his grand news that evening under the cornel-tree, where everybody gossiped at sunset.

By this time he had skirted the southern face of the rock, and passing along its shorter eastern one, had reached the point whence he would strike out over the plain straight for home. But first he naturally turned to glance down the northern side towards his abandoned lodging ; and, doing so, he beheld what smote him with sore dismay. If his enemy had somehow broken prison, and come with long bounds, roaring, to meet him, fear would not have gripped him by the heart as it did, at the sight of a small bent figure in whity-brown, blanket-like garb, who was creeping along in the scanty blue shadow of the rock. For he recognised in it his little old mother, and he knew that she must be on her way to the fatal live trap close by. Would he ever be able to stop her?

Zella had found shelter from the storm among the sand-hills not far off, whence she had struggled out, half-smothered and dazed, and urged by much anxiety as to how her invalid might have fared through it. She was now hastening towards him, as she supposed, at her best speed, little dreaming that each step she took increased the distance between them, till it threatened to become infinite.

Breð shouted his loudest after her, but his voice had grown thin and weak, and she was very deaf, and greatly preoccupied with hopes that she would find him none the worse, and not fretting at her long delay. He hurried in pursuit, but his knees shook, and his feet dragged leadenly as in a nightmare. Her swift pace enraged as well as dismayed him, and he toiled on panting maledictions mingled with entreaties. Soon he saw that he might despair of overtaking her in time. But just at the last moment a flame of hope shot up. For on the very threshold of the terrible cave her sleeve was caught on the thorns of a flaring scarlet cactus which blazed in a rock crevice; and she halted for a moment, and half turned round, to disengage herself. It was a vain hope. Quickly she twitched herself free, and passed in at the black entrance. Two voices, frightful to hear, issued from it. A few seconds later, Breð, fleeing for dear life, followed her in.

Not until the brief dusk of the next evening did Moum-mando find it convenient to arrive with his camel at the cave in the Split Rock. And there at the entrance he and his companion, young Thoul, stood amazed, for from within arose, to their salvation, a noise of ramping and roaring that would have deterred the most zealous messenger. By-and-by, a great paw came out of the opening; and Thoul declared that he had caught glimpses of tawny hide and shining eyes. The two men did not, however, make long observations, but sped home through the falling night to report how the cave was in possession of a furious wild beast, whose victims, in all likelihood, Zella and Breð had become. Thither, at dawn, flocked the Jarbekians to investigate, and the tenancy of the Lion was soon proved beyond dispute. That it was involuntary on his part seemed equally clear; and there could be little room for doubt that the former occupants had perished.

But these conclusions were not the result of any rash researches. For three or four days, during which roars and howls and moans were to be heard proceeding from the captives' cell, neighbours stood without, deploring the fate of Zella and her son, and speculating about the extraordinary and inexplicable circumstance by which it was attended. Then silence fell upon the cave; and several days after, two youths, stouter of heart and slighter of frame than their fellows, took torches and went in to explore. There lay the huge, brindle-maned brute, stiff and stark, and close by, in like case, the bodies of the old woman and the young man. The lion, it would seem, had not touched them after he first struck them down. His passion for his lost liberty had, indeed, overborne his craving for food, and he had disdainfully left his prey to lie unheeded. This abstinence, according to Jarbekian views, added one more uncanny feature to the mysteriousness of his presence in the inaccessible cave. "For," said Moum-mando, "did anybody in the light of this sun ever hear of a brute-beast that would kill not caring to eat? That belongs to the wise customs of our kind."

"Not of all—over there," observed Pondri, pointing with a very swarthy hand to the south, from whence he had migrated, "I have seen strange things, but they were easier to understand than this. Measuring that space myself, I find it is barely a two-fingers'-breadth anywhere."

None of the Jarbekians, of course, knew anything about the opening and shutting of that other doorway, and they therefore lacked a clue to any natural explanation of the matter. But a supernatural one was not far to seek, as everybody knows that lonesome places such as the Split Rock are most commonly haunted by evil beings. Here, then, was a characteristic bit of their arts and crafts; and the practical moral drawn was that it would be well to keep as clear of them all as possible. Therefore they refrained from removing the bodies of their ill-fated friends, and from carrying off the lion-skin, which would else have been a highly-prized trophy.   And after performance of some quaint rites, insisted upon by orthodox elders, for the propitiation of the surmised demon, they built up the entrance to the cave securely with stones.   So there rest the mortal remains of three companions in misfortune, and their rocky sepulchre is looked upon as a precinct to be shunned, even at high noon. But when safe at home among their groves and vineyards, the neighbours to this day — for these things happened not many years since—will discuss the strange mischance, which remains, and appears likely to remain, the puzzle of Jarbek.

THE MOCKERS OF THE SHALLOW
WATERS

THE old man who told me this story one day last
May, while I waited in his little shop to avoid
an unseasonable snow shower, sells stationery, photographs, and other such things on the quay at
Therapia, pleasantest among the summer resorts
that fringe the shore of the Bosphorus. He is a
Greek, but speaks French more fluently than his
native tongue, and it was in French that he related
to me what befell the young man whom I shall
call Achmet, since my informant stipulated with
obvious anxiety for the suppression of the real
names of persons and places in all repetitions of
the tale. I do not know why the old Greek laid
such stress upon the point, unless it were because
a member of his own family was slightly and briefly
connected with the curious incidents which he so
seriously narrated.

Achmet dwelt in the small town of Egrigatsch,
not many miles inland from Beikos, which confronts
Therapia on the Asiatic shore of the bay. He was
generally respected by his neighbours as a steady,
sensible young householder, and his circumstances
were fairly prosperous, his revenues being mainly
derived from a sleeping partnership in a firm which
did business in miscellaneous Oriental produce down

55

at Galata. All had been going smoothly in his modest establishment, which, at the time I speak of, comprised a wife and two small children, when a slight domestic difficulty arose. Achmet, for two or three years past, had employed as a general factotum a youth named Kassim, an uncouth-looking lad, who was commonly supposed not to be "all there," and whose services were consequently secured somewhat under market price. But although he certainly displayed no remarkable intelligence, Kassim did well enough, until it happened¯that, upon the death of Achmet's wife's grandmother, he was sent to the adjacent village of Terlikoi, to fetch home a legacy which had thereby accrued to his employers. This consisted of a camel's head-stall and saddle-cloth, and its arrival at Achmet's house proved a cause of dissension ; for Mrs Achmet at once declared that the silver balls, which had adorned the forehead-band, constituting the only valuable portion of the bequest, had been feloniously removed by the bearer, and in confirmation of her assertion, she pointed out the holes left in the red leather ; while Kassim, on his part, indignantly pro-tested that he had delivered the goods exactly as he had received them. The altercation which ensued raged long and shrilly, being made longer and shriller by the appearance on the scene of Kassim's little old mother, Chelkha ; and the upshot of it was that the youth abruptly quitted his situation, and that both mother and son shortly afterwards departed from Egri-gatsch, breathing out, as several neighbours reported, deep maledictions against Achmet and all his house.

Thereupon some months passed, marked by no noteworthy event, save that Mrs Achmet became afflicted with an inflammation of the eyelids, for which she tried many remedies without obtaining any relief. Then, one morning, as Achmet wended his way to the bazaar, he was surprised to see old Chelkha coming towards him, for she had been supposed to have left the town for good, and he had heard nothing of her return. Achmet, a peace-loving, easy-going man, had taken but little part, personally, in bringing about the rupture with Kassim, the difference having been conducted chiefly by the two females; and he now saw no reason why he should not speak civilly to the crooked little old woman She met his advances amicably, and told him, in answer to inquiries, that her son had got employment as a porter in Stamboul, but that as the work did not suit his health, he thought of setting up as a pedlar. Of her own present business at Egrigatsch she volunteered no account, but asked politely after the health of Achmet's family, and expressed much concern when he mentioned his wife's trouble with her eyes. " I 'll be bound that she has not tried crushed *miraftis* root," she said; and when Achmet replied that he did not so much as know it by name, she explained how the *miraftis* was a sort of small flagger, sometimes, though rarely, to be found growing by the margin of streams or pools. "And," continued Chelkha, "if I err not, a sufficiency of it may be gathered not far from here. At most seasons, you will find a clump or two of it about the shallow waters yonder. I can no longer stoop to pull up

the roots, for the curse of the Fore-seeing rests on
my back-bone, but I could point out to another the
leaves that belong to the plant. It is a sovran cure,
bruised and blent with olive-oil and tamarind-juice,
for all burning of the eyelids. If the Effendi were
disposed to walk thither in the course of this day,
bringing something wherewith to dig among the
roots, Chelkha would guide him to what he sought.

Old Chelkha had always enjoyed much renown for
lore in the therapeutical properties of herbs and
simples, and this inclined Achmet to think- hopefully of her prescription. He was really anxious
to benefit his wife, and he had no especial
business on hand for that evening; so he agreed
with the old woman to meet her at the Shallow
Waters about the hour of sundown, and proceed in
quest of the healing *miraftis*.

The Shallow Waters are a cluster of three or four
insignificant pools, situated in a flat plain which
extends to the west of Egrigatsch. It is a doleful
barren tract, suggesting by its aspect a brick-field so
long deserted that all heaps have become obliterated;
while the dusty, deeply-fissured surface has received
an indiscriminate baking. The pools are, perhaps,
a quarter of a mile beyond the farthest outlying
houses of the town, with nothing intervening, except
here and there a stunted plane-tree, or the sombre
pyramid of a cypress. Achmet kept his appoint-
ment punctually, and arrived in sight of the Shallow
Waters when the hot August sun was burning very
near the horizon's rim, and all the tree-shadows
slanted, fantastically lengthened out, across the plain.

So did old Chelkha's, as she stood waiting for the Effendi beside the summer-shrunken pools. When Achmet joined her, she declared herself confident of soon finding *miraftis* in abundance, but upon searching along the muddy banks, she entirely failed to fulfil her promise, for it appeared that the sparse growth of grasses and reeds which fringed the water's edge showed no traces of the peculiar streaked leaves distinctive of the plant.

At last, after they had several times made the circuit of all the pools, fruitlessly poking and groping among the weeds, Chelkha came to a stand beside the smallest of them, a saucer-like depression, scarcely larger than an average puddle, and began to stir its film of water round and round with the long staff which she carried. Achmet at first supposed that she was doing so in quest of roots, but as she continued her stirring long and, to all appearances, aimlessly, he grew impatient. Yet he felt as if he could not take his eyes off the revolving staff. However, when the stirring had gone on for, it might be, ten minutes or more, he shook off with an effort whatever spell or fascination it was, and, turning on his heel, he said—" It seems to me that this is but idle work and waste of time ; moreover, it is getting late, and the dusk will shortly be upon us. We must give over the search for to-day, with none the less thanks, Chelkha, to you. Perhaps we may light upon the plant elsewhere to-morrow."

In reply to this the old woman uttered such an extraordinary sounding chuckle that Achmet turned again to look at her, as she stood, only three or four paces distant, on the other side of the little pool. Her head was as usual covered by her grey striped *yashmak*, the folds of which were drawn closely about her face, leaving merely a narrow slit between them. But through that now protruded something which looked uncommonly like the tip of a tongue thrust forth in derision; and even while he was staring the harder to see whether such were really the case, this object seemed suddenly to alter in shape, to grow larger and darker in colour, and, at the same instant, the mantle folds fell back, revealing the visage *not* of old Chelkha, but of *a camel*, a hideous, black-muzzled camel, ferociously grinning and lolling out its tongue.

Achmet was naturally confounded at this monstrous sight; and before he could attempt to rally from the shock, the prodigy which caused it had vanished. The veiling *yashmak* was again in its place, with Chelkha's dark eye twinkling at the accustomed hole, and she rejoined so exactly in her wonted tone and manner, without desisting from her stirring, "Let the Effendi have but a little patience; we may still chance on what we need ere we leave the Shallow Waters," that the young man could not but think his eyes must have momentarily deceived him, dazzled perhaps, by the obliquely falling rays. But his attention was almost immediately engaged by another strange spectacle. For now, happening to glance towards the horizon, he became aware that a dark form of considerable bulk was in rapid motion far off against the brightness of the yellow evening sky. He followed its course as it swept along from west to east, until it disappeared behind the buildings of the town, whence it presently emerged in full career, and continued its circling rush, now, however, at a perceptibly diminished distance. Again, with an incredible swiftness it skirted the plain, was lost to view for a brief space beyond the interposing roofs, and again passed from behind their screen, but this time at a point so much nearer the pools that, despite the eye-baffling speed of its movements, Achmet could no longer remain doubtful as to what he beheld.

It was a shaggy-haired black camel, gigantic of size, and bestridden by someone who, though shaped in human fashion, certainly could have been no mere mortal rider. For as the huge brute plunged and bounded onward, the figure of him whom it carried was seen now to shoot up into colossal vastness, now to cower down and shrink into the dimensions of a pigmy, with a grotesque yet horrifying effect. Nor were the phenomena displayed meanwhile by old Chelkha much less uncanny than those which accompanied this portentous apparition, since, still incessantly stirring the turbid water round from left to right, she seemed to keep her gaze fixed upon the monster's movements, punctuating its progress by the utterance of a fiendish chuckle. And at every repetition of the hideous sound, the *yashmak* folds parted asunder to show more or less of—culminating horror—the grinning camel's face.

A feeling of indescribable terror and despair seized upon Achmet. He tried to move, but his limbs were as lead and stone ; to speak, but lips and tongue refused their office; his plight was as that of one whom the hellish drug oorali has bereft of all faculties save torturing sense.   He could only stand helplessly watching the bat-like gyres of the dreadful pair, camel and rider.   These drew in, round the Shallow Waters as centre, with ever shortening radius, and with a rapidity, albeit the speed had begun somewhat to slacken, which wrought Achmet to a benumbed frenzy.   Round and round the creature wheeled, now no longer passing out of sight beyond the town, but dashing headlong through it, as if the solid walls were nothing more substantial than trails of smoke. Another sweep, and the circumference of its circle lay on the hither side of the nearest house; another, and the cypress-clump, distant hardly two furlongs, was excluded.   The extraordinary and frightful features of the unearthly rider became clearly discernible, while with frantic contortions and grimaces he writhed up and writhed down from dwarf to giant, and back again, while the gibbering and hissing with which he urged on his beast waxed by degrees louder and louder.   Yet still the unhappy Achmet stood root-fast, powerless to make a step or utter a sound, staring blankly at the approaching camel, or the end of the old hag's revolving staff.   What terrific Beings those forms might embody, he durst not conjecture, and, nevertheless, must needs surmise.

And now the elongated shadow flitted over him as it passed, and now a little shower of pebbles, spurned by the heavy splay foot, fell splashing into the pool beside him, and now the jingle of the silver ornaments, which he saw bobbing on the great shaggy forehead, rang sharply in his ears. . . . A few strides more, and the diabolical-looking pair would be upon him. But before that awful crisis in his fate occurred, a flood of humming darkness seemed to surge up around him, and, whelmed in a tide of unconsciousness, he recked not what happened next.

At this point, therefore, the story owes its continuity to the evidence of some other persons, who just then arrived upon the scene. These were a small body of men, mainly a remnant of a large pilgrim band which was returning dispersedly from its visit to holy places. Among them, however, was my old Greek's brother, Spiridion, who lived near Egrigatsch, and who had accidentally fallen in with and joined the party on his way home. They reported that as they rode into sight of the Shallow Waters, at sundown, they noticed a large dark object rushing in circles round about the pools, which, upon advancing a little farther across the plain, they perceived to be a camel of supernatural size, ridden by some creature of most unaccountable aspect. But while they were still too far off to observe anything very distinctly, the beast and its rider halted for an instant, apparently quite close to one of the pools, whereupon, almost immediately, an appalling screech was yelled out, and the camel sped on again, fleeing away with great bounds to the eastward, until it vanished in the dim distance. All the beholders, however, averred that as it went it bore *two* riders, of whom one had the semblance of a gigantic veiled woman. In much alarm and perplexity, the pilgrims now continued their advance over the solitary plain, and when they reached the pools, it was to discover Achmet lying senseless by the margin, convulsively clasping a muddy, weed-entwined spade. Finding that all efforts failed to restore him, they conveyed the unfortunate young man into the town, where, after many hours, he regained his senses, and was able to describe the strange experiences he had gone through. It may be remarked here that two small boys, who had beguiled the sunset hour with the pastime of pelting stones at a big melon which grew on the top of a garden-wall in the outskirts of the town, were badly scared, in the midst of their amusement, by the rushing past them of a huge black quadruped, whereas none of the other townsfolk beheld any-thing unusual. Moreover, it appeared that nobody except Achmet himself was cognisant of old Chelkha's return; in fact, a friend of his subse-quently swore to having met the old woman on the Sultan-Validi Bridge, crossing over from Galata to Stamboul, at the very time when Achmet believed himself to have had his interview with her by the Shallow Waters. Be this as it may, certain it is that she has since then been seen or heard of by no dweller in Egrigatsch.

("Those Turks," quoth the old Greek, with a touch of disdain, racial and religious, in his tone, "will have it that their near approach, newly come from their holy places, and bearing with them sacred relics, put to flight the evil thing—mocker or spectre —ere it could work its will on poor miserable Achmet. A Christian man may, of course, be permitted to hold a different opinion. And yet," he continued, meditatively, "if a Turk could drive off the like by any means, I should be slow to disparage him or the places of his superstition"; a sentiment in which I hastened to concur.)

For several months after his mysterious adventure, Achmet was, to all appearances, none the worse. But as time went on, he began to manifest a curious propensity for stirring round, with a stick or with his hand, any standing water that he chanced to see, whether in pool or puddle, tank or cistern. And his doing so was invariably followed by his presently falling into a profound cataleptic trance. This propensity grew by degrees into a positive craze, and he went about seeking for opportunities to indulge it; so that, although the members of his household did their best to keep him out of the way of this peril, the seizures became of more and more frequent occurrence, with markedly ill results alike to his body and mind. At length, when nearly two years had elapsed, a particularly interesting trial happened to be held one day at Egrigatsch, and as the afternoon wore away, Achmet's household, his wife, his sister, his servant, slipped out one after the other to linger about the door of the little *Konak*, and to pick up the latest intelligence as to how things were going inside. It is supposed that he took advantage of his house being thus left empty, to make his way unperceived out-of-doors, and wandered off beyond the limits of the town, and over the deserted plain. But all that ever came for certain to the knowledge of his neighbours, was that

E

towards sunset time, a few loungers near the precincts of the mosque heard a succession of fearful shrieks proceeding from the direction of the Shallow Waters, and upon hurrying thither, found all still as the grave, and by the brink of a pool the dead body of Achmet, lying with garments bemired and torn, and the mark of a great splay foot imprinted lividly on his breast.

"What brought the miserable young man's fate into my mind just now," said the old Greek, as he carefully curled a small sheaf of unmounted photographs round a wooden roller, "was that I saw his brother Alischan here to-day. He was bound for Skutari on business about Achmet's tomb, for he has a friend who keeps a stone-cutter's shed in the great cypress-grove over there, and who is carving him a head-stone on reasonable terms; making quick work of it, too, it seems, as I hear it is nearly completed."

"Why, how long is it since this happened?" I asked, somewhat startled by his remark, as I had vaguely taken it for granted that the fantastic events which he had so circumstantially described might be relegated to at least the softening twilight of a generation or two past, and did not claim a place in our broad noon-shine as a story of to-day.

"Let me consider," said he. "Achmet died—ah! yes—it was three days before Easter; a little over a month ago."

At this moment a wailing whistle sounded, warning me to hasten out and meet the *Schirket-i-Hairiji* steamer, which came zig-zagging across the blue water, fluttering its red-starred and crescented flag, and making a mighty commotion with its floundering screw. In a few minutes it was splashing on Asia-wards. The shower had blown off, and the warm sun gleamed on waves and sails. Veiled women laughed and chattered behind their gaudily-curtained screen. An Albanian sweetmeat-vendor perambulated to and fro in a snowy fustanella, with a tray of pale-green angelica stalks, and other unrecognisable stickinesses. All was cheerfully bright and commonplace for the Bosphorus. Yet, as I looked towards the brown ridge rising behind Beikos, crested with a broken line of gaunt and sombre trees, and as I thought of how a certain lonely plain, with pools in it, lay visibly somewhere beyond them, I had a very narrow escape of the often inevitable "more in heaven and earth . . ."

AT KRINORI

(A MESOGAIAN SKETCH)

DURING a solitary pedestrian tour through Attica, I lost myself one afternoon among the bleak Laureionian mountains of the Mesogaia, and turned in at a very humble little *xenodocheion* to ask my way and avoid a passing shower; when, having ascertained that I was not near anywhere in particular, I ordered a bottle of *Krasì retsinàto*, and sat down to consider the situation.

The only other occupant of the room was a splendidly handsome young Greek, with something seafaring in his aspect, and a complexion more deeply bronzed than is usual even under those southern skies. He greeted me pleasantly and frankly as I took a seat near him; but when soon afterwards several peasants entered the room, and sat down at the other end of the table, his demeanour changed; for, turning his back upon the party, he leaned his head on his hands, and even pressed them against his ears, as if to shut out the sound of the newcomers' voices. In fact he did this so effectually that the landlord, having addressed a question to him vainly twice or thrice, had to poke him in the back before he could extract the required answer. This seemed to remind the young man that I might think

68

his conduct strange and uncivil, and he presently said to me in an apologetically explanatory tone: "The truth is, sir, that I've been at sea for not much under two years, and I've not heard a word from home since last harvest—twelve months and more—and there are many things might happen in twelve months. And, somehow, the nearer home I get, the more things come into my mind; and Kara's scarcely an hour's walk from here. Well now, sir, it so happens that I've no acquaintance with any of those fellows, but they're talking about places and people that I know; I catch a name every now and then, and I daren't listen to them. I can't tell you exactly how it is, but I have the feeling that I might hear a bit of bad news all in a minute if I did. Saint George! to consider what one of them might blurt out in five words, thinking no more of it than if he was bidding me good-day. Says he, maybe, with his mouth full of olives, or slicing away at the loaf: 'The day old Ioannidês died,' or 'At the wed——' Bah! what I mean is that I'd rather be weathering Cape Matapan on a ten-inch plank than sitting and listening to them; and if this rain—— But, by Our Lady, here's Loukos Zarkos himself!"

Loukos was a youngish man of low stature, in a blue blouse and red fez. He had a swarthy countenance, with Jewish features of the unhandsome type, accompanied by a receding chin and shifty, twinkling eyes. I had seen him standing near the door for two or three minutes before my companion observed him, and looking in our direction with, as I thought, a disconcerted expression; but he now came forward beaming smiles and ejaculating joy: "What is this? Andreas Ioannidês alive and well! A bit of good luck, indeed; but I can scarcely believe my eyes, for, let me tell you, your friends had come near giving you up for lost."

"Well, I'm not lost out-and-out, you see," said Andreas, laughing with some constraint, "but we had the devil's own weather all last winter; and then I got the fever, and was laid up two months in hospital at Smyrna. I thought at one time I'd seen my last of Port Peiraios. However, I'm all right again now."

"Ah, by good luck! Then I suppose you've not made your fortune this voyage?"

"Oh, for the matter of that, I've done well enough. I've brought home the price, at any rate, of that bit of vineyard yonder above Melnera, if so be it's still in the market."

"I'm overjoyed to hear that, truly," but the speaker's lengthened visage belied his words. "And now I suppose you're on your way home to the old folks. I saw your father somewhere last week looking as strong as a barley-fed bull.

"Ay, ay, I'm bound for Kara just now; but I'll look in at Krinori one of these days—before very long either, I hope. How are things going there?"

"Oh, jogging along much as usual. Georgios and I have had middling luck of late. The sponge-fishing turned out pretty well last time; the boat came in from Famagousta yesterday, and Georgios has been down at Peiraios seeing after things—you might have met him—but I expect him home to-

morrow or next day. As for me, I've come this far
after a lot of fowl that I hear are to be had a
bargain a bit farther up this road; you can make
a good profit on the creatures, if you buy them
up cheap, and send them on to Athens by rail,
when——"

"And what news is there among the neighbours?"
interrupted Andreas.

"Nothing much. I don't know whether you've
heard that the old Elissa died last vintage?"

The old Elissa's demise evidently was not one of
those sudden blows which Andreas had apprehended,
for he only said with composure: "Poor old soul;
may she rest in peace!" and waited for further
intelligence.

"Then, just at the new year Nikandros Rodopoulos
lost his best ox; and since before Easter he's been
courting the Widow Manetou at Koropi; he'll be a
lucky man if he gets her. Folks say——"

This was more to the purpose. Andreas changed
colour perceptibly, and his eyes flashed wider open
as he said quickly: "Ah, but his daughter, his
children—what do they think of a stepmother?"

"Well, as for the girl," began the other, speaking
with a sort of confused hesitation, "it won't, I suppose, make so much difference to her, you see, after
all—being married out of the way——"

"Married!" Andreas pushed back his chair with
a sudden jerk, and as its legs grated upon the flagged
floor, I said to myself that the bit of bad news had,
sure enough, arrived. "Maro Rodopoulos married!
And who may her husband be?"

"Her husband?   Oh well—why who should it be else," said Loukos, still stammering and hesitating, "but Georgios — my brother?   That's what her father's heart's been set on this long while back. It's an old story at home by this time; though, of course, it's news to you!"

"Well, then, good luck go with them all!" said Andreas, taking a great gulp of his *Krasì retsinàto*, and thereupon rising abruptly. "The shower's over, so good-bye to you, or I'll not be home at supper-time."

"But we'll meet again — you're coming to Krinori?" said Loukos interrogatively; and he watched for the answer with a furtive anxiety in his twinkling glances.

"Not I, indeed; when a man has only a week on shore, he'd rather spend it with his relations and friends than tramp over the country for nothing at all."

"Only a week—to be sure that's a very short while for you to be with your old father and mother—and after such an absence. Certainly nobody could expect you to leave them. But I had no notion you were to be off again so soon."

"The *Olga* sails for Odessa on Saturday, and I'm second in command if I choose. I'm not likely to throw away a good berth in a hurry."

With these words Andreas was striding out of the room; and I presently saw his lofty head pass across the small-paned window; an admirable study for an irate Apollôn. The ugly Loukos sat sipping his wine meditatively for some minutes longer

before he went his way; and I shortly afterwards
took my departure, intending to push on to Liopesi,
a village some fifteen miles distant, and little expecting to fall in again with my chance companions.
In this I was mistaken, however, for towards dusk
I put my foot into an unusually deep rut in a
lonely lane, and sprained my ankle so severely
that I was quite unable to continue my pilgrimage;
in which distressful plight I was overtaken by
Loukos Zarkos with his ox-cart, who offered me
a lift to his home at a place called Krinori, where
he stated that he owned a room—a spacious and
splendid room!—with a bed—an excellent and
handsome bed!—both entirely at my service. I
was, under the circumstances, glad to accept his
offer; and long after dark we arrived at slumber-
ing Krinori, where the room and bed much tran-
scended my hopes, by proving to be quite clean
and fairly comfortable.

Accident having thus brought me to Krinori,
both place and people took my fancy, and I remained there for several days. Krinori is situated
in a small valley shaped like a daisy-petal, and
filled with olive-groves and vineyards, which run
up the slopes of the encircling hills. At the rounded
end are grouped the cluster of cottages forming the
little hamlet, which is so insignificant that it pos-
sesses no chapel, or even tavern, of its own; its
inhabitants depending for those advantages upon
a slightly larger village in a neighbouring valley.
The building of which my room formed a part
was the largest in the hamlet, where it occupied

a central position, and it was then tenanted jointly by the brothers Zarkos, to whom my chamber belonged, and by an elderly couple named Arphoutos. The cottage fronted the south-east, and round two sides of it ran a creeper-wreathed verandah sheltering a wooden bench, which commanded an uninterrupted view of the straight, white, shadow-flecked road leading up the valley, and of the two or three small cottages on either hand. Upon this bench, my sprain precluding much locomotion, it became my custom to spend the greater portion of the day, but not usually alone. For as it was early June, months before the grapes or olives could be gathered, the Krinorians had much spare time on hand, and were often pleased to bestow their leisure upon me. On these occasions they discoursed to me so freely about their own and their neighbours' domestic affairs, that I soon learned more than one curious story; but at present I will speak only of some particulars gathered about the family Rodopoulos, which comprised a father, two small sons, and a daughter, Maro. The latter, whom I saw for the first time on the second morning after my arrival, as she passed by on her way to the well round the corner, was tall and slender, and looked about eighteen, but was probably a year or two younger. She was also exceedingly beautiful; not simply pretty, but perfect, from "the delicate Arab arch of her feet" to the soft black tresses that coiled richly round her small classically shaped head, leaving a dusky down to shade her great lustrous eyes, and blow away from the faultless curves of cheeks whose clear tint, though not sun-browned, made you think of the open air whenever she came into a room. Maro's beauty was patent and indisputable, and its effect was only heightened for me by a certain wistful melancholy in her expression, which harmonised very well with what I had learned, or fancied, respecting her circumstances. For it will be remembered that my present landlord's conversation at the inn had already put me in possession of the facts that she was motherless, and menaced with a stepmother, and that she had recently made a match more, it would seem, in accordance with her father's views than with her own. Her looks, too, were all the more important data, because they remained the only information about her frame of mind that I obtained at first-hand, as, after the manner of Greek girls, she kept strictly in the background; and, saving an occasional shy καλ' ἡμέρα, I had no speech of her during my whole visit.

I was not, however, left solely to conjectures; other sources of enlightenment were open to me, and from amongst them all I was able to gain a tolerably clear insight into the state of affairs. For instance, Maro's youngest brother, Dêmêtrios, commonly called Mêtri, a brown-faced, dark-eyed child of about seven, at once struck up a warm friendship with me, and favoured me with much of his society and conversation. At noon of the day when I first saw Maro, he had established himself near me on the grass with a huge hunch of bread and a short stumpy cucumber, his midday meal, during the progress of which he occupied himself in pointing out to me various objects of interest in the surrounding landscape : the Arphoutos' mule tethered under a plane-tree ; his father's dog barking at the old Spero's pigs ; the lilac-bush which was struck by lightning last autumn, and so forth. While he was thus engaged, Maro came by again with her two-handled pitcher, whereupon he observed : " And that's my sister."

" Ah, your married sister ? " I said, not unwilling to pursue the subject, but Mêtri's answer was unexpected and puzzling. " No indeed, she's not," he said, " Maro's not married. They're talking about it often, but she says she never will be ; not if she lives to be as old as a crow."

" Not married ! " I thought to myself, " then what was the meaning of Loukos Zarkos' assertion at the inn the other day ? He had stated distinctly that she was married to his brother. Were there two Maro Rodopouloses in this little place ? " My curiosity took a keener edge, and I was glad to perceive that Mêtri seemed inclined to enlarge upon the topic with a copiousness and fluency which called for little comment or question from me.

" Father wants her to marry Georgios Zarkos," he said, " and Georgios wants to marry her too, I think. I don't know why she won't ; I would if I were she, for he always brings her sweetmeats when he comes home from anywhere. She always gives them to me ; she says she doesn't like them. Anyhow," he resumed after a large mouthful of cucumber, "father says he can't afford to keep her any longer, since we've lost the ox. It was a terrible thing for him to die, but he'd had a most awful cough all the winter, like this"—here Mêtri produced a series of truly alarming sounds—"and then one morning we found him lying in the stall with all his legs quite stiff; so now we've no ox, only a donkey."

"And so," I observed, "as your father can't afford to keep your sister any longer she must marry?"

"No, no," said Mêtri, wagging his head in a decided negation which he clinched with two emphatic nods, "she says she won't—never, never. And father says she will have to go and live with brother Stavris up at Salonika, and mind the children; but she doesn't want to do that either, and cries, and says it is so far off. Stavris has a wife and a shop, but we never saw them, and one has to go there in a ship. But if Maro married Georgios, he would give us another ox; and father says her head is as full of folly as if it had been sown out of a bottomless sieve, and that it's time she got rid of it. *I* think she's a great fool. Do you know what she did last Thursday? Old Spero was going to Koropi, and I saw her giving him the last *pentára* she had left out of the *drachmé* father gave her at the new year, just before the poor ox died; and I thought she was sending for *loukoumia*—in fact, I was certain she was sending for some, because she looked at me several times, and then at the *pentára*; and I even pulled her sleeve, and said I liked the pink sort best, but she only muttered to herself: ' It's the

last one I have.' And what do you think she'd sent
for after all? A lot of nasty little candles to burn in
the chapel, not another thing. I'd have liked to have
smashed them all up. It's true that she begged
a handful of Karouba-beans for us from Kuria
Arphoutos to make up, but seven Karouba-beans
aren't much; and what's the sense of nasty little
candles? Yánni" (his brother two or three years
senior) "says he supposes she's going to be like
the old Zachara over yonder, who's always burning
candles to bring back her husband from the sea,
which is a very silly thing to do, because his ship
went down off Cape Maléa in a great storm one
winter ever so many years ago. And now Maro
hasn't a *lepton* left to buy anything."

"Then do you think your sister also wants to
bring back somebody from the sea?"

"How can she want to bring somebody back,
when there isn't anybody away? It's just all
nonsense, and besides that she won't swing with
the other girls in the evening, or dance, or do
anything one likes. And I can tell you sometimes
she's as cross as a scorpion, and you never can
know when she won't begin to cry about nothing
at all. Last night she cried because blind Athanasios
played on his fiddle. He came back here yesterday
for the first time this year, for in the winter he lives
with his mother away at Lefsina, and in the summer
he goes about with his fiddle and sings. He sings
vintage songs all the while, because he can't see that
the grapes aren't half ripe; why even the *soultanina*
won't be fit to gather for the next two months nearly,

father says. But last night when he came round to our door playing beautifully, Maro wouldn't listen to it, but begun to cry, and ran away into the garden ── My life!" Mêtri exclaimed here, breaking off the thread of his narrative, "I heard something, didn't you!"

The squeak of a fiddle did sound distinctly from a clump of trees not far distant, and Mêtri, bolting his last bit of cucumber, was off like a shot to join blind Athanasios's audience.

The child's naïve, though fragmentary and lop-sided, relation had interested and perplexed me, so that I felt anxious to supplement it by further details about the Rodopoulos family; and I was soon enabled to do this, as Petros Arphoutos, in his blue blouse made his appearance, with the evident intention of spending that day's *siesta* in a chat, the course of which I easily steered towards the desired topic. Petros spoke of Rodopoulos *père* as an honest fellow and a good neighbour, who had had bad luck ever since his wife died, poor soul! three or four years back. But he went on to express marked disapproval of Nikandros' unaccountable weak - mindedness in permitting Maro to throw away her chance of so well-to-do a husband as Georgios Zarkos, who had been courting her for the last six months without effect. This was all the stranger, considering that the girl's presence in his house was an obstacle in the way of Nikandros' own wishes with regard to the wealthy widow Manetou, who stood out that she would not set up housekeeping along with a grown-up daughter. "However," proceeded Petros,

" I think he's determined at last to get both weddings over out of the way before the vintage begins, or else to pack Maro off to her married brother at Salonika, who would keep her to mind his children. Certainly, I'm glad that my children are all out in the world, for they're a troublesome crop to raise. Not that I'd ever have let mine set themselves up against me in such a fashion. Refuse Georgios Zarkos indeed! Perhaps the Diadochos would suit her, or the Patriarch of Constantinople!"

But though Kurios Arphoutos' strong opinion respecting the great eligibility of Georgios as a *parti* was generally shared by the little community, it was evident that the brothers Zarkos were far from popular at Krinori. Nor was this much to be wondered at, as not only were their manners and appearance unprepossessing, but their circumstances were calculated to raise a jealous feeling among their neighbours. The brothers, like everybody else, owned and tilled a few *hektars* of land; but, unlike anybody else, they were not wholly dependent for their livelihood upon the produce of their fields. They were men of various resources, concerning which I could only vaguely gather that they had shares in several trading vessels and other mercantile ventures, often calling for the presence of them at Port Peiraios or elsewhere. Now this, albeit, doubtless not necessarily iniquitous, was enough, when taken in conjunction with their churlish and niggardly habits, to make them the subject of much unflattering surmise; and I may mention, among the least sensational of current rumours, the statements that

Loukos had a wife and family at Port Peiraios, and
that when Georgios visited Athens he wore a black
coat and silk hat, and frequented the fashionable
Kafeîon toû Solônos in the Plateîas tês Omonoias.

Anna Lavriades, a kindly middle-aged dame, who
lodged next door to the Rodopouloses, and who not
long since had nursed Georgios Zarkos through a
serious illness, was the only one of their neighbours
to whom I ever knew them to show any disinterested
friendliness. Indeed, during my visit, Loukos
actually presented her with one of his cheap hens.
The creature was, it is true, very lame and dishevelled looking; still, the gift showed a good
intention, and made an immense impression upon
its simple-minded recipient.

I had little direct communication with the brothers,
but I was not seldom a listener to their discourse,
for their room was separated from mine merely by
a many-chinked boarding, through which every word
spoken in either apartment found its way unimpeded;
moreover, my favourite seat was on the bench close
by their unglazed window, inside which they spent
most of their spare time, smoking very large and
atrocious cigars, procured from some Italian port,
and talking to one another in sullen, grumbling
tones. As I was always careful to apprise them of
my proximity, which they persistently disregarded,
I had no scruple about listening to their remarks:
and I can truthfully own that I rarely heard them
say a good word of anybody, or express gratification
at anything which did not involve the annoyance or
injury of some other person.

F

I was sitting in my usual place in the evening, soon
after my conversation with Kurios Arphoutos, when I
heard Georgios, who had just returned from Athens,
imparting his news to Loukos as they ate their supper.

"Give me the cheese.   I saw a man down at
Peiraios the other day, whom I'd rather have met
going feet foremost."

"There are many such."

"I was dining in the Odos Miavleôs, when who
comes swaggering in, as if the whole place belonged
to him, but Andreas Ioannidês of Kara.   I hoped
we'd seen the last of that young scamp."

"I could have told you better than that." .

"And what do *you* know about it?   Nothing, I
should suppose."

"Saw him two days ago, up at Thelgros, on his
way home, with a pouchful of *drachmai*."

"The devil!   Then I wish both he and they were
at the bottom of the Hellespont.   Has he been here
yet?"

"Not he; and won't be, thanks to your brother
Loukos."

"That's likely, indeed!   Why, he'll be after the
girl first thing, confound him!"

"Not when I've told him she's safely married.
His face was worth a mile's walk to see."

"You told him Maro was married?"

"Exactly so, and to yourself, no less."

Hereupon there was an outburst of wrath from
Georgios, followed by an angry wrangle; Georgios
expressing, with many uncomplimentary epithets,
his dissatisfaction at his brother's lapse from truth:

on the grounds, first, that Andreas would probably
avenge himself by some act of violence on a successful rival ; and, secondly, that he must soon learn at
Kara how he had been misinformed ; while Loukos
combated the former objection as inconsistent with
Andreas' character, and the latter as guarded against
by his brief stay at Kara, and the ignorance about
Krinorian matters there prevailing. Then there was
a pause, after which Georgios began in a mollified
tone : "Do folks here know the fellow's come
back ?"

"I told them nothing about it. You may manage
your own affairs yourself."

"Bah ! I'm thinking it'll be better to give out that
he's come home. It's my belief that the notion of
his coming for her is what makes the girl so obstinate,
and keeps her father shilly-shallying. But if they
knew he was at home, and didn't come next or nigh
them, Rodopoulos would put that out of his head ;
and as for Maro, she's as proud as anybody, and if
she found that Andreas had thrown her over, why,
rather than seem to be breaking her heart after him,
she might——"

"She might take you out of spite, as it's plain
enough she never will out of liking. Well, that'll be
a bit of news for you to tell them when you go to see
her to-morrow. I wonder, by the way, that you
don't bring her a brooch, or a handkerchief, or some
bit of finery instead of that sweet stuff only fit for
brats. Girls don't think anything of it."

"And I wonder where I'd get bits of finery at
thirty *lepta* a pound. The girl's given trouble enough,

the Saints know, without one's ruining oneself for her entirely. I might drop a hint, too, about his having got married abroad. You're not the only man in Krinori that can tell lies."

"Perhaps I'm the only one that would bother his head about your concerns, and get nothing but abuse for his pains."

Herewith their discourse died away in brief muttered snarls, and the rest was silence.

On the next day nothing that I need note occurred. I was left more to my own society than usual, because as two holidays were impending, people were for the most part occupied in finishing up odd jobs about their little homesteads. Maro passed by at the accustomed times with her earthenware *amphora*, and on each occasion I thought that her beautiful sad face looked sadder, and that her movements were more listless and dejected. However, as I saw the brothers Zarkos working busily all day among the artichokes and pumpkins in their small garden, I knew that she could not yet have been visited by Georgios on his sweet and bitter mission.

But on the following morning I missed her from her water-drawing, and I saw nothing of her family until, in the course of the forenoon, Mêtri appeared to me in a state of stickiness wonderful and fearful to contemplate, with his hands full of an adhesive mass of what looked like toffee, but which was, he told me, composed of figs, almonds, honey, aniseed, and dried grape-skins, and was exceedingly delicious. .

"Georgios Zarkos brought it to Maro last night,"

he said, as he sat down at my feet; "and I found
it thrown away in a corner this morning, and the
string round it wasn't even untied. I've got it
nearly all, because Yánni doesn't like it much, which
is a lucky thing. Georgios stayed for a long while
last night," he continued; "but he was in a great
rage when he went away, because Maro wouldn't
say that she'd marry him, and she said she'd rather
go to Salonika, even if the ship went to the bottom
before it got there. And father said it was a serious
misfortune for him to have such a headstrong child,
who wouldn't do a hand's turn to save him from
being ruined by his losses. And Georgios said
there weren't many men who'd offer to take her
without a penny, and give money's worth for her
into the bargain; and he said he supposed the
truth of the matter was that she couldn't think of
anybody except Andreas Ioannidês. But Maro said
that Andreas was no more to her than the wind on
the hill-top; and Georgios said that was so much
the better, for he'd heard a man at Port Peiraios
say that Andreas had left a pretty wife behind
him at Smyrna; and he said that at any rate, wife
or no wife, it was easy to see that Andreas hadn't
a thought of anybody at Krinori, for if he had, he
wouldn't have stayed a month at Kara, without
setting foot in the place. And Maro said that it
made no difference to her who came to Krinori,
or who stayed away, but there were some people
there that she wouldn't grieve after if they took
themselves off, and didn't come back in a hurry.
And then Georgios got up and banged the door

after him, and didn't say good-night or anything.
I remember Andreas Ioannidês very well," Mêtri
went on, after an interval of meditative munching;
"but he hasn't been here for years and years and
years. He is taller than anybody else; I can get
into the top-branch of our big olive-tree there off
his shoulder. And once he gave Yánni a tin whistle
and a whirligig when he was getting well of the
fever. I wish he'd come here again, but Maro said
this morning that he never would, never again;
and she cried a great deal, and said that she wished
she was with our mother, who's buried where all
the cypresses are, at the other side of the hill over
yonder; you can't see them from here, so there's
no use looking. And she said that she'd send us
plenty of *loukoumia* from Salonika, and new kites
too; mine's to be a red dragon, and Yánni's is to be
green, but he hasn't made up his mind about the
shape. She said that, because he began to cry too,
when father said she was going to Salonika next
week. Yánni says that father's going to be married
himself, and stepmothers are always the crossest
kind of women, so he'd rather go away with Maro.
But I think it would be much better if Maro married
Georgios Zarkos, for I daresay he's in a good
humour again by this time. And old Spero says
it would be a fine thing for us all."

Having made this communication, Mêtri gave
himself up to inarticulate enjoyment of his sweetmeats, until he departed in quest, I fancy, of more
substantial fare. Soon after he left me, I managed
to hobble as far as the low broad-topped wall which

skirted the white road close by, and here I took
up my position, partly to escape the odour of
Georgios Zarkos' never-ending cigars, for he had
elected to spend this day in the seclusion of his
own chamber, and partly because I wished to obtain
a nearer view of the villagers, as they returned in
their holiday attire from chapel. I had not sat there
long before I was joined by Nikandros Rodopoulos,
with whom I had never hitherto conversed at any
length. He was a fine-looking man of about forty-
five, whose good-tempered face formed a species
of explanatory commentary upon that failure of
his to adopt more arbitrary measures in arranging
his family affairs, which was deplored by his auto-
cratically-minded neighbour, Ioannês Arphoutos.
The subject of conversation which he almost immediately broached was Salonika. About this place,
its situation, and the best method of proceeding
thither, he seemed anxious to collect what informa-
mation he could, and the scantiness of his original
stock may be inferred from the fact that he regarded
me as a reliable authority on the grounds of my
familiarity with the neighbouring city of London.

"I'm afraid I'll presently have my daughter on
her way there," quoth Nikandros, after I had done
my best towards making clear to him the relative
positions of the modern Babylon and the ancient
Thessalonikê, illustrating my explanations by an
impromptu map of Europe sketched with the point
of a stick in the deep dust at our feet, "though it's
not what I could have wished by any means. But
you might as well count on a March wind as a

girl's mind, and you'll find larks' eggs on Christmas morning as soon as wit in——"

"You speak of your daughter's refusal of Georgios Zarkos?" I said, striking athwart the current of Nikandros' proverbial philosophy.

"Exactly so, sir. I don't wonder that you should think it an extraordinary thing. But you'd have been surprised, I can tell you, to see the obstinacy of the girl last night when Georgios was with us, for we both talked to her till we were as hoarse as ravens, both I and Georgios, and, as we say, sir, he can speak plain who has a golden tongue. And what did we gain by it all? Not a civil word would she give him from beginning to end, any more than if he'd been a rogue of a pedlar trying to take her in with the worst bit of stuff in his pack. Nobody can wonder that he went off in a passion. And all she'd say when he'd gone was that she hoped he'd keep away for a long while, as she'd rather see the wood-devil's father-in-law coming into the house than he."

"I suppose the truth is," said I, "that she has a dislike to him."

"But nobody ever asked her to like him; to marry him merely, instead of behaving like a sense-less creature."

"And you are certain that she has no other reason for refusing him?"

"Well, to tell you the truth, up to the present time I'd been thinking that she might happen to have some idea in her mind about a young fellow, a sailor, from a place away among the hills, who

came courting her two years ago. Not that he'd
have been a match equal to Georgios Zarkos; far
from it; you don't find men with shares in half-a-
dozen boats, and a soap-factory, and a marble
quarry, round every turn of the road. However,
he was a fine lad enough, and his parents are
honest people, with a tolerable vineyard; so I said
that I'd make no objection, provided that he
brought back a bit of money from his next voyage,
and settled down on dry land, for I shouldn't wish
my daughter to be a second Widow Zachara.
Well, but then he went off and stayed away so
long that we all thought he'd found his way to
the bottom somewhere; and now, I hear, he's at
home again. But it seems he's changed his mind,
or, what's more likely, has come back no richer
than he went. For he's never sent us a word or
come near us, and that doesn't look much like
courting. Georgios, indeed, tells some story about
Andreas having got married abroad, but that may
be true or it mayn't. Anyhow, as it happens, it
doesn't make much difference either way, for Maro
says that Andreas Ioannidês is nothing at all to
her, and that she forgot all about him long ago."

"Goodness forgive you for that statement, Miss
Maro," I thought to myself; but aloud I said, "And
when did she tell you this?"

"Oh, last night. Mention happened to be made
of him while Georgios was with us, and she said
she never wished to set eyes on him again. So I
see I was quite mistaken when I imagined that her
mind might be running on the young fellow. He's

nothing to her at all," repeated Maro's father, with an air of conviction which made me think somewhat meanly of his insight into character; and while I doubted whether I should enlighten him as to what was, I believed, the true state of affairs, the present opportunity slipped away. For Nikandros, who had looked down the road, exclaimed in much surprise, "Guiding Madonna! who is coming this way but Spiridion's Thekla? Now, what may bring her here? And however did she travel all the way from Kara? Not on foot, poor soul, I should imagine."

I looked where he did, and saw at some little distance the approaching form of Spiridion's Thekla. She appeared to be an elderly woman, miserably lame and crooked and bent, and clad in ragged, fluttering black garments, which, together with her long staff and dishevelled locks, gave her a weird and almost witch-like aspect.

"Eh, now, but that's a pity, truly, it's a pity to see," was Nikandros' next remark, as he stood watching the halting progress of the new-comer; "and to think what a handsome lass she was only four or five years ago—as straight as a reed, and as light-footed as a goat; much such a one as my girl Maro. Why, it seems but yesterday; and now look at her lurching along like an over-rigged schooner in a side wind."

"Did you say only four or five years ago?" I asked in surprise, as she looked about fifty, and though I was familiar with the early withering of Eastern beauty, the transformation here seemed too complete to be thus accounted for.

"Ay, sir, scarcely so much," said Nikandros; and then, while she stopped and talked to some children on the road, he told me the main fact in the history of Spiridion's Thekla, which was that a runaway horse had one day knocked her down and drawn a heavily-laden cart over her, crushing and maiming her past all possibility of cure, though many months' suffering had ended in a certain measure of recovery, thus enhancing the misfortune; "since," proceeded Nikandros, "it's hard to tell what can become of her if she should happen to outlive her old father, who's the only soul belonging to her. For though they're respectable people, and akin somehow to the Ioannidês family, they're poor, very poor. Spiridion doesn't own the bit of land he farms, and he finds it no easy matter to get a living out of it at all; and Thekla, the unhappy girl, can do little to help him, though she does more than she's fit for, creeping about on the earth like a wounded plover, to grub up the stones and weeds. If it hadn't been for that mishap, she needn't have waited long for a husband, I'll be bound. There wasn't a prettier girl in Kara than Spiridion's Thekla. The young men had no need to be looking in other places for a handsome wife."

By this time the lame woman had limped up to us; and scanning her face for vestiges of its marred beauty, I could see little of it in the wasted, pain-furrowed features; but her eyes were still young and very magnificent — large, dark, and strangely bright, with their dilated pupils and luminous grey irises. There was youth, too, in the tones of her sad voice, as she responded briefly to Nikandros'

voluble greetings, and, panting for breath, and
evidently dead tired, seated herself near us on a
large detached stone which he pointed out to her.

The dust of her journey lay thick upon her poor
garments, and even powdered the black locks which
straggled from beneath her faded yellow kerchief.

"Well, well, Thekla," Nikandros began, "I never
-was more surprised than when I saw you coming
down the road. Surely you can't ever have walked
all the way from Kara?"

"No, only from Melnera; I got a lift in a cart
that was going there."

"But that's six miles, if it's a step; over-far for
you. And what may have brought you such a
journey?"

"I came — because — oh yes, because I thought
somebody here might happen to have a bush of the
Kandian barberry with the berries ripe. They're
green still at Kara—we're later up there—and I
want some to make a syrup for a cough I've had
all the year; barberries are a great remedy, they
say."

"Well, to be sure, I should have thought you
might have found some nearer home. And this is
queer weather to be coughing."

"Oh, a cracked pipe can but squeak whatever tune
you play on it."

"That's true enough. And how did you leave
the good folk at Kara?"

"Very well, all of them. But what's this I hear,
Nikandros, about a wedding at Krinori?"

"Now, by Saint Georgios, how should I know what

folk say?" said Nikandros, smiling self-consciously,
as Thekla raised her great shining eyes to his face,
"no doubt the widow Manetou and I may have
talked——"

"But, no," interrupted Thekla, "I meant your
daughter—Maro, I believe. We heard the other day
that she'd married one of the brothers Zarkos."

"Then you heard what's little likely, unluckily,
to come to pass. It's true that the girl has had
the chance, but she's fool enough to fling it away—
won't look at the man. Why, so far is it from a
marriage, that I'm sending her off next week to
her brother Stavris, at Salonika. The English
gentleman has just drawn this splendid picture to
represent her journey," said Nikandros, pointing with
pride to the scrawl in the dust; "and anybody may
wonder at the madness of a girl who'll set off to
strange lands when she might have a rich husband
at home. Not but what the married have their
troubles as well as the single, Thekla; we musn't
forget that. And who told you the story?"

"The Kuria Ioannidês; it was her son told her."

"Ah, the young Andreas! I knew he was at
Kara, though he has never shown himself here."

"He came home only five days ago; he had the
fever at Smyrna, and that was what kept him so
long away. But he's talking of leaving again to-
morrow or next day to join his ship."

"That's a short holiday, certainly. It looks, too,
as if there might be some truth in a story I heard
about him—that he'd left a wife somewhere abroad.
Do you know whether it's true?"

"There's not a word of truth in it—I know well."

"That's likely enough.   Well, how would the idle folk pass their time if there were no lies to tell? But you mustn't sit here, Thekla.   Come up to our house—it's only a few steps this way—and get a bit to eat."

"No, no, thank you, Nikandros," said Thekla, sighing wearily; "I'll go no farther; and, indeed, I must be on foot again very soon, or I'll lose my chance of the cart, for it's to leave Melnera before dark, and I get on but slowly.   I'll just sit here a bit, and then go the way I came."

"But that's folly; you'll never be able to start off again without a longer rest.   And, may I ask, do you intend to go home without those wonderful barberries after all?"

"Ah, Saint Anna!" said Thekla, laughing unmirthfully, "how I forget things!   I believe the heat of the sun confuses my head."

"Well, we've none ourselves, but I can easily get you some out of our neighbour's garden.   I see you've brought nothing to carry them in; however, I daresay we can manage somehow.   I'll send one of the children with them directly, and a drink and a bit of food."   Nikandros turned away in the direction of his house, murmuring to himself: "If I had the unhappy ox, now, and if the poor ass wasn't lame, I could give her a lift.   I wonder could I by any means get the loan——"

After he had gone, Thekla sat motionless, leaning her head on her hands, only raising it now and then to decline the hospitable invitations of a few women

who, seeing that she was an acquaintance of the
Rodopoulos family, ventured to approach the un-
canny-looking stranger. Before many minutes had
passed, Maro was seen coming from her house, bringing the barberries wrapped up in a large crinkled leaf,
deftly skewered at the corners with cactus-spines,
and also carrying a wooden plate of bread and olives,
a thick-rimmed tumbler of wine, and a small water-
jar. She was very pale, and there were dark shadows
under her eyes, yet her fresh young beauty contrasted
strangely with the marring of the face, haggard and
lined, towards which she stooped to offer her refresh-
ments. Thekla drank the wine and water thirstily,
but would only crumble a little bit of bread; and
when she had finished, she got slowly to her feet,
saying: "Thank you, many times—Maro Rodopoulos,
is it not? I must be on my way again." Then
looking hard at the girl she added: "Can I bring
any message for you to Kara?"

"Oh no, indeed!" said Maro, averting her head
with a haughty gesture. "What message should
I have for Kara? No friends of mine live
there."

"I'm good for little now, to be sure," said Thekla,
leaning on her long staff, and speaking in a solilo-
quising tone; "but, at least, I can carry a message
as well as another; that I know."

"What did you say then?" said Maro, looking
round quickly with a sudden rose-colour, "That you
had brought me a message?"

The other shook her head. "I brought none,"
she said, half-reluctantly as I thought. "However,

that wouldn't hinder me from taking one back, if so be anybody happened to have such a thing."

But all the light had faded out of Maro's face, as she turned away, saying sadly: "Not I, indeed. Good-bye, and a prosperous journey." And Spiridion's Thekla began to limp painfully down the dusty track, where the sunbeams still blazed hotly between the slowly expanding shadows of the grey olive-trees.

In the very heart of the following afternoon, when rays are richest and shadows bluest, I thought to myself, as I sat by the door, that Krinori had never looked fairer. Few of its inhabitants were abroad, for it was a holiday, and many of them were prolonging a *siesta* within doors ; but the sound of song and fiddle proceeded from a clump of shady plane-trees at a little distance, where blind Athanasios was performing amid an appreciative audience.

The singer's voice had just died away for the last time, in a strange incomplete-sounding modulation, when I became aware that somebody was moving along the deserted road, though still so far off as to present merely an indefinitely human aspect. I began lazily to watch the advancing figure, and as I did so, it all at once flashed upon me that this was no other than Andreas Ioannidês. Yes, without doubt it was Andreas himself, but Andreas in his very smartest clothes, looking handsomer than ever, and also both eager and cheerful, as if bound upon some agreeable errand. Having made this discovery, my aimless and languid curiosity changed into so keen an interest that I breathed much more freely when I had seen the new-comer take the left-hand

turn leading to the Rodopouloses' cottage, stride up
the narrow cactus-hedged path, and fairly disappear
beneath the black arch of the open doorway; after
which, further observations being impossible, I had to
content myself with speculations as to what ridding
of baneful doubts and setting straight of tangled
fate-threads might be in progress on its other side.

There had been much slanting and shifting of
lights and shadows, before I found an opportunity
of verifying my conjectures; for full two hours
lingered by, and still Krinori lay sleepily basking,
with none of its inhabitants astir. Then I saw,
coming briskly towards me from the direction of
her dwelling, next door to the Rodopouloses, the
good - natured Dame Lavriadês, who, ever since
my arrival, had taken my sprained ankle under
her special charge, treating it with many curious
concoctions of carefully-culled simples. Just now,
however, she was so pre-occupied with another
subject that she hurried over her customary minute
and sympathising inquiries respecting the progress
of her patient, and forthwith continued: "Well, sir,
and have you heard the last piece of news? Why,
here's young Andreas Ioannidês from Kara, whom
we all thought was gone to the saints could tell
where, sitting as comfortable as you please in
Nikandros Rodopoulos' kitchen. And what do
suppose he's come for? Nothing else but to carry
off the pretty girl Maro, who, he says, was promised
to him two years ago. He's brought home a
sackful of money, and means to buy a bit of land
and take to farming. Nikandros told me all about

G

it just now, when I looked in at them, for it occurred to me that they might happen to be short of something for supper, and might like a couple of our fine artichokes. He's as pleased as can be, poor man! It's Georgios Zarkos who'll look crooked at the match; but, as the saying is, a man who can buy a gold ring will find a finger to put it on easily enough—his turn'll come. But for my part, I'm glad of the young fellow's luck."

"They'll be a handsome couple," I remarked.

"Ah, well, we musn't take beauty for more than it's worth. However, Andreas is a fine, honest lad. I told Maro I'd be well satisfied if my girls got as good husbands, when they were of an age for it, but she looked as if she thought there wasn't another such in the world. Eh, sir, that's the way they are at the beginning! And just to see the silver necklace he's brought to her: all little balls and chains, and with blue stones in the clasp of it as big as the tip of my forefinger. Well, well, good luck to them, and good evening to you, sir! I must be running back, as I promised Maro to look after their supper for them; in truth she's so taken up with him that she's as likely as not to let him go hungry."

Anna had already turned away, when she suddenly wheeled round, with a recollected appendix of news: "You'll remember the poor lame creature who made her way here yesterday? She'll never be seen again in Krinori, that's certain, for she died—the Madonna have mercy on her!—this very morning. So Andreas told us; you must know he was a sort of kinsman of hers. Likely enough that long journey was the death of her, for it seems she somehow missed the cart going back, and had to walk a wonderful number of miles. Still, Andreas says she was at his father's house very early this morning, telling them all the news about us here in Krinori. And scarce an hour afterwards a neighbour went into her kitchen, and found her sitting there, in the middle of washing some heads of lettuce—stone dead. The affair delayed Andreas a bit, or he'd have been here earlier."

The brief twilight was vanishing, and the stars were beginning to prick through in little radiant rosettes above the tree-tops, when a small procession emerged from the Rodopouloses' dwelling. First came Andreas and Maro, followed at a discreet interval by Nikandros with the little boys; the family evidently intended to set their guest upon his homeward way. I certainly never had seen a handsomer or happier-looking pair than were those two young people, as they passed slowly between the cobweb-coloured olives towards the tree-clump where blind Athanasios was striking up his oft-repeated song:

"The vine with its clusters laden
    Each bough to the black earth dips,
Dark, dark as the locks of my maiden,
    And sweet as her lips."

The party had passed almost out of sight, when I heard heavy boots clump into the room behind me, where they were joined a minute afterwards by a similar pair. Then there rose through the open window the familiar surly drone of the brothers Zarkos' discourse.

"I told you the young scoundrel would be here before long."

"There are many who can foretell yesterday's wind and weather.   He might have come for aught it mattered, if he'd left that cursed lot of *drachmai* behind him."

"I wish he and they were at the bottom of the sea."

"So do I most heartily."

"And her fool of a father with him.   I met him just now grinning like a zany."

"I'll tell you a notion I have, Georgios: cut him out with the widow at Koropi."

"Curse the widow at Koropi!"

"You might curse worse things.   Anyhow you owe that fool Nikandros an ill turn."

"That's true enough."

"And may I be hung if I don't think a beggar's daughter no such wonderful treasure.   The Widow Manetou, now, has land."

But there was no answer to this.   And in the silence which ensued I heard blind Athanasios still thrumming and singing away unweariedly:

> "Dark, dark as the locks of my maiden,
>   And sweet as her lips."

A CAPRICE OF QUEEN PIPPA

NO story has ever yet come to its end, nor has
any had a beginning, so far as we can tell, but
that caprice of Queen Pippa marks an important
stage in this one, and is a convenient point whence
to look backward and forward.

The little state of Dendringia was then being
reigned over by King Bernard and Queen Clara, a
very worthy youngish couple, who both, especially
the King, were great poultry-fanciers, and most
zealous in promoting the improvement of varieties
throughout the kingdom. Their Conservative Court
Journal had a leading article on the subject about
once a week, besides repeated descriptions of the
Royal fowl-yard, character-sketches of the Superin-
tendent, and illustrated interviews with everybody
in any way concerned. With the right men in the
right places, and the right hens sitting on the right
sorts of eggs, what people had ever been so blessed
as the Dendringians? Whereas the Liberal press
made jokes and drew caricatures. Now, Philippa,
the Queen-Dowager, who could not endure to be
called anything but Queen Pippa, had leanings
towards Radicalism, and a decided abhorrence of
poultry; and this happened to have been aggravated
by accidental circumstances, just at the time when

101

her lady-in-waiting read out to her the name of Count Elvering in a morning's list of fashionable arrivals at Carmenfort.

"Elvering?" said Queen Pippa, "oh, then, I declare we must ask him to dinner; Markwen must find out whether there is a Countess now. My impression is that there was, and that something happened to her. It's ages since I heard anything of them; but this man's—his aunt, she must have been—Anna Stilton was always my great crony; we were like sisters—*elder* sisters," she added, remembering how long it was since poor Anna's death, but, as usual, not over-careful to convey her meaning with precision.

After an absence of some fifteen years, Count Elvering was revisiting the gay world of Carmenfort on business. He had come a long journey, as the royal residence lies on Dendringia's sunnier southern frontier, while plunged deep among its northern pine-woods, which are spectral with drifted snow for months every winter, stands Castle Elvering. The erection of that overgrown, out-of-the-way pile had set the Elverings several stages on a persevering progress towards impoverishment. Always they had lacked the qualities of a fortune-building race, and rarely were they deficient in the opposite propensities. In most generations they produced at least one thriving specimen of the prodigal. But their nearest approach to the miser—that unpopular saviour at a pinch of a financially-foundering house —would be some scholarly-minded brother, who, while his kinsmen were busily getting (on credit), and spending (on account), and faring sumptuously into insolvency, dwelt obliviously among his books, not discriminating between oatmeal and ortolans, nor concerning himself with affairs further than earnestly to desire that he need never think at all about them.

The present head of the family had inherited some germs of this abstracted mood, but they did not fully develop until after the melancholy end of a matrimonial venture, by making which he proved that he was not wedded to learning in true scholar's wise as the sole love and lady of his life. For, when no longer a very young man, he married a girl in her teens, and lost her before she was twenty. Valerie Beaumont, daughter of a dignitary at Carmenfort, being possessed of brilliant beauty and an exquisite voice, had appeared with them one night at the Court Theatre in an ambitious operatic rôle, and had failed utterly, through a paroxysm of stage fright. Whereupon immediately she had married Count Elvering, an old family friend, and gone away to live amid an uncritical audience of pine-trees. This was an obvious *non sequitur*, the consequences of which Society predicted with varying details. But what actually followed was, that one morning when Count Elvering, solitary in his Castle, expected her home from a visit to her father's house, a letter came instead, explaining how she would return no more to him, and the baby Countess Phyllida, and her faithful nurse Lunelle. After which he did retreat into his studies with an inaccessibility not rivalled by the most recluse of his ancestors, and devoted

himself to his monograph on the epigrams of the
Augustan Age. It grew slowly and slowlier, like a
tree, and sheltered him from himself for many a
year.

All this while, however, his daughter and his
orphan nephew Leopold were lodged somewhere
beneath the Castle's half-acre or so of ruinous roof.
Now and then a faint rustling of leaves at the far
end of the long library reminded Count Elvering of
Count Leopold's existence. Countess Phyllida he
saw so very seldom that he was amazed one day
when he suddenly confronted in the courtyard what
seemed an earlier edition of her mother, poorly clad,
and singing a quaint folk-song. Her notes were as
clear as a thrush's, and as soft as a wood-quest's,
yet Count Elvering begged her to cease that disagreeable noise, which was subjectively quite a correct
description, and went on his way, thinking about
several things. He had long vaguely intended to
marry his daughter some day to his heir, Count
Leopold, upon whom the bulk of his encumbered
estate must devolve; but since Countess Phyllida
existed in his mind as a sedate baby, not many
months old, the matter had seemed by no means
urgent. Her surprising growth all in a minute,
however, changed the situation, and suggested that
it might be well to observe whether her cousin
Leopold had grown likewise. He had, it appeared,
and might be considered a fine-looking young fellow
enough, though rather inky and dusty, and inclined
to stoop. But Count Elvering was again somewhat
taken aback when, upon entering into conversa-

tion with his nephew, he found the young man's
fancy altogether engrossed, apparently, by Professor
Ochlenschläger's theories about the Homeric di-
gamma. The fact was that the youth, startled as
much by his uncle's remarks as if they had fallen
from one of the cobwebby folios, had talked volubly
and with exaggerated emphasis about the subject
nearest to hand. Still, Count Elvering was not
without reason for thinking that it really looked
as if the line were to end in one of those hermit-
scholars; and in that case how could he carry out
his intention of establishing his daughter for life out
of harm's way in her old home? Accordingly, he
forthwith resolved to go and consult his man of
business at Carmenfort about the possibility of
making some provision for her; a sense of respon-
sibility being so new and burdensome to him, that
his first impulse was to shake it off as promptly
as he could.

On the evening when Count Elvering, much
against his will, was bidden to dinner, Queen Pippa's
grievance about the palace poultry still lay among
her uppermost ideas, which habitually supplied the
subject of her conversation, appropriately or otherwise, as the case might be.

"I hope *you're* not fond of cocks and hens, Count
Elvering?" she said. She had taken a fancy to
him, and had importantly offended two personages
by insisting that he should sit beside her at dinner.
"My poor son is sadly afflicted with a craze for
the creatures. I was nearly driven wild last week
when I was staying with them—for my sins. Where-

ever you turn, you come upon something screeching
or squawking. But the first night I was wakened
before my head was on the pillow — you know it
gets light at unearthly hours now—by the wretches
setting up a hallelujah chorus in my ear." The Queen
here crowed two or three times realistically enough,
to the astonishment of several stranger guests. "I
thought one must have got on the roof, and we
had all the sentries and the watchmen and everybody tramping overhead for an hour. But where
do you suppose it was all the while? Some incredible idiot had carried a crateful of Cochin China
monsters up to the dressing-room in mistake for
one of my gown-baskets. I was nearly deafened
before they found it. They're not like rational
beings—my son and his wife I mean, not the fowls.
I am sure you are not plagued, my dear Count,
with such pests up there in your charming, cool,
silent pine-forests. Is there anything so refreshing
as solitude and silence?"

"I fear they produce nothing more useful than
screech-owls," said Count Elvering. "But I could
promise that your majesty would be undisturbed in
our old library, unless, indeed, like the scholar
Mentzelius, you could hear a bookworm flap its
wings and crow like a cock." He felt bound to
say something felicitous, and fancied for a moment
that he had done so, as Queen Pippa said: "Oh,
delightful, delightful!" and tapped him on the
shoulder with her spoon. She had a portly presence with which playfulness harmonised scarcely
better than a *bébé* fringe; however, it was generally

her pleasure to put on both. "Charming, charming!" she said. "My dear Count, do you know I have a thousand minds to pay you a visit this summer—this very month; the heat here is growing unendurable; I am wild for the green woods. Just a picnic sort of visit, you know; to hear your crowing bookworms, and eat omelets of screech-owls' eggs—seriously I will."

And seriously she did.

So poor Count Elvering came presently posting back to his desolate old castle, to make what preparations he could for this invasion, the threat of which had fallen upon him like a thunderbolt from a November mist. Bad were the best, such short notice he had, and such slender resources in an establishment where everything betrayed the no-rule of an impecunious master living in the Augustan Age. By dint, however, of a fortnight spent in going to and fro like a troubled spirit along the nine miles of execrable road between the Castle and the nearest town, Grauberg, a grim, decaying place in a mining district, he completed arrangements which he hoped might enable him to board and lodge the royal party for a week without irreparably damaging the honour of his honse, whatever might be the effect upon his daughter's possible portion. His immediate concern about that young person took the form of stringent injunctions that she should confine herself strictly to her own apartments, and on no account appear to any of the visitors. "Nor go shrieking about," he added as an afterthought, remembering her song. That the child looked much disappointed, and more like her mother than ever when he issued these commands, was a fact which made him insist all the more peremptorily upon them.

Countess Phyllida was indeed not a little morti-fied and cast down. This extraordinary event had seemed to promise her a sight, at least, of things very new and strange, and when one's fifteen long years have never before brought a chance of the like, it is sad to have it snatched away. Old Lunelle, too, her only and one-idea'd companion, was un-wontedly dismal and moody these times. She would bring back from visits to the bustle below-stairs a face criss-crossed with regretful wrinkles, and sit brooding dolorously over milk spilt years ago. Her talk was about the oddness of any per-sons, who could keep away from it, coming to a place where you might listen all day to those dreary plagues of wood-pigeons *oo-oo-ooing* in the black of the trees there, like so many old wives round a bier, till your heart was broken. And how, for her part, only a promise to stay with the child had prevented her from hearing the last of them long ago ; and how there had never been any such fine doings in her poor young lady's time, who was fairly moped to death, with his Excellency squatting in his study like a spider in his web, and turning the door-key like a pistol snapping if he heard a step outside. "Just moping to death she was, she that the world ran after at home. And you, Countess Phyllida, no more company to her than a blind kitten," Lunelle would say, and her reproachful tone would strike Phyllida with remorse for her own social deficiencies, which were really not inexcusable, as at the time referred to she had been but a few months old. So the hours passed heavily and querulously in the low-ceiled, moth-fretted chambers, huddled away among the mazes of the oldest north wing.

But Queen Pippa arrived in very good spirits one radiant July evening, and said next morning that the cooing of the wood-pigeons was the most soothing sound imaginable; it made her think of angels snoring. And a day and a half passed gaily, but then rain set in, which sadly disorganised all Count Elvering's painful impromptu *al fresco* arrangements. It looked terribly as if the fine weather, upon which they were based, had untowardly broken up. Perhaps this was why, as the procession went dinnerwards across a wide hall, Queen Pippa said to the Count: "Ah, what a place for private threatricals, my dear Count! Has Master Bottom his loom anywhere about your woods? Oh no, to be sure, he lives with that funny Falstaff in the Forest of Arden. I'm devoted to Shakespeare; know him by heart. There's nothing so enjoyable as atrocious acting, when it really is atrocious. These people of mine, now"—waving round her suite—"unluckily are quite useless in that way; neither good enough nor bad enough to be amusing. Do you think any of the others have dramatic gifts? Your bishop, for instance? I'm told that the Bishop of Norenstock takes off all his clergy in a sort of comic dialogue after dinner most delightfully; and

I have seen our Regius Professor of Pastoral Theology do a skirt-dance with a tablecloth." But the guests that Her Majesty had consented to meet, were all, even the Bishop, serious and solemn persons, from whom no such contributions to her entertainment could be hoped.

And the veiled light of the next morning showed pale mists creeping closer out of the forest, and where the great trees stood severally on the lawns, spinning a woolly white cocoon round each, in a fashion from which the weather-wise of the place drew the gloomiest auguries. Before breakfast had begun, raindrops were rapping out notices that open-air amusements could not be in the order of that day, but refrained from suggesting any substitutes. Under these trying circumstances things did drag a little. At luncheon, from which Count Elvering was unavoidably absent on business in Grauberg, conversation languished rather dismally, until towards its end somebody started the speculation whether tomtits could be trained to walk like hens instead of hopping along. Whereupon somebody else observed how awkward it would be if people could move only in hops, especially when waiting at dinner. And the Queen's equerries, and her private secretary, and two or three of her ladies, began on the spot to give a practical demonstration of the inconveniences by hopping round the table to hand dishes. They hopped so high, with such disastrous consequences to jellies, and creams, and carpet, that if the party had been a nursery or schoolroom one, it would have broken up in dire

and well-merited disgrace.   As it was, however, they
rose much exhilarated, and Queen Pippa proposed
that they should divert themselves by exploring the
Castle.

Thus it came about that, in the course of this
wet afternoon, a noisy little crowd burst without
warning into the faded blue room, where a young
girl, whose sad-coloured, unseasonable garments were
as a withered brown calyx to a fresh flower-bud,
was sitting on the low window-seat half asleep.
She had long been looking out into the heavily-
swaying drenched tree-tops, and wishing she had
something else to do; and now the rustling and
gleaming of brilliant costumes and uniforms—th.
Queen was wearing heliotrope silk, relieved with
cactus-scarlet velvet—seemed as uncanny as if a
flock of great gaudy birds had suddenly flown in
through the lattice.   An elderly waiting - woman
started up in the background, manifestly disconcerted at this visit of unceremony; but Countess
Phyllida was scared into a severe and stately
mien.

"Whom have we here?" said Queen Pippa,
striking an attitude of surprise, which was unfeigned: "the Sleeping Beauty in her chamber?
Upon my word, it looks very like it.   What great
eyes you have, my dear, and that thunder-cloud
of hair.   Quite a strong likeness to the Count,
too.   But he spoke of her as a mere child.
Does he always keep her shut up here, I wonder?
However, the fairy godmother has come to find
her.   And now that the beauty is awake, I'm afraid

she thinks her fairy godmother a terrible sort of thing."

"I'm sure nobody could think you any such——" Countess Phyllida began, but she was interrupted in the middle of her speech, exemplifying once more how much better is the half than the whole. She was going to add: "For you are a great deal too fat for a fairy."

The interruption was the entrance of her father, who had returned from Grauberg, and hurried in just too late to prevent an undesired discovery. His wishes were now to get the Queen out of the room as speedily as might be; but Her Majesty, curious and pleased, was not easily moved on.

"Well, Count," she said, "no wonder you look a little disgusted." Count Elvering straightway smiled, the smile that is necessarily slightly too broad, because it has to overlap underlying chagrin. "Here I've come upon something you had hidden away very craftily indeed. But now you'll have to let me carry it off with me, on loan at least, when we go home."

"Your Majesty can see for yourself," the Count said depreciatingly, "how unpresentable——"

"Presentable?" said Queen Pippa. "Why, that's a matter of a few new frocks. As it is, I only wish poor Clarry" (the Queen Consort) "had half that air of the *grande dame*. But *she* takes after all the Alten-Oberfelds, who, I always think, are the most hopelessly plebeian-looking set of people in existence. Their latest photograph — that family group—is fearful to behold. Such hands, such ears!

I call it the Elephant and—my goodness!" said the Queen, subsiding into a dismayed whisper, and moving away, "I do believe Madame Dix was within hearing, and she repeats everything to *everybody*; you might as well talk into a walking phonograph. And I have noticed that people are so touchy sometimes. But this child, if I had her at Carmenfort——"

"Ah, Queen Pippa, you would spoil her for a poor forester's wife," said Count Elvering, continuing warily to guide her steps towards the door.

"What absurdity! Much chance of that, if our young millionaires have as many eyes in their heads as coins in their pockets. That's not it exactly, is it? though, indeed, they'd want them all—the eyes I mean—to spy her out, buried alive down here. And it's really wrong. Oh, to be sure, I remember hearing of some family arrangement; she was to go along with the estate. But I don't approve of that at all. I believe in romance and love at first sight, if possible. You'd far better marry yourself, Count; marry an heiress, and put this place in repair: make it just habitable. Of course, it's charming at present, quite charming, and most comfortable. I don't mean *that*," stammered the Queen, for once become conscious of having said a foolish thing, and staring fascinatedly at a window full of smashed panes, until she tripped over a loose board in the flooring. "Only —only, you know, money is sometimes convenient," she ended, lamely, so much discomposed, that she thankfully allowed her host to begin upon the

H

subject of his morning's expedition. It had been
to secure the services of a travelling theatrical
company then visiting Grauberg. And he had
returned in a position to suggest that Her Majesty
should be graciously pleased to command a performance at the Castle for the following evening.
"From the appearance of the manager, whom I
interviewed," he said, "I should infer that the
atrocities of his troupe would leave little to be
desired." And Queen Pippa, still self-reproachful,
expressed in her happiest terms the liveliest gratification at the prospect.

A few hours later, when all dangerous persons
were safely dining, Countess Phyllida ventured out
among the trees. Towards sundown, the rain had
ceased, and a wide golden-amber shining came on
through the woods from the far west, burning like
a flame, yet brooding like a wing. With all its
glades and dells, the forest seemed a vast house
of many chambers storing jewels of light, and
threaded by long alleys, where the steady green
shadow seldom flickered. The clear freshness of
the evening air, sifted through a myriad million
aromatic pine-needles, and breathing over the twinkling wet leaves and grasses, was softly fragrant to
her after a day wished away in musty, beetle-browed
rooms; and a thrush singing liquidly from a tangle
of briar-roses gave a mellower voice to seemingly
more hopeful views of the present time, than did
old Lunelle, with her disconsolate creak of reminiscences. Countess Phyllida roamed about for a
while contentedly enough. Still, it was all very

lonely. Even her favourite friendly Spitz was out of the way. The green, goldenly-lighted dells that she looked into were empty, every one; nothing stirred except leaves and shadows; and as she turned homewards with the dusk dim on her track, she felt disappointed, she could not have told of what expectation.

However, she was presently cheered by falling in with Count Leopold, whom an invasion of indoor haunts had driven to unwonted wandering abroad. They were good friends, for he liked his cousin very well, whenever he happened to think of her— which he sometimes did when he saw her; while to her his chief defect appeared to be that, like all men and boys, so far as she knew them, he cared most for unintelligible books, and seldom emerged from an unapproachable library. His talk to her turned much upon his studies, whereby she had picked up some familiarity with the phrase-ology of classical lore; and in the misapplication of it, she showed an ingenious ignorance, which she perceived to give him pleasure. She enjoyed making him laugh at her, which argued good nature on both sides. It had never occurred to him that she was a beauty; but once it did strike him that her profile resembled a mythological heroine's in an engraving of antique gems, which he brought to show her, and which she reluctantly considered frightful.

This evening he began to carve their initials in Greek characters on the trunk of an elm tree, while she sat between its mossy roots in the last long blink of the sun.   When he had just finished a mis-shapen *Phi*, he remembered a bit of news. "We're to have a play here to-morrow night," he said.

"*They* are, I know," said Countess Phyllida.

"Oh, nonsense! Of course you must be there too," he said, replying to her wistful emphasis.

"But I mustn't be seen, you know, any more than if I were the snaky woman with all the hideous heads that everybody had to pelt with stones," Countess Phyllida said mournfully, illustrating her prohibition by this somewhat inaccurate reference to a repellant legendary character.

"Never mind. Let me see. There's the little gallery where the old organ was. It's right opposite where they'll have the stage, and you'd be quite out of sight in it, if you had a hundred hideous heads. I'll manage, never fear," said Count Leopold, with a touch of self-importance at a novel sense of practical efficiency.

So Countess Phyllida after all went indoors much cheered by her outing, and full of wonderful expectations for the morrow, scarcely likely, however, to be realised, since her cousin, as a forecast of what they were about to witness, had described to her as graphically as he could a performance of the *Agamemnon* of Æschylus in the ancient theatre of Dionysius.

All the next day workmen did rough carpentering with loud thumps in the empty, echoing hall, and at dusk the Montglaçon Dramatic Company drove up through the rain with their properties in a

tarpaulin-tilted van, which gave some of them the
sensation of a miserable reverse—perhaps reversion—
of fortune; it was so like going to a fair. Their
performance, nevertheless, was a marked success,
though not from the sarcastic point of view which
Count Elvering had suggested to the Queen. This
was due, indeed, almost solely to the leading lady,
Madame Almeria, whose vivid beauty, if somewhat
on the wane beneath the prying sun, shone un-
dimmed behind those primitive footlights, in violet
velvet cloak and tunic, with all the other lovely
garnish of a melodramatic boy. Her rôle in the
Perjured Page had been selected by the manager,
with a fine sense of the unfitness to present company
of such things as the *Desperado of Golden Gulch*,
and *Tiara, or Tatters*; and there were touches of
inspiration that night in her acting and singing,
which impressed even her colleagues, and took the
Queen by storm, thus carrying, of course, the whole
position. Hidden away up in the dark little organ-
gallery Countess Phyllida's grey eyes grew larger,
like stars at dusk-fall, as they watched every revelation of this wondrous new world ; and Count Leopold's
gaze was not less rapt and ardent, though he at first
deplored the absence of masks and chorus. Yet nobody was affected in at all the same degree as, strange
to say, Count Elvering. He sat staring at the
stage as if he had seen a ghost, so Madame Dix,
the observant, reported, and made a hasty exit
after one of the most powerful scenes, looking, to
cite the same authority, like a ghost himself.

Thus it chanced that the master of the house was

out of the way when Queen Pippa requested an interview with Madame Almeria, and bestowed upon her a golden bangle with a splendid true lover's knot of pearls and emeralds, instead of the more trivial turquoise pin, which in cooler moments she had dedicated to the encouragement of Art. This star, she now declared, must certainly be brought from its obscurity into the light of day; and she at once began to revolve measures for the making of Madame Almeria's fortune, and the marring of the Montglaçon Dramatic Company.

In the passage near the green-room door, Count Elvering by-and-by came bewildered face to half-defiant face with, presumably, a ghost indeed; for he said: "Valerie?   Good heavens!—*Valerie*!   But you died the year after—in the winter."

"That time at Moscow?" said the ghost, who was wrapped up in an old waterproof, ready for a wet drive back to Grauberg, "So I made them give out; but it was only my voice. I've often been sorry that that was all, and I see that you are too; however, the van will be at the door in a minute. It was very bad luck for the new *prima donna* to sing Zerlina twice in *Fra Diavalo*, and Marguerite once—that was all—and then catch cold at rehearsal; that Latin sort of sore throat.   Now I can sometimes venture upon just a little song, if there is a dance to help it out.   When I am too hoarse, I dance a bit longer, and they like that quite as well.   But it is ages since I have sung as I did to-night."

"I don't understand," said Count Elvering.

"Why, when I lost my voice," she said, "I had to live somehow—at least it seemed necessary to me—and as acting never was my strong point, it was not easy for me to get on. In fact, I didn't. I got *down*—to country fairs sometimes, with caravans and merry-go-rounds. However, at least, I kept myself alive. I shouldn't be here entertaining royalty if I were dead."

"Nor unless you were mad," said Count Elvering.

"I may be," she said, "but with a sort of method on this occasion. Our manager would have turned me adrift very promptly if I'd made any difficulties. Your terms are so magnificent, you know. We had pancakes for supper last night on the strength of them, and I expect to get some arrears paid, and a clean suit for Ronaldo—this is disgraceful." She protruded a cotton-velvet cuff, which was stained and frayed.

"Don't let me detain you any longer," said Count Elvering, and was turning away, but she intercepted him and caught his sleeve.

"The truth is," she said, "that I came to see the child, little Phyllida."

"Whom you might have been seeing every hour of every day through all these years," said he.

"Yes, yes, and what else?" she rejoined, "there are so many hours and so many days. I did stay nearly one whole year here. I believe it would never have come to an end if I hadn't gone. Nobody to speak to, nothing to do; a jingling wreck of an old piano, that I was afraid to touch, and—resignation if I sang. . . No, I could not

come back to it once I had got away," she said
after a slight pause, as though to revise her sketch
of domestic felicity. "And then the Delmoronis
offered me another chance of what I'd always set
my heart on. And I had it, too, twice, for perhaps
five minutes; made a great crowd hold its breath
to listen. Sometimes I dream of it still; but awake
one is wiser to think of something else. Yet, whenever I'm at all fairly well off, I wish I'd taken
little Phyllida with me."

"God forbid!" said Count Elvering.

"He might forbid her worse things," she said.

"Than dancing in a showman's booth?"

"She would have run no risk of that; it is not
my bad luck that she has inherited. Her voice,"
Madame Almeria said wistfully, "will be lovely. I
heard it last winter, when we were three days at
Grauberg. Of course I had no—no engagement
here, but I tramped over one morning for a sight
of her. It is much too far, and I was half-dead,
though I got a lift in a baker's cart. I waited by
the gap in the yew-hedge, where she'd pass with
her pigeons' food, and, as luck would have it, she
was singing all the way down the walk. My voice
never promised so well, I believe. It will be a sin
if she does not get training. And this time I am
off without getting a sight of her at all. I am sure
it might have been managed better if Lun—...
And you are going to marry her to that dusty,
sleepy-looking, bookish boy?"

"Why should I trouble you with our family
affairs?" said Count Elvering.

"I seem to have left her tethered in a dismal cobweb. Let her at least go to Carmenfort first for a while," she said, "with that absurd, good-natured old Queen. She has taken a great fancy to the child, and has been talking about her ever since she saw her yesterday."

"Who keeps you posted up in these things?" said Count Elvering. "Ah, that old woman— Lunelle."

"I am a fool," she said aloud to herself.

"A matter of opinion," said he. "But no doubt it will in future be more convenient for that faithful domestic to reside with her employer."

Steps sounded close by, with a call for Madame Almeria, who sped away to her equipage. On the morrow Lunelle, too, was driven off, smiling grimly, under a dripping umbrella. She expressed to the lad who drove the trap an unfulfilled hope that she might never more meet with the dismal smell of those dreary pines.

And next day the old family coach, ordered out in a sudden hurry, lumberingly conveyed Queen Pippa from the scene of a silence and solitude to enjoy which the concerted war-whoops of all Dendringia's chanticleers would hardly have frayed her back. Yet she did assure her host at parting, with flattering emphasis, that she seemed to have been spending *ages and ages* in the Garden of Eden, and thought she would never feel quite wide-awake again.

Then Castle Elvering grew quieter, and the wood-quests crooned louder than ever, and to Countess Phyllida the days became very lonesome and long,

for her father followed the Queen to Carmenfort
almost immediately, taking with him his nephew,
who was about to come of age, which involved some
lawyers' business.   Count Elvering set out with the
intention of doing a piece of business on his own
account ; but, arrived in Carmenfort, he heard such
a tempting report of a commentary on Martial,
lately grubbed up in a library at the obscure town
of Arkwald, that he postponed everything else, and
hurried off thither in hopes of a prize.

Meanwhile Count Leopold, on his part, was
beginning now to learn that the world had not
been wholly committed to script and print, a discovery which appeared to him interesting and worth
following up.   The acquisition of his mother's small
fortune gave him the means of doing so moderately,
and he presently informed his surprised uncle, who
had supposed the shy and silent youth to be pining
for escape from the haunts of men, that he thought
of visiting Wilnalinden, a fashionable watering-place,
where Queen Pippa was then quartered.

His intention perhaps sprung from his knowledge
that Madame Almeria, late of the Montglaçon
Dramatic Company, had through her Dowager-
Majesty's influence obtained an engagement there,
and was performing nightly with much *éclat*.   At
any rate, upon his arrival he lost no time in putting
himself under the spell which she had thrown over
him that first night at Elvering.   Things in general
looked so wonderful through its glamour, that the
coincidence did not strike him as especially remarkable, when he lit upon the old familiar face of

Lunelle in the character of Madame Almeria's
waiting-maid. A happy coincidence it was for him,
as he had always been rather a favourite with the
peevish old woman, who now admitted him to the
glory and joy of an interview with her mistress.

" I always liked poor Count Leopold, Miss Valerie
—my lady," she said. " He was a quiet, civil-spoken
child, and gave no trouble. How he ever found
his way here is more than I can tell, for he 's
mooned all his days in that old library, till he 's
as ignorant as the mice in the walls. But here he
is, with a bunch of pink and white tulips bigger
than his head. He 'll be disappointed if I don't
let him in to give it; and then you can bid him
run off again as soon as you like."

Count Leopold found Madame Almeria in private
life a less young and beautiful person than he had
imagined, and she by no means sought to prolong
his illusion. As it faded, however, it was replaced
by a sentiment of genuine friendliness. For Madame
Almeria was kind to him in a motherly sort of way,
which he had never experienced before, and which
his present position, out alone in a strange new
world, put him in just the mood to appreciate.
Right glad he was often to let Lunelle shut him
in from the alien bustle outside the street door,
and to spend a while talking with her mistress about
Elvering. That was the subject upon which their
conversation generally turned, by Madame Almeria's
choice, and she seemed to take a special interest
in anything that concerned his cousin Phyllida.
She asked more questions than he could answer

about her occupations and amusements, and showed so much surprise one day at learning that he had not yet written to her, that he sent off a letter by the very next post. Countess Phyllida's reply, extremely brief and laboriously ill-written, stated that the weather was wet, and she was quite well. As it struck him that Madame Almeria seemed somewhat aggrieved and disappointed at this being all he had to report, he showed her the little note to prove that he had suppressed nothing; and she must have forgotten to give it back, at least she never did so. On another occasion she said to him : "Your cousin has an exquisite voice," and wished she could send her a mandolin to sing to. But Lunelle, who was present, declared she had never thought Countess Phyllida's voice any such great things that there was any need to be strumming accompaniments to it. So he could not conjecture how Madame Almeria had formed her high opinion. Her solicitude, however, was to some extent infectious, and he found himself regretting that Phyllida should be left lonely and moping away in the old forest Castle, where, to quote Madame Almeria, "She can have no out-of-door resources in such weather as they have up there" (for by this time winter had set in, and Madame Almeria had migrated to the Gaieté at Soldoro), "when the clammy dead leaves stick to the soles of your shoes, and the howling winds come to tear up the white fog, that's stiff with frost, and you see the black fir-tops all round nodding and wagging over it, like the plumes at everybody else's funeral, till you more than half wish it was your own."

"Why, you never were at Elvering in the winter, madame, were you?" said Count Leopold.

"Oh, one knows what such places are like," she replied.

And Count Leopold said, and thought: "It is a shame to leave her there so long all alone." Yet his newly-realised liberty continued to pre-occupy him, and the turn of the year saw him still tarrying in the south.

Meanwhile Count Elvering, though the contents of the Arkwald library did for many a week divert his mind from the business which had been the main object of his visit to Carmenfort, was not altogether oblivious of it, and eventually found an opportunity for transacting it. On his previous visit, when discussing Countess Phyllida's far from brilliant financial prospects with his man of business, the latter had casually remarked that Baron von Stritt's two slenderly-dowered daughters had lately been provided for in the neighbouring Convent of Saint Serena, the Monitress. "It is a charming little spot," Herr Linfeld said; "and the portion required is wonderfully reasonable. The Sisters support themselves to a considerable extent by their garden. Their cucumbers and vegetable-marrows are famous. And they are all highly well-born."

Count Elvering knew the exterior of Saint Serena's Convent, a small white house in a hollow planted with shrubs, most of them tall and sombre, threaded by walks, where the Sisters' habits of serge and linen went to and fro, bringing a moonlight gleam into broadest noon.   Some events which had occurred since that conversation inclined him to look upon the convent as a desirable place wherein to establish his daughter.   It were a better plan, he thought, than a marriage with her cousin Leopold, even if that could be brought about.   Viewed in the light of past experiences, he saw how completely that might fail to avert from the family's pride very mortifying shocks.   What if the annals of Elvering had once again to record the erratic proceedings of a stage-struck bride?   Certainly such a risk would be obviated by her enrolment among the sisterhood of Saint Serena.   Therefore he had a highly satisfactory interview with the Mother Superior, during which his plans for his daughter's future ripened as rapidly as a peach in a July sun, and at which it was arranged that when once spring weather made travelling pleasant, a lay Sister should be despatched to fetch Countess Phyllida from among the cushat-haunted woods of Elvering.   It really never occurred to him that he need consider her sentiments upon the subject any more than if she were some dusty little volume which he was transferring from one shelf to another.

One, May day Madame Almeria, after a rehearsal at Soldoro, found a hurried-looking scrawl on a post-card awaiting her.   It was from Count Leopold, and only said: "My uncle has just told me that Ph. is to go into a convent here, and they are to fetch her to-morrow. But I am sure she would hate it." And on that evening Madame Almeria's performance was announced to be prevented by a sudden attack of influenza. Madame's maid, indeed, was of the opinion that it would have been a deal better to let things take their chance; a reckless view of the case which did not, however, affect her mistress's proceedings.

Next evening Countess Phyllida was coming along a narrow, thicket-walled path, with a bundle of fragrant thorn-boughs in her arms, the fleece of white blossom on them lying as thick as the wool-fillets on a suppliant's wand. She had just reached an open glade, where several overgrown rides converged, likely to be crossed by anybody passing between the Castle and the forest. It was steeped in the flushing light of a May sunset, which turned the grey trunks of the beeches into columns of rosed silver, and as she stepped across the circle of sunbeams, they seemed to clothe her all in a fleckless shimmer, though her white home-spun was really powdered with yellow lichen-dust, and stained with the juice of fresh green leaves. She had of late shot up very tall and slender, and her eyes were large and melancholy. As a sort of farewell to the youth which she felt slipping away from her, she had gathered up her dark hair into heavy silken coils. Over it she wore a little poppy-coloured shawl like a peasant girl's.

The months since Queen Pippa's visit had been the loneliest in all Countess Phyllida's sixteen years, and haunted by wistful regrets for the happy past, when she had always had a gloomy-tempered old companion, and sometimes an absent-minded young one. Now, as she stood still beside a broad twig-feathered elm-trunk, she let her bundle of foamy-blossomed sprays drop on the carpet of wood-sorrel and moss. "It's not worth while to bring them in," she said to herself. "There's nobody to see them." Then she looked up and saw where some carved letters showed clearly, a low relief in pale brown on the crinkled, speckled rind. And she remembered that evening before the play, when Leopold had chipped out the *Phi* and *Lambda*, discoursing the while mostly about a theory of his own that the fluting on ancient Greek columns was originally a conventional representation of bark. At the time it had bored her a little, but in the retrospect it seemed all delightful sunshine. So, remembering, she drew a fond and rueful finger along the tracing of the initials, and then for the sake of that dear, lost day, leaned her cheek against the rough inscription caressingly, as if she were touching the soft plumage of one of those little wild birds who last winter had often saddened her by lying in a piteous rufflement of feathers on her frozen path.

Just at that moment somebody, who at her approach had slipped behind a berberis-bush close by, plucked a companion's sleeve and pointed, with a whisper. But a crackling leaf had already whispered less discreetly, and Countess Phyllida glanced round to see her cousin Leopold, who had sped softly down the moss-muffled path,

standing almost at her elbow. Whereupon, following her first impulse, she fled away from the tree,
as if whirled off by a sudden gust. But her flight
was not far. "Wait—stop, Phyllida," Count Leopold
called; "you mustn't play hide-and-seek now. I've
something serious to tell you." And then their
voices moved slowly away in earnest conversation.

"So his young Excellency has come headlong too,"
Lunelle said, following Madame Almeria from behind
the bush. "Well, to be sure, there's sometimes a
great deal of running after little enough. It was he
carved those outlandish letters in Hebrew or some
such heathen way. Countess Phyllida could read
them no more than you or I."

"And so that's how it is," Madame Almeria said,
and sighed. "Well, maybe it is all the better. Only
I suppose she won't stay with me long; and I had
hoped—— He can come back with us, too. But
there must be no delay, for the others may arrive
at any moment."

"They wouldn't drive from where we passed them
in much less than a long hour in that lump of a heavy
coach," said Lunelle. "They won't be here yet a
good while."

"Bread and water, and little whitewashed cells,"
said Madame Almeria, hurrying away. "Don't forget
we are to talk about all that. Yet, I daresay, indeed,
there will be no need for us to frighten her into
coming."

And when shortly afterwards Count Elvering
entered the glade, escorting a black-veiled, placid-
countenanced Sister Monica, nobody was there to

be seen, nor all along the paths which they paced until the twilight began to spin grey webs, and Count Elvering gave up the quest impatiently, remarking that he hoped the good Sisters would cure his daughter of her roving fits. He had wanted her so seldom in the course of her life, that he might reasonably feel aggrieved at her being out of the way on this special occasion.

At that moment she formed one of a quartette who were driving rapidly towards Grauberg.

"Have you heard the latest news?" said Madame Dix to Queen Pippa, who was sofa-ridden owing to a heavy fall from her first cycle.

"If it happens to be anything about Toulouse geese or Rouen hens, *don't* tell me for mercy's sake," said the Queen. "I've just had poor Clarry here for half-an-hour clacking and cackling, till at last I asked her if she didn't think hard-boiling the eggs before they were hatched would be likely to strengthen the chickens. So she went away to tell everybody that I've got concussion of the brain."

"*Impossible!*" Madame Dix said, with conviction; "But it's partly about one of your own pets— Madame Almeria."

"Oh, as for that," said Queen Pippa, "I haven't been in a theatre for months. Since I took to cycling, I've been so stiff and sleepy in the evening, that I should dislocate my unfortunate neck if I tried to sit out a one-act comedietta—worse than my ankle, you know, and that's nuisance enough. But what about Madame Almeria?"

"Well, it's also about Count Elvering—another pet, I believe."

"Elvering?" the Queen said, much as she had done nine months before. "Oh yes, the man who beguiled me up to that fearful place of his last summer. And what about him?"

"There's his nephew, Count Leopold Elvering," said Madame Dix.

"Really, a great many people seem to be mixed up in it," said Queen Pippa; "and I don't remember him at all."

"A gawky, short-sighted sort of boy," said Madame Dix. "And then there's his cousin, Phyllis, or some such name."

"Patience of saints! *Is* there anybody *not* implicated?" said the Queen. "I do remember *her*; a pretty child with wonderful hair, very long, and very untidy."

"Perhaps her father thought it *too* long," said Madame Dix, "and that may have been why he wanted to make a nun of her here in the Convent of Saint Serena."

"The old Bluebeard!" said the Queen. "But after all, if she was to live for life up there like a lost hermit among those pines and wood-pigeons, it may be the best thing he could do with her."

"But he can't do it," said Madame Dix, "for it appears that when she and this boy heard of the arrangement, they eloped, and went off straight to Madame Almeria at Soldoro, where they are now."

"And why on earth to Madame Almeria?" said the Queen.

"Possibly because, you see, she happens to be

the girl's mother. My dear Queen Pippa, if you bounce up that way, you'll double-dislocate your unlucky ankle. And it's not as if there was any great scandal. She was one of the Von Tenkels, a beauty with a splendid voice, and ran away from Elvering a year or so after her marriage to go on the stage, for which she had a passion. But she did not succeed, and it somehow got about that she was dead. She had come down pretty low in the world, as you saw, when you picked her up. It was a quaint idea of hers to go and act at the Castle, and the situation must have been quite thrilling. Isn't it a pity that we didn't know at the time? However, I fancy she's hardly likely now to accept another engagement at Elvering."

"She'd be moping-mad if she did," said Queen Pippa, "or very soon afterwards at any rate. And upon my word, as I said before, I think the little girl might have a less dreary time of it here at the convent."

"She would have had to renounce all prospects of riding," Madame Dix said impressively, specialising her argument. "A Sister seems to be one of the few things that are not possible on a cycle."

"Ah, well, yes; and of course that does make all the difference in the world," Queen Pippa said earnestly, as if she were uttering rather a pious sentiment, and feeling it, too. And, after a short pause, she added solemnly: "In that case, I don't see what else she could have done."

So the match might be considered to have received, at least in a modified form, the Royal assent.

AN ADVANCE SHEET

Quapropter cælum simili ratione fatendumst
Terramque et solem lunam mare, cetera quæ sunt,
Non esse unica, sed numero magis innumerali.—LUCRETIUS.

MANY years ago I lived for some time in the neighbourhood of a private lunatic asylum, kept by my old fellow-student, Dr Warden, and, having always been disposed to specialise in the subject of mental disease, I often availed myself of his permission to visit and study the various cases placed under his charge. In one among these, that of a patient whom I will call John Lynn, I came to feel a peculiar interest, apart from scientific considerations. He was a young man of about twenty-five, of pleasant looks and manners, and to a superficial observer apparently quite free from any symptoms of his malady. His intellectual powers were far above the average, and had been highly trained; in fact, the strain of preparing for a brilliantly successful University examination had proved the cause of a brain fever, followed by a long period of depression, culminating in more than one determined attempt at suicide, which had made it necessary to place him under surveillance. When I first met him he had spent six months at Greystones House, and was, in Dr Warden's opinion, making satisfactory progress towards complete re-

133

covery.   His mind seemed to be gradually regaining
its balance, his spirits their elasticity, and the only
unfavourable feature in his case was his strong taste
for abstruse metaphysical studies, which he could
not be prevented from occasionally indulging.   But
a spell of Kant and Hartmann, Comte and Hamilton,
and Co., was so invariably followed by a more or
less retrograde period of excitement and dejection,
that Dr Warden and I devoted no small ingenuity
to the invention of expedients for diverting his
thoughts from those pernicious volumes, and our
efforts were not unfrequently rewarded with success.

My acquaintance with him was several months old,
when, one fine mid-summer day, I called at Greystones
House after an unusually long absence of a week or
more.   The main object of my visit was to borrow
a book from John Lynn, and accordingly, after a
short conversation with Dr Warden, I asked whether
I could see him.   "Oh, certainly," said the Doctor;
"I'm afraid, though, that you won't find him over-
flourishing.   He's been at that confounded stuff,
Skleegel, and *Ficty*, and *Skuppenhoor*"—my friend
is no German scholar, and his eccentric pronuncia-
tion seemed to accentuate the scornful emphasis
which he laid upon each obnoxious name—"hammer
and tongs ever since last Monday, and you know
that always means mischief with him.   To-day,
however, he has apparently taken to Berkeley and
Herbert Spencer, which is a degree better, and he
was talking about you at luncheon, which I thought
rather a good sign; so perhaps he may come round
this time without much trouble."

Having reached John Lynn's apartments, however, I did not feel disposed to adopt the Doctor's hopeful view. For though he appeared outwardly composed and collected—epithets which, indeed, always sound a warning note—there was a restlessness in the young man's glance, and a repressed enthusiasm in his tone, whence I augured no good. Moreover, I found it quite impossible to steer our conversation out of the channel in which his thoughts were setting ; and this was the atomic theory. I did my best for some time, but to no purpose at all. The atoms and molecules drifted into everything, through the most improbable crevices, like the dust of an Australian whirlwind. They got into sport, and politics, and the current piece of parochial gossip—which really had not the remotest connection with any scientific subject—and the latest novel of the season, albeit the time of the modern metaphysical romance was not yet. So at length, abandoning the bootless struggle, I resolved to let him say his say, and the consequence was that, after some half-hour's discourse, which I will not tempt the reader to skip, I found myself meekly assenting to the propositions of the infinitude of the material universe, and the aggregation and vibration of innumerable homogeneous atoms as the origin of all things, from matter to emotion, from the four-inch brick to the poet's dream of the Unknown.

"Now, what has always struck me as strange," quoth John Lynn, who at this point leaned forward towards me, and held me with a glittering eye, which to the professional element in my mind sub-consciously suggested the exhibition of sedatives—"what strikes me as strange is the manner in which scientists practically ignore an exceedingly important implication of the theory—one, too, that has been pointed out very distinctly by Lucretius, not to go farther back. I refer to the fact that such a limitless atomic universe necessarily involves, in conformity with the laws of permutations and combinations, the existence, the simultaneous existence, of innumerable solar systems absolutely similar to our own, each repeating it in every detail, from the willow-leaves in the sun to the petals on that geranium-plant in the window, whilst in each of them the progress of events has been identically the same, from the condensation of gaseous nebulæ down to the prices on 'Change in London at noon to-day. A minute's rational reflection shows that the admission is inevitable. For, grant that the requisite combination doesn't occur more than once in a tract of a billion trillion quintillions of square miles, what's that, ay, or that squared and cubed, to us with infinite space to draw upon? You'll not overtake the winged javelin. But, of course, this isn't all. For it follows from the same considerations that we must recognise the present existence, not only of inconceivably numerous Earths exactly contemporaneous with our own, and consequently arrived at exactly its stage of development, but also of as many more, older and younger, now exhibiting each successive state, past and future, through which ours has already proceeded, or at which it is destined to arrive. For example, there are some still in the palæolithic period, and others where our Aryan ancestors are driving their cattle westward over the Asiatic steppes. The battle of Marathon's going on in one set, and Shakespeare's writing Hamlet's 'Is life worth living?' in another. Here they've just finished the general election of eighteen hundred and ninety - something, and here they're in the middle of the next big European war, and here they're beginning to get over the effects of the submergence of Africa, and the resurrection of Atlantis—and so on to infinity. To make a more personal application, there's a series of Earths where you at the present moment are playing marbles in a holland bib, and another where people are coming back from my funeral, and saying that that sort of thing is really an awful grind, you know."

"Oh well," I said, in a studiously bored and cold-waterish way, "perhaps these speculations may be interesting enough—not that they ever struck me as particularly so. But what do they all come to? It seems to me quite easy to understand why scientists, as you say, ignore them. They've good reason to do that, with so much more promising material on hands. Why *should* they waste their time over such hopeless hypotheses—or facts, whichever you like?"

"Then, conceding them to be facts, you consider that they can have no practical significance for science?" said John Lynn, with a kind of latent triumph in his tone.

"Not a bit of it," I promptly replied. "Supposing that this world *is* merely one in a crop, all as much alike as the cabbages in a row, and supposing that

I *am* merely one in a bushel of Tom Harlowes as strongly resembling each other as the peas in a pod, what's the odds so long as these doubles— or rather infinitibles—keep at the respectful distance you suggest? If they were to come much in one's way, I grant that the effect might be slightly confusing and monotonous, but this, it would appear, is not remotely possible."

"But I believe you're quite mistaken there, Dr Harlowe," he said, still with the suppressed eagerness of a speaker who is clearing the approaches to a sensational disclosure; "or would you think a fact had no scientific value, if it went a long way towards accounting for those mysterious phenomena of clairvoyance—second sight, call it what you will— the occurrence of which is generally admitted to be undeniable and inexplicable? For, look here, assuming the facts to be as I have stated, the explanation is simply this: the clairvoyant has somehow got a glimpse into one of these *facsimile* worlds, which happens to be a few years ahead of ours in point of time, and has seen how things are going on there."

"Really, my good fellow," I interposed, "considering the billions and quintillions of miles which you were talking about so airily just now, the simplicity of the explanation is scarcely so apparent as one could wish."

"However, it's an immense advance, I can tell you, upon any one that has hitherto been put forward," he persisted, with unabated confidence. "Why, nowadays, there's surely no great difficulty in imagining very summary methods of dealing with space. Contrast it with the other difficulty of supposing somebody to have seen something which actually does not exist, and you'll see that the two are altogether disparate. In short, the whole thing seems clear enough to me on *à priori* grounds; but, no doubt, that may partly be because I am to a certain extent independent of them, as I've lately had an opportunity of visiting a planet which differs from this one solely in having had a small start of it—five years, I should say, or thereabouts."

"Oh, by Jove! he's ever so much worse than I thought," I said to myself, considerably chagrined; and then, knowing that to drive in a delusion is always dangerous, I went on aloud: "What on earth *do* you mean, Lynn? Am I to understand that you are meditating a trifling excursion through the depths of space, or has it already come off?"

"It has," he answered curtly.

"May I ask when?" with elaborate sarcasm.

"Yesterday. I'd like to give you an account of it—and if you'd take a cigar, perhaps you'd look less preposterously: We understand-all-about-that-sort-of-thing-you-know. You really don't on the present occasion, and it is absurd, not to say exasperating," quoth John Lynn, handing me the case, with a good-humoured laugh.

I took one, feeling somewhat perplexed at his cheerfulness, as his attacks had hitherto been invariably attended by despondency and gloom; and he resumed his statement as follows: "It happened in the course of yesterday morning. I was sitting up here doing nothing in particular;

I believe I supposed myself to be reading a bit of the *De Natura Rerum*, when suddenly I discovered that I was really standing in a very sandy lane, and looking over a low gate into a sort of lawn or pleasure-grounds. Now, let us take it for granted that you 've said I simply dropped asleep—I didn't, all the same. The lawn ran up a slope to the back of a house, all gables, and queer-shaped windows, and tall chimney-stacks, covered with ivy and other creepers—clematis, I think : at anyrate there were sheets of white blossom against the dark green. It 's a place I never saw before, that I 'm pretty certain of ; there are some points about it that I 'd have been likely to remember if I had. For instance, the long semi-circular flights of turf steps to left and right, and the flower-beds cut out of the grass between them into the shape of little ships and boats, a whole fleet, with sails and oars and flags, which struck me as a quaint device. Then in one corner there was a huge puzzle-monkey nearly blocking up a turnstile in the bank ; I remember thinking it might be awkward for anyone coming that way in the dark. Looking back down the lane, which was only a few yards of cart-track, there were the beach and the sea close by ; a flattish shore with the sand-hills, covered with bent and furze, zig-zagging in and out nearer to and farther from high-water mark. There are miles of that sort of thing along the east coast, and, as a matter of fact, I ultimately found out that it can have been no great distance from Lowestoft—from what corresponds with our Lowestoft, of course, I mean.

And I may observe that I never have been in that part of the world, at least, not nearer than Norwich.

"Well, as you may suppose, such an abrupt change of scene is a rather startling experience; and I must frankly confess that I haven't at present the wildest idea *how* it was effected" ("Hear, hear," said I), "any more than you can explain how certain vibrations in the air are at this moment producing sounds, causing in your brain other vibrations, which we would call a belief that I am either raving or romancing. But the strange feeling—which in itself proves that it wasn't a dream, for who ever is surprised at anything in one?—wore off before long, and I began to make observations. As for the time of day, one could see by the shadows and dew on the grass that it was morning, a considerably earlier hour than it had been here when I quitted Greystones abruptly; and the trees and flowers showed that it was early summer. Nobody was visible about the place, but I heard the scraping of a rake upon gravel somewhere near, whence I inferred the vicinity of a gardener. After standing still for what seemed a considerable length of time—I had forgotten to put on my watch, and so could only guess—I resolved upon committing a trespass to the extent of seeking out this man, in hopes of thus gaining some clue to the maze of mystery at the heart of which I had suddenly been set, and as a preliminary I framed several questions ingeniously designed to extract as much information as possible without betraying my own state of bewildered ignorance. But when I tried to carry out this plan, it proved quite impracticable. The gate at which I stood was unlatched, the banks on either hand were low and apparently most easily scalable, yet I found it by no means possible to effect an entrance into those pleasure-grounds. My attempts to do so were instantly frustrated, repulsed, in a manner which I am totally unable to describe; some strange force, invisible and irresistible as gravitation, arrested every movement in that direction, almost before it had been telegraphed from brain to muscle. In short, a few experiments demonstrated the fact that while I could proceed unchecked to right or left along the shore, I was absolutely prohibited from taking a single step farther inland. How far my limits extended to seaward, I naturally did not fully investigate, having once ascertained that the water's edge did not bring me to the end of my tether. It was a sort of converse of King Canute and the waves. Here I was between the deep sea and—I will not say the Devil—but, at any rate, a manifestation of some occult Power, such as mankind, during a certain stage of development, is prone to identify with that personage. I had been, as it were, set down in a fixed groove, out of which I could no more pass than I could now transcend the three dimensions of space.

"Having clearly recognised this state of things, I next bethought me of making my presence audible, with a view to attracting thither the possible guide, philosopher, and friend, whom I might not go to seek. This expedient, however, failed even more promptly than the other; I couldn't utter a sound.

Then, like old Joe, 'I took up a stone and I knocked at the gate'; and such is the strength of association, that I continued the process for some time before it dawned upon me that my hammering produced no noise whatever. It is true that soon afterwards a ridiculous-looking small terrier came trotting round the corner; but his bored and indifferent air only too plainly proved his arrival to to be *non propter hoc*. I vainly endeavoured to attract his attention, whistling phantom whistles, and slapping my knees, and even going to the length of flourishing defiant legs; but the mountain could not have been more disregardful of Mahomet than he of me. And, as if to show that this arose from no natural imperturbability of disposition, he presently saw fit to bark himself hoarse at a flock of sparrows. Altogether it seemed sufficiently obvious that in these new scenes—where and whatever they might be—I was to play the part merely of a spectator, invisible, inaudible, intangible; and, furthermore, that my opportunities for looking on were subject to rigorous circumscription, approaching that experienced by the boy who peers under the edges of the circus-tent and sees the hoofs of the horses. Still, unsatisfactory as I might consider this arrangement, I had no resource save to acquiesce therein; nor could I, under the circumstances, think of anything better to do than to keep on loitering about the gate, waiting for whatever might happen next.

"What happened next was that a glass door in the house opened, and out of it came two ladies, in one of whom I recognised, as they walked towards me down the slope, my eldest sister, Elizabeth. There was nothing in her appearance to make me for a moment doubt her identity, though it did strike me that she looked unusually grave and— yes, decidedly older—and seemed to have lost the pleasant freshness of colouring which mainly constitutes what the Irish call 'pig-beauty.' I was then inclined to attribute this impression to the queer old-fashioned-looking dress she wore; but I must now suppose her attire to have been whatever *is to be* the latest novelty for that particular summer. The other girl puzzled me much more, for although there was certainly something familiar to me in her aspect, I couldn't fit any name to her uncommonly pretty face and figure; and it wasn't until I heard my sister call her 'Nellie' that the truth occurred to me—it was Helen Ronaldson. She, you know, is a sort of cousin of ours, and my mother's ward, and has lived with us most of her life; so there was nothing surprising in finding her and Elizabeth together. The curious and, except upon one hypothesis, unaccountable part of the matter is, that whereas I saw her a few months ago in the guise of an angular, inky-fingered school-girl of fifteen or sixteen at most, yesterday she had shot up to twenty or thereabouts, had, I believe, grown several inches, and had undoubtedly turned into a 'come out' young lady. I must say that she had improved very much during the transformation; I should never have thought Miss Nellie had the makings of such a pretty girl. Not that it's a style

I particularly admire; too tall and dark for my taste, and I should be inclined to predict her ultimate development into a fine woman—rather an aversion of mine, but distinctly handsome all the same.

"Well, they went about picking flowers for a long time, without coming near enough for me to overhear what they were saying, which I was extremely anxious to do. But at last they came down the path, running along inside the boundary - bank, and sat down to sort their roses and pinks on a garden-seat, behind which I found no difficulty in taking up a position well within eavesdropping distance. I'd begun by this time to suspect how matters stood, and was consequently rather uneasy in my mind. One can't find oneself suddenly plumped down five years or so ahead of yesterday, without speculating as to how things—and people—have gone on in the meantime. So much may happen in five years. The situation produces the same sort of feeling that I fancy one might have upon finding oneself intact after a railway accident, and proceeding to investigate who among one's fellow-passengers have held together, what number of limbs they still can muster, and so on. Of course I was not sure that I would learn anything from their conversation; they might have talked for an hour without saying a word to enlighten me; but, as good luck would have it, they were evidently discussing a batch of letters received that morning from various members of the family, about whom I was thus enabled to pick up many more or less

K

disconnected facts.   It appeared, for instance, that my sister Maud was married, and living in South Kensington.   My brother Dick, who has just got a naval cadetship, was in command of a gunboat somewhere off the Chinese coast.   Walter seemed to be doing well on the horse-ranch in the Rockies, which he's hankering after at present — all satisfactory enough.   The only thing that made me uneasy was that for some time neither of them mentioned my mother, and it really was an immense relief to my mind when at last Elizabeth said:

"'I see, Nellie, that we haven't got any sweet-pea, and the mother always likes a bit for her table'; and Nellie replied:

"'We must get some before we go in.   Her cold seems to be much better this morning.'

"'Oh yes, nearly gone.   There's not the least fear, I should think, that she won't be able to appear on Thursday.   That would be indeed unlucky; why, a wedding without a mother-in-law would be nearly as bad as one without a bridegroom, wouldn't it, Nellie?'   Nellie laughed and blushed, but expressed no opinion, and Elizabeth went on: 'Talking of that, do you expect Vincent this morning?'

"'I don't quite know.   He wasn't sure whether his leave would begin to-day or on Wednesday— that is, to-morrow.   He said that if he got it to-day, he would look in here on his way to Lowestoft.'

"'Oh, on his way; rather a roundabout way from Norwich, I should have thought.   Do you know, Nellie, I'm glad that you'll be quartered in York next winter. I believe there's much more going on there than at Norwich, and you can ask me to stay with you whenever you are particularly gay. There, now, you've mixed up all the single pinks that I had just carefully sorted from the double ones—what a mischievous young person you are!'.

"From these last remarks I inferred two facts respecting Vincent, my youngest brother, now at Rugby, neither of which would I have been at all inclined to predict. For one of them was that he had entered the army, whereas he has so far displayed no leanings towards a military career. I should say that his tastes were decidedly bucolic, and, moreover, I can't imagine how on earth he is to get through the examinations, as his only books are cricket bats and footballs, which won't help him much even for the Preliminary. But I think there are still fewer premonitory symptoms of the second fact—that he was about in the immediate future to contract a matrimonial alliance with Helen Ronaldson. Why, the idea's absurd. I remember that in the days of their infancy, being nearly contemporaries, they used to squabble a good deal, and at present I believe they regard one another with a feeling of happy indifference. In Vincent's last letter to me he said he was afraid that he would find the house awfully overrun with girls when he went home, which was, if I'm not mistaken, a graceful allusion to the circumstance that Nellie's holidays coincide with his own.

"However, likely or unlikely, I had soon conclusive proof that such was actually the case, as

Vincent himself arrived, not easily recognisable, indeed, having developed into a remarkably good-looking young fellow, got up, too, with a regard for appearances not generally conspicuous in hobblede-hoys of seventeen. The discreet way in which Elizabeth presently detached herself from the group and went to gather sweet-pea, would alone have led me to suspect the state of affairs, even if the demeanour of the other two had not made it so very plain before they walked round a corner beyond the range of my observations. But they were scarcely out of sight when there appeared upon the scene a fourth person who took me utterly by surprise, though, of course, if I had considered a little, it was natural enough that I—I mean he—should be there. All the same, it gives one an uncommonly uncanny sensation, I can tell you, to see oneself walk out of a door some way off, stand looking about for a minute or two, and then come sauntering towards one with his hands in your pockets—I 'm afraid my pronouns are rather mixed, but you must make allowances for the unusual circumstances which I am describing. No doubt my feelings resembled those of the old fellow—Zoroaster, wasn 't it ?—who ' met his own image walking in a garden,' and if so, he can't be congratulated upon the experience ; one gets more accustomed to it after a bit, but at first it 's intensely disconcerting. I 'm not sure whether in such cases we see ourselves as others see us : I should fancy so, for I noticed that I looked ex-tremely—I must hope abnormally—grumpy ; I don't think I was improved either by the short beard he had set up, not to mention several streaks of grey in my hair. Just then I saw Elizabeth crossing the grass to speak to me—I don't mean to myself, you know, but to him — and I heard her say: 'You're a very unfeeling relative! Have you forgotten that this is my birthday, or do you consider twenty-four too venerable an age for con- gratulations?' (This, by the way, fixes the date exactly: it must have been the twenty - third of June, five years ahead from to-morrow. I regret to say that in reply he only gave a sort of grunt, and muttered something about anniversaries being a great bore; and I remember thinking that if I were she I'd leave him to get out of his bad temper myself—I say, these pronouns are really getting quite too many for me.

"Your own name is rather a convenient length, why not use it?" I observed; and he adopted the suggestion.

"Well, then, Elizabeth and John Lynn strolled aimlessly about for a while, but soon went into the house, and after that I saw nobody else, except occasionally the gardener, for what seemed a very long period. I had nothing at all to do, and the time dragged considerably. The strip of beach on which I could move about was hot and glaring, and disagreeably deep in soft sand; yet, for want of better occupation, in the course of the afternoon, I walked more than a mile along it in a northerly direction, until I came to a dilapidated-looking old boat-house, built in a recess between two sand- hills, and just beyond the line I couldn't cross.

Having reached this point, and perceiving no other objects of interest, I slowly retraced my steps towards the pleasure-grounds' gate. By this time it must have been four or five o'clock, and the weather, hitherto bright and clear, showed a change for the worse. An ugly livid - hued cloud was spreading like a bruise over the sky to the south-east, and sudden gusts began to ruffle up the long bent grasses of the sand-hills on my right hand.

"When I came near the gate, several people were standing at it, apparently watching two men who were doing something to a small sailing-boat, which lay off a little pier close by. Elizabeth and Nellie, and my other sister Juliet, were there, and Elizabeth was explaining to an elderly man, whom I have never succeeded in identifying, that Jack and Vincent intended to sail across to Graston Spit—she pointed over the water to a low tongue of land at no great distance — which would be Vincent's shortest way to Lowestoft. 'In that case,' said he, 'the sooner they're off the better, for it looks as if we might have a squall before very long, and the glass is by no means steady to-day.' Whereupon ensued a short feminine fugue on the theme of: 'Perhaps it would be wiser for them to give up the idea — I hope they won't go — Jack could drive him to the station, you know—Don't you think it would be much wiser if——' in the midst of which they both arrived, and naturally scouted the suggestion that they should abandon their sail, John Lynn, whose temper seemed to have somewhat improved, asserting that they would have a splendid breeze, and that he would be back again in an hour or so. Accordingly, they hurried over their adieux, and lost no time in getting off, taking no man with them.

"They had been gone perhaps three-quarters of an hour, when the 'splendid breeze' made its appearance in the shape of a furious squall, which came hissing and howling on with remarkable suddenness and violence, and brought the girls, who were still out-of-doors, running with dismayed countenances to look over the gate to seaward. The sweeping gusts bore to me fitful snatches of anxious colloquies, the general drift of which, however, seemed to be towards the conclusion that the boat must have got over before the wind sprang up, and that Jack would, of course, wait there until it went down. As the blasts moderated a little, they were accompanied by driving sheets of large-dropped rain, which again sent the girls scurrying indoors, and I was left to my solitary peregrinations and reflections. These latter ran much upon the boat and its occupants, who must, I thought, be having a rather nasty time of it, unless they had really landed before the squall; for both wind and tide were against them, and a surprising sea had got up already. I consider myself to know something about the management of a boat, and I supposed that my strange double or fetch might be credited with an equal amount of skill; otherwise their prospects certainly looked blue enough, as Vincent has had little or no experience of nautical matters. I reviewed the situation, standing where the shallow foam-slides seethed to my feet, and I found myself contemplating a catastrophe to that John Lynn with a feeling which I can't either describe or explain. After a while, I began to pace up and down the beach, now in this direction, and now in that, and I must have continued to do so for a considerable length of time, as light was thickening, when, on turning a corner, I again came in sight of the old boat-house, to which I had walked before. Almost at the same moment, my eye was caught by some dark object to seaward, elusively disappearing and reappearing between the folds of grey vapour drifting low upon the water. They were very blinding and baffling, but a longer rift soon showed me plainly that it was a small boat in sorry plight, in fact, filling and settling down so fast, that her final disappearance would evidently be a question of a very few minutes. There was nobody in her, and I thought to myself that if anyone had gone overboard in that sea, he must assuredly have preceded her to the bottom. And I felt equally convinced that she was no other than the boat in which I had seen the two Lynns embark.

"This opinion proved to be both right and wrong : she was the Lynns' boat, but the Lynns had not gone to the bottom. On the contrary, they were just then safely emerging from imminent danger of so doing. For I now became aware of a human form, which, at not many yards' distance, was making slow and struggling progress through the swirling surf towards the water's edge, and had already reached a place shallow enough to admit of wading. As I ran forward, not to assist, having long since ascertained that I could by no means demonstrate my presence, but merely to investigate, it turned out to be John Lynn, half-carrying, and half-dragging along Vincent, who was apparently insensible. I had an awful scare, I can tell you, for he flopped down on the sand when I— when John let him go, in such a lifeless, limp sort of way, that I thought at first the lad had really come to grief. However, I suppose he had only been slightly stunned ; at any rate, in a minute or two he sat up, and seemed none the worse. But when he got to his feet, it was evident that he had somehow damaged one of his ankles—sprained it badly, I should say—and he could hardly attempt the feeblest hobble. 'Here's a sell,' he said, 'especially as we seem to have landed in unknown regions.' All this time the rain was coming down in torrents, and it was blowing so hard that you could scarcely hear yourself speak. 'It's a good step—more than a mile,' I heard the other say. 'Do you think you could get as far as the old boat-house ? You see it there opposite to us. Then you'd be under shelter, while I run back and find some means of conveying you home.' This suggestion seemed sensible—though I say it who, I suppose, shouldn't —and they made their way haltingly to the boat-house, which, judging by the cobwebby creaking of the door, had not been entered for many a long day, and into which I was, of course, unable to follow them.

"Presently John Lynn came out alone, and set off running towards the house at a really very creditable pace, considering the depth of the sand and the weight of his drenched garments. I had found a tolerably sheltered station under the lee of a sand-bank, and I decided to wait where I was for his return; but I had to wait much longer than one might have expected. The twilight turned into dusk, and the wind dropped, and the sky cleared, and a large full-moon came out, all in a leisurely way, but there was no sign of anybody coming near us. I couldn't account for the delay, and abused John Lynn a good deal in consequence of it. I know my wits sometimes go wool-gathering, but I'm certain I should never have been such an ass as to leave another fellow sitting wet through for a couple of hours — enough to give him his death, I said, for one always takes a pessimistic view of things when one's being kept waiting. Of course it was possible that he might have found all our womankind in hysterics—though from what I know of them I shouldn't think it particularly probable—but, even so, he should have managed to send somebody. Vincent, too, was evidently getting impatient, for I heard him shout 'Jack' once or twice, and whistle at intervals in a way which I knew betokened exasperation.

"At last John Lynn came posting round the corner, apparently in no end of a hurry, but not a soul with him, though he'd been away long enough to have collected half the county. As he ran up to the boat-house, I saw him taking out of his pocket something which gleamed in the moonlight, and was, I'm pretty sure, the top of a flask, so he'd at any rate had the sense to bring some spirits. I wanted to find out whether any more people were on their way, and forgetting for the moment that the boat-house wasn't in my reach, I went after him to the door. And there two queer things happened. In the first place, I got a glimpse, just for an instant, but quite distinctly, of—*you*, Dr Harlowe; and immediately afterwards an extraordinary feeling of horror came over me, and I began to rush away, I don't know why or where, but on—on—until the air suddenly turned into a solid black wall, and I went smash against it, and somehow seemed to wake up—sitting here at this table."

"That's the first sensible remark you've made to-day," I said, in the most soothingly matter-of-fact tone that I could assume; "only why do you say *seemed*? I should think it was perfectly obvious that you did really wake up—or is there more to follow?"

"Then I dreamt it all?" said he.

"All of it that you haven't evolved out of your internal consciousness since then, in thinking it over," I replied with decision.

"Oh, well," said my young friend with a certain air of forbearing superiority, "as it happens, I dreamt it no more than you did. But if you prefer it, we'll call it a dream. At any rate, it wasn't a bad one. I should feel rather uncomfortable now if it had ended disastrously; however, as far as one can see,

nothlng worse seemed likely to come of it than
Nellie's being obliged either to postpone her wedding
for a week, or to put up with a hobbling bridegroom.
Then, as to those disagreeable sensations at the conclusion, I dare say they would be quite explicable if
one knew the details of the process by which one is
conveyed back and forward; some phase, no doubt,
of disintegration of matter.   But you said, didn't you,
that you wanted to borrow *Walt Whitman*?   Here he
is—mad Martin Tupper flavoured with dirt, in my
judgment; however, you may like him better."

During the remainder of our interview John Lynn
conversed upon miscellaneous topics with such perfect
composure and rationality, that I began to think less
seriously of his relapse.   I reflected that, after all,
many thoroughly sane people had been strongly
affected for a time by vivid and coherent dreams,
and I felt no doubt that in his case the impression
would wear off in a day or two.   As I went out, I
communicated these views to Dr Warden, who was
disposed to agree with them.

This proved to be my last conversation with John
Lynn.   For that very evening I was unexpectedly
called away by business, which obliged me to spend
several months in America; and upon returning, I
found that he had left Greystones House cured, and
had gone abroad for a long tour.   After which, I
heard nothing more about him; so that the days'
"petty dust" could accumulate with undisturbed
rapidity over my recollections of the man himself,
and our acquaintanceship, and his curious dream.

In the early summer, five years later—my diary fixes all dates—I happened to be wandering along the eastern coast, and arrived one evening at a remote little seaside place in Norfolk, which rather took my fancy with its many gabled farmhouses and comfortable *Cock and Anchor*. The next morning, the twenty-third of June, was, I remember, brilliantly fine, and tempted me out with my photographing gear—a much more cumbrous apparatus than at the present day. My negatives turned out better than usual, and as it was a new fad with me, I became so deeply absorbed in my attempts that I allowed myself to be overtaken, a good way from home, by a violent storm of wind and rain, which came on suddenly between five and six o'clock. I had an extremely unpleasant walk home with my unwieldy camera and other paraphernalia; and having got into dry clothes, and ascertained that several of my most promising plates had been destroyed, I did not feel enthusiastically benevolent when the landlord appeared in my room with a statement to the following effect: A young man had just druv over in the dogcart from Sandford Lodge—Mrs Lynn's place below—wantin' Dr Dixon in the greatest hurry to the old lady, who was took awful bad—for her death they thought; but Dr Dixon had had a call seven miles off Stowdenham ways, and couldn't be got for love or money. "And so, sir," proceeded my landlord, "believing as you be a medical gentleman, I made bold to mention the suckumstance to you, in case as how you might think on doin' summat for the poor lady."

Common humanity, of course, compelled me

so to think, albeit human nature—that equally common, but very different thing—mingled some heterogeneous elements with my thoughts; and the consequence was that I at once set out again through the rain, which still fell thickly.

The young man in the dogcart was excited, and communicative of mood, and upon the way told me several facts explanatory of the state of affairs in the household towards which he was swiftly driving me. The family, he said, had been at Sandford Lodge for about a couple of years, and were well liked in the neighbourhood; everybody'd be sorry to hear of their trouble, and, to be sure, it was a terrible thing to have happened; it was no wonder the mistress was taken bad at bein' told of it sudden. Why, hadn't I heard them talkin' about it up above? Sure, the two gentlemen had been out sailin' that arternoon in their little boat, and was caught in the squall and capsized, or else she ran on a rock, it wasn't sartin which, but anyway she'd gone down clever and clean. And Mr Jack had somehow manidged to swim ashore; but his brother, Mr Vincent, a fine young gentleman in the army, there wasn't a sign of him—and he about gettin' married to one of the young ladies just the day arter to-morrow. But with the tide runnin' out strong as it was then, the corpse might never happen to come ashore at all. Indeed, they were in an orful takin' altogether down at the Lodge, and just before he come away, they'd found the mistress lyin' all of a heap in the landin', and couldn't get her round again

by any means. So it 'ud ha' been a bad job if he'd
had to come back without Dr Dixon or nobody.

By this time our short drive was nearly at an
end. "Coming this road," said the young man,
"the quickest way to the house is round by the
back." So saying, he drove a few hundred yards
down a deep-rutted, sandy lane, debouching on the
seashore, close to an iron gate, at which he pulled
up. "There's a turnstile in the bank to your left,
sir," he said, as I alighted, "and then if you go
straight on up the lawn, you'll find the porch-
door open, and there's safe to be some one about."

I followed his instructions, feeling a curiously
strong impression of familiarity with the place at
which I had arrived—the sandy bank, the gate,
the slope running up to the creeper-draped gabled
house, standing out darkly against the struggling
moonbeams. A common enough illusion, I reflected, but it was now without doubt unusually
powerful and persistent. It was not dispelled even
by my pricking my hand severely in brushing past
a puzzle-monkey, which brandished its spiny arms
in front of the turnstile; and the sensation
strengthened as I walked up the steep lawn,
threading my way up flights of turf steps, among
flower-beds cut fantastically into the semblance of
a fleet of boats and ships, with sheets of white
blossoms glimmering for spread sails, and scarlet
ones gleaming for flags. I felt convinced that I
had never seen the device before; and yet it
certainly did not seem new to me. At the door
I was met by two girls, who looked stunned and

scared, but who reported that their mother had recovered from the long fainting-fit which had so much alarmed them. They brought me upstairs to the room where she was sitting; and the first sight of the miserable face which she turned towards me served to heighten my perplexed state of what may be called latent reminiscence. For I was at once struck by its marked resemblance to a face which I had in some past time frequently beheld, but which I now completely failed to single out from among a hurriedly summoned mental muster of my friends and acquaintances. And so thick a fold of oblivion had lapped over my recollections of the persons and events which would have given me the right clue, that although I knew I was speaking to a Mrs Lynn, I could make no instructive application of the fact.

I found the interview dreary and embarrassing. Mrs Lynn was so far recovered that her health called for but little professional discourse, and yet I feared to appear unsympathetic if I hastened away abruptly. Accordingly I sat for some time, delivering myself intermittently of the common commonplace, "and vacant chaff well meant for grain," which is deemed appropriate to such occasions. At length I bethought me of terminating the scene by producing a visiting-card, which I handed to Mrs Lynn, murmuring something about a hope that if I could at any time be of any service to her she would—— But before I was half through my sentence, she started, and uttered an exclamation, with her eyes fixed upon the name and address. "Harlowe—Greystones," she said; "why, it must be you who were so kind to poor Jack when he was with Dr Warden!"

As she spoke, a ray of recognition shot into my mind. Could it be?—yes, certainly it could be no one but John Lynn's mother—of course I remembered John Lynn. Indeed, there was as strong a likeness between her and her son as there can be between an elderly lady and a young man. I was, however, still unable to recall the occasion upon which he had, as I now began to feel dimly aware, given me a somewhat minute description of this place and its surroundings; and then had not the driver told me that the family had lived here for only two years? My perplexity was but partially removed.

Mrs Lynn appeared to be strangely agitated by her discovery of my identity. She sat for a minute or two glancing from the card to me, her lips moving irresolutely, as if upon the verge of speech into which she dared not launch forth. Then she looked quickly round the room, which was empty, her daughters having been called away, and thereupon, with the air of one snatching at an opportunity, she turned to me and said: "Dr Harlowe, I must tell you something that has been upon my mind for a long time." She continued, speaking low and rapidly, with many nervous glances towards the door, and sudden startled pauses upon false alarms of interruption: "Perhaps you may have heard that my youngest son Vincent is going to be married." (The tense showed that she had not yet learned to associate him with "the tangle and the shells.") "Their wedding was to have been the day after to-morrow, his and Helen Ronaldson's. She's my ward, who has lived with us all her life; and they've been engaged for nearly a year. Well, Dr Harlowe, my son Jack—you know Jack—has been at home, too, for three or four years, and some time ago I began to fancy—it was scarcely more than a fancy, and I've never said a word about it to anyone—a feeling on his part of attachment towards Nellie. I hoped at first that I might be quite mistaken, but latterly I've thought that hardly possible. What I believe is that it sprang up gradually and insensibly, as it were, and that he never realised how matters stood until the time of his brother's engagement. And since then I think —I fear—he has at times—just occasionally—shown some jealous feeling towards Vincent—and those two used always to be such good friends. Not often at all, and nothing serious, you know; I'm sure none of the others have ever noticed anything of the kind; and indeed it may be only my own imagination; it's an idea that, under the circumstances, one might easily take up without any real reason."

"Very true," I said, because she looked at me as if wishing for assent.

"But that's not what I particularly want to tell you," she hurried on. "To-night, soon after he came back from that miserable boat, I was in here, when I heard Jack running upstairs, and I went to the door to speak to him, but before I could stop him, he had passed, and gone into his room. Just outside it he dropped something, and I picked it up. It was this!" She took out of her pocket a small gold horseshoe-shaped locket with an inch or so of broken chain attached to it. One side of its case had been wrenched off at the hinge, showing that it contained a tiny photograph —a girl-face, dark-eyed and delicately featured.

"That's Nellie," said Mrs Lynn, "and it belongs to Vincent; he always wore it on his watch-chain. So if he had really been washed away, as they said, I don't understand how Jack came to have it with him. I don't see how he could have got it, do you, Dr Harlowe?" queried this poor mother, leaning forward and laying a hand on my sleeve, in her eagerness for an answer.

"He might have been trying to rescue his brother —to pull him ashore, or into the boat, and have accidentally caught hold of it in that way," I suggested. "It looks as if it had been torn off by a strong grip."

"Do you think that may be how it was?" she said with what seemed to me an odd mingling of relief and disappointment in her tone. "When I had picked it up, I waited about outside Jack's door, and thought I heard him unlocking and opening a drawer. Presently he came out, in a great hurry evidently, for when I spoke to him he only ran past, saying, "I can't stop now, mother." He had some shiny, smooth-looking thing in his hand, the passage was so dark that I couldn't see exactly what. I went into his room, and the first thing I noticed was the drawer of the writing-table left open. I knew it was the one where he keeps his revolver, and when I looked into it, I saw that the case was empty. The revolver is gone; he must have taken it with him. Just then I suddenly got very faint, and they say I was unconscious for a long time. One of the maids says that she saw Jack running down towards the beach, about an hour ago. I believe numbers of people are there looking out. I said nothing to anyone about the revolver—perhaps I ought to have done so. What can he have wanted with it? I've been thinking that he may have intended to fire it off for a signal, if the night was very dark. Don't you think that is quite possible?"

"I don't know—I can't say," I answered, without, indeed, bestowing any consideration upon Mrs Lynn's somewhat unlikely conjecture, for at this moment a whole sequence of recollections stood out abruptly in my mind with a substantial distinctness, as if my thoughts had been put under a stereoscope.

"Can you tell me whether there is a boat-house at some little distance from here along the shore? An old boat-house that hasn't been used of late, standing back near some sand-hills—perhaps a mile along the shore—in a rather ruinous state, built in a hollow between two banks," I went on, impatiently adding what particulars I could, in hopes of prompting her memory, which seemed to be at fault.

"Yes, yes, there *is* one like that," she said at last; "in the direction of Mainforthing; I remember we walked as far as it not very long ago."

"Some one ought to go there immediately," I said, moving towards the door.

"Why?" exclaimed Mrs Lynn, following me; "is there any chance that the boys——?" But I did not wait to explain my reasons, which, in truth, were scarcely intelligible to myself.

Hurrying down the lawn, and emerging on the beach, I fell in with a small group of men and lads, of whom I demanded in which direction Mainforthing lay. To the right, they told me by word and gesture, and one of them added, pointing in the opposite direction, where a number of dark figures, some with lanterns, were visible, moving along the margin of the far-receded tide. "But it's more that a-way they think she must ha' been when she went down." I explained that my object was to find the old boat-house, whereupon they assured me that I would do so easy enough if I kept straight along by the strand for a mile and a bit, and two or three of them accompanied me as I started.

The stretches of crumbling, moon-bleached sand seemed to lengthen out interminably, but at last, round a corner I came breathlessly upon my goal. The door of the boat-house was wide open, and the moonlight streamed brightly through it full in the face of a youth who, at the moment when I reached the threshold, was standing with his back to the wall, steadying himself by a hold on the window-ledge beside him, and looking as if he had just with difficulty scrambled to his feet. He was staring straight before him with a startled and bewildered expression, and saying " Jack—I say, Jack, what the deuce are you up to?" in a peremptorily remonstrant tone. And not without adequate cause. For opposite to him stood John Lynn—altered, but still recognisable as my former acquaintance—who held in his hand a revolver, which he was raising slowly, slowly, to a level as it seemed with the other's head. The next instant I had sprung towards him, but he was too quick for me, and, shaking off my grasp on his arm, turned and faced me, still holding his weapon. "Dr Harlowe! You here?" he said, and had scarcely spoken the words when he put the barrel to his temple, and before the echoes of the shot had died on the jarred silence, and while the smoke-wreaths were still eddying up to the boat-house roof, he lay dead at our feet with a bullet in his brain.

The coroner's jury, of course, returned their customary verdict, perhaps with better grounds than usual. Upon my own private verdict I have deliberated often and long, but without arriving at any conclusive result. That crime upon the brink of which John Lynn had undoubtedly stood —was it a premeditated one, or had he taken the revolver with some different intention, and afterwards yielded to a sudden suggestion of the fiend, prompted by his brother's helpless plight? This question I can never hope to answer definitely, though my opinion inclines towards the latter hypothesis.   Upon the whole it seems clear to me that by his last act my unhappy friend did but "catch the nearest way" out of a hopelessly complicated maze of mortal misery.   Furthermore, I cannot avoid the conviction that but for his narration to me of his strange dream or trance experiences, a fratricide's guilt would have been superadded to the calamities of his mind distempered, and his passion "by Fate bemocked."

THE FIELD OF THE FRIGHTFUL BEASTS

M AC BARRY bore a heavy weight on his mind
through a part of his summer at Clonman-
avon, which, being only the sixth one in his life,
seemed to him a season with remotest beginning
and end. He was visiting his great-grandmother,
Mrs Kavanagh, who for each of his years could
have given a baker's dozen of her own, and still
have had several left over; and through the glowing
July days the old lady worked away, steadily and
swiftly, at sundry woollen garments, sometimes expressing a fear, as her needles clicked, that she
would hardly have them all ready for the boys
before the cold weather began. The youngest of
these boys would never see fifty again, and Mrs
Kavanagh knitted the faster whenever she thought
of her Johnnie's rheumatism. To Mac, on the
contrary, it never occurred at this time that the
days were ever going to be otherwise than warm
and long, with hummings in the sunshiny air;
neither did he concern himself about anybody's
tendency to aches and stiffness. His cares had
a quite different cause.

It was one of his great-grandmother's household
laws that he should every morning take a walk,
attended by Kate Heron, the housemaid; and

Kate, duly carrying out this decree, would fain have supplemented it with another, to the effect that their walk should always bring them along Madden's Lane. For that thick-hedged thorough-fare ran past no less than two little dwellings, toward whose dark half-doors her feet instinctively turned. And on their first few walks she met with no opposition to her wishes. Mac, knowing nothing about the topography of the neighbourhood, had not any alternative routes to prefer, and was content to amuse himself with the shaggy-coated small terrier, Gaby, while Kate's large flowery hat bobbed in deep conference with emerging shawled heads, or vanished altogether for a few minutes, diving into shadows beneath the shock of thatch and wavering blue smoke plume. But one morning, when they were on their way home, and had come near the corner of the road which was only a hundred yards or so from his great-grandmother's gate, Mac made a very dreadful discovery.

He happened to glance up at the top of the wall along which they were passing. A very high old stone wall it was ; three, or perhaps four, superimposed Macs would scarcely have reached to a level with its parapet, yet over it he saw pro-jecting the heads of two cows and a sorrel pony gazing down calmly into the road. The sight filled him with dismay ; in fact, he was almost startled into betraying horrified surprise. " My goodness, Kate ! " he began, forgetting his dignity so far as to pull the fringe of her amber-bordered brown shawl.

"What ails you at all, Master Mac?" Kate said, recalled from some rather far-off meditations of her own. However, he recovered his self-possession in time.

"Nothin' ails anybody," he replied stiffly. "I was only wonderin' why they can't find somethin' better to do than to stand there gapin' at everybody that passes on the road, which is no concern of theirs."

"Ah, the crathurs!" Kate responded absently.

What had really struck him was the thought of how prodigious must be the stature of the beasts to whom those prying heads appertained. For how otherwise could they look over that great immense wall, as high nearly as the house? Mac, all unversed in Rabbinical legend, had never gauged "the just dimensions of the giant Og," and recked nought of colossal storks wading with immeasurable legs; which was doubtless well for his peace of mind, since such lore would have revealed portentous abysses to his imagination. Even as it was, he stood gravely aghast. Towards all animals his sentiments had hitherto been most friendly and fearless; but that somehow seemed only to aggravate the present circumstances, making more odious the belief that the attractive and estimable tribes of horses and cattle had stalking among them creatures of proportions so unsightly and grotesque. The fact, however, could not be doubted. When he passed that way, there almost invariably he saw ranged a row of heads fearsomely far above his own, the more placid and contemplative wearing immobile horns; the more alert and observant twitching sensitive ears. Mac wondered whether it was their legs, or their necks, or both, that were so preternaturally elongated; but he felt that in any case they must be hideous to behold, and he shuddered inwardly at the notion of what night-mare - like shapes those interposing stones must screen. Once, indeed, he fancied that he caught a glimpse of something like the head of what ought to have been a very *little* girl appearing over the edge in a flappy white sun-bonnet; but the figure which this compelled him to imagine was so monstrous that he hastily averted his eyes, and tried to persuade himself that they had deceived him.

Of course, he mentioned the matter to nobody. Self - respecting children never do confide their haunting terrors to elders, possibly derisive of them. No chance of gaining coveted protection and de-liverance from the torment of fear can justify one in running the risk of appearing ignorantly ridiculous to those who presumably know all about everything. So Mac preserved a scrupulous silence, in which his alarms had ample scope to root themselves. The nearest approach he ever made to the subject was once, when he remarked to Tim Brennan, the coachman, as they were driving over Clonmanavon Bridge—he had only just forgiven Tim's offer to let him hold the end of the reins—" I suppose, now, you never see cows walkin' about here who are so tall they couldn't fit in under that arch?"

Unluckily, Tim took the question as a sort of

challenge, and replied, "Well, sir, I wouldn't say that the most we keep hereabouts couldn't make a shift to get through it middlin' aisy for any size there is on them. Not but what I've seen an odd one now and again might be very apt to stick half-ways, unless they was after takin' a bit off of the horns of her—ay, she would so. We've plinty of powerful big cattle in Clonmanavon."

This answer gave cold comfort to Mac, who had hoped to elicit an assurance that abnormally huge quadrupeds were at any rate extremely rare in the neighbourhood, and exclusively confined to the one gruesome place which he called in his thoughts "The Field of the Frightful Beasts." Failing in this, he could not tell but that many of them might be at large close by, and the continual likelihood of falling in with one spread a heavy cloud over all his open-air hours. The dread seized possession of him, and grew more harassing every day. He was constantly peering through gates and gaps to see whether they led into pastures infested with uncanny herds. When the click-clack of horses' hoofs sounded on the road, he scarcely dared look at what was coming, lest it should prove to be a steed with spidery legs and snaky neck, shaped like the ungainly shadows thrown when the low sun is drawing caricatures.

It was quite natural that the actual sight of the wall with its frieze of protruded heads, which were sometimes so numerous that he could not well count them, should have the effect of intensifying these detestable impressions; and Mac's experience being such, he very soon began to shrink from turning the corner that brought them into view. Kate Heron presently found herself wondering: "What at all had set Master Mac agin walkin' anywheres except Crumloughlin ways, that was no better than an ugly boggy ould bit of a boreen, wid nothin' in it good or bad to bring anybody trapesin' there." But she wondered to little purpose, as Mac did not feel called upon to offer any explanation for his new departure. In the course of his only childhood he had acquired independent and masterful habits, and he now saw no reason why he should not choose his own way. Therefore he set a resolute face northward every morning, calling, "Hi, along this way," to Gaby, who generally bolted in the wrong direction, and replying decisively to Kate's proposed amendments, "No, my friend, that other's a horribominable old road." This was, so far as it went, a simple solution of his difficulty. Before long, however, complications occurred, which placed him in a serious dilemma.

One morning, just outside the gate, they met Lizzie Egan, Colonel Hodson's nurserymaid, wheeling along two fat little twin girls, whose drowsy heads nodded in their big white-frilled bonnets like a couple of fantastic giant blossoms. After a short preliminary gossip, Lizzie said: "Was you hearin' lately how poor Mrs Reilly is?"

"Sure, I haven't had e'er a chance since Sunday," said Kate, "and then she was only pretty middlin'."

"Deed, then, the crathur's to be pitied. And had she heard a word at all from Willie?"

"At that time she hadn't; but for aught I know she maybe might agin now."

· "Well, he'd a right to be ashamed of himself, anyway. Takin' off like that, and lavin' the poor ould woman frettin' in disthraction till she isn't the size of a hedge-sparrow. Jimmy Collins was tellin' us he seen her one day last week, waitin' at the post-office, and he said you could ha' just given her another double up, and slipped her in at the slit of the letter-box handy, she was that stooped and wizened away to nothin'. Sure, Willie might aisy throuble himself to send her a line of a letter to say where he's went. That's the laist he might do, let alone not havin' the manners so much as to ax whether the boy he was after murtherin' might be dead or alive."

"Och, for that matter," Kate said, "people say the divil takes care of his own. Sorra the notion Alec Sweeny had of dyin', nor wouldn't if it was off of ten forty-fut ladders he was shook."

"Oof, then, it's little call Mrs Reilly has to be disthressin' herself about that Willie of hers aither; if that's the way of it, *he's* safe enough," said Lizzie. "I'd ha' called in goin' by to see how she was, only that we aren't very great these times, you know. She heard me mother passin' some remark on his conduc', and bitther as sut she's been agin us ever since. But I thought you were along be her door most days."

"Sure, not at all. What's come over Master Mac there I dunno, but pitchforks wouldn't get him along that road. Nothin' ll suit him except streelin' off up the lanes at the back of the house. If he's axed to turn that corner, you might think you was offerin' to take him into disolit wildernesses. He won't look the way it is," Kate said ruefully.

"He's frightened of Molloy's big dog—him below at the Bridge, that comes out barkin' and leppin'— that's it, you may depind. Sure, I do sometimes have the work of the world gettin' Miss Carrie past him," said Lizzie. "Screechin' she'll be like as if you was ringin' a little pig. The baste wouldn't hurt man or mortal, but it's the great coarse bark he has, like a door slammin', or a little clap of thunder, that scares the children when they're small. And it's apt to be what's took the young fellow."

"Very belike it is then," said Kate. "There's no end to the foolishness of them before they've got the wit."

"Or afterwards aither," said Lizzie. "The more sinse they have the less raisonable they'll behave themselves, accordin' to my experience." And with that they parted.

Mac was positively bewildered with disgust and indignation. He had overheard all this discussion, while apparently helping Gaby to climb up the gate-post, and the scandalous conjecture so coolly made by Lizzie and adopted by Kate came to him like a sudden blast of scorching air. Afraid of a barking dog! Placed in the same category with a crying baby! A calumny so outrageous could not be too energetically refuted. But how was this to be done effectually without facing the visible horror of the Frightful Beasts?—an ordeal which he could not contemplate with equanimity. One point alone was clear enough ; he must modify his simple plan of merely avowing a dislike for Madden's Lane as a sufficient reason for shunning it. That would now leave him open to disgraceful imputations. Yet it was difficult to devise a better one.

All the rest of the afternoon he pondered the subject inconclusively, and was so much pre-occupied with it at tea-time that his great-grandmother asked him if he was sleepy, thus crowning the insults of the day. He replied politely and reprovingly : " If a Person was sleepy, I suppose he 'd have the sense to go to bed, no matter *how* early it was—even if the sun was shining straight into his cup of tea—and not think it fine to sit up blinking like an old owl."

" You see, you were so quiet, my dear," his great-grandmother said, half-apologetically, feeling herself set down, and misappropriating the old owl.

" It would be a queer thing," said Mac, " if a Person couldn't keep himself awake inside without making a noise outside, like a clock tickin' to show it was goin' on. I rather wouldn't be talkin' all the while as if I was wounded up with a key."

But next morning Mac made an important announcement on the door-steps. " Gaby 's to choose where we 're goin' to-day," he said. " In fact, I think I 'll always let him choose. For you see, Kate, it 's only a quarter as much our walk as his, because he goes it on four legs and both of us on only two. So if he chooses it will be a great deal fairer. We 'll just watch which way he 'll turn."

Kate, remembering what direction Gaby always seemed disposed to take, was so well satisfied with this arrangement that she felt no wish to cavil at Master Mac's logic or arithmetic; and a sparkle lit up her melancholy grey eyes as she thought to herself how surely she could call this morning at Mrs Reilly's. It was, however, too hastily kindled, and was extinguished speedily. For when they all three reached the gate, Mac suddenly picked up a pebble, and flung it as far as he could towards Crumloughlin, indeed nearly toppling over head foremost with the vehemence of his throw. And, of course, Gaby needed no bidding to be off in a rapturous whirl upon its track. Whereupon Mac said complacently, "There, you see he wants to go this way," and set forward with the air of one acting from a strong sense of duty.

"Ah, now, Master Mac, weren't you the conthrary child to go do that?" Kate called after him remonstrantly. "Sure, how was the baste to know his own mind, and you disthractin' him wid peltin' stones about the road?"

But Mac continued to stump along inexorably. "I promised poor Gaby we'd go wherever he liked," he said in a highly moral tone, "so I wouldn't disappoint him now on any account." And Kate could only follow him with chagrin, rightly foreboding a meditated repetition of the manœuvre upon all such occasions in future. As for Mac, though he did his best to believe in his own disinterested deference to Gaby's wishes, he more than half-suspected that he was behaving somewhat

M

meanly; and, despite his virtuous airs, his mood
continued to be partly crestfallen and partly defiant,
as he trudged along in brown holland suit and broad
straw hat, through the hot sunshine, preceded by the
cheery terrier, and followed by the reluctant maid.

The success of his stratagem was, moreover,
destined to be transient. On the very next morning,
when he was looking at a volume of Du Maurier's
society pictures in the hall, he heard his great-grandmother's time-worn treble calling from the breakfast-
room door to Kate a-scrub on the steps outside.
"Oh, Kate," it said, "I find we are short of eggs.
I wonder could you get some anywhere to-day when
you are out with Master Mac?" and Kate replied
with great alacrity: "Ay, sure, ma'am; there does
be mostly a good few at the Widow Reilly's down
beyond the Bridge. Grand layin' hens she has in
it." And, "You might bring me a dozen, then,
please," said Mrs Kavanagh.

Mac's heart sank as he listened to this dialogue,
which seemed to fix inevitably the direction of that
morning's walk. He said to himself that Mrs Reilly's
hens were nasty old beasts, and he wished to goodness Gaby had ate them all the last time he was
waiting there for Kate to finish, just asking what
way she was, which usually took a wonderfully long
while. Then they couldn't have been laying any
detestful eggs for people to go and fetch. But as
the hour for setting out drew near, he became
alive to the futility of such aspirations, and at
length he desperately determined upon a bold,
practical step.

About a quarter before twelve o'clock, while he knew Kate to be still finishing her sweeping down of the back stairs, he beckoned silently to Gaby, who obeyed with his broadest grin, and they went quietly out of the house together. Mac purposed to give his attendant the slip and go his own way, which certainly should not lead to the precincts of the "Frightful Beasts." He was well aware that the proceeding would be most gravely discountenanced by the authorities, but he could not for a moment weigh their disapproval against that row of horrible high-reaching heads; and he had long regarded the assumption that he required a caretaker at all as one of those vexatious anachronisms, which a Person found himself so frequently called upon to point out. His independent expedition thus would subserve a twofold end, asserting a principle as well as averting a miserable hour.

It started prosperously enough. On his way down the avenue Mac successfully eluded notice by slipping behind a laurel when overtaken by the pony-carriage in which his great-grandmother was driving to inquire for Lady Olive Despard's bronchitis. But when he came to the front gate, it happened that a fawn-coloured, sharp-nosed collie was in the act of trotting past, upon observing whom, Gaby, inflated with a sense of being on his own premises, stood in the middle of the gravel sweep and made contemptuous remarks. Of these the stranger took no notice whatever, and Gaby misconstruing this forbearance, being himself neither conspicuously prudent nor magnanimous, was ill-advised enough to venture on a short rush towards him, with yaps of insufferable import. The natural consequence was that in another moment he saw the collie dancing at him open-mouthed, whereupon he lost his head, and, instead of fleeing into the more obvious refuge, bolted away down the road, with his enemy's nose grazing his craven heels.

Mac followed in pursuit of both, filled with con-sternation, which increased as he found how rapidly he was being left behind. Round a corner the two dogs whisked, into a grassy-rutted cart track, and by the time he had raced through the open field-gate at its end, they were out of sight, and his only clue was a sound of yelping far and farther ahead. Guided thereby, he ran along, skirting the hedgerow with its high-grown fringe of late summer weeds, and clambered over stiles, in and out of another empty hay-field, on the margin of which something scudded away, hopelessly beyond the reach of his shouted commands and menaces. He was so bent upon the rescue of the recreant Gaby, that he never once thought of whither he might be going, or with what creatures he might fall in, considerations which would otherwise have lain uppermost. Next there confronted him a tallish plastered wall, with flat slabs projecting sparsely from it for steps. Up these Mac heaved his inadequate legs in a dislocating manner, and he plumped down on the other side into a rustling bed of nettles.

When he got to his feet again, he perceived that he was in a field-corner, where, on the one hand, wall and hedge meeting at a sharp angle, and on the other a grassy slope swelling up, narrowly circumscribed the view. It was a place in which he had never been before, and his route thence seemed by no means clear to him. But as he stood perplexed, Gaby himself, safe and unmolested, trotted into his ken a little way up the slope. He was panting still, but had recovered sufficiently to sniff about intermittently with a business-like air, as if surmising rabbit-holes. Apparently, however, he had for the time being abandoned himself to evil ways, as when Mac called to him gleefully, he left his master's shouts unheeded, without even pretending not to hear, and after a little desultory jogging to and fro, ran quickly off out of sight over the swarded ridge. This line of conduct distressed and annoyed Mac, who, now that he was relieved about the dog, began to reflect uneasily upon his strange surroundings and possible neighbours. What if some Frightful Beast came ambling down that hill at him, or strode abruptly over the hedge close by? He did not feel by any means sure either that he recollected his way home. In short, if he would have self-confessed it, forsaken Kate's arrival at this juncture would not have been unwelcome. On the whole it seemed to him that he had better start once more in pursuit of Gaby; so he began to scamper up among the clumps of ragweed and thistles, uttering calls as he went, which betrayed more perturbation of spirit than he guessed.

Near the top of the slope his path was crossed by somebody who came out from beneath the boughs of an elm-tree, in whose noon-stunted shade he had been sitting. It was a tall, dark-faced young man in a labourer's dusk-coloured suit, with a blue bundle and a blackthorn.

"Fine day, sir," he said to Mac. "Would you be lookin' for anybody?"

"For a shaggy little disobedient wretch, that won't ever mind a word one says to him—at least, he sometimes won't ever—I think it's rabbits he's hunting," Mac replied, breathlessly. In his hurry he forgot to touch his hat until the end of his sentence, when he supplied the omission with much correctness.

"Maybe, now, that might be himself over there," the young man said, taking a glance round, and then pointing to a place where Gaby was, in fact, skirmishing, nose to ground.

Mac suddenly climbed up on a fallen log, which brought the truant into his field of vision as well. "So it is, I declare," he said. "I was lookin' the wrong way before."

"He's after the rabbits, sure enough," said the young man; "but he'll soon tire of that. It's only of a very odd while there does be e'er a one down these fields. Belike you come here along wid somebody?" he suggested, surveying Mac, who, reassured by company, had sat down on the log to rest, and presented an appearance rather less portly than might have been expected in a person whose age lacked not more than ten months and one week of six years.

"Oh no, I'm exercisin' Gaby quite by myself

to-day," said Mac. "Kate Heron does come with us sometimes, just because it's sociabler, you see."

"Oh, Kate Heron, bedad!" the young man said, and looked round him again.

"She isn't here to-day," said Mac. "I told you only sometimes."

"So you did, sir," said the young man.

"And because it's sociabler," said Mac.

"Ay, sir, to be sure," said the young man, "and is she gettin' her health these times? and her sisters, and her father?"

"I don't know about *them*," said Mac. "But to the best of my b'lief Kate's perfitly well. It's Mrs M'Quaide, the cook, that thinks she'll drop off her two feet some fine day, she's so killed with standin' over the heat of the blazin' fires."

"And is there any talk, sir, at all—of Kate gettin' married?" the young man asked, swinging his bundle about by the knotted handkerchief ends.

"If you do that with it, it'll untie, and everything come flingin' itself out head foremost," Mac said warningly. "And there may be talk, and a great deal of talk, but people don't go about repeatin' whatever gossip they may happen to hear downstairs."

"Sure, not at all, sir, be no manes," said the young man. "I only axed the question of you because—you see I'm just after trampin' over from the town of Greenore; off in Scotland I've been this last couple of months, and maybe I'll be steppin' on again, and not stoppin' here any time— it just depinds. I've met ne'er a sinsible crathur yet to be tellin' me aught I want to know, and I've as many as ten minds this minyit to turn back the way I come. So I was wonderin' what news there might be in it since I quit, such as buryins or marryins, or any talk of the like."

"Oh, of course, news isn't gossip," said Mac. "It's an entirely diff'rent thing. If it's news, I shouldn't mind tellin' you anythin' I heard talk about. But I think there hasn't been much about marryins or buryins, at least since I came to stay here. Let me consider"—and Mac considered with his chin in the air, and his over-large hat set very far back on his head. "Oh, I know there *is* great talk about one thing, only it happened before I came, and that's the row there was when they were buildin' Mr Carden's rick. It was what you may call a row, for one man actually went and knocked another off the top of the ladder, because he got annoyed at somethin', down on the paved stones, and no thanks to him if he wasn't killed dead on the spot. They're always talkin' about that—Kate and everybody."

"Are they, sir, bedad? And what do they be sayin,' everybody and Kate?"

"Oh, but Mrs MacQuaide says nobody need mind a word of Kate Heron's, because she used to be speaking to Willie Reilly—that's the man that got annoyed—and so that's the only reason she sticks up for him now. Not that she's got any great call to be troublin' her head about him, Mrs MacQuaide says, after his runnin' off the way he did, and never so much as sendin' home tale or tidins of where he

was gone to.   Poor Alec Sweeny was worth ten
of him, she says—the man who got knocked off;
he was always pleasant.   And she'd twice as soon
be marryin' him, if it was her, as a cross-tempered
firebrand like Willie Reilly.   It's *news* that I'm
repeatin,' you know."

   "Why, to be sure—not a word of gossip is there
in it at all, sir.   But what does Kate Heron say?"

   "She says that Alec Sweeny had a right to have
held his fool's tongue, instead of to be givin' impudence to other people, and then nothin' would have
happened anybody."

   "And true for her, the Lord knows," the young
man vehemently said.   "What business had he to
be blatherin' about what didn't anyways consarn
him, when he was bid keep himself quiet?   Supposin' a man did be chance put the collar on wrong-
ways up, and he harnessin' in the divil's own hurry,
it's no more than might aisy ha' happint himself, or
any other person, that he need take upon himself
to be bawlin' it up to young Maggie Heron, where
she was treadin' the rick, and ready to run home
wid the story to Kate and the rest of them the
next thing she done, as he well knew, so he did; he
done it a-purpose, and the divil's cure to him," Mac's
new acquaintance asseverated, again swinging his
bundle recklessly round.

   At this unexpected heat Mac felt slightly taken
aback, though he observed without discomposure:
"If I was you I'd put it down out of my hand
altogether, if I couldn't keep from flourishin' it
about.   But besides that, the woman where Kate

goes to get hairpins says that Alec Sweeny was
only jokin', the way he had, and no reasonable
person would have thought bad of it. And Tim
Brennan says in his opinion it's likely enough they
both had drink taken, and neither the two of them.
nor the one of them, rightly knew what they were
doing. And Dick the postman's sister says she
always had a sort of liking for poor Willie Reilly,
but there was no denyin' he had an ugly passionate
temper, and you couldn't know what minute he
might be flarin' up in a fury, any more than you
could tell by lookin' at it when a steam-engine would
be lettin' a screech out of it. And old Mrs Walsh
said she'd be long sorry to see a daughter's child
of hers married to the likes of him, that might up
and hit her a crack some fine day she'd never get
the better of. I think old Mrs Walsh is Kate
Heron's grandmother."

"She is, sir, she is; and, begorrah, she only said
very right," said the young man.

"Well, but afterwards, when we were going home,
Kate was saying to a girl we met on the road that
she'd daresay all the while Alec Sweeny slipped
his foot by accident, and the lock of hay fallin' on
him had nothin' to say to it at all; and Willie
Reilly never intended him any harm; and if the
truth was known, he *didn't* make a wipe at him
with his pitchfork.

"I'd give more than a little," said the young man,
"to think that was the way of it. But I know
betther."

"It was an immense high rick, I b'lieve," said

Mac.   "Joe Malone said anybody tumblin' off the top of it would be apt to be broke to jomethry—jomethry means somethin' like a dissected map."

"It was so; and be the same token, there it is glimpsin' through the trees fornent us," said the young man, pointing across a breadth of pasture land to where a yellow gable-end gleamed through an opening in a cloud of round-crested elms.

"By Jove! and is that the real one he fell off?" said Mac, gazing with much interest and a little awe. "And were you there too?"

"Part of the while I was, sir," said the other gloomily.   As he stood staring at the distant rick, his memory brought him back to the noon of a hotter day, not very long past, when he had been at close quarters with it, pitching hay, in fact, on the top.   He recalled the glowing glare of the June sunshine, that seemed to clutch at anybody who stepped into it out-of-doors, and to hold him faster and tighter the longer he stayed under it; and the strong scent or the clovery hay that came wobbling up to him in heavy bundles on the end of Alec Sweeny's fork.   And then he recollected how, just when everything was at its most scorching point, he had heard Alec beginning with a shrill cackle of laughter to relate the story of the ridiculous blunder committed by Willie Reilly that morning while hastily harnessing the cross jennet, and how he himself, finding peremptory injunctions to desist of no avail, and stung by the titters of Maggie Heron, had resorted to the more vigorously repressive measure of hurling down upon his too communicative colleague a blinding and smothering forkful. A spasm of rage made his thrust of fierce-looking steel prongs so much more than merely reckless that Alec had probably been lucky to drop out of his reach, tumbling sheer off the tall ladder thud upon the stones, amid the shrieks and shouts of all beholders. "Och, murther!—Och, mercy on us all! —Och Holy Virgin!—The man's kilt—he's dis-throyed!" But there the scene shifted, for a guilty consciousness of that furious moment had prompted the assailant to flee, scrambling down on the other side of the rick, without waiting to know whether a result so fatal had actually supervened. Before continuing his flight over seas, he did contrive to learn that Alec Sweeny's fall had not killed him outright anyway; but during his two months' absence at the Scotch harvesting he had had no home news. Now, being just returned to Clonman-avon, whether he would there remain or again decamp must depend upon what turn several things had taken; and he wondered how far he might trust the report given by this queer, old-fashioned talkative little imp of a child, who was evidently the belonging of some Quality staying up at old Mrs Kavanagh's, and under the charge of Kate Heron. Meanwhile Mac had resumed:

"Well, then, you know, everybody declared every mortal bone in his body was broken. But were you there when Dr Crampton came and said the most that ailed him was that he'd wranched his ankle round? So he wranched it right for him again, nd Mrs MacQuaide thinks that if Alec would have

taken advice he might be well mended by this time;
but he must needs go off with his foot to old Christy
Hughes, the cow-doctor, and get him tinkerin' at it.
And in my opinion he was a very great fool to do
any such thing. For it's no business of Christy
Hughes to understand about the legs of human
persons; they're no more like cows' legs than the
legs of chairs and tables. By the way," said Mac,
sidling along the log nearer to where the young
man stood, "about how high was the highest cow or
horse that you ever saw anywhere—near here, for
instance?"

"Sure, the same as e'er a one you'd see in it, sir,
I should suppose," said the young man. "But you
was tellin' me the news about Alec Sweeny's fut?"

"He's got very little use of it yet, poor man!—
very little at all," Mac replied, shaking his head so
solemnly that his hat fell off backwards. "If you
meet him on the road he's stumpin' with two sticks
as slow as a snail. It isn't like anybody really
walkin'; you'd think it was somethin' standin' there,
and nearly tumblin' over every minute. Christy
Hughes made a fine botch of it, whatever he did
to him. They say it's a wonder if he's ever fit for
anythin' again, and Dr Crampton says his only
chance is not to put his foot to the ground for the
next couple of months. Only Tim Brennan says
it's easy talkin', but how's a man to get his livin'
without wages for that length of time. So Alec
makes a shift to go as far as the place where they're
breakin' stones; that's all he's able for now. It
would be pretty detestful to get one's living by

breakin' stones on the road, with a black thing on to keep the splinters out of one's eyes. Alec always takes his off when he sees us passin', but it looks ridic'lous."

"I 'm as sorry of that as anythin'," said the young man, "as sorry as anythin', supposin' that made a hair of differ. It 's cruel, now, what 'll take and happen in a moment of time, and nobody intendin' any great harm maybe, if you come to consider, but, och! sure the Lord knows where you 'll ha' got to afore you 've e'er a chance of doin' that—somewheres you never thought of bein' very belike. . . . And so you do be meetin' Alec Sweeny on the road now and again, sir? And has he and Kate Heron anythin' to say to one another these times at all?"

"I can't be repeatin' every single thing. People sayin' 'What way are you?' and 'It 's a fine day,' when they 're passin' isn't news," Mac said with some sternness.

"'Deed, no, sir," assented the young man.

"Really, I don't think I remember anything else," said Mac, reflectively. "They talk sometimes about Willie Reilly, the annoyed man's mother; and Rose, the other housemaid, says what she thinks baddest of, is his leavin' the poor old woman there all this while, frettin' herself sick, and never writin' her a line to say what 's become of him."

"And did you say she was took bad?" said the young man. "It 's running over I 'll be across the fields; that 's the shortest way."

"Oh, she got news yesterday from her daughter

away in Chicago, who's doin' grandly, and sent
her an order of money, and that's heartened her up
finely, Rose says. But it's no thanks to that Willie
Reilly. In fact, nothin's any thanks to him, I believe,
and if he stayed out of this altogether," Mac said, in
the tone of one making a familiar quotation, "it 'ud
be no great harm."

"I'd ha' wrote fast enough, and so I would," said
the young man; "only I thought she'd be writin'
back, and the truth is I was in dread of what she
might he tellin' me news of—somebody after dyin',
or gettin' married, that 'ud be worser to my mind.
Troth, if I'm not as good-for-nothin' as I can stick
together, get me one that is."

At this moment a shrill alarm of barking and
yelping arose from Gaby, and he was seen to be
digging violently close under the wall at a little
distance.

"He's got one," Mac exclaimed; and ran off,
followed by the young man, passing on the way
several perfectly normal head of cattle, which were
peacefully sauntering and grazing. The field wall
was here rather low all along, and in just one place
the soil about the roots of a willow-tree which grew
against it banked it up to such a height that standing
there, a person as tall as Mac could easily look
over it. By the time they arrived, Gaby had dis-
appointingly abandoned his excavations and roved
farther on, leaving Mac nothing more interesting
to do than ascend this small mound, and see what
might be on the other side of the wall. What there
was gave him a shock of surprise, for instead of

merely looking across into another field, he found himself staring down into a road, which lay ever so far beneath. It was a narrow road, with a sharp bend in it a short way to his left, and a long straight stretch on the right; and he felt vaguely aware of some familiar thing in its aspect. By-and-by he identified that feature as a dark stone cross standing in a recess of the bank just opposite. Very old and ancient it was, a block which the wild weather of many a century had rough-hewn again into almost its primitive shapelessness. Mac remembered it quite well, and the three rude granite steps upon which it was mounted, with a sloe-bush sprouting from a crack in one of them; the recollection was somehow disagreeable to him, yet when or where he had seen it he could not immediately think.

As he was puzzling over this point, a figure came into sight at the farthest end of the road, slowly approaching.

"Oh, here's Alec Sweeny himself," said Mac; "and he's walking lamerer than ever."

The young man, who was leaning against the willow-trunk behind him, stooped forward to watch, and began muttering half aloud: "Ay, bejabers, lame he is. It's the bad offer he's makin' at gettin' along at all, and he that ought to be keepin' himself quiet, if he's to give himself e'er a chance. Goodness forgive me, I'm thinkin' I have the man bravely disthroyed. But I'll halve me six pound ten wid him, I will so; or if me mother doesn't want it, he might take the whole of it and welcome, then he could lie up for the winther, and he might git a sound fut under him agin the spring.   Faix, now, it's a quare dale aisier crookenin' things than straightenin' thim again.   And sure a man's to be pitied when he's so be his nathur that he'll flare up in a blaze inside him all of a suddint minyit, till he's no more notion what he's after doin' than the flames of fire has of what they're after burnin'.   Many's the time I do be thinkin', and I takin' a scythe or a rapin'-hook in me hand, that the divil himself only knows what desthruction I mayn't ha' done on some mislucky body afore I quit a hold of it.   But Alec Sweeny had no business to be risin' the laugh on me, if he *was* thinkin' of Kate Heron, and be hanged to him.   If I thought she was thinkin' of him, it's his neck I'd as lief be breakin' as his ould ankle.   And as I was sayin', sooner than get news they were marryin', I'd hear tell he was in his grave, and his murdher's sin on me sowl—I would so.   That there is at the bottom of me heart I well know all the while, if I cocked twenty diff'rint lies atop of it, and the Ould Lad's got good raison to be proud of me and the likes of me.   Och, wirra, but the man looks powerful poor and weakly in himself.   Halvin' them pounds 'ill be the laist I can do, and little enough.   They'd ha' set Kate and me up grand in our housekeepin' next Shrove, but sorra the bit of me'll ax her now till the year after, and afore then she's very apt to ha' took up wid somebody else; and a good job for her—and maybe it's a good job too for every bone in his body that I dunno who he is.   Sorra a word I'll ax her."

N

The young man fell silent, and shrank back a little farther under the boughs as Alec Sweeny came by. He was a tall, large-framed, young man, too, but looked gaunt and pinched; his coat, greenishly discoloured, hung baggily from sharp angles, and his limp was so dolorous that the beholders felt relief when it stopped and he sat down on the steps of the old cross, staring drearily into the dust at his feet. Almost at the same moment, round the nearer corner, came Kate Heron, in her homely brown shawl, and the incongruous bedizened hat due to her position in the service of Quality. She was walking rather hurriedly, and carrying an empty basket errandwise; but at the cross she hesitated, and then halted, saying: "It's a fine mornin', Alec."

"Whethen, now, what need is there for her to be stoppin'?" murmured a malcontent voice from above. "A good-day goin' by 'ud ha' been plinty."

Kate's greeting, indeed, apparently gave satisfaction nowhere, for Alec Sweeny seemed just to grunt in acknowledgment without raising his eyes.

"And I hope you're gettin' your health somethin' better now, Alec," Kate added after a slight pause.

At this, Alec Sweeney not only looked up, but scrambled abruptly with painful haste to his feet. "See you here, Kate Heron," he said. "Do you take me for a born fool? Or do you think I don't know as well as I know me own name the only raison you'd spake a civil word to me is considherin' I'm an ould show of a cripple, that it's a charity for a dacint body to be passin' the time of day to? Sorra another raison have you. Sure you wouldn't be lookin' the side of the road I was on. And let me tell you, I'd liefer be listenin' to me ould hammer crackin' the stones. So you may just keep your fine talk for any that 'ud care to be pickin' it up out of the dirt, as if it was ha'pence you were throwin' a blind beggar. Sorra the other raison." And he hobbled away with reckless lurches, still muttering.

"Set up himself then, bedad, and what other raison had he the impidence to be expectin'?" commented an overhearer. "Och, but he's the misfort'nit lookin' bosthoon. And if that's the way he'll be biddin' me keep me ould pounds to meself, what am I to do at all to set things straight and contint me own mind?"

Kate Heron had lingered looking after the lame man as if pondering upon this rebuff, but had just turned to go her way, when Gaby, who was now running to and fro along the wall-top, barked fiercely at a robin, which caused her to look up and recognise a well-known broad-brimmed straw hat. "Guide me to goodness, Master Mac, and is it up there you are? And me lookin' for you every place, and thinkin' then the mistress must ha' picked you up in the avenue, and took you drivin' wid her."

"You might have *knowed* I was goin' to-day on my walk with myself," Mac replied with dignity, chiefly for the benefit of his new acquaintance in the background.

"And what at all brought you up there? Ah,

now, Master Mac, you're the ungovernable child. Don't be lanin' over the edge of the ugly high wall, there's a darlint. How'll I get you down out of that ever? For it's breaking your neck you'll be if I take me eye off you to run round to the gate."

"He's right enough, Kate; you needn't be dis-thressin' yourself," said the young man, stepping forward.

"Saints above—it's not Willie Reilly?" Kate said, doubly startled: "sure nobody'd ha' thought of seein' you, and we all expectin' you home every day of the week for this long while. And where at all have you been that you weren't writin'?"

"If you'd run round to the gate below, *machree*— no, I mane just plain Kate Heron—I'd be fetchin' the little gintleman along to meet you, and it 'ud be handier tellin'," the young man suggested, and Kate acted accordingly.

"I daresay that *would* be the best way of goin' home," said Mac. "It must be rather near lunch-time. Gaby, where've you got to?" He looked around him for the dog; and as he did so he made a remarkable discovery. Close by, a little knot of beasts were standing with their heads over the wall; two or three cows, and a sorrel pony, whose face with its white streak somehow seemed unpleasantly familiar to him. Where had he seen it before? Why, looking over a wall just like this one. But was not that the wall of the Field of the Frightful Beasts? Could it be possible that he was actually inside it? "And I declare to goodness," Mac said to himself, "we used to be passin' that stone with the steps—and there's the old white horse lookin' over too. They *aren't* Frightful; they're only standin' on the high bank. But how was a Person to know that a wall would be pretendin' it was the height of a house along the road, and then turn into a little quite lowish one on the wrong side?"

This view of the matter was such a new and agreeable light to him, that he naturally wished to flash it on; so he began: "Do you see that little black cow there?"

But his companion, who was thinking of different things, misconceived the motive of the question, and replied: "Sure you needn't mind her, sir, she wouldn't hurt anybody. It's only the flies tormentin' her makes her put down her head that a way." An answer, which led Mac to keep half the width of the field between himself and insulting insinuations as he proceeded towards the gate.

There Kate Heron awaited them, and one of the first remarks that Willie Reilly made to her was—

"I'm not axin' you, Kate; troth, nor won't I this great while. But d'you think, now, you'd think entirely too bad of waitin' for me as long as to a year from next Shrove? Till I get meself a thrifle broke of me outrageous temper, and till I gather another odd few pounds instid of them here that I'm intindin' for Alec Sweeny; and till I've kep' the pledge for awhile, for truth it is I've no call to be stirrin' meself up wid dhrinks, that's deminted enough whether or no; and till I've some sort of sartinty in me that I'm not widin the turn of your hand every instiant whatever of behavin' no betther than a ragin' hyenna. I'm not axin' you, mind you. But if I had a notion you wouldn't ha' took up wid anybody else agin then——"

"Saints and patience, Willie!" Kate said, as airily as she could, "that's a terrible great hape of things you're to be gettin' done between this and then. You'd be hard put to it, I should say, in a dozen twelvemonths, let alone one."

"I'd conthrive it, if that was all," he said. "But it's too long a len'th of time to be expectin' of you altogether. Somebody else'll be axin' you; and then if I keep out of the raich of doin' murdher on someone, that'll be the most I'll manage. Ay, but it's too long entirely."

"For the matter of that I'd wait a year and welcome, or ten year, or twenty, I'd wait *contint*," Kate said, with an earnestness upon which her hearer might have put a somewhat discouraging construction. But he did not, and rejoined—

"Glory be to goodness! then we'll do grand after all. It's steppin' along I'll be now to see me mother, and after that I'll go straightways and make all square wid poor Alec Sweeny. Sure a rest for his fut's all he's wantin'; dancin' jig polthogue he'll be at our weddin' one of these fine days."

He had set off, but after a few quick steps faced round to add, in a tone slightly conscience-

pricked, "Mind you, Kate, I'm not axin' you,
nor goin' to." Then he started again at a brisk
trot, which became a positive gallop as he de-
scended the grassy slope.

"He might have the sense to know that
tearin' along like that's the very way to make
them run at him, if that's what he's afraid of,"
Mac, watching his departure, observed with super-
cilious vindictiveness; "and one would suppose
anybody could easily see that they're not
Frightful beasts at all."

That evening Mac and his great-grandmother
had cold chicken at tea instead of eggs; for the
morning's adventure had put them so completely
out of Kate's mind, that she aimlessly brought
home her basket "as empty," Mrs MacQuaide
averred wrathfully upon discovering the omission,
"as your own *stookawn's* head is of wit. And
what am I to be poachin' now for the misthress
to-night?" It was a brilliant sunset hour, and
the long rays again slanted straight into Mac's
creamy cup; but this time is was the old lady
who seemed rather dull and abstracted. She
had heard on her drive that morning how her
old friend Lady Olive's chronic bronchitis had
been suddenly cured, and her thoughts kept
running on the news.

"We can't have been much older than you,
my dear, quite small, small children, the first
summer her people came to Lisanards, and that
would be about the year '26. It's a long time

now since she's been well enough to see anyone, but it gave a sort of object to one's drive to go and ask if she had had a good night. Well, there could be no other end to that."

"You must come down the fields with me instead, great-little-grandmamma," said Mac.

"Oh, my dear, my days for running about in the fields were over long ago."

"I *don't* run about," said Mac; "not unless somethin' partic'lar happens. I was in a very nice one to-day, where there is a pond, and part of an old car, and a black little donkey that won't let you go very near it. You'd like it when you got inside. There's a plank across a ditch, and steps up a wall, quite easy."

"Stiles and ditches, my dear child," said his great-grandmother. "Do you want me to break all my old bones?"

"That sounds very much like just a 'scuse," Mac said, with some severity. "There's only two stiles, and you needn't tumble down into the nettles unless you put your foot on the wrong stone. And as for the Frightful Beasts, if that's what you're thinkin' of, I really can *not* imagine who put it into your head that there were any such things."

A LONG FURROW

AT one time it seemed as if there were going to be "a rael ould shindy" just inside the gate leading into the cow-lane out of Big Cross-corners, which Mr Mahony was ploughing for potatoes. It was a likely enough opportunity for such an occurrence—half-an-hour or so before sunset on a bright, east-windy March day, when work had ceased, but a little dawdling appeared expedient on the way back to the farmyard, where "Himself" might otherwise call attention to the fact that the six o'clock bell wouldn't be ringing this good while yet. In these odd corners of leisure, the tempers of people who have ploughed, or hedged and ditched from early morning in a cold and hungry wind, are apt to shrink, and censorious grow their views of anything that precedes food and shelter. So now there was some captiousness in the senior ploughman's criticisms upon the performance of young Brien, who had been driving the second pair of horses. "Och to goodness, look at that, lads!" he said, pointing across the broad brown field, where a low sun shone iridescent upon the burnished clods, and rosed the white flecks of the sea-gulls scattered peering among them. "What sort of ould show would you call it at all? Is it be way of bein' a dacint straight furrow, or is it the edge of a wave

201

of the say? Or would you suppose he was makin'
an offer at scrawmin' his name wid the ploughshare?
Them's fine pot - hooks and hangers, begor. Very
belike he disremembered he wasn't up at their
iligant National Schoolhouse yit — it's no great
while anyway since he war." His sarcasms were
needlessly caustic, still, they would not have necessarily produced any recriminations, as young Brien,
too humble - minded to think of protesting against
a prize-winner at ploughing matches like Pather
Meehan, no matter how grossly he might exagger-
ate one's deflections from the right line, stood silently
by the drooping heads of the old greys, Kitty and
Rose, and formed with them a meek and patient
trio.

But unluckily Tip Hanratty, who, mind you,
had no notion of handling a plough *at all*, took
upon himself to continue: "Sure, it's steppin' across
the counthry to Connaught he'd a right to be.
That 'ud be just the place for him, where they
have their pitaties planted in their little ould lazy-
beds, you could cover over wid the tail of your
coat: a dhrill wouldn't ha' room to run crooked.
Faix, you'll find plinty of parishes up there, where
they haven't so much as a plough on e'er a one of
the town-lands. You'd be laughin' to see nothin'
goin' on the roads but the little ould asses throttin'
under the big loadins of turf; they're the only
sizable things they have in it at all—thimselves and
their ould bogs."

Whereupon Mick Loughlin, who, as Tip very well
knew, was a Connaught man, flared up and said,

among other things: "Is it laughin' you'd be? Bedad, is it so? Troth, now, you'd be meetin' as good goin' the roads there as ever you met in the dirty county Wexford, ay would you, and betther than you'd be able for, or the likes of you."

To which Tip rejoined, wonderingly: "Och, it's the great talk the man has entirely. Sure, they was able, at all evints, to be puttin' him out of jabberin' there, to come here givin' impidence to them that has somethin' else to do besides mindin' him." Whence it seems more than probable that the matter would have gone farther rapidly, had not somebody interposed. This was old Felix O'Beirne, sitting on an inverted wheelbarrow to watch the sun slip down; and he could interpose with effect for several reasons: Because he was a person of consequence, being brother-in-law to Mr Mahony's mother, and a visitor at the farm; because he, too, was a Connaught man, owning a forge off away at a little place called Lisconnel, among the blackest of the bog-lands; and because the renown of his exploits in the war of '98 still enhaloed him after half-a-century. Moreover, having seen much serious fighting in his time, he was always inclined to discountenance amateur wrangles and scuffles, which seemed to him an aimless waste of valuable material. Accordingly, he made haste to remark, "Well, now, I wouldn't say but I've squinted down plenty crookeder furrows than the young chap's; and it's a fine len'th too. But was I ever tellin' yous of the longest one ever I set eyes on? Bejabers,

that was the quare story. I do be often thinkin' of
it when I'm in the pitaties."

It was, in fact, a very favourite reminiscence of
Felix's, and, partly in the interests of peace, he
dwelt upon it now at considerable length, as he sat
confronting the flush of the sunset, beyond the
broad, evenly-ridged field.   He was looking with
his mind's eye across the wide expanse of fifty
chequered years into another field, broad, likewise,
but not bare and brown ; and into another day,
not on the bleak threshold of spring, but under the
glowing azure canopy of early summer.

"If it wasn't only for John Callaghan's pitaties
that year bein' such a grand crop," he said, "we'd
ha' had a poor chance of doin' what we done ; but,
bedad, in the four corners of the land you'd have
had a hard job to find a finer-lookin' one. Scarce
a plant had missed in the len'th and breadth of it
all, and ne'er a gap was there in the green—you
might as well have looked for houles in the smooth
of the say. A rael credit it was to poor Norah
Callaghan and her *pistrogues*, she that would be
plantin' a half-dozen of hin's eggs in a one of the
dhrills whenever the pitaties were sowin', by way
of drawin' the good out of the lands round about
into their own bit of field—so she said. Troth, it's
the comical notions people take up wid.   Some
whiles, it does be like as if they'd a mind to let on
they'd a hand in everythin', good or bad. And the
less they can do, the quarer they consait.   But
sure, what great harm ? Anyhow, they were the
iligant pitaties.

"The way I come to see it, was that I'd a score or so of pike-heads to be bringin' from our own place to Carrickdonel. Thravellin' wid them I was from Marcraney to Loughnalone under a load of cabbages. Bedad, it's stranger cart-loads than me and me pike-heads were goin' through the counthry in those days. And if it wasn't be raison of me havin' got lamed for a bit wid a poke in the leg, I'd ha' had somethin' else to do besides carryin' pike-heads, that manner of way; for our lads were havin' great work just then in the county Wexford. Howsome'er, it was better very belike that I come to Loughnalone the time I did. For when I got there, latish in the day, when one's shadow was about the len'th of a pike-staff, in a bad state I found them all. The redcoats was after comin' the evenin' before, and wid most of the boys off in Wexford, few enough was left in it to be hinderin' thim of whatever divilment they plased—a big throop of them, the West Corks. Ugly it was, goin' by, to see the bits of black thatch smokin' and blazin' wid nothin' unless the sunlight to be puttin' it out; and uglier things than that I seen, ay did I.

"But Owen Connor's little place, that we was bound for, bein' convaniently out of harm's road down at the lonesome ind of a *boreen*, had took no hurt in the night's slaughterin'. The Lord knows it's glad I was when I set eyes on his daughter Margaret, and she cryin' her own out of her head sittin' be the door. And a good few of the neighbours was in it too, that tould me all the bad news, and, begor, bad you might call it.

Troth, now, the sharp end of me pike remimbered it agin a militiaman many a time after—and may God forgive us all, that had the makin' of us.

"There was a dale of their doin's it seemed no use to be considherin' then. But Owen Connor and the other two along wid- him was a diff'rent matter ; just a chance there might be of conthrivin' somethin' for them. You must know the most of the throop was after marchin' off wid themselves out of the place about mid-day, and they'd left the sargint and five or six men at John Callaghan's house be the Lough, in charge of three prisoners they'd took, and the three was Callaghan himself, and Owen Connor, and Dan Tobin. The captin wasn't for hangin' *thim* offhand, because of a notion he had that they might be givin' information first. So keepin' them he was to send on to that black divil, Judkin Butler at Trenchestown, a good step farther down the Lough. That was all any of us knew for sartin ; but there was talk of a party of redcoats comin' to fetch them off be wather, and in coorse none of us could tell the hour or the minyit that they might be quittin' out of it. So if we was to thry do a hand's-turn for them at all, we'd a right to make haste, or else whatever weeny chance there might be 'ud swim into nothin' like a dab of snow on a hot hearthstone.

"Only the worst of it was, that what wid the boys away in the Wexford army, and thim that was away farther than Wexford—rest their sowls —since the night's massacreein', we'd scarce any left able for more than talkin' ; och, the women, the crathurs, sure if they knew the differ between sinse and nonsinse, there'd seldom be a word out of them —and just wastin' time. There was Owen's brother, Joe Connor, and Eugene Walsh, and Pat O'Shaughnessy, and ould Christy Flynn, that we misdoubted of bein' soople enough to come along. But says he to us: "Is it keepin' me out of me chance yous 'ud be, after what happint last night?" and sure we couldn't go agin him. Thim was all we had.

"To be sure there was another young chap in it, and himself nobody else than Bernard Creagh from Moynessan. But sorra a sound out of him about comin' wid us; and maybe none of us was very wishful he would. For there was quare ugly stories goin' about him, and I knew more than one that 'ud make bould to declare he was no better than an informer. However, those times most of the neighbours did be sayin' he come of very respectable people, and they'd be sorry to believe any such a thing of him; afterwards some of thim had raison to be sorrier along of him, bedad. Anyhow, he was standin' there lanin' agin the wall at the back of everybody, wid a face on him as black as thunder, and all the while starin' like one bewitched at little Margaret Connor, where she was sittin' in disolation on the form at the door. Faix, it's not long she'd ha' put up wid him, if it hadn't been she was too much took up wid the dhread she was in about her ould daddy to be heedin' anythin' else. Sure 'twould break your heart to see her, and herself other whiles a dale apter to be laughin' as lightsome as a bird

wid ne'er a throuble in the world on its mind. So
her uncle, Joe Connor, stopped a minyit, and we
passin' by her goin' out, to be sayin' what he could
to hearten her up; and little enough that was, if
he would ha' been tellin' the truth.

"And says he to her : 'Ah, now, mavourneen, you
needn't be frettin' your heart, and cryin' your eyes
out, that's the brightest shinin' in the parish—yet
a while you needn't. Sure we might git him out
of it right enough, be some manner of manes, wid
the help of God. Maybe you'll prisintly be seein'
him steppin' safe and sound down the boreen. And,
bedad, Maggie machree,' says he, 'I'm thinkin' it's
as much as a *Thank'ee kindly* you'd be sayin' to
us, you crathur, for bringin' you home your ould
daddy.'

"And what at all would you suppose Margaret
ups and says? 'Is it a thank'ee?" says she.
'Sure, God knows I'd *marry* any man that done
his endeavours and conthrived to save him away
from them murdherin' hounds — ay would I, and
welcome.'

"So wid that Biddy Ryan, her married sister,
that was sittin' beside her, got pullin' her sleeve,
and biddin' her whist-a-whist. 'Is there no shame
in you?' says she to Maggie. 'It's as good as
makin' an offer you are to Felix O'Beirne, for right
well you know there's sorra another bachelor goin',
only he.'

"But ne'er a bit Maggie minded her, nor a diff'rint
word would she say except: 'Ay would I, to-morra,
and welcome.' And says I, in a whisper, passin'

by them, that as for makin' offers, 'twas what I'd been doin' ever since I set eyes on her last Easter twelvemonth, so Biddy'd no call to be talkin' foolish. And when I'd stepped outside, and was pullin' a grand long - handled pike down out of a hidin'-houle in the thatch, I was thinkin' in me own mind that liefer than bring bad news back to Margaret Connor, some sort of a houle I'd find for meself—a little round one, maybe, that's so to spake a door to a bigger-sized under sod. But it's not much likelihood there looked to be of our gittin' home wid any good to tell; and less it looked when we come to a place at the other end of the boreen, where we had a clear view across the fine pitaty-field I was spakin' to yous of, over to Callaghan's white house.

"For it stood on a little grassy spit of land, wid the wather on two sides of it, and just the pitaties stretchin' up on the others to the door and windies. Ne'er a dyke nor a ditch was there, nor a screed of hedge; and them widinside sure and sartin to be keepin' a sharp lookout—themselves and their cara-bines. Be the same token, that very minyit of time, as we was spyin' cautious through the privet-bushes, out at the front door stepped a one of the redcoats, and begun pathrollin' up and down. So what great chance could there be of ourselves, wid nought betther among us than an ould horse-pistol, ever gittin' up close enough to put our lads in the way of quittin' quick and aisy be the road of a dacint bullet, that was the best luck we was hopin' for thim? Shot down we'd be afore ever we come

o

widin pike-raich of a militiaman, and divil a thraneen
of use to Owen and the rest.

"That's what we was thinkin', standin' and lookin'
over, when all of a suddint a notion lep into me
mind, and about spakin' of it I was, only somebody
came up behind me, and tapped me on the shoulder;
and who should it be but Bernard Creagh, and he
pantin' like a dog runnin' after a stone.

"'Quit out of that, Felix O'Beirne,' says he to
me, 'git out of me road.   You've no call here,'
says he; 'it's men that know their way about,
we're wantin', instead of strangers to be blunderin',
the mischief can tell where, and desthroyin' other
people's chances.'

"'Strangers,' says he; and I that knew every
inch of the place as well as himself and betther,
after that again.   So says I to him what was he
blatherin' about at all?   And as for the way, only
too plain it was, and nothin' ailed us but to know
how to set about gittin' over it widout takin' up a
bigger loadin' of lead than we could be carryin'.
And I bid him keep aisy, and not be showin' himself where he might be seen thro' the bushes.

"But says he to me: 'You've no call here,' he
says; 'let other people be mindin' their own business,' says he; 'Owen Connor's nothin' to you.'

"So then Joe Connor tould him to git along wid
himself, and be hanged to him, and to hould his
fool's tongue.   'Nobody's spakin' agin your lendin'
a hand,' says he, 'if you're to be trusted.   But lave
Felix O'Beirne here alone, and don't be interferin'
wid your betters.'

"Och, murdher, but it's rael wicked Bernard looked at him and me, whatever'd come over him, and wid that he took one caper across to the other side of the boreen, and in he slipped among the bushes there as fast as a ferret into a rat houle. Eugene Walsh passed the remark that he thought the chap was a thrifle deminted. 'And if he is, it's the *best* thing he is then,' says Joe Connor; 'I wouldn't trust him,' says he, 'the len'th of that fine big straw Felix is after pullin' out of poor Owen's thatch.'

"And then I tould them what I was goin' to say was that the only way we'd e'er a chance of gittin' across the field. would be crawlin' in low under the green of the pitaties. For 'twas a grand height growin' over the furrows. Some places there'd be room enough for creepin' in the threnches on your hands and knees; and where there wasn't, 'twould be lyin' flat and wrigglin' along. 'It's the finest cover at all,' says I; 'bedad, we might be five fishes swimmin' down at the bottom of the Lough for any notion them up at the house had we was comin' next or nigh them, till we'd up and lep out at the door, like frogs from under a swathe of hay. Here by the bushes,' says I, 'would be a handy place for slippin' in; and sorra another plan good or bad I see a sign of.'

"And the rest of them was of the opinion that, at all events, we might as well be givin' it a thrial.

"So we got into the field very convanient behind the bank of the bit of a headland wid the privet-bushes thick on it. And the four men went, a

pair of them, aich follyin' the other, in a couple
of the furrows, but down along the one in the
middle, between them,. I took be meself. Sure,
now, as like as anythin' it was to stoopin' in under
a weeny green wood, wid all the branches flourishin'
themselves together above your head, and lettin' on
they were the right-sized trees, and you were the
wrong-sized man, till you might consait you were
after growin' into some quare discripshin of a giant.
Thinkin' I was, that if be accident I thrimbled
them a thrifle, passin' below, nobody could tell but
they were only shakin' in the win' blowin' over them.

"And I had me pike thrailin' along wid me, no
fear but I had. Maybe it wasn't the handiest thing
to be bringin', but somehow I always had a great
wish for a pike ; there's nothin' I'd liefer be handlin'.
Bedad, now, this minyit of time I'd give more than
a little to think I'd ever git the chance to be carryin'
a one ; but I question will I. It's a great while
since I've heard any talk about them ; I dunno
what betther yous have got these days instead.
For och, men alive, where'll you see a purtier sight
than a good few of them comin' along under the
clear moonlight, wid a shine on the heads of them
like as if they was after raichin' down so many stars
out of the sky? And if I'm not mistook, they'll
be out again one of these fine nights, though it
mayn't happen while I'm to the fore. Contintin'
meself I must be wid remimberin' fifty years back
the way I am now. Tellin' you the truth, I do
be forgin' meself an odd one yet now and agin, just
for diversion, after all the ould horse-shoes.

"Howiver, 'twas no obsthruction to me at all that time in the pitaty-dhrills. The only thing bothered me was me left knee, that hadn't got rightly soople yit after the prod a yeoman gave me at Three-mile Rock, and come agin me a bit at the creepin'. So wonderin' I was would the other men be gettin' ahead of me, and listenin' could I hear them stirrin' in their furrows. But never a sound I heard, till at last the notion come in me mind—wid hearin' or how I dunno—that there was something creepin' after me. And I conthrived to take a squint back along behind me, that was no aisy matter; and, sure enough, I seen somebody comin'. Who it was I couldn't tell, but, sez I to meself, 'twould be one of our own lads anyway for sartin. And prisintly, after a while, I looked agin, and who was it but Bernard Creagh?

"Well, now, I'd as lief he'd ha' sted out of it, and that's a fact; but there he was, slitherin' along like a weasel at a great rate intirely. Faix, 'twas a rael curiosity to see him pullin' himself on, wid the two hands of him clutchin' from one side to the other of the dhrills. 'Twasn't very long I'd be keepin' ahead of him, I well knew. And the next time I looked back agin, it's very near he'd slithered, very near. And be the same token, what had he stuck in the grin of his clenched teeth, except the biggest clasp-knife you ever beheld, and it open ready. Throubled you'd be to say which was shinin' brightest, the long blade of it, or the two glarin' eyes of him; but the both of thim together had an oncommon ugly appearance. 'It's mischief he's manin',' sez I, 'and it's murdher he's manin'—and it's meself he's manin'.'

"So it's the tight houle I was in, you may percaive. For turn round to face him I couldn't, widout standin' up on me feet; and if I done that, liker than not the militiamen 'ud see me, and there'd be an ind of e'er a chance for Margaret's father and the rest of them altogether. All I could do was to be peltin' on wid meself the quickest I could conthrive, and considherin' the ould furrow was bound to not be runnin' much farther. But sure I might considher as much as I plased; divil a sign was there of an endin' to it. You wouldn't believe the quare len'th it seemed; rael onnathural. And me afeared to be liftin' me head the way I'd know whereabouts we'd come, and lookin' behind me every minyit, and seein' the grin and the shine comin' slitherin' nearer and nearer.

"And the last time I done so, 'twas be great good luck, begorrah. For that same instiant me lad takes and shifts the big knife out of his mouth into his fist, and a grab he makes at me left leg wid the other. Only just soon enough I was dhrawin' it in, or he'd ha' had me caught. But when it come to that work, I made me mind up I must be thryin' somethin', good or bad, if he wasn't to have it all his own way, stickin' me like a pig. So I shortened me hould on the pike-staff, and I let one back-handed dhrive at him as best I could—glory be to goodness, I always had a powerful stren'th in me wrists. Take him or lave him it was, for I couldn't see to be aimin' be any

manner of manes; and I made sure at first I'd
missed him cliver and clane, 'cause sorra the feel
it had of goin' through anythin' wid a bit of
substance in it, till the point run into the crumbly
clay. Och, it's as plased as anythin' I was when
I felt the tug on the handle like a mackerel at the
ind of your line. And, bedad, as good luck would
have it, the point had just skivered through and
through all the folds in his coateen and shirt under
one arm of him, and pinned itself into the ridge
alongside of him, the way an inch he couldn't be
stirrin' backwards nor forwards, till he'd riefed the
ould rags off him, and that he wouldn't manage in
a hurry, lyin' cramped in a narrer thrench. Ne'er
a scrape he had himself—maybe, more's the pity.
But sorra a hand's-turn could he be doin' against
me, unless it was wid raisin' bawls and roars, and
that he dursn't for his life. Just one elfish sort of
howl he let, when he seen me crept nigh out of
his sight; and that done us no harm, for be then
we were close up to the house at last, and through
wid the hidin' and crawlin'. The worst of the matther
was lavin' me pike behind me, that I did be at
somethin' of a loss for the use of. But me hands
was strong, as I was sayin', they was strong. And
we'd prisintly enough to be carryin' widout it.

"Ay, bedad, that was the right way we come, and
a good job we made of it too. Dead drunk a couple
of the North Corks was, and another not much
betther; it's little talk there was out of *thim*. And
we'd no great throuble wid the rest aither; not but
what one of thim got a chance first of puttin' a bullet

through poor Christy Flynn's head.   Howane'er, considherin' the desolation thim divils had made for him to be goin' home to, belike 'twas the best thing could aisy ha' happint him.   And when we were thrampin' across the field back agin, we had a sight of a crathur all in tatters leggin' it off, and stoppin' for to shake its fists at us, like a scarecrow gone out of its sinses.   And that was the last any of us saw of Bernard Creagh for many a long day, though there's plinty more I could be tellin' yous about him afterwards.

"So we brought Margaret her daddy home after all to her wid no harm took, and you might ha' thought the crathur was goin' daft too wid con- tintmint.   And you may depind I wasn't long delayin' before I was remindin' her of what she'd promised.   And maybe she wasn't anyways greatly disthressin' herself over it—maybe she wasn't.

"But och, there's your workmen's bell ringin', and me discoorsin' here all the evenin'," Felix said, growing old, and getting up; "more betoken I've sat till I'm as stiff as a one of thim gate-posts. It's the bad hand I'd be these times at creepin' in pitaty-furrows.   Not but what I'd make an offer at it yit, if I was put to it—ay would I so."

MOGGY GOGGIN

IF Moggy Goggin had lived among genteeler people her name would probably have been smoothed out into Margaret Geoghegan ; but Society in and about Lettercrum made small pretensions, and Moggy Goggin, with roughly-compressed gutterals, she was to her neighbours, except when they spoke of her as an "ould crathur." This they were rather apt to do, as she was a person of no social importance, dwelling all alone in a very tumble-down shanty, formerly a shepherd's, huddled under the bank at the end of Long Leg, one of Matt M'Cormack's fields. She had been established there for several years, yet nobody seemed to know much about her, beyond that her near relations had all died or otherwise "quit out of it." Her cousins, the M'Cormacks, were, indeed, better informed, better than they cared to let on, being fairly prosperous farming folk, and disposed to resent the circumstances that connected them with such an extremely poor old woman. As a matter of fact, Mrs M'Cormack was her half-sister's daughter, but they never owned anything more than a vaguely remote cousinship ; and Moggy, who was not an encroaching person, advanced no claim to closer kindred. Although only two or three fields lay between her and the farmhouse, her appearances at it were few, and

217

would have been fewer, had not Sally, the youngest girl, had certain looks and tricks of speech that reminded her of her own favourite sister, Norah, in a way which made her feel young again for a minute, as she sometimes did when the birds all began to sing together very suddenly, after a spring shower, under the eaves of a low-flashing sunset.

One early autumn morning, however, Mrs M'Cormack, looking out from her back door, said with dismay: "Och to goodness, if there isn't that ould torment of an ould Moggy Goggin comin' through the field. What at all's bringin' her at this hour of the day, and it not ten o'clock? I declare she's never from under one's feet. Annie, girl—och, she's not here—Sally, then, run and see what she's wantin', and maybe she might turn back. But I'm afraid of me life she'll be meeting himself and me nephew that's out and about somewheres—and Matt's no more gumption than a three-year-old; he'd let out who she was as soon as look at her!"

Mrs M'Cormack had special reasons for dreading such a disclosure. They had partly arrived a few days before in a letter from this stranger nephew, Thomas Martin, of Archmount, Illinois, U.S.A., just returned on a brief visit to the old country. It said, among other things: "Perhaps you may not have had the news that poor Aunt Norah Jackson died of pneumonia last Thanksgiving Day at Lambertville. I saw her a week previous, when she entrusted me with her savings to bring home to this country, which I was then about visiting shortly. Her wish was that her sister Margaret, if still living, should have the money; but otherwise her late sister Sarah's daughter Julia, or, namely, I take it, yourself. A friend of the family informs me that he believes old Margaret Goggin is lately deceased, and likely she is, as being the eldest sister she must have reached a great age, but doubtless you can let me know. If this is so, I can hand over the cash to you when I come to your place. It amounts to a trifle over two hundred pounds."

As Mrs M'Cormack had read the last words her eyes gleamed wistfully. The handing over of two hundred pounds struck her at this time as such a particularly desirable transaction. For then her favourite son, Dick, could make a match of it with Kate Neligan, who had a fine fortune, and they might settle down comfortably close by Tullyglen, instead of which it seemed as if the poor lad would have to take off to the States and seek a fortune for himself before the new year. It was provoking to think that only the superfluous existence of old Moggy Goggin rendered the better arrangement impossible. "Lately disaised, bedad!" Mrs M'Cormack said to herself bitterly; "ne'er a much she is, or sorra the sign of it on her. Sure if she was good for anythin' she'd ha' been dead these twenty years. But them's the sort of people that live for ever and ever, like a fish in the well. And what at all would the likes of her do wid a couple of hundred pounds?" As Moggy's livelihood depended mainly upon the precarious weekly sales of her poultry's eggs, she would no doubt have thought it not impracticable to find a use for the sum; but Mrs

M'Cormack answered the question in her own way: "She wouldn't know what to be at wid it. You might as well be trowin' it in the river. I wonder, now, who was tellin' Thomas she was dead? Aisy enough she might be, and nobody the wiser—and she livin' away in a bit of corner, out of the world."

To this question no answer was forthcoming; but the result of her meditation upon it was that in replying to her nephew's letter she made no mention of old Moggy—it would be time enough to tell him when he came—and that to her family she said nothing about the tantalising nearly-acquired bequest. On the morning before Thomas Martin's arrival, however, she remarked during breakfast: "And you needn't be talkin' about ould Moggy Goggin before your cousin. Maybe she'll keep out of this, be good luck, the few days he's here, and I hope she may, for the dear knows she's no credit comin' about any place, the show she is in her ould rag of a shawl, and th' ould shoes of her lookin' ready to drop off her feet; it's barefut I'm always expeckin' to see her comin' streelin' over one of these days."

The young M'Cormacks carried out this injunction dutifully, and the subject of Moggy Goggin was avoided in the presence of their visitor. But one of the first things he said to his hostess next day, when, fortunately, nobody else happened to be within hearing, was: "And so me ould grand-aunt Margaret Goggin's dead!" Mrs M'Cormack set down the bowl she had in her hand with a clatter, which left it uncertain whether she assented to the statement, and he went on: "Well, it seems more reasonable that the bit of money should come to you. With your fine family growing up, you'll find plenty of uses for it. Anyway, there it is, and I can pay it over to you whenever you like."

Mrs M'Cormack hesitated for a moment. Something she must say, and she felt that what she said must be of fateful import. She was just beginning to speak when she heard her husband's step approaching, and her speech turned into: "Don't—don't say anything about it to him." Her nephew stared at her with surprise, which grew into comprehension, as he nodded knowingly, and said: "All right, Aunt Julia." And next morning she had a delightful roll of bank notes in her possession. Moreover, she had learned, with loud regret and mute relief, that her nephew and his two little boys must depart on the Saturday, and as here was Wednesday, she could look forward to her anxiety being soon safely ended.

Therefore it was now most contrary that just when matters were proceeding so smoothly the old woman's perilous presence should intrude itself upon the scene. "She's comin' along—ay, the mischief doubt her, she is," Mrs M'Cormack said, looking out with disgust. "If Sally had the wit of a blind beetle, she might ha' contrived to turn the ould torment back. The Lord knows how long she'll stop here blatherin', and those two may be landin' in on top of her every minit of time."

Old Moggy, it appeared, had come to report that her heart was broke wid the brindled bull up in Long Leg. "I thought I'd just tell you the way he's carryin' on," she said apologetically. "For when he come out first into the field he was paiceable anough. But this last week or so it's outrageous he's been. Times and again he's run at me; and, you know, ma'am, I have to be crossin' the strame and the corner of the Mount Field to get to the road gate, and it's thereabouts he's keepin' continyal. Bedad, I believe he has his eye on the house watchin' till I come out. Yesterday he had me afeared to stir a step the whole day, and I wantin' to get down to town wid me few eggs. They're sittin' in the basket yet."

"Sure he's only a young baste, scarce full-grown," Mrs M'Cormack replied, testily unsympathetic to this complaint.

"Young he is," said old Moggy. "'Deed, now, it seems only the other day I would be seein' him in the yard here, not the size of anything. But he always was a passionate little crathur, and more betoken, I distrust them brindly-coloured bastes. Never a one of them I knew but was quare in its temper, and quare's no name for him. This mornin' he stravaded away wid himself off beyont the mount. John Cleary was tellin' me he seen him above there, or else I wouldn't ha' got the chance to slip over here at all, for it's in dread of me life of him I am."

If Moggy had but known, she could scarcely have put forward an unluckier fact, so far as her own purpose was concerned. For upon hearing it, Mrs M'Cormack said to herself: "More power to him then; it's a charity, there's something to keep her out of this." And she immediately resolved that no matter how the brindled bull might see fit to conduct

himself, he should remain at large until her nephew
had fairly gone. But to Moggy she said suavely
enough: "Ah, well, I'll spake to Matthew about it,
and he'll regulate him. He's busy these times wid
the last of the oats. But if that's the way he is, it's
home wid yourself you ought to be runnin', or else you
couldn't tell where the baste might be agin you got
back."

"Thrue for you—faix, and I ought to,' said
Moggy, taking the hint as she was intended to do,
if not altogether as it was meant, and she turned
ruefully to face her homeward way. "I'll go along
wid you," said Sally. But Moggy declined the
offer, saying, "Sure not at all, child. Where'd
be the sinse of havin' him runnin' at two of us
instead of one?" And her mother, having sent
her off to wash up the dairy things, stood watching
the old woman out of sight with anxious hopes
that she might meet nothing on her journey back;
but she was not thinking of the bull. Now that
she had that roll of bank notes stowed away upstairs,
she somehow found the aspect of "ould Moggy
Goggin," doubled up in her ragged grey shawl
and greenish black gown, more repellant than ever,
the possession of wealth having, no doubt, endowed
her with finer sensibilities.

Moggy herself fared on with hopes and fears,
which grew acuter as she approached Long Leg.
It is a long narrow field with a bend in the middle
of it, and flowed through by a stream, beside which
there are thorn and briar bushes. The bull, she
thought, might be waiting for her round the corner;

and when it was safely turned, her cottage looked dreadfully far off across the stretch of green, while danger might lurk behind every clump.   And, in fact, she was at least fifty long yards from her door when the ominous shrill roar sounded, and the bull came trotting gaily through the gap in the hedge out of the adjoining field.   She was only just in time to shut herself in before the rushing tramp went by outside, with a baffled bellow that scared her even in her security.

All the rest of the day she remained in a state of siege, her enemy choosing to graze so close by that to strew her hens their supper seemed quite a hazardous venture, and the gathering of their eggs was an impossibility.   On the morrow he gave no signs of changing his quarters, and from hour to hour she looked out, vainly hoping for the approach of relief in the shape of men sent to drive him off.   Nobody came, and she was left a prisoner, fretting over the impracticability of reaching the town, where she might replenish her small store of provisions, for not only her dwindling grain of tea and sugar, but her heel of a stale loaf, and her flaccid bag of meal had begun to look poor indeed.   The September sun went down in an amber glory on her alarmed vexation, and rose again on the same posture of affairs.   Apparently the brindled bull found the herbage in that corner of Long Leg very much to his taste, and by noon Moggy had grown so desperate that she sometimes said "Shoots" faintly, and flapped her apron in his direction as she stood at her door.

But when the shadows had stretched into a deep border along by the hedge, the beast, who for some time past had been stalking restlessly to and fro, crossing and re-crossing the stream with querulous roars, began to move steadily towards the Mount Field, and presently disappeared from view. Moggy was just wondering whether she dared set forth on her expedition, when something new came in sight. A party of three people were walking up Long Leg. It consisted of a fair-bearded man, in a light brown suit, with hat and boots which were both black and glossy (rale iligant), and two small boys, in a sort of fanciful sailor costume, more iligant still. These were Thomas Martin and his youngest sons, who had come out for a stroll. It was churning day at the farm, and the master had given his hand a rather nasty cut with a reaping-hook in the course of the morning, which caused much bustle and confusion in the household, and made Thomas think it advisable to take the children out of the way. Their presence was reassuring to old Moggy, and she resolved upon going. "I'll caution the strange man about that baste," she said to herself, as she went into the house to get ready. But she found that the handle of her basket was broken, and dim eyes and tremulous hands made its repair a work of time, and when she emerged again, it was to stand aghast; for the interval had brought back the bull with aggravated circumstances. Something had wrought the natural arrogance of his temper to a pitch of frenzy, which transformed him in demeanour from a hectoring

P

bully to an example, half-terrible, half-grotesque, of
the tyrant in his rage.   He advanced with rapid
strides, lashing his tail and lunging aimlessly with
his wide horns at invisible objects by the way.
The gravest feature of the case was that he seemed
to be making straight for the smallest of the children,
little Jack, who had strayed off while his father's
thoughts were occupied with vague reminiscences
of a place seen at five years old, half a lifetime ago.
The child had become horribly aware of the beast
just as Moggy appeared, and she sent a quavering
call, bidding him run to her, much the nearest
refuge.   Jack's panic, however, was blind and deaf,
and he evidently meant to rush after his father and
brother in the opposite direction, destroying his
chances of escape.   So she risked a bold sally,
captured him and began to tug him, heavy and
resistant, towards her house.   It was a terrifying
race, with the thud of hoofs gaining on them so
fast, that she felt as if her feet were taking root.
Once, at least, all seemed lost, only the pursuer
paused to demolish with swinging strokes, a clump
of ragweed, which gave them a fresh start.   But a
little farther on they were hopelessly overtaken ;
and, as a last resource, Moggy, snatching off her
old shawl, flung it in the bull's face.   By good luck,
one of the largest of its many holes caught on a
horn, so that the folds hung down blindingly ; and
while they were being furiously rent and tossed
and trampled into shreds, the old woman and the
child escaped safely indoors, where they were joined
by the other two fleeing from the opposite direction.

Thomas Martin was volubly grateful for Jack's
rescue, but old Moggy said: "Ah, sure, not at all.
It's sorry I'd ha' been if anythin' happened the little
crathur. I declare now the two eyes he has in his
head is the livin' image of me poor brother Johnny.
the time he was the same size. And for the matther
of that, it was only the ould shawl kep' the baste
off him. Saints above! look at the quare work
himself there's havin' wid it, tatterin' it he is into
nothin' you could give a name to."

"Well, ma'am, you shall have the best to replace
it that money can buy," averred her visitor; "and
you must tell me who I'm to send it to."

"Why, Moggy Goggin's what they do be callin'
me," said the old woman. "But I mind me mother
sayin' it was Margaret I was christened be rights."

"Margaret Goggin—well, now, that's extro'nary.
And are you anything then," he said, "to the
M'Cormacks here, at the farm?"

"Sure, Julia M'Cormack was daughter to me
half-sister, Sarah Finny, she that died a few years
ago at the ould place in Westmeath," said Moggy.
"But it's cousins we are these times, and not much
talk of that, for, you see, they're getting on finely,
and I'm diff'rint."

"There's bound to be talk of it, though," said
Thomas. "To think now of Aunt Julia playin' such
a trick on me, and takin' the money." He thought
of it for a while perplexedly, and then began to
compare with Moggy notes upon family history,
which soon placed her identity beyond a doubt.

"'Deed, but the States is a great place for people

to be gettin' their deaths in," she said ; for her grand-nephew's news had been largely obituary. "It was there me poor sister Norah went out to, and married David Jackson, but she'll be gone this long and long ago—never a word I've heard from her."

"Not a great while," he said ; "something under a twelvemonth, anyway."

"Glory be to goodness!" said Moggy, looking relieved ; "frettin' I was thinkin' of all the time I was delayed of follyin' her, but sure I won't be long after all."

"Oh, come now, Aunt Moggy! I hope you'll be here many a year yet," Thomas said, meaning encouragement, "and she's left you a legacy — a handsome one, too — something over two hundred pounds. So you've every reason to take a new lease of life."

"'Deed, has she? That was very good of the crathur," said Moggy, rather abstractedly.

"A very tidy sum indeed : it will set you up in fine style," he went on expatiating. "You haven't any great shakes of a place here, but you'll be able to move out of it now, and fix yourself com-fortable," he said, critically surveying the dark little room, with its mud floor and smoky rafters.

"Ah ! sure, it's terrible work movin', said Moggy ; "I'd liefer not be gettin' that sort of a legicy. And, plase goodness, it's scarce worth me while to be settlin' meself too comfortable anywhere hereabouts."

"But, bedad now," she said, after reflecting for a few moments ; "if I had as much as a couple of odd pennies in the week, that I could be givin' little

Larry Flynn for doin' me messages in the town, 'twould be a great thing entirely,· for the road's gettin' a weary long lenth wid itself. And then I needn't be troublin' me head aither about the bull. Ay, rael grand it 'ud be," she said, with a gleam of satisfaction. " But here I am, forgettin' the tay all this while ; sure the childer 'll be starved," she exclaimed, and started into a bustle of preparation, against which Thomas Martin protested in vain.

The tea itself, although the very last pinch of black dust went into the pot, had not much strength to boast of ; but there was still enough brown sugar left to make it quite to the taste of her great-grand-nephews at all events. While they were drinking it, three men appeared in the field armed with pitchforks, ropes, and other implements, evidently designed for the coercion of the brindled bull, who was presently seen being led away in captivity. Old Moggy stood at the door to watch the departure of her enemy through the pleasant green field, which the sunsetting light had strewn with spangles of clear gold and flecks of soft shadow. " I declare now," she said, " I 'm sorry the crathur's to be put out of it be raison of meself. Only it's a pity he couldn't ha' kep' himself paiceable. What call had he to be runnin' at a body that wasn't makin' or meddlin' with him, and plinty of room for the both of us ? But some quare notion he'd got into his head of the whole place belongin' to himself; and that's naither nathur nor raison," concluded Moggy Goggin.

When the Martins returned to the farm, Mrs M'Cormack was looking out for them with some anxiety, which had been aroused by hearing in what direction they had gone, and which had made her send the men after the bull. But worse than her worst fears were confirmed, when her nephew replied with marked coolness to her greeting: "Thank 'ee, Aunt Julia, the children aren't hungry. They're just after having their tea with their old aunt, Moggy Goggin. The bull drove us into her little place down there." She knew at once that the discovery had been made, and it was hardly necessary for him to add: "I find that I was under a misapprehension about that legacy, and needn't be troublin' you to take charge of the money any longer." In great bitterness of spirit she mumbled something about fetching it down, and went upstairs to do so. As she came back along the passage with the notes in her hand, her husband called at her through an open door, "I seen them drivin' in the young bull. I've a notion of sendin' him to the fair at Bagnalstown on Thursday; cattle's goin' well this week." But she said to herself, going on her way regretful and unrepentant: "Troth, thin, it's the quare price you'll have to get for him, me good man, or else he'll be the dear baste to us, an' himself the raison of better than two hundred pounds goin' off us to that ould pest of an ould Moggy Goggin."

COCKY

COCKY M'CANN was behaving ill, as, indeed, he had done more or less habitually all through his seven years or so. On this February morning, however, his misconduct had reached the point which his neighbours described as "beyond the beyonds altogether," and which generally led to the intervention of some one in authority.

"What at all's he at now?" his mother said, uneasily, as across her doorway gossip came a sound of shrill shrieks, mingled with a cackle of too familiar laughter.

Mrs Walsh, who, bound for market, was passing the time of day, fell back a few steps to reconnoitre, and reported: "It's disthroyin' your bit of a shawl he is, ma'am, and tirrifyin' Mrs Farrell's childer out of their siven sinses."

Cocky had, in fact, draped head and shoulders with a skimpy black shawl, and, thus arrayed, was reiterating short rushes towards two very little girls, who were seated on the bank close by. He approached them with flapping arms, in long hops, after the manner of the alighting crows, whom he had often seen last summer shut themselves up like pairs of black-polished shears and drop into the green or gold of the adjacent oat-field. His performance was rather successfully realistic, but the

231

small children did not by any means appreciate it, and it at length made them break into ecstatic screams, which brought their mother scurrying to the rescue from over the way. While bearing them off, she hurled many voluble reproaches at Cocky, whom they seemed to soothe, as he shook down his mother's shawl into a puddle and sauntered on. He was following in the wake of a little top-knotted hen, very white and clean, who had just picked her steps fastidiously across the road.

"It's outrageous he is," Mrs M'Cann said, apologetically, looking after him. "But sure I had him spoiled all the days of his life, thinkin' I'd never rair him, he was that wakely, till he's that unruly in himself he's a tormint grown to man and baste. Chuckens is the only thing he won't annoy if he gets the chance. He was always terrible fond of chuckens. 'Deed, when he was littler, I did be hard set to keep e'er a weeny one alive at all, wid the way he'd be pettin' them. And the bawls of him whinever he found he had the bit of life squeezed out of a one of them—och, murdher! But now he's took up intirely with his little white top-knotty hin. If anythin' happint her, we'd have the quare work."

"The Widdy Goligher has the very moral of her," Mrs Walsh said. "Top-knot and all: you might think the two of them come out of the one egg."

But the Widow Goligher was a person at the mention of whose name Mrs M'Cann's mouth would close suddenly as if with a strong spring, the expression of her countenance seeming to convey that it was on some disagreeably flavoured morsel. For

she and the widow were black out, and had been
so ever since the autumn, when the widow had
seen cause to consider that Mrs M'Cann had unfairly
forestalled her in securing the promise of Mrs Vesey's
sour milk for pig-feeding. It was a feud not likely
soon to die out, as its embers were fanned every
week on Mondays and Fridays, when Mrs M'Cann's
supplanting bucket went by Widdy Goligher's door.
So now Mrs M'Cann chose to ignore Mrs Walsh's
remark, and proceeded: "It was be raison o' that
—his bein' so fond of the chuckens—he got the
name of Cocky, for be rights he's called Bernard,
after Himself, poor man."

"And you've no news of him yet, ma'am?" said
Mrs Walsh.

"Sure not the sound of a word. His ship was
due in Liverpool the middle of October, and here's
the beginnin' ind of February—I dunno what to say
to it."

Mrs M'Cann's husband was a sailor; she said a
mate, but her neighbours said, *a mate, bedad!* which
is quite a different thing. However, for the last
month or so, in the course of which his ship had
become alarmingly over-due, they had been saying
it was much if the crathur ever set eyes on him
again, and they had temporarily waived the question
of his rank.

"If I was you," Mrs Walsh continued, "it's makin'
inquiries I'd be meself at the shippin' offices up
in Dublin. I wouldn't let them get the notion they
was to be dhrowndin' people promiscuous about the
world, and nobody passin' a remark."

"Sure that's the very thing I'm about doin', ma'am," Mrs M'Cann said. "I've sold the chest of drawers for our fare, and we're goin' up to-morra to stop wid me married sister in Crampton Lane."

"Lands sakes, will you be takin' the young chap wid you?" said Mrs Walsh.

"Why, to be sure, ma'am. Who'd I be lavin' him wid? He'd have their places ruinated wid his mischief before he got me back turned, let alone that I'd be disthracted in me mind wonderin' what villiny he was at. It's a poor case, ma'am, to be shipwreckin' your mislucky husband every minyit of the day and night, widout lavin' a child behind you as well, settin' fire to other people's houses, or conthrivin' disthruction on himself, the dear knows how."

"Ay, bedad, it is so. But you'll find him fine and throublesome to you up in Dublin, if I'm not mistook, ma'am," Mrs Walsh said, gathering up her basket to go.

She was not at all mistaken. In fact, Mrs M'Cann's difficulties with her travelling companion began that same evening, when Cocky said: "What'll I bring Toppy in?"

"Mercy on us all alive!" said his mother. "Is the child deminted? Takin' Toppy that far! Sure, she'd be dead twyste over before we got half-ways, and your Aunt Lizzie'd be ragin' mad if we went and brought a hin flutterin' about her house. Mrs Murphy here says she'll keep her eye on Toppy and the rest of them for us."

"If I seen her offerin' to keep her ugly ould eyes on Toppy, I'd knock the two of them into one,' Cocky said, darkly.

"Well, then, Mrs Kavanagh would," said his mother.

"I'm thinkin' the ould male-bag 'ud do," Cocky said, deliberatively.

The ensuing stormy discussion ended in Cocky's suddenly abandoning the controversy with a cheerfulness which would have seemed suspicious to a more discerning person than his mother. Suspicious, too, next morning was his insistence upon himself carrying the covered market-basket, and his running back to the house with it after they had started, on the pretext that he had left his knife in a crevice of the wall; and then his lagging behind all the way to the station, and loitering aloof on the platform until the train came up. So successfully, however, did he carry out all these stratagems, that not until she had gone 'some distance on their long railway journey was Mrs M'Cann's attention caught by a slight rustling within the basket, which she found to contain Toppy, alert, and interrogatively peering. Cocky coolly admitted that he had made room for her by bundling out most of its other contents, and he listened blandly to his mother's reproaches, while he fed Toppy with bread crumbs. Nevertheless, retributive justice was even then keeping time with inevitable punctuality upon his track.

Within a few miles of Dublin, where night had already fallen, a stop was made to collect tickets, which were presently demanded at the door of the

M'Cann's compartment by a guard, lantern in hand. Now the lid of Toppy's basket was insecurely fastened down, leaving a chink through which her prying head happened to bob up just at the moment when the round yellow-glaring eye turned its flash of light in at the open window. Perhaps she may have taken the illumination for a strange dawn in the midnight; perhaps she may have merely acted upon a sudden panic; but at any rate the result was that the stow-away all at once came fluttering forth, with a pro-digious whirring of wings, and, before any one well knew what had begun to happen, had hurled herself into the blackness of the wild wet night which moaned outside. A brief white flapping across the flare of a neighbouring lamp, and a single tail feather left in his unavailing grasp at her, was the last Cocky saw, was all he retained, of his too-well-beloved Toppy. He would, of course, have followed her head foremost, but the train was already in motion, and a large-framed farmer, who sat next him, repressed him with one heavy hand as effectually as if it had been a paper-weight laid upon a rustling leaf.

"Aisy, man, aisy," said the farmer. "There's losses in every trade, and you'll readier come by another little hin than a new neck bone."

Cocky was really stunned by the magnitude of his disaster; and the big Dublin railway terminus, that vast cavern full of mysterious panting and shrieking, succeeded by clattering streets, where great luminous globes hung aloft, pearly and diamond-pierced, and ranged golden stars flung chains of light across and across the black water, all helped further to overawe

and bewilder him, so that he went to bed with unwonted meekness, in a sort of dazed nightmare. But
next morning he awoke with all his wits about him,
and a firm conviction that he would find Toppy as
soon as he could get out-of-doors. So, when his
mother had started on her inquiries along the Quays,
strictly forbidding him to stir, he eluded observation,
and, slipping downstairs, made his way into the
streets.

To a visitor fresh from life-long residence in Ballylogan's solitary cabin-row they would have seemed
a strange and startling experience, had he not been
pre-occupied by one engrossing purpose, which left
him no leisure to marvel or fear. He was looking
out all the way for traces of chickens, and as he went
he called at intervals, "Toppy, Toppy." In his
pocket he had a crust, filched from the breakfast-table,
wherewith to regale her on their happy meeting.
But he passed by what appeared to him endless rows
of houses, all with closed doors, and no way round
to the back, before he came upon something that
raised his hopes. This was an extraordinarily
immense window, with white letters on it, and in it
a pyramidal heap of many eggs—dozens and dozens.
Evidently, therefore, hens must exist somewhere
close by, and, if so, what more likely than that Toppy
had for the time being taken up her abode among
them? Moreover, the crowning egg of the pile was
a very brown one, exactly like the eggs of Toppy.
Cocky needed no further evidence. Into the shop
he stumped, and confronted across the counter, an
elderly, stout woman, in a black cap with purple

ribbons, who was the wife of P. Byrne, family grocer and provision dealer.

"Where," said Cocky to her, "do you be keepin' your hins—ma'am?" he added, on reflection that civility might be his best policy.

"What hins?" said Mrs Byrne.

"Thim that lays your eggs, of coorse," said Cocky.

"Och, run away wid you—we've no hins," said Mrs Byrne.

Cocky's eyes, which just cleared the top of the counter, blazed angrily over it, but he had not yet abandoned politeness, "Mind you, I don't say you're after *stailin'* Toppy on purpose," he said, with much self-restraint. "She might ha' flew in among your chuckens last night unbeknownst, and got mixed up wid thim like. You must own a power. And you're welcome to keep the egg, though you've no call to it all the while. I want to look through thim and see——"

"Quit," Mrs Byrne said, drumming on the counter. "There's nothin' for you here."

"You ould thief of the world," said Cocky, thereupon letting himself ago, "have you no shame in you, to be standin' up there tellin' black lies? Just you wait till I get in the pólis to you that I have at the door."

"Here, Pat, put the little miscreant out of it," Mrs Byrne called to some one, who proved to be a youth big enough to hustle Cocky away with no more ado than if the black-headed, fierce-eyed urchin were an ordinary ingredient in the dust he was sweeping up.

Near the door were standing a ragged little girl and two smaller boys, interested beholders of Cocky's unceremonious expulsion. "Look you here," the little girl whispered to him, confidentially, "if it's anythin' you're after *takin'* on thim, you'd do right to run for your life. That's the pólis." She pointed to a portly uniform stationed at the nearest corner. But Cocky said: "Bejabers, I'll get him to her," and darted off, making straight for the place of peril.

The children stared after him with a sort of horror, as if watching one bent upon his own destruction; and, still staring backwards, moved off in the opposite direction, as if from the vicinity of something probably explosive.

Constable 89 A, being twitched by the sleeve, looked down a long way, and perceiving a small, peaky face, full of fury, said: "Well, me big man?"

"You're to come and take up herself inside there," said Cocky. "She's got Toppy's egg in the windy, that flew out of the train last night on me; and has her keepin' somewhere along wid her own bastely ould hins—it's wringin' the necks of thim I'll be, and givin' me impidence, and tellin' lies in there like the ould outrageous robber she is; and you'll know her be the top-knot on her head."

"It's a lunatic child, begorrah," Constable 89 A said; but before he had decided how to deal with the matter, Cocky was seized upon by a distracted woman in a greenish plaid shawl, who swept him off, protesting that "he had her heart-scalded and torminted," and that it was "a poor case to have the steamboat companies dhrowndin' your husband or you in the rowlin' says, and no more talk about it than if he was a fly in a bowl of skim milk, widout your bould brat of a child takin' upon himself to go to loss in the streets of Dublin, where the first you'd hear of him he'd be flattened under a one af thim jinglin' thrams."

For Mrs M'Cann had returned from a fruitless quest among puzzled clerks, to find a crown set upon her afflictions by the disappearance of her evil, but only son.

Travelling home next day, she felt utterly cast down by the result of the expedition, which had turned out all failure, from her vain inquiries about the missing ss. *Brackenburg*, to the mortifying conduct of Cocky, who had been upon his worst behaviour, and had very unfavourably impressed his Dublin relatives. But Cocky's spirits had risen, because he was buoying them up with the fixed idea that when he got home Toppy would be there waiting for him. Toppy, he declared, could fly much faster and farther than the train, and knew her way back a deal better than the likes of whoever he happened to be addressing. Of course, he only brewed bitter disappointment for himself by such impossible imaginings, and when, upon his arrival, he learned that "sight nor light" had been seen of any little white hen, he collapsed into a melancholy of strange persistence. The sole hope in life to which he clung was the possibility that Toppy might yet return, and nothing would he do but sit all day long on the bank beside his door looking out for this event. The tail - feather, all that remained to him of his pet, he kept constantly with him, and the spectacle of him crouching out in the bleak March winds and sleet showers, mournfully contemplating that relic, wearing now stumpy and grimy, cast a gloom over his end of the row. In fact, the dejection of the M'Canns became at this time quite a weight upon the minds of their neighbours in Ballylogan. For, as was often remarked, "you couldn't go by their door but there'd be poor Mrs M'Cann standin' lookin' the eyes out of her head for him comin' down the road that was as like as not streelin' about at the bottom of the say, and a step farther you'd see that mischancy imp of a Cocky sittin' frettin' himself into fiddle-strings over his ould crathur of a fowl. 'Twasn't nathural; and like enough he wouldn't be very long after his poor father."

None of them felt sincerer commiseration than the old Widdy Goligher from a bit down the lane, Mrs M'Cann's unsuccessful rival in the matter of sour milk, and proprietress of a hen the very moral of the so-lamented Toppy. She had petted and prized this bird not a little, a fact which, perhaps, sharpened the edge of her sympathy with Cocky's tribulation; at any rate, as she watched the moping of him and his mother in these early spring days, she began to think of parting with her. Her thought passed through several stages of development until it took the form of: "He's a mischievous little spalpeen, but I niver seen him doin'

Q

anythin' agin anybody's chuckens, I'll say that for
him. Sure, he's frettin' himself sick for nothin';
and it's my belief the poor father's dhrownded on
them all the while. I'll be apt to let him have her."
But in the evening, when she was feeding her fowl,
second thoughts intervened: "It's his own one he's
wantin'. If I went for to offer him mine, as like as
not it's impidence he'd be givin' me. And more
betoken if I send her away, what'll I do wid the
settin' of Black Minorcas ould Lady Rachel's after
promisin' me?"

At this point matters halted for some time, partly
because her possessions were so very few. Then—it
was the same day that she passed by and saw how
Cocky had a little refection of cold-potato crumbs
spread on the bank beside him in readiness for
Toppy's return—she advanced another step: "He
mightn't ever tell but she was his own one, if we
put her in the bit of a shed there unbeknownst
over-night. There wasn't scarce a feather's differ
between the two of them. He'd be as sot up as
anythin' consaitin' she was flown back after all.
Anyway, we might thry it. I'll spake to Mrs
M'Cann to-morra'."

Mrs M'Cann, when spoken to, made little demur.
The acceptance of a favour from the Widow Goligher
was not indeed without its bitterness; but her pride
had fallen with her fortunes, and she felt serious
anxiety about Cocky. So she feared he would be
too cute for them, but agreed to try the experiment.

It succeeded to admiration. When Cocky found
the pretender roosting comfortably upon the long

desolate perch, he declared with many vehement asseverations that she was his own Toppy; that there was not another hen like her in the whole of Ireland, and that he saw the gap in her tail where he had pulled out the feather. His exultation was unbounded. He could hardly be withheld from scattering to her half his meals, and he poured derisive scorn upon everybody who had prophesied against her restoration.

A day or two later he chanced to stroll indoors, and found the Widow Goligher talking to his mother. Whereupon he planted himself in a defiant attitude before her and said: "Yah, hah, ould Widdy Goligher, that thinks she's the only one in the world owns a white hin, and Toppy sittin' there on the roost this minyit, worth twinty dozen of her dirty little ould ugly-looking 'scarecrow.'"

"Goodness forgive you, Cocky, but you're the ungovernable, ungrateful child, and poor Mrs Goligher after bringin' you—" his mother had begun, when the widow interrupted her, dreading indiscreet disclosures.

"Here's a clutch of eggs, Cocky, *avic*," she said, pointing to a large hay-lined basket, "for you to be setting under your Toppy. They're a grand sort."

"Toppy doesn't want to be bothered sittin' on any such blamed ould thrash," replied Cocky. "She'd a dale liefer be walkin' about wid herself. Git along wid them."

"Ah, sure, I was thinkin'," the widow said artfully, "it 'ud be a good plan to purvint her of strayin', in case she had e'er a notion in her mind of takin' another fly off away to nobody-knows-where. The eggs 'ud be as good as a pound weight on aich fut of her, keepin' her down safe for you."

Cocky reconsidered the question for a while from this point of view. "You may lave them," he said, turning on his heel. Certainly, Mrs M'Cann had some grounds for deploring his defective manners.

But her graver trouble was happily ended that very evening, when who should walk in at the door except Bernard M'Cann himself, whom nothing worse had befallen than broken-down engines, tardy tugs, and tedious repairs, causing ominous delay. So that Cocky had perhaps a somewhat narrow escape of missing the benefits which accrued to him from the Widow Goligher's condoling mood. For the sun of our neighbour's prosperity does sometimes tend rather to bake than melt us.

Be that as it may, although Cocky did acquire his hen and his clutch, the following incident makes it seem somewhat more than doubtful whether anything ever came of the latter. It happened a day or two after the return of his father, to whom Mrs M'Cann, as she surveyed some new gaudy-hued foreign handkerchiefs, observed: "Well now, that one wid the puce-colour in the border is what you may call iligant. I declare to goodness, I think I'll be givin' it to ould Widdy Goligher. Oncommon good-natured she was about decaivin' poor Cocky wid her little hin. If I seen him anywheres about, I might be persuadin' him to run down wid it to her—or else I might be lavin' it wid her meself

this evenin', and I passin' her door wid the pig's
bucket. Like enough, Cocky'd only be desthroyin'
it. I wonder where he is all this while, so quiet?"

Cocky was, in fact, at that very moment in the
shed, impatiently watching the placid Toppy; and
he might have been heard to murmur discontentedly,
"It's my belief the crathur's sick and tired of
sittin' on thim ould eggs. I've as good a mind
as ever I had in me life to be smashin' thim wid
a stone. But if it's only the hate brings thim out,
maybe I could hurry thim up a bit wid givin' them
a rinse through a sup of hot wather. Bedad, I will
so to-night, when me mother's went after the milk,
and the kettle's sittin' handy on the hob."

AS LUCK WOULD HAVE IT

SOME of you may have heard how, last St Patrick's Day was a year, very old Mrs Rea, who had fully determined to celebrate it by an excursion from Letterowen to Dublin, found herself, almost at the last moment, obliged to put off her travels for a twelvemonth, and let Dinny Fitzpatrick go instead. Of course, so long a postponement made the ultimate carrying out of the project more or less doubtful, a fact of which her friend and contemporary, Julia Carroll, did not fail to keep her in mind, often dwelling upon the many odd things that might happen, that would send ould bodies like them thravellin' a dale farther than Dublin, a long while sooner than next March. Julia was led to repeat such remarks partly by disapproval of Mrs Rea's plan, and partly by a certain pleasure which she herself took in the prospect of that longer journey. "If one had e'er a notion at all," her friend would sometimes grumble, "what manner of road they'll be taking a body." But Julia would rejoin serenely: "Ah, sure, 'twill be quare if it's not more agreeable at all evints than them rackety ould thrains."

However, when St Patrick's Day came round again, on her long-meditated expedition Mrs Rae did go, in a way. But *in a way* it was, as people say, meaning, in a way not of their own. For she went less on pleasure than on business, and rather melancholy business too. It was connected with a very deplorable accident which had befallen Dan Fitzpatrick about a month before. Dan was the oldest of the young Fitzpatricks, and the best liked of his family, who were generally regarded as persons to be respected for their quick wits and upright dealing, and mistrusted for the crossness of their tempers. Hot they unquestionably were, some in a flaring, some in a smouldering fashion, both detrimental to friendliness and good-fellowship. Only Dan was an exception, being a big, soft-hearted, easy-going man, not over-clever, a safe subject for pleasantries, and a maker and mender of peace. So there were regrets both at home and abroad, when during the past summer Dan went away to work in the city of Dublin, at the other end of the country. The neighbours said about this proceeding that Dan was a great fool to do any such thing; that Dublin was a place where you couldn't tell what might be after happening to a person before you'd hear a word of it, no more than if they were in the States; that Maggie M'Grehan was at the bottom of it for sartin—you might depend sorra aught else would have made Dan, that thought such a heap of his own people, go take off with himself away from them all, high wages or low wages. They also said, in selecter conversations, that Maggie would liefer have got Dan's brother Dinny, and only when she saw that he would have nobody but her sister Norah, she settled her mind to put up with Dan—who was too good for her, they often added.

There was some truth in this gossip. At anyrate,

it was true that Dan's departure to Dublin had been
caused by a conditional half-promise from Maggie
M'Grehan.   She would have nothing to say, she
declared, to ten shillings a week and living in an
ugly little hole like Letterowen, that she was sick of
the sight of; but if a man was earning decent wages,
and in a place where you were not apt to get moped
to death entirely, it would be a different pair of
brogues.   Furthermore, she admitted that the man
might be Dan Fitzpatrick.   Whereupon, off one
August morning he went to look for a job of well-
paid work which was offered on a Dublin railway.
His hope was that by Shrovetide he would be in a
position to fetch home a wife, and for some time this
seemed likely enough.   But now the latest news of
him that had reached Letterowen was the woful
story of his being run over on the North Wall by a
dray, with the resulting loss of his right arm.   This
calamity, having trampled all Dan's prospects into
the dust, cast a shadow over the festivities with which
the wedding of his brother Dinny and Maggie's
sister, Norah M'Grehan, was attended at Shrovetide,
just a fortnight before St Patrick's Day.   Everybody
supposed at first that the occasion would be a specially trying one to Maggie, with her bridegroom that
was to have been lying maimed in hospital, and
people wondering how at all he would contrive now
to keep himself, let alone a wife.   They were quite
ready to bestow sympathy and condolence; but
Maggie lost no time in making it plain that these
would be completely thrown away upon her.   So
prompt was she indeed about disclaiming any per-

sonal concern in the disaster, that Letterowen presently buzzed and clacked with reports of her
heartless demeanour.

"Would you like to know what I heard her sayin'
meself on'y this mornin'?" to the Widdy Cornish
said Mrs Hannigan, on the Sunday after the sad
tidings had arrived. "Kate M'Grehan was telling
Mrs M'Cann, from Ballylogan, and they goin' in to
eleven o'clock mass, and, sez Mrs M'Cann, 'Och, but
is it his *right* arm the poor man's afther losin'?'

"''Deed is it,' sez Kate.

"'Ay, bedad,' sez Maggie, 'you may trust Dan
Fitzpatrick to make a rael botch of a thing when he's
about it. That's most all he was ever good for,' sez
she. And a grand blue scarf round the throat of her
that minyit that the crathur sent her in a prisint at
the new year."

"She'll be takin' up wid somebody else before
Easter, you'll see," the Widdy predicted.

"It's quare, now, the differ there is in the same
people," said Mrs Hannigan. "For Norah and Kate
are kind-hearted girls, the both of them, and Maggie
herself's friendly-spoken enough when she plases.
A pretty slip of a crathur she is, too. You'd never
think, to look at her, that she'd be apt to talk so
unfeelin'."

"Ah, she's no nathur in her, sorra a bit; that's
what ails her," said the Widdy Cornish. "And if
she was all that poor Dan's got shut of, maybe he'd
ha' no great loss. But his hand—och, the unlucky
bosthoon, what'ill he do at all?"

This question was often asked just then in Letter-

owen, and as often left unanswered. It seemed so
puzzling, in fact, that the neighbours commonly gave
it up, falling back upon commiserations of Dan and
censure of Maggie, neither of which was much to the
purpose. There was one person, however, who could
find no relief in such unpractical measures for the
sorrow of her heart, and that was the mother of
Dan, an infirm old woman, with few resources at her
command. She came creeping up to Mrs Rea's door
two or three sunsets before St Patrick's Day, and
quickly made it clear that the object of her call was
to ascertain whether Mrs Rea still kept her purpose
of going on the cheap railway excursion up to Dublin.
" They're advertisin' it this good while below at the
station, you might ha' noticed, ma'am," she said. " So
I suppose you'll be off fine and early the way you
was intendin'."

Last year Mrs Fitzpatrick had been among the
most earnest of Mrs Rea's advisers against the
venture, on the ground that it was no thing for an
ould body at her time of life to think of doing. But
now, inconsistently enough, she added suggestively,
watching Mrs Rae's face with anxious eyes : " The
fare's oncommon raisonable, that's the truth ; it's a
great chance. If I was able for it at all I wouldn't
be long runnin' up," and her expression grew piteously
woe-begone when Mrs Rae replied : " 'Deed, then,
ma'am, I've as many as twenty minds to not stir a
fut. You was all tellin' me last time I was too ould
for jiggettin' about the world, and very belike I am
so. I'd git more wid less goin', as the cow said, and
they drivin' her to the fair."

Several circumstances had combined of late to make Mrs Rea less energetic and enterprising than usual. To begin with, she had, in the course of poetical justice, caught "a rael bad could intirely," no make-believe like what she had feigned that time twelvemonth, that Dinny Fitzpatrick might visit Dublin in her stead; and this had left her depressed and languid. Poor Dan's mishap, too, had a discouraging effect; and the weather threatened to be unkind.

"Ah, to be sure, you must plase yourself, ma'am; it's nothin' to me," Mrs Fitzpatrick said, in deep dejection. "I was only thinkin'—you'r threatenin' it so long—you might have the notion yit. And I was only thinkin', if bechance you had happened to ha' wint, you might maybe ha' left an odd thrifle of a few things for me wid that poor child up at the hospital, and brought me word what way he was lookin' at all, and if there was e'er a chance they'd be lettin' him home to me any time. It's ould ages since I seen a sight of him. Ne'er another one there is I could be axin'; they're all took up at home wid themselves and their foolery and no talk of goin'. But sure what matther at all about it? I'd ha' ped anybody's fare and welcome."

But after all she was not going to be disappointed in that way. Mrs Rea's ardour for roving, though it had flagged somewhat, was by no means extinct, and now this proposed errand stirred it up and gave it fresh fuel, at which it kindled again as warmly as ever, so that to Mrs Fitzpatrick's great relief she answered—

"Pay the fare to your great-grandmother's cat. Sure, ma'am, dear, it's as plased as anythin' I'll be to go see poor Dan. He and I was always great since he wasn't the size of a frog-hopper. And anythin' you was wantin' to send him, I could be takin' along in me basket as aisy as lookin' at them."

So Dan's mother went home half-comforted, and spent the evening in packing up and unpacking some small parcels, that would certainly be ready in good time. It seemed to her a step towards getting back her son, who was twice as valuable now that everybody had begun to say he would never be fit for anything again. "Glory be to God, he has his two feet on him yet," she said to herself, as she folded up a pair of socks.

By the time that Mrs Rea was setting off in the early grey of St Patrick's morning, her big, old, much-battered market-basket had grown more than half-full of different things. For, when Letterowen heard of her mission, many of the neighbours entrusted her with various little presents, chiefly fair-complexioned fresh eggs, and swarthy lumps of tobacco, but including an old, long-treasured Christmas card from the Widdy Cornish, and a postage-stamp, which Joe M'Keown had kept in an empty match-box for the last five years without finding occasion to affix it. The Christmas card was ironically extravagant in its gilt good wishes, and Mrs Rea had been charged with dozens of others that Dan's well-wishers could send only in a still more portable form. Yet notwithstanding that, when she had added her own substantial round of girdle cake, there remained but little spare room in her basket, and though her memory was stored with many a "And Mrs Carroll bid me say," and "Your brother Dinny tould me to tell you," she felt as if something important lacked. Maggie M'Grehan had given her no message, not a word; "And," thought Mrs Rea, "the crathur up there 'll be lookin' out for a one, that I know right well."

She was careful, accordingly, to introduce the subject of her expedition whenever she fell in with Maggie, and, on St Patrick's eve, meeting her at the shop, and finding that hints, broad and broader, produced no effect, asked her point blank whether she had e'er a message for Dan.

"And what at all have I to say to sendin' messages to Dan Fitzpatrick?" Maggie demanded, with ostentatious surprise.

"You'd plenty to say to his goin' up to Dublin and gettin' himself destroyed," said Mrs Rea.

"Did anybody ever hear such blathers and nonsense? As if I was after biddin' the man take and rowl himself under the ould cart-wheels," Maggie protested, flouncing angrily away.

But a bit later on that same evening she presented herself in Mrs Rea's kitchen, with some little shame in her face, and in her hand a pink-glazed cardboard box, with a strip of looking-glass in the lid. "'Twas Dan Fitzpatrick sent it to me awhile ago for houldin' hair-pins," she said, laying it on the table, "so I was wonderin', Mrs Rea, as you had talk of carrying messages, if you'd think bad of takin' it back to him, and just tellin' him I've no use for it. I don't want people to be passin' remarks about me gettin' prisints from him these times."

Maggie had tried very hard to put her new blue scarf into the box; but she possessed so few others, and this one had such a lovely satiny gloss and was of so becoming a colour that she really could not.

Evidently Mrs Rea did think very badly indeed of the proposal. If she had been requested to swallow the box whole, she could scarcely have eyed it with more disfavour. "Troth and bedad, will I do no such a thing," she said, waving it off her table as though it were red-hot. "If that's the only word of kindness you have for him, you may thravel off and be takin' it to him yourself. And it's my belief you might thravel a dale farther after that agin before you find e'er a body little-good-for enough to match wid you—a heartless baggage as ever I set my eyes on," she commented, as Maggie retired hastily with her rejected commission.

But Mrs Rea had again to set disapproving eyes upon Maggie M'Grehan only a few hours afterwards, n, the bustle of bundling into the early morning cursion train having subsided, they found themselves seated opposite to one another in the same compartment, and along with Maggie was Con Goligher, affable and insinuating; obviously she had taken up with somebody else. Perhaps they would have the face to go and see Dan, Mrs Rea thought; however, it appeared that they were going no farther than Powerstown Junction, where they alighted, and relieved her for the latter half of her journey from the duty of staring stonily over their heads.

The first thing Mrs Rea did upon arriving towards noon in Dublin was to lose her way completely, or rather utterly fail to find it. For a very long hour she was astray in the bewildering streets, and not before she had been grievously affronted by a lady, who interrupted her preliminary " I beg your pardon, ma'am," with a glum " I 've nothing for you," and not until she had begun to feel hopeless, as she desperately clutched her basket's worn handles, of ever again beholding another familiar object, did the wide hall of the right hospital receive her, and a wonderfully pleasant-spoken young nurse assure her that Daniel Fitzpatrick might be seen in a ward close by.

It was, on the whole, a joyful meeting. Her pleasure at the almost despaired-of sight of a friend, and the unexpected discovery that he was well enough to be up and dressed, took the edge off Mrs Rea's melancholy observations of how gaunt he looked "wid the face of him gone to nothin' in his beard," and then that woful empty sleeve. Dan, on his part, was delighted at a glimpse of Letterowen ; and he had, moreover, good news to communicate— no less than that he had just got his discharge, and would be setting off for home in another hour or so. "Great argufyin' I had wid Dr Clare," he said, "before he was contint to give me lave. But I tould him of the terrible chape fares there would be on the thrains. runnin' this day, so the end of it was I had him persuaded I might, and I'm goin' on the two-thirty from the Broadstone."

"Glory be to goodness, Dan; then I'll go along wid you, and we might have a better chance of findin' our ways out of it," Mrs Rea said, hopefully. They were sitting at a window by the head of Dan's bed in the long bleak ward, and she looked out over the grey roof ridges with a doubtful expression, as if she were contemplating the billows of a perilous sea which had to be crossed.

"Och, that'll be grand," said Dan; "only then, ma'am, you'll ha' seen scarce a sight of Dublin at all—the Phanix, and the Pillar, and——"

"Man alive," said Mrs Rea, "it's the quare sights of this place I'll be behouldin' wid my good will. Sure, wasn't I thrapesin' thro' it and thro' it and round about it just now like a sthrayed heifer, wid me head in and out of a dozen big doors till me heart was broke, and sorra the dacint-lookin' thing I seen in the whole of it, only a fine hape of turf they have sittin' beside the canal, close be the edge of the wather there, wid the little ripples tug-tuggin' at the image of it, like as if they was tryin' to pull it in pieces and wash it away back to wherever it come from. Rael nathural it looked. I was sayin' to meself I'd give a dale meself to be stookin' sods that minyit on our ould bog at home."

"Ne'er a one'ill I be cuttin' this year," Dan said, with a sudden droop of his head, as if something had fallen on it. "Bedad, it's the quare bad offer I'd be makin' at it now, ma'am, wouldn't it?"

"Oh, boy, dear, maybe you might be doin' somethin' betther," Mrs Rea said, feeling the vagueness of her encouragement.

"I dunno what at all it's apt to be, thin," said Dan. "There's such a power of things you want to take your two hands to, let alone a left one that needn't set up to be the half of a pair, not be any manner of manes. I'd ha' had more of a chance if they'd took one of these ould brogues on me," he said, looking down at his feet. "For I might ha' conthrived to stump about after me work in some sort of a way. But, sure, now I may thramp to the world's end, and what 'ud I do when I got there? Walkin's no more use to me than it 'ud be to this ould chair. Howan'e'er, 'twas as luck would have it, ma'am, and that's all can be said. And, well now, yourself was the rael dacint woman to come see me. And what way did you lave them all at home?"

Mrs Rea was more than willing that their discussion should turn upon the news of Letterowen and the contents of her basket, and at first the distribution and display of them went on glibly and satisfactorily. "Grandly your mother is looking, ay is she so, *considerin'*. And them's the socks she knit you; and she bid me tell you not to be frettin' about anythin' but come straightways home to her the first minyit you could. Och, it's quarely plased the crathur 'll be this night. And your brother Dinny and Norah M'Grehan are doin' finely. He's sendin' you a bit of rael Irish twist. They've got Martin O'Connor's little house at the turn in Brierly's boreen, and Mr Hamilton's just after givin' Dinny another shillin' a-week to do the odd jobs of carpenterin' up about the place."

"Ay, bedad, Dinny was oncommon handy wid

R

the tools," said Dan. "It's lucky 'twasn't him it happint to anyway. That would ha' been a pity and a half."

But after a short while Mrs Rea began to feel that they had not changed the subject for the better. It would have been easier to deal with Dan's gloomiest forecasts of his future than with the wistful glances that watched the parcels coming out of her basket, and the expectant pauses which lengthened after each of his leading questions. "And how's poor Johnny M'Grehan gettin' on these times? I haven't any news of them this great while. He would be disthressed wid the sevare weather last month. . . . But it's plased he'll be to have Norah settled so near. . . Did you say there was any talk about Kate's goin' out to service? It was rael good-nathured of her to be sending me the bunch of colts-foot; an iligant smell it has off of it. And *Kate* it was that sent it, ma'am?" Once she caught him in the act of stealthily groping round the inside of the basket with his clumsy single hand, and although he, with a sort of laugh, declared himself to be only counting how many eggs she had brought him, she knew only too well that he was really trying to feel whether there still remained some little packet over-looked. But everything had been delivered, even the postage stamps, and Mrs Rea, with that in her mind which made her garbled statements sound as false to herself as they were disappointing to their hearer, rejoiced when it was suddenly found that the time for starting had arrived, and they had to bustle away from the hospital to the terminus.

On his way home Dan was silent, and seemed to be meditating. Their crowded train was a slow one, that stopped wherever it could find an excuse, and Mrs Rea noticed that at all the stations which were large enough to own a bookstall Dan emerged from his reveries, and kept eager eyes upon it as long as it was in sight. The garish litter on counter and shelves evidently had some fascination for him. Yet Dan's tastes were by no means studious. At length, as they were steaming slowly out of Bally- lavin, he muttered, half-aloud: "They had a one in it there, right enough; I seen it hangin' up, if the ould naygurs would but stop aisy and give you a chance to be gittin' it. But, sure, you never can tell that they won't be slitherin' off agin wid them- selves on you before your feet's firm on the platform. They've no more consideration now than a blast of win' goin' by," Dan grumbled, with the querulousness of a convalescent.

"What ails you then, man," Mrs Rea said, partly overhearing, "that you're murmurin' there like an ould pitaty-pot on the boil? What at all was you wantin' to git? If it's a newspaper, there's very apt to be one of thim little chaps wid the baskets yellin' past the windy the next place we come to, and you might have a chance thin."

"'Twas just one of them sixpenny purses I'd a mind to be gittin' they have on the stalls," said Dan. "Mostly there do be plenty of them hangin' up along with the straps and other con- thraptions."

"And what for would you be throwin' away your

sixpinnies buyin' purses, wid little enough to put in them?" Mrs Rea said, thriftily reproving.

"Well, I was thinkin'—thinkin' I was," said Dan. "I'd like to be bringin' one home to—Maggie." He tried to take the name out of its long silence naturally and unconcernedly, but did not quite succeed. "I haven't got her e'er a hap'orth," he said. "Nor anybody else for the matter of that. But you see, ma'am, she wasn't sendin' me anythin' be you, and she might be takin' it into her head 'twas be raison of that I didn't, so I'm not wishful she would. 'Twould ha' been diff'rint if you was after bringin' anythin' at all. But I'll tell you the notion I have, ma'am. Very belike she was thinkin' bad to be annoyin' you wid carryin' parcels thravellin' that far, though, 'deed, now rememberin' a word in your head wouldn't ha' throubled you much—and she has a little prisint keepin' for me all this while, the crathur, at home. I'll find it when I git there. Mightn't that be the way of it, ma'am, wouldn't you think?"

"Och, I do be thinkin' many a thing," Mrs Rea replied; and, though her words were vague, she had before her so distinct a vision of a shiny pink cardboard box no doubt waiting ready, that she added, with some bitterness in her tone: "If them that was good for nought got lost, and them that was little good for went to find them, there'd be a dale of empty sates in chapel of a Sunday mornin'," a cynical sentiment of which Dan was too much pre-occupied to make any particular application.

Soon after this the two travellers found themselves

at Powerstown junction, with half-an-hour to wait for the train which should bring them to Letterowen. This station is not a large or much frequented one, yet to Mrs Rea, despite her Dublin experiences, it seemed an imposing scene, full of bewildering bustle, at which she preferred to look on from a bench somewhat secluded, niched between a lamp-post and an automatic machine. The grey day was nearly done, and the west, clearing for sunset behind her, flung over her head a sheaf of long ruddy rays, which slanted across to the opposite platform, and glanced at the many-tinted literature displayed upon Messrs Eason's stall. "Bejabers, ma'am," Dan said, catching sight of it as he sat, "I'll be steppin' over there and thryin' have they e'er a purse in it at all. We've plenty of time, no fear."

"But how'll you git across all thim, lad?" she said, pointing to the network of shining metals by which their strip of platform seemed to be enisled. "Don't you go for to be settin' your feet on a one of thim rails, whatever else you may do; you niver can tell the instant or the minyit there mightn't be an ingin comin' up threacherous at the back of you, and sendin' you to desthruction. The accidents there do be in the papers is enough to terrify you."

"Sure, I'll go be the bridge," said Dan. "Sorra the accident there'll be. I've had enough of thim, bedad, to last me for the rest of me life."

Accordingly, Mrs Rea watched the tall gaunt figure of Dan, in his loose-grown old coat, glimpsing away up and down the latticed bridge. And the next thing she saw was the gleam of a brilliant blue scarf, and there at her elbow stood Maggie M'Grehan, with Con Goligher close by. "Musha, good gracious, and is it yourself, Mrs Rea?" said Maggie. "You're early back from Dublin!"

"Ay, it's meself," Mrs Rea said, stiffly, "and there's more than me back to-night from Dublin, too. Lookit, d'you see yonder?" She nodded towards the bookstall, where Dan, with his back turned to them, was bargaining.

"Och to goodness, if it isn't Dan Fitzpatrick," Maggie exclaimed, so loudly that Mrs Rea, not-withstanding the broad expanse of rails said, "Whist," apprehensively. "Don't have him to be seein' you now the first thing, and he comin' home wid his misfortin, if you've settled in your mind you'll have no more to say to him. Be steppin' on wid yourselves, you and Con, before he turns round and gets a sight of you, there's a good girl," Mrs Rea said, in her anxiety con-descending to entreaty.

But Maggie, tired and disappointed, and dissatis-fied with herself and her holiday, was as perverse as a fractious child; so she replied, "Musha, cock him up. What's Dan Fitzpatrick that I should be botherin' meself gettin' out of his way?" And, instead of moving on, she plumped down on the bench, saying—"There's room for you, too, Con Goligher."

"Well, then, you Con," Mrs Rea said, desperately, "you're a good-nathured fellow I believe; git along wid yourself anyway, and that 'ill be the next best thing."

"I don't see why at all," said Con, who, to do him justice, would have been less obtuse if he had not taken the edge off his sensibilities with too many glasses of whisky. "Let Dan Fitzpatrick go where he plases. I'm not afraid of him, or any man in the county Cork."

Mrs Rea uttered a despairing "wirrasthrue." The time for saying anything more to the purpose had gone by. For Dan had concluded his purchase, and, whether allured by that gleam of blue, or merely acting with the recklessness of a railway man, was coming, in disregard of all rules and bye-laws, straight back across the line. The low sun's rays blinked dazzlingly into his eyes, and may have blinded him to the fact that the down express was just going to run through ; or he may have miscalculated the distance ; or perhaps he did not allow for the drawback that his empty sleeve and one hand full of a little parcel would be to him in scrambling up on the platform. At all events, he was a second or so too late to elude the sliding swoop, which swept him as far away as if it had been a wave from a shoreless sea.

Maggie M'Grehan, shocked and sorry and remorseful, wailed lamentably on the twilit platform. "Och, poor Dan, the saints may pity him. There wasn't anythin' he wouldn't ha' done for me, I well know. Och, I wisht he'd never gone off to Dublin. I wisht I'd sint him e'er a bit of a word —I wisht I had."

Con Goligher was trying to pacify her. "Sure

'twas no one's fault," he said; "it couldn't be helped. 'Twas as luck would have it."

"Ay, to be sure," said Mrs Rea, who was standing by. She could not keep out of her mind the thought of that little pink box, and she added: "As luck would have it, for sartin. But I dunno if his luck isn't as good as yours, Con, me man."

HER BIT OF MONEY

I SHOULD not have been surprised any day in the course of the sketch-making summer which I spent at Carrickcrum, if one of my neighbours had stepped in to ask would I lend a hand with the painting of Mr Rochfort's front gate, or put the name on Farmer O'Shaughnessy's new tilting-cart. Such an incident would have seemed to me rather encouragingly appropriate to a progress famewards, and I should have treasured up the anecdote, including, of course, a gracious compliance on my part, for future use in the "Autobiography" or "Recollections," which I shall no doubt eventually feel myself called upon to compose. So I really thought that something of the kind was going to happen when one wet afternoon Joe Lenihan, a handy youth of the village, visited my cottage, accompanied by a poor-looking, elderly woman, whose name I did not know. For their manner showed that they were come on business, and that it concerned my profession appeared plainly from the way in which he pointed out my works to her, while I was taking off intolerably muddy boots in the passage.

"That's the one I was tellin' you about," I heard him say to her; "the plate of griddle-cakes stood on the bit of patchwork, and the little ould blue milk-jug wid the spout cracked off it beside them.

That's a good likeness now; you couldn't mistake it."

By this description I recognised a small study of still-life, which hung over the chimney-piece; and Joe's friend was discerning enough to reply:

"'Deed, then, it's uncommon tasty. You might be nearly smellin' them bakin'."

It seemed, however, that their errand did not involve any commission. Judy Tandy had just slipped in on her way to market to tell me that they had a very quare manner of ould picture in it up at her sister's place on Doonakileen townland, and they'd be as plased as anything, if I didn't think bad of stepping over some day to take a look at it.

"You maybe mightn't ha' happint to ha' seen the kind it is, sir; though," said Judy, glancing flatteringly round the studio, "they're a grand collection you have here, and them little cakes bates all."

It was, I fear, with some sacrifice of truth to politeness that I assured her of how glad I should be to inspect this work of art on the earliest opportunity. I am certain, at any rate, that such opportunity would never have occurred, had I known beforehand what lengths of what miry ways stretched between me and my intention. But my notion was only vague of the distance to Doonakileen, and an unoccupied afternoon arrived, on which I had nothing apparently better to do than betake myself thither.

On the way I fell in with Joe Lenihan, while I

was hopelessly trundling along the adhesive ruts of a deep boreen, and he exhorted me to keep stepping out, if I wanted to get on at all.

"If you stand still," said he, "it's stickin' fast under you your feet 'll be, like a postage - stamp that's dhried afore you can shift it off the wrong envelope."

As we walked on together in accordance with this principle, Joe gave me some information about the household at Doonakileen Farm, with whose affairs he was intimately acquainted, his father being a near neighbour and frequent counsellor.

"For sure, how would a couple of ould women make an offer at regulatin' anythin' rightly, onless they could be gettin' a bit of advice from a man now and agin that knew what was raisonable? Sure it isn't the nathur of them," quoth Joe, "to have as much sinse mostly as 'ud keep a blind horse from strayin'."

One of these naturally incompetent persons, Mrs Lymbery, to whom the farm belonged, was further incapacitated by bad health, which for many years had prevented her from getting about at all. According to Joe's recollection, which went back, perhaps, two decades, she had never set foot out-of-doors; and ever since her husband's death, more than a dozen years ago, her sister, Mrs Tandy, had been managing things. She was doing middling well, Joe admitted, though he evidently thought poorly of ould Judy Tandy, who had married to disoblige her family.

"And the man she took up wid—in the army

he was—as great a villin as you'd aisy find, if you went to look for one. Run off from her he did, as soon as he grabbed hould of her bit of money, and left her there wid the imp of a child on her hands, that grew up, be all accounts, no betther than his father. Anyway, he took off wid himself too, the first minyit he was of a size to be earnin' a hap'orth, and what's become of aither of them I dunno. Some people do be sayin' she hears of an odd while from the son; but if she does, it's nothin' good, you may depend, or else it's whillalooin' over it she'd be to man and baste, like an ould hin set up wid a new-laid egg—but never a word out of her about him. So her sister lets her live wid her. And this is the gate, sir, and there's herself above in front of the house.

Joe continued floundering on his way, and I turned into a cart-track, where the ruts, though as deep, were less complicated. Potatoes grew on either side of it, and a drill of them was thriftily prolonged to run under the windows of the narrow white-washed house in what would usually have been a flower border. Mrs Tandy, who wore a battered Japanese straw hat, tied on with string, was hoeing among the dark-green clumps as I came up, and when she had said: "Och, glory be to goodness, sir, I'm very glad to see you; and did you rowl your-self over on the little wild thing?"—by which she meant my new Imperator Shuttlebury-Cardensworth roadster—she showed me indoors.

Mrs Lymbery, who was discovered in the little parlour, propped up with pillows on a high-backed,

antique settle, looked less old by several years than
her weather-beaten younger sister, and had a somewhat apathetic manner and expression, whereas Mrs
Tandy seemed rather harassed and flurried.   This
old-fashioned settle was the only interesting object
in the room, the picture I had come to see being
a terrible thing worked in tent-stitch, with insertions
of pink satin for face and hands, and with bugle
eyeballs.   It represented some ecclesiastical dignitary
in full canonicals, and my attention was especially
invited to the gold and silver tinsel threads tarnishing
in his mitre and crozier and cope—all of which I
admired hyperbolically, and presently parted from,
as I supposed, forever.   But fate had decreed otherwise ; for next morning I missed a much-prized
note - book, and thereupon distinctly recollected
having taken it out of my pocket in Mrs Lymbery's
parlour to jot down a praiseworthy bit of moulding
on the top of her couch.   So a few hours later saw
me once more on the Doonakileen road, eager to
reclaim that shabby and well-beloved companion.

It was just about sunsetting when I reached the
farm, but, of course, still broad daylight—extremely
broad, indeed, at the front of the house, whose
windows blinked with every burnished pane as the
long amber lances broke against them.   At first sight
nobody was visible.   However, in a minute or two,
a barefooted girl pattered down the passage, and
surveyed me with a dismayed countenance from
beneath a black haze of hair.   Upon my asking to
see Mrs Tandy, she paused irresolutely for a moment,
and then, with a sort of desperation, as of one between

two fires, she suddenly thumped on the left-hand
door, calling :

"Mrs Tandy, ma'am! Mrs Tandy, it's the strange
gintleman agin!"

As immediately afterwards the handle began to
turn inside, the girl shrank away behind me, so that,
when the door opened a cautious chink, I alone
appeared.

"Och to goodness, sir! come in wid you quick,"
Mrs Tandy said. And the lock clicked behind me
before I knew where I was.

I had stepped into a darkness that almost took
away my breath, so abrupt and unexpected was the
transition from the sun-dazzled passage into the
murky room—for the parlour window was shuttered
and curtained so closely that not a ray penetrated,
and the only artificial lights provided consisted of
two smoky candles. They rose through the gloom
from a small table beside the settle on which Mrs
Lymbery still lay propped up, and their dull, yellow
flame was flaring very close to her wrinkled face.
But one might have thought it to be illumined by
something more — some sort of radiance kindled
within, that lit it up eagerly. No longer placid, as
on the day before, it seemed to be all twitching and
twinkling with many mobile lines and a pair of eyes
that glittered keenly. The candle-light fell strongly,
too, upon her hands, which were busily occupied.
She was apparently sorting or arranging some small
articles that she had spread out on her lap; and as
my sight adapted itself to the dimness, I perceived
that these were golden coins and silver, with a few

bank-notes, lying on a red flannel-lined wicker tray. They had evidently been taken out of a grey linen bag, with a running string of green braid, which gaped hungrily on the table by an empty japanned tea-caddy, whose brass padlock was of surprising bigness. The coins, which were mostly sovereigns, nearly covered the bottom of the tray, and Mrs Lymbery, dipping the tips of her fingers among them, and letting them slip through, wore the rapturous look of one enjoying an exquisite sensation.

A faint chinking sound accompanied the action, and Mrs Tandy, upon hearing it, said, "Tchuck, tchuck!" in a distracted manner, and hurried over to her sister. "Arrah now, woman," she said, remonstrantly, "can't you be aisy and quit fiddlin' wid it? They might hear it jingling at the end of the parish."

Mrs Lymbery was not much impressed by this grossly exaggerated statement—at least, so I gathered from her replying:

"Jinglin' how are you? Ah! don't be talking foolish." Then, observing me, she said: "And is it yourself, sir? You're kindly welcome. But if it's after another look at himself there you've come, she'll have to be throwin' back th' ould shutter, for thim two dipts wouldn't show you a stim. Judy has a quare notion agin e'er a spark of light whiniver I'm goin' over me bit of money."

"Welcome he may be," Mrs Tandy said; "but there was Rose Duggan as near bouncin' in on top of us along wid him as anythin'."

"And supposin'?" said Mrs Lymbery. "What great matther for that?"

"And she gabbin' about it to ivery crathur in the place? And the next thievin' thramp goin' the road steppin' in here convanient, whin there wouldn't be a sowl in the house except yourself, that hasn't stood on your feet this last ten year? And he doin' murdher on you, lyin' where you are this minyit, and away wid himself and the money-box afore man or mortal knew it was happ'nin', the same as I do be tellin' you out of the newspaper times and agin? Battherin' the head off you handy he could be wid the butt-ind of the poker if he hadn't thought to bring a big bludgeon of a blackthorn along wid him. So there you 'd be."

Mrs Tandy was evidently producing an often-exhibited bugaboo, and I fancied a shade of fright beneath the defiant mien with which her little old sister listened.

"Och, but she 's the terrible headsthrong woman, sir," Mrs Tandy continued, turning to me. "Ivery day of me life I 'm bargein' at her to sind it in to the Bank, where they 'd keep it rael safe, the way nothin' 'ud happin her or it. Bedad, they wouldn't be long puttin' the thramp out of it if he offered to walk in there. But sure I might as well be biddin' the soverins and shillins take and rowl thim-selves out of the house like so many weeny cart-wheels goin' to the forge to git shod. And isn't it a pity now, sir, that she won't listen to raison?"

"No doubt, the money would be safer in the Bank," I said, conscious that both the old women had hopes staked on my reply.

"Thrue for you, sir," Mrs Tandy said, triumphantly, while Mrs Lymbery's countenance fell.

"I dunno what good it 'ud be to me thin at all," she said, disconsolately. "If I wouldn't get e'er a sight of it—that's a plisure in itself, let alone touchin' it—I'd as lief be not ownin' a pinny!"

"But they'd pay you interest on it," I said. Upon which Mrs Lymbery remarked: "What at all's that thin?" and Mrs Tandy tried unsuccessfully to look as if she knew, so I explained.

"Well, suppose you send them a hundred pounds, the Bank would send you thirty or forty shillings every year that you left it there."

"Listen you to that now, woman alive," said Mrs Tandy. "Thirty shillins, or liker forty! And the hundred pounds just what you've got there, wid seventeen and sixpence over, that you could be keepin' to look at. It's the savins, sir, that poor Mr Lymbery left behind him. And, indade, now herself's been the lucky woman, whativer she may say, that she's never had to spind away a ha'penny of it. Not even the year the two heifers died on us, and I thought for sure and sartin she'd ha' had to be makin' out the rint wid some of thim. But I conthrived it right enough."

"Troth and bedad, me good woman, sorra the rint, or anythin' else, they'd ha' gone for," said Mrs Lymbery. "Not if all the heifers in the county Roscommon took upon themselves to go die. So there's for you, me dear!"

"Ah! thin have it your own way; it's all one to me. Goodness knows it's little I care," Mrs

s

Tandy said, bitterly. "And maybe you'll be contint when you have all the ould miscreants in Connaught walkin' off wid it down the road there. That's a dale betther than gittin' intherest on it out of the Bank, to be sure."

"Woful I'd be missin' it all the while," Mrs Lymbery said, sadly, as she noiselessly fingered the piles of coin. "And how could I tell they'd be keepin' it safe, when I wouldn't git the chance of behouldin' it year out and year in? They might be lavin' it litterin' about anyhow; and as like as not they wouldn't so much as show it to you, Judy if I sent you thravellin' in now and agin to be lookin' after it. But, at all ivints, I'd never set eyes on it any more, and cruel lonesome I'd be without it—me one tin-pound note, and me two five-pound notes, and me fourteen single notes, and the gould and silver shinin'—sure, it's a picture!"

"And, bedad, I wish to goodness you had thim in a picture, you crathur, the like of the one Mr Hamilton here done of the little cracked jug and the plate of cakes—the livin' moral of thim it is. For sure, if you had that, you could be consowlin' yourself ivery minyit of the day lookin' at thim, the very way they are this instiant; and thin you'd be contint enough to let thim be put safe out of the raich of the robbers and thramps."

"I maybe might," Mrs Lymbery said, half doubt-fully. "'Twouldn't be the same thing altogether, but one might make a shift wid it."

That was how I came to paint the little study in oils, "Her Bit of Money," which I had, not long afterwards, the pleasure of seeing marked " Sold " at the Van Wergk Gallery exhibition. The subject rather fascinated me from the first moment that Mrs Tandy's wish suggested it. There seemed to be many possibilities in that red-lined tray, from which gold and silver gleams responded to the smoky orange and yellow of the down-flickering candle-light, enisled in a murky pool of shadow. The notes looked inviting as they lay spread out, or more or less closely rolled — a clean Bank of Ireland note, with crimson lettering and wreath of dwindling masks ; smaller provincial notes, crumpled and grimy, and curiously repaired with the selvages of postage-stamps. And I at once determined that in my picture an old, lean, wrinkled hand should rest upon the rim of the tray, and seem about to pick up a coin.

Mrs Lymbery acquiesced in a somewhat resigned manner when I spoke of my willingness to carry out her sister's suggestion. But Mrs Tandy showed a sort of relieved joy, which made it obvious that the fears she had been expressing were unfeigned When I returned to the sunset glow, with my recovered note-book in my pocket and this newly-acquired design in my head, she followed me out, I thought, that she might utter her satisfaction more freely. She couldn't tell me, she said, the trouble it would be off her mind if her sister was persuaded to put the bit of money out of harm's way, and she believed there'd be a good likelihood of that if the picture was painted ; 'twould pacify the crathur finely. I had settled to begin it on the next afternoon, and I took leave of her at the gate, not expecting to see her again till that time. But a few yards down the winding lane I found it necessary to repair a trifling puncture in my tyre, and while I was busy with a sticky little bottle of cement, I became aware of voices close by. I had stopped just opposite to a gap in the high, furzy bank, on the other side of which I now saw that Mrs Tandy had joined a youngish man, who was sitting on a fallen tree-trunk, with his feet deep among nettles and thistles. He looked between thirty and forty, and was rather stout, with a Roman-nosed large face framed in frilly black whiskers, and black hair that rose into a peaked crest on the top of his head. His expression was aggrieved as he fanned himself with his cap. Mrs Tandy stood beside him in apparent dejection.

"Begorrah, thin, if I'd ha' known all there'd be was a couple of shillin's," I presently heard him say, "I'd ha' thought as much as twyste, anyway, afore I come thrampin' over from beyant Corrymines, and the sun fit to roast an ox alive the most of the while. Bejabers, the stones on the road was like hot pitaties, and I startin' off. Couldn't you ha' wrote me word you'd nothin' worth bringin' me over for, and ha' sint it to me in stamps?"

"Ah! sure, Dicky lad, I thought bad of puttin' you off whin you'd said you was comin'," Mrs Tandy replied, in an apologetic tone. "And, tellin' you the thruth, it's wishful I was for a sight of you; but next time I'll send it in a letter. And, 'deed now, the two shillin's is ivery ha'penny of ivery pinny I

have to me name, for me few hins was layin'
scandalous all this month, as if they consaited eggs
was tuppince apiece, instead of sixpince a dozen
—and the Gaffneys makin' a compliment of takin'
thim at that. Arrah now, sonny, don't be losin'
thim yourself in the long grass."

"Your few hins are laying scandalous bad," said
Dicky, who was contemptuously tossing the small
coins on the palm of his hand. "And how many
has me ould aunt got, I'd be glad to know, let alone
butther and bastes, and all manner?—and money
saved up, I wouldn't won'er. Ay, there's talk of that."

"It makes no differ to you and no differ to me
what she has and what she hasn't," Mrs Tandy said.
"And thim that talks of savin's has little to talk
about."

"Doesn't it, begorrah?" Dicky said, sitting up
with a jerk, and pocketing the shillings. "Thin
maybe it won't be so one of these days. Plinty of
differ it's apt to make. Yourself and your few hins!
Where was it you said she kep' it—under her ould
head where she's lying?"

"Och, boy dear! don't be talkin' foolish and wild,"
Mrs Tandy said, with consternation in both look and
tone. "And wouldn't she be the deminted woman
to keep it anywheres out of a press wid a lock? A
good stiff turn it has on it too—sthronger than the
one in ·the room above. But come along, honey,
out of that just as far as the yard, and I'll be runnin'
in for a sup of sour milk for you: there's a beautiful
pan sitting inside. The girl'll be gone home again
now."

Mr Dicky expressed his opinion upon the merits of sour milk as a beverage in very uncompromising terms, and he did not seem disposed to stir. But at this point my repairs terminated, and with them my eavesdropping, so that I do not know how the interview ended.

Next day the picture was begun, and during several sittings continued to make satisfactory progress. As the work advanced my pleasure in it grew, flattering me with a hope that I was making a good job of the Rembrandtesque lights and shadows which played over the poor little hoard. Only one slight hitch occurred. It was caused by Mrs Lymbery's wrinkled left hand, which, in pursuance of my original design, I had introduced emerging from the gloomy background and gripping the edge of the tray. For she objected to this, and protested against its presence. She declared that it gave her the notion of somebody grabbing at her ten-pound note, and looked that nathural, it made the flesh creep on her bones. Therefore, after vainly attempting to convince her that it really represented the guardianship of her treasure's rightful owner, I agreed to expunge it from my canvas, and her approbation of the painting was restored.

These sittings, which took place at intervals of five or six days, extended over a period of several weeks, and were, I believe, regarded as somewhat festive occasions by the two old dames. Mrs Lymbery enjoyed the recurrent excuse for gloating over her riches, and it was evident that the longer I took about the business the better she would be pleased. On the other hand, Mrs Tandy rejoiced to see the task actually in progress, but looked on with an undisguised impatience for its completion. Thus the gratification of both was tempered, as such things are wont to be.

One afternoon, when I had nearly finished, I arrived rather later than usual at the farm, and found Mrs Tandy just going out. She had made all preparations for the sitting, and said that she must take a run down to see what was doing in the mangold field, but would be back in next to no time to make the tea—which she had left, I saw, brewing itself into black bitterness on the hob. However, she was gone a long while. My work did not prosper on that afternoon. In fact, the japanned tea-caddy, with its big brass padlock, which formed part of the composition, gave me so much trouble, and had to be painted out so repeatedly, that at last in disgust I set the canvas on the sill outside the shuttered parlour window, where it might dry in the hot sun, while I poured out for Mrs Lymbery the cup of tea whose delay she had begun to lament.

When I went shortly afterwards to fetch in the picture, I heard a sound of voices and steps approaching before I reached the door, and, standing on the theshold, I saw appear round the corner of the house Mrs Tandy accompanied by the dissatisfied Dicky. Both of them at once caught sight of the object on the window-stool, which startled Mrs Tandy into horror-stricken ejaculations :

"Och murther! that oughtn't to be there at all. Sakes alive, to go cock it up there for iverybody to be seein' it comin' by! Is it mad the man is altogether, and I biddin' him continual to niver let on we had a brass bawbee in the place?"

She was rushing forward to remove it, but Dicky fenced her off with his walking-stick, the end of which he propped against the house-wall, while he proceeded to scrutinise the picture narrowly.

"The laws bless us!" he said. "Well, now, but that's what you might call somethin' like a fine little whack of money—poun' notes and shiners and suff'rins, and a one of them a tenner, no less! And the whole of them all ready to gather up handy. I'd say be the look of them that they'd just stepped out from inside there; and I wouldn't wonder now if that's where the pattron of them is this minyit."

"Ah, come along out of that wid yourself and niver mind thim," Mrs Tandy said, pulling him by the sleeve. "They're on'y some ould invintions a poor deminted sort of body that comes about the place of an odd while does be dhrawin' out of his own head—ay, bedad, that's the way of it. Sorra a pattron he has at all. Where'd he be gettin' one? Just divartin' himself, he is."

"It's great ould talk she has out of her, to be sure," Dicky said, meditatively, still fending her off with a crook of his elbow, and continuing to stoop over the picture. "Look-a-now at the ould bag they was emptied out of; and I'll bet me best brogues that's the shiny black box it's kep' in when it's put up. Rael convanient it 'ud stand on the high shelf of the dresser, or maybe over the fireplace; and the grand padlock it has on it, too!"

"Goodness grant me patience, but I dunno what bewitched him to go do such a thing as lave it there, when you might as well be lookin' at it all showin' itself off in the lookin'-glass! But as for standin' it on the dresser, that 'ud be the fine foolery, too, wid her good locked press in the corner, and no throuble on'y to keep the kay somewheres safe— supposin' all the while there was anythin' to lock up, and long sorry I 'd be to say there was. Arrah now, Dicky man, can't you be comin' along? I tould you you 'd no call to folly me this far, and the deminted body mightn't be best plased if he seen us passin' remarks on his ould conthrivances. Come on, Dicky jewel!"

Mrs Tandy's voice and countenance expressed such miserable apprehensions, connected apparently with the proceedings of "Dicky jewel," that I thought it kinder to make my appearance, upon which he at once beat a retreat, and had vanished round the corner before I reached the window. Of course, I was met with upbraidings for my reckless exposure of the painting, about which I had been warned "times and agin niver to let on a word to man or mortal." It was uncommonly lucky, and no thanks to me, Mrs Tandy declared, that there hadn't any-body chanced to come by except herself and a very respectable, quiet, poor lad, who 'd hold his tongue sure enough.

"And isn't himself grown the big up-standin' man, sir? Six-feet-two, I believe they call him, in his stockin 's."

After this incident, I noticed a perceptible height-

ening of Mrs Tandy's impatience for the completion
of the picture, and she had not much longer to wait.
In a few days more I could carry it home, bound by
many promises of most cautious secrecy to put a
finishing touch or so, and make a replica for myself.
This, likewise, was soon accomplished, and one
afternoon I had thought of bringing the original
back to the farm, but put off doing so upon finding
the varnish not yet quite dry.   However, on that
same evening an extended ramble brought me near
Doonakileen, and I purposely took a way through
Mrs Lymbery's land, thinking that if I fell in with
Mrs Tandy I would tell her she might expect " Her
Bit of Money " to arrive upon the morrow.

It was now so late in the season that the misty
beginnings and ends of the days smelt of the autumn,
and a dim violet bloom had crept over the sober
green potato ridges, with an effect which is, as I
have learned from experience, particularly difficult
to produce.   The fields all lay lonesome, and I saw
nobody, until at last, as I was skirting the edge of
a mangold patch, a whiff of extra strong tobacco,
wafted over the sodded dyke on my right hand, drew
my attention that way, so that I perceived on the
other side of it Mrs Tandy's acquaintance, Dicky,
basking in the company of a black little pipe under
the far-darted western sunbeams.   But he did not
seem an appropriate person to entrust with my
message, and I faced home, leaving it undelivered.

When I got there, I was not a little surprised to
find Mrs Tandy standing in the kitchen, where
fire-flickerings had begun to get the better of the

lack-lustre twilight. She had evidently only just arrived, panting and dishevelled, from a hurried journey, and my first theory was that she might have run over in hopes of finding her picture ready. It proved to be quite wrong, however. For to the increase of my perplexity she drew from beneath her striped shawl the familiar grey linen money-bag, and thrust it into my hands. Then she broke volubly into a woful tale:

"Och, Mr Hamilton, it's the bad news I'm afther gettin' this day. There's me poor son Dicky, that's stoppin' away up at Corrymines, a good step beyond our place; he's wrote me word he's took that sick the docthor's no opinion of him, and he sez I'm to be comin' over the minyit we're done the milkin', if I've e'er a fancy to be seein' him alive at all. Och, me darlin' lad, goodness may pity him! So I'm skytin' over to him this instiant. Only you see, sir, me mind was disthracted wid the ould sisther at home there, lavin' her that helpless; for if she has the girl wid her itself, what sinse is in the pair of them? And I done me best to thry could I persuade her to let me hide the key of the press away somewheres safe, but sure not if I was to go down on me knees to her—sorra a place else'll suit her except under her ould fool's head and the pillow— and there's nowhere they'd be apter to look. So what did I do, but I took and whipt the bag out of the caddy, behind her back, and I put in a sizable lump of a stone, the way it wouldn't feel too light, and I've jammed the wards of the little padlock kay on her, so that if she does git the girl to hand it out to her, and gab it all over the parish, she won't be able to open it any way till they're bet sthraight, and I might git back afore that. She'll be contint wid the feel of the weight. But I've brought the bag to you, sir, supposin' you wouldn't think bad of keepin' it wid you just till I'm able, plase goodness, to clap it into the Bank out of raich; and the dear knows I'll be glad of that same."

"Mrs Tandy," said I, "was it your son Dicky that I saw with you the other day up at the farm looking at the picture?"

"'Deed it was so, sir," said she; "and lovely he was lookin' that time, the crathur. You'd niver ha' thought there was like to be a ha'porth ailin' him."

"Well, Mrs Tandy," I said, "when I was in your mangold field about an hour ago, I saw him sitting under the bank smoking very comfortably, and unless I'm greatly mistaken, he hadn't much amiss with him then."

Mrs Tandy looked hard at me for a moment, and I could see one fear chase another out of her face, as shadows flit over the field furrows on a windy day. Then she said:

"I'll be steppin' home."

"I'll go with you," I said, stuffing the bag into my coat pocket, which, upon reflection, seems rather an imprudent thing to have done; but at the time neither of us thought about it.

At first, I could scarcely keep up with Mrs Tandy's rapid striding; and when presently she had to slow down, she could waste no breath on conversation, though now and then she muttered gaspingly what seemed to be prayers mingled with self-reproaches. Before we reached Doonakileen, all the daylight had ebbed away, but an ample segment of a large honey-coloured moon was steadily surmounting an eastern mist-bank, and gradually sharpening the blurred outlines. Not a living creature did we see on our road, until, when we were in Mrs Lymbery's demesne, a figure was descried crossing a field, whereupon Mrs Tandy remarked:

"If there isn't that girl Bridget! Och, the little-good-for-nothing! And that's what she calls mindin' the house."

A short way farther on, as we were traversing the meagre sally-plantation within a few perches of the front door, somebody came bolting towards us along the path, and that somebody was Dicky, who had a small black box in hand.

I attempted to arrest his progress, but I must admit that he tripped me up with much prompt dexterity; and when I regained my feet he was out of sight. His mother, however, was pulling me by the sleeve, and saying fervently:

"Thanks be to goodness—och, thanks be to the great goodness! he's not after killin' her dead, anyway—for there she is screeching rael powerful, and sure she'd be apt to not, if she had murdher done on her."

The shrillest of shrieks were indeed issuing from the house, and in the parlour we found its poor old mistress frantically bewailing her loss, to which the rifled press bore witness, smashed open, evidently, with a rough-and-ready poker. Wrath and terror had so forcibly seized her that it was long before she could by any means be rescued from their bewildering grip. Even the production of her money-bag only partially appeased her, and certainly did not make clear to her the true state of affairs. This I know, because when she had at last become comparatively tranquil, and I wished her good-night, she looked from me to her fondly-clutched treasure, and murmured, shaking her head slowly :

"Well, now, I do declare! I'd niver ha' thought it of him, and he a gintleman—I niver would!"

While Mrs Tandy, appealing to me with an agonised look for the preservation of her secret, said, with desperate boldness :

"Ah, sure, whoever it was done it, meant it just for a bit of a joke."

And to the present day that is, I fear, the most favourable construction put upon my behaviour by Mrs Lymbery, though I am conscious of deserving better of her—for I took timely steps calculated to diminish the probability of another visit from her nephew Dicky; and I myself hung "Her Bit of Money" in full view on the parlour wall; and I effected the lodgment of the real "bit" in Clondrone Bank, where she happily believes it to be stowed away in the securest of presses, still in its grey linen bag and japanned caddy, which Mrs Tandy picked up in the lane.

Yet, notwithstanding all these services, the last time I called upon the two old ladies I had the mortification of overhearing Mrs Lymbery's soliloquised "Well, now, I wouldn't ha' thought he'd go do such a thing!" Whereupon Mrs Tandy, who had acquired complete confidence in my discretion, observed, with singular effrontery:

"Sure, what matther, when it was on'y be way of a joke?"

SOME JOKES OF TIMOTHY

THE earliest of them that was memorable may be considered his first step towards the reputation he eventually reached, since, had he not played it—a practical one it was—the chances are that he would never have endured so much leisure for propounding jocular views of things on the bridge of Kilanesk. Just at the time, however, this result was quite out of sight, round many a corner, and its more immediate consequences failed to amuse anybody.

It was a sunny afternoon in March, and Timothy had been for some little time diverting himself by dropping turf-sods down the Widdy Meleady's chimney. The feat was just difficult enough to be interesting, as the black-rimmed smoke-hole opened in the end of the Widdy's mossy thatch farthest from the tall bank, against which her little house stood, with its roof slightly below the level of the lane, so that Timothy had to aim carefully and often at the delicate blue smoke-plume. He knew that the result of success would well repay his pains, experience having taught him what would follow upon the flight of a missile down the dark mouth. Open would fling the house's door, and forth would hobble its very ancient little old mistress, who would shriek up to him shrill threats and reproaches and lamentations, and totter furiously about her small yard below him, like a wasp with sticky wings, while he rolled in laughter on the swarded bank, and waited for her to go indoors that he might resume his bombardment. In fact, he was acting on the penny-in-a-slot principle, albeit this March day fell long before railway platforms were enlivened by scarlet automatic machines.

But even the simplest machinery gets out of gear sometimes, and now a sort of hitch occurred. For when next the dark clod had gone skimming true to its mark, the door did, sure enough, fling open, but the person who came bolting out was not the little old decrepit woman with her ineffectual hobble, and futile menaces. On the contrary, it was her great-nephew, Dan M'Grenaghan, a renowned racer and wrestler of the neighbourhood. At sight of him Timothy said: "Murdher alive," and darted off up the hill behind him, on the last run he ever took. For in his headlong hurry he tripped over the furze-masked edge of a disused stone-quarry, out of which he was drawn with a leg broken in so complicated a fashion that "the docthors had to take it off for repears, and very belike they may be tinkerin' at it yit," as Timothy used to say afterwards when relating his disaster. A long time elapsed, however, before he learned to turn out the facetious side of the incident.

Still, notwithstanding its woful associations, he did once again play his favourite turf-and-chimney joke. It was on the fine May morning when he first made his way on crutches as far as the Widdy Meleady's cabin, with the help of two little O'Gradys,

T

who were several sizes smaller than himself. "Sling one down on her, Tim," urged Paddy, as they rested on the bank, and a broken sod lying handily within reach, tempted him to comply. Down it went with great precision, and out came the old Widdy. But when she saw Timothy she said: "Och, sure it's him divertin' himself, the crathur," and returned indoors without another word. That was, perhaps, the bitterest moment in all Timothy's life.

Then, before many months had passed, another misfortune overtook him. It had been on his track for some time, and may have literally come up with him all the sooner by reason of his lameness. For his mother's health, which was failing at the time of his accident thenceforward declined more rapidly, and her fretting over the prospect of leaving him "alone in the width of the world, without so much as his two feet to stand steady on," no doubt hastened the arrival of the dreaded parting. Not that she was so forlorn as she might have been. The shelter of at least two neighbouring roofs interposed between Timothy and the grim white walls of the dreary House away at Allenstown. For in Kilanesk lived the families of her brothers-in-law Paddy O'Rourke and Nicholas Crinion, of whom she often said self-reassuringly, that, "at all events, neither of them would let her own child and poor Larry's go to loss." In this belief she remained unshaken, practically, even when she felt most despondent; but she could not always forbear to recollect that her sister Biddy O'Rourke "did be sometimes as cross as a weasel," and that Nicholas Crinion's wife was "as near and

close as she could stick together, and so were them
she came of; sorra a one of the Sheehans but was
the makins of an ould naygur." And she knew well,
that for many a long day, seven-year-old Timothy's
comfort must depend mainly upon the disposition
of the woman of the house. To set against these
disquieting considerations, she could reflect that
"Biddy's husband was a big, soft gob of good-nature,
without e'er a tint of bad temper in him, even when
he had a drop taken," and that Nicholas Crinion
"had always been a rael dacint, quiet man, and no
better brother than he had her poor Larry." So
that upon the whole she might have reviewed her
little character-sketches with tolerable equanimity.

Nevertheless, it is a fact that she spent rather a
large part of her last months at Kilanesk in scheming how to propitiate the kinsfolk with whom she
was to deposit the dearest thing she owned. But it
must not be supposed that she sought to do so by
enlarging upon the value of this treasure. That
would have been a crude and inept device. In
those days she was constantly drawing comparisons
between the qualities, mental and moral—no competition was now, alas, possible as to physical—of
Timothy and of his cousins, the young O'Rourkes
and Nicholas Crinions. "Ay, bedad, Biddy," she
would say to her sister: "It's the fool poor Timothy
is at his figures compared with your little Nannie,
that's quick as lightnin' flashes, and she only a
twelvemonth oulder than him. 'Deed, it's the poor
offer he'd make at sayin' his twice times the way her
father had her, when they come to see us last Sunday."

"Her father hasn't so much sinse as you'd crack a cockle wid," Mrs O'Rourke would reply grimly. But it was her habit to be grimly pleased.

Or Mrs Nicholas Crinion might happen to call upon her invalid sister-in-law, and then Mrs Larry would not fail to point out in how many desirable properties Timothy was excelled by his cousins. "Sure you'll not have much throuble gettin' *them* places, Lizzie, when they're any size at all. It's plased people'll be to employ them, and they that willin' and biddable. But poor Timothy was always as foolish as if he hadn't plinty of wit. Playin' thricks was what he'd mostly be givin' his mind to. Not but what he's quiet enough these times, the crathur. And keepin' an eye on the child he could be, or goin' on a bit of an errand, if it wasn't far to spake of, and no great hurry about it—and not pourin' outrageous, Lizzie, the way he would be drownded entirely hobblin' so slow under it. And anyhow you'd scarce notice him sittin' contint in a corner."

To which Mrs Nicholas, unluckily, was rather likely to rejoin: "Ah sure, my childer's brought up to know right well that work they may git, or hungry they may go"; a view of the matter other than what Mrs Larry had hoped to elicit.

On one of these occasions, Timothy, after the visitors had departed, came and looked sternly at her, leaning on his crutch. "There's no child to be keepin' an eye on," he said.

"Sure, not at all, I was only supposin', be way of a joke," said his mother.

"Where's the sinse of supposin' nonsinse?" Timothy demanded, and withdrew, not waiting for an answer, which would hardly have proved satisfactory.

But his mother reserved her great stroke of policy until she felt that the time remaining at her disposal for the execution of her designs had become very strictly limited. Then she expended a long hoarded sum of "three thruppennies" upon sugar-sticks and bull's-eyes, and bade all the young O'Rourkes and Crinions to a feast. This took place in mid-wintry weather, with deep snow all round, including a small drift, like a wonderfully white pillow, just inside the wide-chinked door. The stark cold had made her cough so much worse that she was obliged to keep her bed, whence she could only issue hoarsely-whispered exhortations to Timothy to be liberal in distributing the sweets, and admonitions to behave himself like a good child. To do Timothy justice, he was quite spontaneously disposed to comply with the first part of her injunctions, and he dealt out streaky white sticks and treacly black balls in no niggard spirit. The latter and vaguer half of his instructions were not perhaps so scrupulously obeyed. At least, some parts of his behaviour did not strikingly resemble that of a conspicuously good child.

Towards the close of the entertainment, when Mrs Larry's house was filled with an odour of peppermint that could almost be seen, and when anything one touched seemed inclined to adhere, Nicholas Crinion looked in on his way from work to ask how his sister-in-law was, and expressing

regret at finding her so indifferent altogether, sat
for some time by the hearth, where the red firelight
glowed redder as the outer world grew all a colourless
black and white. The remoter parts of the room,
however, were left in a dusk dim enough to cast
a veil over the proceedings of Timothy and his
cousin, Mick O'Rourke, who were busy at something
near the door. Presently Timothy came forward,
and to his mother's gratification, very politely offered
his Uncle Nicholas a long white sugar-stick, one end
of which was neatly wrapped up in newspaper.

"Och no, thank'ee kindly, Tim, me man," Nicholas
said, blandly. "Sure, I lost me sweet tooth ould
ages ago, and I question will I ever find it again.
Ait your bit of candy yourself."

"But I'd a dale liefer you had it," Timothy
persisted, affectionately. "Put it in your pocket,
anyway, and be bringin' it home."

"Sure, not at all," Nicholas said, hurriedly stuffing
both hands down his pockets, to prevent a possible
intrusion of the unwelcome gift. An ill-advised move,
as he found; for Timothy, suddenly saying: "Och,
bejabers, but you must have it!" thrust the white
stick, which had already begun to drip suspiciously,
down the back of his uncle's neck, while his con-
federate, Mick, jumped ecstatically up and down on
the snowdrift at the door, scattering moist flakes
about the room. No one who has experienced the
sensation of a lump of half-melted snow slithering
along his back like a horribly agile slug, its progress
only accelerated by the vain attempts of a groping
forefinger to arrest its downward career, will under-

estimate the constraint which Timothy's uncle put upon his feelings when he appeared to be pleased and exhilarated by this instance of his nephew's pretty wit, and protested with sincere - sounding laughter that the young rapscallion had had the better of him that time, at all events. But perhaps most people would have done likewise, had they too caught a glimpse of Timothy's mother's face, watching the scene with the expression of one who beholds a last hope wantonly destroyed. Nicholas's well-feigned sportiveness lulled that fear to rest, and enabled her to breathe again as freely as her circumstances ever permitted. Still, she felt that an unjustifiable risk had been run ; and later on in the evening, when they were alone, she said remonstrantly to Timothy, who was finishing a bull's-eye in much comfort by the fire : " It's a terrible child you are, Tim, for jokin' and playin' the fool, and it's too free you make sometimes intirely."

Timothy so deeply resented what appeared to him the injustice of this rebuke, that he hastily swallowed his diminished sugar-ball, thriftlessly, and at some risk of choking, to retort, " And I'd like to know who was makin' jokes yourself about mindin' childer, no great while ago ? " And this gibe—such is Fate's fine sense of the fitness of things—was almost the last speech that Mrs Larry had of her son Timothy.

At his mother's wake it was settled that Timothy should be provided for conjointly by his uncle, Nicholas Crinion, and his aunt, Biddy O'Rourke, and thenceforward he had his abode under their roofs, sometimes one, and sometimes the other, "just accordin'," as they said themselves. Nobody could have foretold from one day, or even hour, to the next, among which troop of barefooted children he might be included at dinner-time or bed-time; and the tribes both of his Crinion and O'Rourke cousins were so numerous, that one more or less might be supposed to make little difference. This promiscuous arrangement had its advantages and its drawbacks. In one respect Timothy found it decidedly convenient; for the two families lived at opposite ends of the long street, and Timothy discovered that a hasty hobble down it would generally bring him from the O'Rourkes' big black pot to the Crinions' before the last steaming pitaty had been distributed; by which not scrupulously honourable means, he pleasantly supplemented his midday repast. He seldom inverted the order of procedure, because his Aunt Lizzie under such circumstances was apt to be embarrassingly particular in her inquiries as to whether he had already dined. It must be said for Timothy that only while he was at an age when people are naturally very hungry and very selfish did he practise this trick. Later on, he made just the opposite use of his opportunities, and would sometimes come in falsely representing himself to have had a bit down below or up above, as the case might be. On these occasions it was his Aunt Biddy who felt suspicious; but she used to think of her scanty stores and large household, and keep her misgivings to herself.

Thus, in the matter of board and lodging, the dual guardianship worked fairly well. But where clothing was concerned, it had a tendency to introduce the principle that what is everybody's business is nobody's. Mrs Crinion would be of the opinion that, "Supposing Timothy's bit of a coateen had gone to flitters entirely, it was a queer thing if Mrs O'Rourke couldn't contrive to make him up some sort of a one, and she with three boys bigger than he growing out of their rags every minute of the day, until cast off they must be"; while Mrs O'Rourke had, from just the same premises, arrived at the conclusion "That Mrs Crinion, with the most of her childer little girls, had a right to be better able to keep a dacint stitch on him, than a body who had a young rigimint to ready up by some manner of means."

These conflicting views may have had a somewhat adverse influence upon the repairing and replenishing of Timothy's wardrobe. It was, indeed, hardly possible for his tatters and flitters to be wider and wilder than those of his cousins; but the neighbours naturally fancied that they were so, and when in a censorious mood, spoke to each other about the scandalous figure his aunts kept the poor orphan child. Mrs Hoytes once even went so far as to declare it was a public show; and Judy Mullarkey, choosing a subtlèr method of conveying disapproval, ostentatiously presented Timothy with a very old knitted scarlet comforter, all ravelling into threads. But Mrs Crinion promptly ravelled it a little more, and used the wool for mending the handle of her market-basket, where it gleamed conspicuously on the very next Saturday—a thrifty retort which Judy did not fail to appreciate.

Perhaps Timothy may really have been rather unusually tatterdemalion just then, as he and his relatives were going through a spell of hard times. A rainy, blight-bringing summer had conducted them to the threshold of an autumn bleak and menacing. Illness had been infesting them, and at that very moment a dreary chaos reigned in the O'Rourke's household, because its mistress was laid aside with crippling rheumatism.

Timothy's other aunt was at first disposed to think it an additional misfortune when her cousin, Andy Sheehan, came driving along in his donkey-cart one of those frosty mornings. For Andy had long been considered a calamitous member of his family, having wasted his substance and come down in the world. He had started in life as the owner of a small shop and a little bit of land, which, after a few years, he found himself obliged to relinquish, setting out anew with his possessions dwindled into an old donkey and cart, and confirmed tastes for drinking and betting. Thus equipped, he adopted the ill-reputed calling of an old-clothes man which he pursued with scanty profit, and still less credit to himself. So much less, indeed, that his cousin, Lizzie Crinion, had accounted for a recent cessation of his periodical transits through Kilanesk by supposing him to have got into some especially serious trouble with the police. Now, however, it appeared that things had been looking up with him. Bits

of good luck had fallen in his way. He had found
a five-pound note in the lining of an ancient waist-
coat, purchased for fourpence and a three half-penny
mug. Also, he had made a tidy little sum of money
over a horse he backed at the Listowel races. And
he had bought himself a new donkey, and a fine
stock of crockery wherewith to carry on his
barter.

Andy related this to Mrs Crinion at her door ; and
shortly afterwards, when drinking tea by her fire,
while the children minded his property outside, he
remarked that he was looking for a small spalpeen ·
of a boy, to sit in the cart and keep an eye on Nellie
and his wares during the transaction of business. For
want of such a coadjutor, he had had a grand delft
jug stolen off him quite lately, and, furthermore,
Nellie had come near overturning the whole concern,
straying up the bank after grass. " I suppose, ma'am,
you wouldn't think of loanin' me a one of your little
gossoons ? " he concluded, half-jocularly.

"Och, not at all, man, not at all," Mrs Crinion
hastened to reply. " Me Pather 's too big—a fine tall
fellow he 's grown—and me Joe 's a delicate little
crathur—och, not at all." She might, with perfect
truth, have added that she would be long sorry to
send e'er a child of hers travelling about the country
with the likes of any such an ould *slieveen* as Andy
Sheehan, who was drinking morning, noon, and night,
if he got the chance, and had the divil's own temper
when he had a drop taken. At that very minute she
doubted was he altogether sober, and it scarce ten
o'clock.

"There's that one-legged child I seen along wid them, he'd do me right enough," said Andy.

"Is it Timothy? Och, well now, sure, he maybe might," Mrs Crinion said, her mind instantly grasping at the pitaties and farrels of bread that his absence would leave at her disposal. "It's not much he's good for here, the dear knows, except to be aitin'. But he's 'cute enough, mind you, and his leg keeps him quiet. He'd sit in the cart as steady as a rock."

"Well, then, it's comin' this way agin I am to-morra night," said Andy—"I'm stoppin' above for the Drumclune fair—and pickin' up the brat I could be."

Mrs Crinion considered for a moment. "You might so," she said then. "But look-a, Andy, don't be lettin' on anythin' about it to man or baste. For, you see, be raison of his bein' poor Larry Crinion's child, Himself as like as not might take up wid some fantigue agin lettin' him go. And his aunt, Biddy O'Rourke, might be talkin'. But if he just wint off wid you promiscuous, 'twould be like as if you was only givin' him a jaunt, and 'ud prisintly lave him back. So they'd contint themselves wid that notion till they was used to missin' him."

"Ay, to be sure," said Andy; "and then any time, if I wasn't contint, or the brat wasn't contint, I do be passin' plinty of Unions in diff'rint places, and I could drop him at a one of them aisy."

"Ay could you, aisy," said Mrs Crinion. She was still thinking of the pitaties.

Meanwhile Timothy, in complete ignorance of the arrangements that were being made for him, was on his way to do an errand at Lawlor's shop. To him, slowly halting over the bridge, Jim M'Guire, lounging there, bawled: "Och Timothy, man, just stop and tell us which of the ould scarecrows you might be after strippin' of that grand coat you have streelin' round you. Was it Mr Kenny's? For I seen he had an iligant objic' of a one in his barley last time I was passin' through." A gibe to which Timothy's rejoinder came shrill and prompt: "Ay, bedad, had he. But it isn't there now, as you'd a right to know, when walkin' off wid itself it was—the very same way you was a-goin'." And applausive peals followed him down the street.

It would seem as if Timothy's mood must have been particularly facetious that morning. At any rate, when a few minutes afterwards Tom Crosby handed him over the counter a loaf, with the remark: "It's riz a farthin'," he was led into replying too innocently: "Arrah, now, is it any differ in the sort of yaist?"

"I'll not be long learnin' you the differ, if I come across to you," Tom said, sternly, and with such an apparent intention of coming that Timothy turned to flee precipitately, and in so doing dropped the loaf, which rolled thumpingly into an inaccessible corner behind some meal-barrels. He was trying to fish it out with his crutch, propping himself perilously against the counter, when somebody came to his assistance.

This was a much smaller boy, in a grey suit, which, unlike the garments commonly worn by the youth of Kilanesk, did not appear to have been originally designed for an elder and inartistically curtailed.

His hat alone seemed to be somewhat a misfit, and
was set so far back on his head that its broad brim
made him a sort of halo, misleadingly, for his care-
takers often considered him " a very bold child." It
fell off on the floor in his crawling among the barrels,
which drew to him the attention of Maria, the maid,
who was conversing with Mrs Hoytes close by. So,
just as he was handing the loaf to Timothy, she called
to him reprovingly, " Ah, what are you doing there,
Master Mac ? Come out of that with yourself. It's
no way to be behaving, and you a nobleman's
grandson."

" I wish to goodness," said Mac, " that you were a
nobleman's plaguey old granddaughter, and thin you'd
have to be behavin' yourself instead of *bovverin'* other
people."

And Mrs Hoytes said, soothingly : " 'Deed now, it's
the good nature the young gentleman has in him.
And poor Timothy's a dacint little child, that's hard-
set to be creepin' about. Sure, the Crinions and the
O'Rourkes do be very respectable people, livin' here
all the days of me life."

Mac, who was visiting his aunts up at the Grange,
had presently an opportunity of making further
acquaintance with this well-connected youth. For in
the course of that afternoon's walk the sunny grass of
a bank by the river tempted Maria to sit down and
take out her crochet. It happened that Timothy was
at hand, pegging pebbles at a boulder, whose ledged
recesses seemed to promise " troutses," and with him
Mac fell into a conversation, which Maria, on the
strength of Mrs Hoytes's testimonial, and her own

wish to finish her collar, did not feel called upon to
interrupt. As they were moving along to take up
another position of attack, Timothy accounted for his
obvious difficulty in getting over the sliding gravel by
the remark that it was "very unhandy to be lame of
the both of your feet in one," and he went on to
explain how he had lately stepped, with painful
results, on a bit of broken glass.

"Boots," suggested Mac, "would have kept the
sharp edge of it off, and they aren't so much *bovver*,
if you don't let her lace more than every second
hole." He glanced down with complacency at his
own footgear, which, as the fruit of frequent con-
tention with Maria, were fastened on this time-
saving principle.

"The last ould brogue iver I owned," said
Timothy, "went off wid itself on a swim down
the river, and it niver come back."

"But I saw plenty of them hanging up in the
shop," said Mac; "near the buckets they were, and
the legs of bacon."

"Sure, the only body I'd have a chance of buyin'
a one off of 'ud be an ould Lepracaun," said Timothy.

"I happen not to remember his shop," Mac said,
carelessly.

"Och, now, don't you, then?" Timothy said, in
apparent surprise. "The little ould fairy shoe-
maker, that's as wizendy-up and quare-lookin' as
ever you beheld. Sure, I'd ha' thought, if you was
anywheres at all, you'd ha' been apt to see a
Lepracaun. But nobody ever seen him makin'
more than one boot at the one time—that's sartin.

So I'd ha' no throuble wid gettin' him to break a pair for me. It's quare to be watchin' him workin' away, tickin' tackin' wid his little silver hammer, and his leather apern, and he in his grand green coateen, and his red cap wid a white feather streelin' out of it the len'th of your arm, like a bit of a moonbame got crookened."

"Where does he live?" Mac asked, with interest.

But Timothy was surprised again—mortifyingly so. "Musha, good gracious, it is where does he live? Sure, where else would an ould fairy be livin', except it was at a fair? That's the raison of the name."

"*Of course*," Mac said, with dignity, upon receiving this piece of etymological information. "I meant where does the nearest one to you live?"

"Sure, very belike there might be a one in it to-morra at the fair in Drumclune, that's no great way off," said Timothy.

"I've drove there," said Mac. "But perhaps a person who had cut his foot with broken glass, which is very dangerous to leave lyin' about, couldn't walk so far to get anythin'."

"Anyhow," said Timothy, "thim boots th' ould Lepracaun would be sellin', does be terrible expensive. The price thim sort of crathurs do be axin' would frighten you. Keepin' his boot he may be for me."

"Would it be as expensive, I wonder, as two florins, and a sixpence, and a threepenny bit?" said Mac. "And I wonder does he make boot-laces too, or have you to get them from somebody else?"

"Ay, bedad, would it, every pinny," Timothy said.

"Why, there's ne'er a Lepracaun in the counthry but owns a big crock full up of gould that he's got wid chaitin' thim that buys his boots. Look-a, sir, there was somethin' lepped in the pool."

But Mac continued to wonder.

The next morning was all blurred with cold mists, white on the dark hills, blue on the green fields, and leaden-grey overhead. Towards noon, Timothy established himself on the parapet of the bridge, quarters which he preferred to the smoky gloom of a cavernous kitchen, though the drizzle, swarming thickly about him, pricked his face and hands chillily, as if with the alighting of a cloud of half-thawed icy midges. His Aunt Lizzie, on his going out, had exhorted him with unwonted solicitude not to stay stravading round under the wet too late; and she had previously been dilating, without much apparent relevance, upon the good luck of any-body who might get the chance of jaunting through the country in a grand little ass-cart. But Timothy, surmising no connection between these two facts, nor any possible bearing of them upon his own future prospects, heeded them very slightly at the time, and gave them no further thought.

The weather and the fair having diminished loungers, he had the bridge all to himself, until by-and-by Felix Riley came along, driving home three heifers, whose witless heads pointed persistently in wrong directions. Felix now allowed them to drift a bit down the road unsteered by his blackthorn, and stopped for a word with Timothy. "There's

U

apt to be blue murdher up above at the Grange to-day," he said.

"What's happint them?" inquired Timothy.

"Sure, up there, about Martin's cross-roads, I'm after meetin' the little chap that's visitin' the ladies— Master Mac they call him—stumpin' along his lone, which I well know they'd niver countenance his doin'. He slipped out, belike, widout their know-ledge. But when I made free to axe him where he was off to, he answered me mighty stiff that he'd business at Drumclune fair; and that's no place, to my mind, for the likes of him to be sthrayin' in. Sure, he isn't the size of anythin'; and might very aisy be over-run wid the first drove of bastes come his way. So, if you hear anybody axin' about him, you might just say where I seen him. I've me heifers to git home—and, bedad, there's the red one about steppin' into Mr Duggan's."

"It's after the Lepracaun he's goin', I'd bet me life," Timothy reflected, with remorse and amuse-ment mingled. "Sure, he thought every word of the ould blathers I tould him was true. 'Deed, but it's quare the foolery childer'll be believin," he said loftily to himself, from his altitude of nine years.

He sat for a while longer considering in the drizzle, and then he saw George Mack approaching with a high-piled cart-load of hay. "Is it for the fair above you are?" Timothy asked.

George replied: "Ah, sure, not at all. I'm just about slingin' it in the lough over there, for fear anybody might be offerin' to buy it off of us."

"Gimme a lift," said Timothy.

"Och, but you'd niver conthrive to git up that height," said George; "and there's no room on the shaft."

"Right enough, I'd conthrive," Timothy said. And so he did, crutches and all, whereupon the load resumed its waddling way towards Drumclune.

Timothy had not been mistaken in his conjecture concerning Mac, who was about this time arriving at the fair. He found it a rather bewildering place, where many of the people one met seemed to stagger along and bawl in a strange and undignified manner, and where sudden rushes of large beasts came by, with horned heads awkwardly on a level with his own, which some persons—quite other persons, of course—might possibly have found startling. Nor did he anywhere light upon traces of the green jacket and long white feather, of which he was in quest. This gave him a foreboding of failure, and somehow made him the more alive to the fact, of which in his conscience he was well aware, that he should not have set forth upon the expedition un-authorised by his elders.

So that he was feeling slightly forlorn and dis-couraged, when at last he wandered into a little back lane where nothing particular seemed to be going on. At one end of it, into a recess meant for holding broken stones, a donkey-cart had been drawn—the donkey was nibbling a grass bank close by—and converted into a temporary old-clothes stall. Garments of various kinds were hung from the erected shafts, and piled on boards placed counter-wise across it, interspersed with tempting

clusters of the crockery, which often played a leading part in bargains struck for ancient coats and
shawls. The proprietor sat on the low wall behind
it, in a weather-beaten, greenish great-coat.   He
was elderly, small, and wizened, with a deep red
face, and hair several shades lighter; and he said
to Mac: "Fine day, sir.   Might you be a-wantin'
anythin'?"

"A boot I was wantin'," said Mac, who by this
time had almost given up hopes of the Lepracaun;
"but the right place for gettin' it at doesn't seem
to be here to-day."

"Is it a boot?" the old man said, hopping up
with alacrity.   "Sure, I've the grandest stock of
thim to-day, at all.   A pair I have this minyit 'ud
fit you delightful, sir, as if they was made to your
iligant measure."

"But I want only half a pair," said Mac; "and
I want it not to fit me.   I don't know exactly the
size, but one that both my feet would fit into at
once would be about big enough."

"What would you say to that, honey?" the old
man said, clumping down before him a large and
heavy boot, whose travelling days were evidently
nearly done.

"It hasn't any lace in it," Mac said, being disposed to adverse criticism by the term of endearment.

"A lace, sir; is it a lace?   Me sowl to glory,
sure, all the gintlemen ever I knew buys their laces
sep'rit.   Not but what a nice bit of string off of a
parcel looks as tasty as anythin' you could get."

"How dear is it?" Mac inquired, beginning to

pull out his red leather purse with a silver "M"
on the flap.

Eyes expectantly twinkling watched the process.
"Why, that's accordin'," said their owner. "But
it's apt to be as much as all the shillin's a customer
would have along wid him, anyway, and worth
every one of them, and more."

"Would it be more than two florins," the customer
said, laying down the coins, "and a sixpence, and a
new threepenny, and another sixpence; only it's a
queer crumpled-up shape, and Val says it looks
doubtful?"

"Well, now, just to oblige you, sir, I might
contint meself to take it," said the old man; and
a bony clutch was descending upon the little heap
of silver, when another hand intercepted its pounce,
and covered its prey under a firmly-pressed palm.

"Ay, would you, bedad, y'ould robber," the
new-comer said, "if you got the chance."

This was Timothy Crinion, whose equipage had
lumbered past just in time for him to espy Mac at
his bargaining, and to intimate a wish to alight
by dropping a crutch on George Mack's head.

"Git out of this, you young vagabone," said the
old man, "and don't be offerin' to meddle wid the
young gintleman's money he's just after payin' over
to me."

"Och, but yourself's the notorious great chait,
ould Andy Sheehan," Timothy retorted, keeping
one hand resolutely on Mac's property. "Look at
the rubbishy bit of thrash you was takin' all his
shillin's for," he pointed a scornful finger at a

huge chasm in the upper leather of the decaying boot. "You wouldn't give so much as a cracked taycup for three pair of them, and that you wouldn't."

"I 'll git the pólis, and thry what *they* 'll be givin' *you*, you unchancy-lookin' spalpeen," said Andy.

"Git them, and welcome," Timothy defiantly said. But he gripped the money, and calling "Come along," to Mac, swung himself away as rapidly as he could.

Mac naturally followed, but the old man could pursue them only with maledictions and threats, being conscious that the earth was not spinning so steadily as it had done before the contents of a certain black bottle had shrunk and sunk.

Timothy had not much difficulty in convincing Mac of the worthlessness of Andy Sheehan's wares, and the advisability of deferring a purchase to a more favourable opportunity. "For," he urged, "the Lepracaun might happen to be in it some other day, and you wid ne'er a farthin' left. But if yon was wishful to be gittin' a somethin' now, there's me Aunt Biddy 'ud be terrible thankful for a limon. Cruel bad she is wid the rheumatics, and sez there would be nothin' aquil to a limon, when she 's chokin' wid the thirst all night." And Timothy had some trouble in halving Mac's prompt order for a dozen. His most effective argument was a whispered, "Sure, if you git that many, they'll be thinkin' you 're mistakin' thim for a clutch of eggs, and buyin' thim to put under an ould hin."

Then John Harrel, from Carrickmore, the next

place to the Grange, met the two boys just as he was going to drive home in the jennet-cart, and he gave them a lift back to Kilanesk, where they arrived before Mac's absence had caused any serious uneasiness.

And although he had done no business with Andy Sheehan, it seems probable that the frustrated transaction was not without its effect upon the fortunes of Timothy. All that evening Mrs Crinion expected the arrival of her cousin's donkey-cart to carry off the interloping nephew, but it did not come. And when he next appeared in the village some weeks later, he merely vouchsafed a surly Good-mornin', driving past her door, and was already provided with a travelling companion in the shape of a small, oppressed-looking boy. She could conjecture no cause for Andy's change of mind, and ascribed it to "some contrary fantigue," in her ignorance of how Timothy had displayed an inconvenient readiness to pick holes in the goods of his proposed employer. Yet, though she deplored the result, a more disinterested judge of the case might have been inclined to pronounce Timothy "better off stopping where he was," even if his stay promised him no more brilliant prospect than the watching of many miles of clear brown river-water, slipping away beneath Kilanesk bridge.

NOTICE TO QUIT

OLD Arthur Duff sat stiffly down on the steps of the dilapidated summer-house, saying to himself that the children were late bringing him his bit of dinner, for the twelve o'clock bell must have rung long ago, and he somehow have missed hearing it: maybe the wind was the wrong way. As a matter of fact, the wind was at that very moment wafting the sound through the garden as clearly as on any day since he had begun to listen for it, which, boy and man, dated from more than seventy years back; therefore the fault lay elsewhere. Had he not, though tall, been spare and light of frame, he would have found the rustic step in its crumbling decay an insecure seat, for even under his weight it creaked so noisily that two wood-lice and an earwig looked out with some concern from beneath the loosening bark-flakes.

Sitting in the glow of an early autumn noon, the old man had at his feet an oblong plot of fairly smooth shaven sward, dotted with small, round flower-beds. These were rather meagrely filled with rosettes of dwindled asters—white, pink, and lilac— and straggling geraniums, upon which lingered yet a few scarlet blossoms. The plot was bounded by mossy walks edged with ragged box; and beyond that the great garden stretched away about and

about in a wilderness of weeds. Massive ivy-tods
hung heavily over the tops of the high grey walls
as the crest of a wave hangs before it flings itself
prone. In two or three places this seemed to be
happening, where a matted clump had fallen by its
own weight, dragging down with it a scattering of
coping-stones. One of the gaps thus made framed
a glimpse, across a few fields, of the little old chapel
from whose tower the last of the twelve strokes came
clanging. The whole look of the place gave the
impression that a tide of wild life was sweeping in,
encroaching upon, and enisling the painfully - kept
grass-plot, which had been made a last rallying-
point of culture. Its ruinous arbour and decrepit
guardian seemed to presage a speedy submergence.

Some such foreboding was running in the old man's
mind. Perhaps because he felt tired and hungry
after his long morning's work, which had conscien-
tiously begun among the dews at seven o'clock, he
just then inclined to despair of the situation. "It's
givin' up that north walk I'll have to be—I will so,"
he said to himself, staring gloomily before him, with
shaggy eyebrows knit against the sun-dazzle. "Hard
set I am to keep the other three ones anyways clane,
creepin' round them wid the ould scuffle. But sure,
I well know if I lave it alone for a week, throopin'
over the whoule dirty pack of them'll be as fast as
a dog'll throt. And wunst that bastely scutch gits
a 'hould of the dacint grass, you may quit contindin'
wid it. But sure, the mortal truth is, it's time I was
quittin' out. Ten apprinticeships I've put in in it;

and half-a-dozen I've had workin' under me, afore
the ould master wint; and the end of it is I'm left
widout so much as a brat of a boy to be thrashin'
the nettles, and Mrs Kelly has the face on her to
call me the caretaker. It 'ud suit her betther to keep
her tongue off passin' remarks, and remimber to send
a body his bit of food, and she afther takin' upon
herself to say she would. Or very belike the childher
has it sittin' on the roadside this minyit, while
themselves is aitin' the green blackberries out of the
hedges — Och no; here the crathurs are. Well,
Nannie and Thady, what was delayin' you at
all?"

Two small fat children with a little tin can and
a dangled bundle came into view from behind a
dying brown laurel. They were not loquacious
people, and handed over their charges without
making any observation. But they stood opposite
to him and stared.

"Well, Nannie and Thady, what at all 's delayin'
you now?" the old man said again, and again
they gave no reply other than could be gathered
from their continued standing and staring. "Ay, to
be sure!" he said presently, with a start of recollection, and getting to his feet, scrambled up the steps
into the summer-house, whence he emerged bearing
two small windfall apples, which he gave the children,
who thereupon departed as mute as they had come.
Only when they were nearly out of earshot, Nannie
remarked to Thady, who was a size smaller : "If
you gnorr it while you 're walkin' along, you 'll be
nearly chokin' yourself wid the core, the way you

done last time." Thady, however, made a backward kick at her silently, and went on *gnorring*.

When they had gone, old Arthur began his dinner, shaping mouthfuls of cold griddle-bread with his clasp-knife, and drinking hot tea out of the can. The children's mother, Mrs Kelly, with whom he lodged, had lately declared that "wid the air gettin' so thin, it was noways fit for the ould crathur to not have somethin' wid a taste of warmth in it the len'th of the day; and Nannie and Thady might as well be fetchin' it to him as runnin' after mischief through the ditches." It was rather magnanimous of Mrs Kelly to concern herself on his behalf, seeing that he did not conceal a very poor opinion of her as the wife of a man who, many years before, had filled, unsatisfactorily, a subordinate post up there at the Manor. "Joe Kelly," old Arthur was wont to aver, "had been the greatest gawk of a garden-boy of all he ever had under him, and plenty more that sort were than he wanted." Moreover, Mrs Kelly had not long since sunk herself still lower in his esteem, because, on the occasion of his last attack of asthma and bronchitis, she had spoken of him to the new dispensary doctor as a caretaker. Old Arthur had almost choked outright in hoarse attempts to correct the title into "head gardener that was," and he had not yet forgiven the insult. Nevertheless, he owed her many a good turn, and she was at much trouble and some little expense to make the most for him of the seven shillings a week to which he had been reduced by the fallen fortunes of "the Family."

These were in his mind now as he sat consuming his bread and tea: for his eyes had lit upon a skeleton form at a short distance, and he was saying to himself: "Bad cess to that ojus bindweed. Look at the way it's afther smotherin' poor Miss Helen's myrtle, and I disrememberin' to move it out of that, as I was intendin' this time last year. Finely annoyed she'd ha' been about it!" But his attention was diverted by the arrival of an habitual caller, who came hopping over the grass with a round black eye to crumbs, and as many bobs and ducks as a Chinese envoy on his best behaviour. "Arrah now, git out wid you, and come along wid yourself raisonable," the old man said to the robin, after watching its ceremonious approach for a while. "What figurandyin' you have, and lettin' on, and yourself as brazen wid impudence all the time as you can stick together, and sorra a bit frightened of anything."

He had hardly spoken, however, when the bird suddenly darted off in a panic, obviously unfeigned, and hid itself among weedy bowers.

"What's took it at all, then?" said old Arthur; "well, but it's the conthrary one, and I not stirrin' hand nor feet a-purpose for 'fraid of scarin' it. Bedad, if them crathurs had the wit to know the fools they make of themselves flutherin' away demented-like when people's not manin' them a hair of harm, they'd save themselves a sight of throuble come wid takin' notions in their heads."

Yet, though he thus moralised on the spectacle of the fanciful robin, he was himself to be seized anon by a delusion as irrational at least as that which had prompted its flight. For when, a moment afterwards, he became aware that a tall grey-clad figure, whose muffled steps had not reached his duller ears, was standing close beside him, he sprang to his feet, exclaiming in a sort of ecstatic terror:

"Master Chandos! *Master Chandos!* Is it ever yourself?"

"Why, do you know me?" said the stranger, who was a tall, thin, dark-haired young man. "Chandos *is* my name—Chandos Considine. But I don't believe I ever saw you before."

"Well, maybe not, sir, maybe not," said the old man, seeming to collect himself, "it's not altogether likely, if one comes to consider; but just the first minyit I dunno what I consaited. Anyhow, I've seen the mortal image of you, if it wasn't yourself; and a Master Chandos too, he was, and a Considine, in coorse. And more betoken, you come the very way you'd ha' took, supposin' you was him. It's a short step from th' ould buryin'-ground, if you cross the river be the hand-bridge below at Cullen's, and folly along the holly-walk, and in here through the rosery gate forenint the arbour, same as you done, sir; and that's the raison I niver noticed you till you was so close—Master Chandos."

"When did you see him last?" inquired the young man, feeling that he was again being eyed perplexedly. "Did you say he lived here? I never was in this neighbourhood before."

"When I seen him?" old Arthur said, looking away with the expression of one venturing a glance down something perilously high and steep. "It might

be a matter of fifty year since he went off in a decline.
Much of an age the both of us was those times, and
neither of us to say very ould. But, as for his livin'
here, sure, he lived in it as long as he got the chance,
and that wasn't over-long; and where else should he
be now except in the big vault they have over yonder,
along wid all the Considines that ever was?"

"Ah, well! that settles the question, for if once I
get in there, you may depend upon it I'll never *walk*
—not another step, I think," said the new Master
Chandos. He looked down at his boots, which were
dusty, and set his small black bag out of his hand on
the grass, as if he found its weight a burden. "I had
to be in Crossmasheila on business, and I just turned
in to take a look at the old place. A woman at the
gate-lodge told me that the shortest way was by one
of the shrubberies, but I hardly think she would have
recommended it if she had remembered how like a
bit of virgin forest it is. So these, I suppose, are the
gardens?"

"Sure, you may call them so, for the sake of giving
them a name," said their guardian, surveying them
with a disconsolate gaze. "But it's little bether
than tellin' a lie. Nobody'd say it was the same
place at all, if it warn't lyin' inside of the same wall,
and that's fallin' down as fast as it can, wid the ivy
sittin' atop of it. And you can see yourself the holy
show the other ould weed's after makin' of it all,
sthreelin' over everythin'. Do you mind the big—I
mane, there's the big strawberry-bed yonder; many's
the day I've had four or five boys pickin' away on it
the len'th of the mornin', and they whistlin' all the

while to make sure the berries was goin' into the right place—that was how I circimvinted *them*. But och! what all you'd find on it now wouldn't hinder e'er a spalpeen of whistlin' like a blackbird. And me grand row of hollyhocks there wid the white lilies in clumps between them, sorra a thrace of thim's left: now and agin an odd one makes an offer to be comin' up, and 'twould sicken you to see the weeny wizened size it is. And sorra a bush of the roses the ould misthress set such store by but has the life smothered out of it; they might as well be thryin' to grow under the weight of an ould rick-cover. Bedad, it's the quare desthruction poor Master Chandos 'ud ha' thought there was on the place—and yourself's his picture; just the livin' image of him, the way he would be mopin' about here the last summer before he got the bad could that took him off suddint at the end. A lep comes aisy to a body when he's runnin' downhill. . . . Beg pardon, sir, but I won'er what you are to the Family? There was Master Mervyn, that come next to Master Chandos; he married, and lived somewhere outlandish——"

"My grandfather's name was Mervyn," said the stranger. "The same man. But both he and my father died years ago."

"Ay, ay, your honour; so they would," said old Arthur. "The Family was always ready enough at that. And, truth to say, some of them that was longer-lived spent their time doin' their endeavours to lave as little behind them as they could. But none of them equilled Sir Edward at that work—the eldest of them, that owned this place. The horse-racin' ruinated him. I remimber Mr Sullivan, the butler, tellin' me how one time an ould uncle of theirs, that was some sort of judge, was stoppin' at the Manor, and, sez he, after dinner, to Sir Edward: 'It's to the dogs them horses is bringin' you.' And sez Sir Edward: 'What'll you bet that it won't be there and back?' That was all the heed he paid his uncle. So he died in the Bankruptcy Coort, and the property, as I understand, is in it yet. Anyway, his sisters, Miss Helen and Miss Margaret, that was livin' here, had to quit. I'll never forget the pourin' wet day they wint, and meetin' Peter Ryan the coachman in the avenue—that was after dhrivin' them over to Ballycrone—and axin' him what way he'd left the ladies. And sez he: 'Cocked up on a ould jauntin' car, wid a baste under it I wouldn't put to draw a decint pig-creel. And I'd as lief never rub down a pair of carriage-horses agin.' So, whether it was the wettin' or the frettin',' I dunno, but he never had a day's health after, and died widin the month. That now's goin on for twenty year since, and the best part of the time I've had the plisure-grounds and the gardens and everythin' on me hands, and heart-scalded I am wid them all. Belike, your honour, the woman below at the lodge may have tould you I was the caretaker; but she's as ignorant as a blind cow. Head-gardener I've been, wid me pound a-week, and allowances, and as many as six workin' under me, forby boys at jobs of weedin', as she well knows. But yourself's the first one of the Family I've set eyes on for I couldn't tell you how long; and I only wish'd you'd found the demesne in betther order."

"Ah, well! when I've finished making my fortune, I must buy it, and we'll set it to rights again," said Master Chandos.

"Will you, bedad, your honour? That's a good hearin' anyway," said the old man, with a gleam darting into his eyes. "And will you be long finishin'?"

"Oh, I don't expect to get done before the New Year, at all events," the young man said, carelessly, as he stooped to tie a boot-lace.

"And Michaelmas past this week!" said the old man, joyfully. "Sure, the New Year'll be on us in next to no time! Glory be to goodness! I'm a great while considherin' some such thing might happen after I was in me grave, and missin' it all— and now I'm widin three months of it! What's three months? Begorrah, Master Chandos, we'll have our own work cut out for us then, but what matter? 'Twill be grand. Only, if you'll take my advice, your honour, you won't let anybody persuade you to have it all ploughed up slapdash be way of gettin' shut of the weeds. That's no thratement for a garden. You'd do a dale betther to let me hire a dozen or so of dacint men, and set them on it wid billhooks and spades. Och, but it's the immense ould slashin' and thrashin' we'll have at that ungovernable clanjamfry of weeds; 'twill do one's heart good to be seein' it. And then, wunst we have the ground clear——"

Old Arthur launched out into a detailed programme of spring-work in the garden, from which its visitor escaped with difficulty, leaving behind

x

him half-a-crown, and a very safe promise to return as soon as the purchase of the estate had been effected.

But when he reached the entrance of the over-grown shrubbery, the young man paused to reflect, leaning against the gate. Said he to himself: " I wonder, now, did the old chap take it seriously! I half believe so, and I really never meant to make a fool of him. But how was he to know, after all, that I 'm engaged, unsuccessfully, in selling tea, under notice to look out for other employers next month, and with the vaguest idea as to their whereabouts? And, my gracious!" he said, drawing a halfpenny from his pocket, " I 've given him my last piece of silver: I had fondly imagined this to be a shilling. Now I 'll have to walk home. That was another irremediable mistake. But maybe I 'd better go back, and ask about the way, and say something to show that I was just romancing."

So he slowly retraced his steps, stumbling over the wispy grass which laid snares in his path. But when he regained the arbour he saw that the old man had resumed his work, and was digging in a jungle of weeds with an energy which seemed to over-task cruelly the worn-out machinery it set in motion. He was murmuring to himself with a blissful counten-ance. "No—I won't say a word," said the young man; "I 'd as soon ask him to give me back the half-crown!" And as he turned away unobserved, he continued to meditate: " Much better to leave it as it is. Three months are three months; there 's plenty of time for many things to happen; and he mayn't be disappointed though I don't arrive at the New Year!"

PILGRIMS FROM LISCONNEL

YOUNG Mrs Dan O'Beirne, whom the neighbours at Lisconnel still speak of as Stacey Doyne, comes up there every now and again to stay for a while with her mother. These visits generally have for their object either the giving or getting of "company." Mrs Doyne, who is a despondently ailing person, happens to stand in especial need of heartening up, or else young Dan has undertaken a temporary job at some little distance, whither it is inconvenient to carry with him wife and child. But, of course, in so small a place as Lisconnel, "company" does not by any means confine itself to the household in which it is domiciled. Such isolation would be found practically impossible, even if it were sought. The stir of an arrival vibrates from one end of the hamlet to the other—several hundred yards—and the accompanying news penetrates as impartially as sunshine to the fireside of friend and foe. Not that Stacey has any enemies up at Lisconnel. For even Sally, the Sheridans' eldest girl, who had betrayed some touches of spleen about the time "Dan was coortin'," soon afterwards met with a sweetheart of her own, and, though she had used to describe Fergus Tighe disparagingly as "a quare little conthrivance," was presently asserting and believing him to be "worth ten of them big lumberin'

323

fellows, wid their heads cocked up among the thatch," so had thenceforward left off fancying that she hated Mrs Dan.

Sally's next sister, lame-footed Peg, was one of Stacey's particular friends. Peg, a person with troubles of her own, had felt much for Stacey when her prospects were, during some dreary months, darkened by young Dan's unaccountable absence and silence, which ended, after all, in a happy return, and if not literally with marriage-bells, only because the poor little chapel "down beyant" possessed none to ring. Her sympathy at that anxious time actually led her so far as to offer Stacey the loan of her two priceless old flitterjigs of volumes, "Ivanhoe," and a dilapidated song-book, her brother Larry's parting bequest. And, albeit Stacey, who was nearly as illiterate as Peg herself, did not accept, she understood how signal was the mark of friendship.

"Ah no, Peg," she had said; "I might on'y be losin' the laves on you. And sure, tellin' you the truth, it's as much as I can do to spell out a word at all, when I'm givin' me mind to it, but me mind somehow won't take a hould rightly of anythin' these times. I wonder do there be a *great* many people dhrownded in the say crossin' over between this and Scotland—so thank you kindly, Peg."

This trouble of Peg's could never end with wedding-bells—that was certain. All the peals in Christendom clashing together would fail to scare it away. Her lameness itself was less incurable, though caused by an ankle "quare and crooked ever since the day she was born"; and, though it claimed notice at every step she took, it probably haunted her thoughts less persistently than the recollection of the quarrel with Larry, which could not ever be made up in this world—the quarrel about the pitaty planting, which had driven him away into exile so terribly farther than either of them had intended. Circumstances made her peculiarly liable to the sway of such bitter memories. Her painful limp debarred her from the distraction of active pursuits, and up at Lisconnel it is very hard for a body sitting still not to sit, as they say, "with his hands before him." The knitting up of coarse yarn is almost the only manual exercise attainable, and, unluckily, the supply of the material and the demand for the product are both apt to run short long before the worker's leisure. Moreover, the needles, under accustomed fingers, move so all but automatically that their twinkling, regarded as a mode of parrying heart-thrusts of regret or remorse, is little better than just twiddling one's thumbs. Peg used to linger over her socks and long-hose, purposely complicating them with intricate ribbing, and double heels, and fanciful arrangements of stitches purled and turned.

"Sure, girl alive," her stepmother would say to her, "what for would you be botherin' yourself puttin' the like of all them diff'rint pattrons up the legs? Tasty enough they may be, but sorra the extra halfpenny 'll you get for them, no more than if it grew on them be accident; and they take double of the time doin'." And Peg often answered, "I dunno, but maybe that's the raison."

Not seldom, however, either wool or spirits completely failed her, and then she would sit idle through all the daylight on the low bank where, a stone's-throw from the Sheridans' door, the bog pouts up a swarded lip. From this seat she could see, running over the Knockawn, the road towards Duffclane, along which Larry had set forth in the bleak grey of that sorrowful March morning, now years past, with the thought in his heart that he must quit out of it, because Peg had turned agin him like all the rest. If Peg had followed her own inclination, she would often even now have called down the empty road after him—so long after him —that there was not a word of truth in it. But she only sat silent and still.

These hours of idleness made her look what the neighbours call "quare and fretted like." After a spell of them, it might have been noticed that her face grew peaked and faded, until her many freckles seemed to increase in size and deepen in hue, while her wavy red hair hung limp and lustreless, and her grey eyes widened with staring vacantly at nothing visible. A stranger would have found it hard to believe that scarcely a score of years had passed over her woe-begone head.

One of Stacey's visits happened to fall at a time when Peg was moping thus, a forlorn object in the mellow harvest sunbeams that drowsed over Lisconnel, and not to be appreciably cheered by the freshest gossip from Duffclane, nor even by the conversation of a marvellous ten-month-old Felix O'Beirne, who could say *Yah-ah-ah* quite distinctly

at anybody he misliked the looks of. This struck
the young matron as a singularly deplorable sign of
depression, and she sometimes discussed the matter
with her friends, who had no remedy to suggest.
They were talking one evening at Ody Rafferty's,
and Mrs Quigley had just expressed the opinion
that "poor Peg would be apt to fret herself into the
next world before she was much older, for, bedad,
that was the only place she had a chance of goin'
aisy wid her misfort'nit fut, that had her torminted,"
when Stacey said, " I wish she had e'er a chance of
thravellin' wid herself to Tubberbride, over away
between Sallinbeg and Sallinmore. The cures people
do be gettin' somewhiles at the ould well there is
past belief. Mrs O'Rourke, at our place, was tellin'
me her brother-in-law gave it a thrial last Easter,
and came back a diff'rint man altogether, and he
that disthroyed wid the rheumatiz before he went,
he'd be from this till to-morra creepin' the len'th of
the house-wall. She might exparience a fine benefit
yit, the crathur. There's to be a great Pattern in it,
I hear tell, come Michaelmas; and I'd liefer than
nine ninepennies poor Peg was goin'."

Stacey uttered this aspiration quite aimlessly,
without in the least supposing that it would lead to
anything, let alone to Tubberbride. But a few days
afterwards old Ody Rafferty stopped at her mother's
door in his donkey-cart, and thumped on the bottom
of it with his blackthorn to bring somebody out.
"Well, Stacey, me child," he then said, " I'm after
bein' round Sallinmore ways wid a thrifle of the
stuff, so I made it me business to call in at the

wife's sisther's place, that's livin' widin a short mile of Tubberbride. And it's as plased as anythin' they'll be herself bid me say, if you and Peg 'ud sleep the night wid them, supposing you had e'er a notion of thryin' the Houly Well. Great carryin's on they're to have in it at Michaelmas, she sez, wid the Bishop and all manner. I'll be goin' that way meself agin, about then, and I could be landin' the two of yous over there in the ould cart, as aisy as lightin' me pipe. The jaunt 'ud be good for the crathur, if it was nothin' else; sure she's niver thravelled beyond widin the roar of an ass of this place in all the days of her life. And I'd pick yous up agin next mornin' passin' by."

This expedition seemed so large an undertaking to Stacey, and so wildly adventurous to Peg, that much time was needed for thinking it over, and then one essential point had to be settled before the project could be seriously entertained. "The child would come along wid us, in coorse?" said Stacey. "Me mother 'ud mind him the best way she could, I well know, if I took and left him behind. But sure, then, the other childer might get carryin' him about, or he might set off wid himself crawlin' unbeknownst —a won'erful quick crawl he has; there's many remarks it. Anyway, I'd have the dread on me all the while that he was lyin' dhrownded at the bottom of every houle in the bog. I wouldn't be lavin' him." But Ody answered, "Sure, what 'ud hinder you of takin' it along? A crathur that size might as well be one place as another for any differ it 'ud make."

So it came to pass that on a breezy September

morning Ody Rafferty's very dark - brown donkey drew out of Lisconnel his long, narrow cart containing, among other things, Mrs Stacey, Master Felix, and Miss Peg; four jars of poteen, a basket of bog-berries which Mrs Ody was sending as a present to her sister, and, tied up in a blue-speckled handkerchief, the contents of a select library, from which its owner, somewhat to her friends' regret, had not endured to be parted, even for a day. The twelve-mile journey was an extraordinary experience to Peg, who had never before gone one tithe as far, nor realised how the bog would at last turn into fields and hedges, and crowds of such terrible tall trees, with here and there as many as a dozen little houses clustered together, and two or three "grand big ones with windows on the top of their windows, and they the size of doors, same as in the picture on Mr Corr's paper bags." Ody's slow-pacing beast, and springless cart, whose wheels were not an exact match, made the very most of the deep-rutted road-lengths, which led them through this marvellous landscape; and before she reached her destination untravelled Peg felt as if home lay many ages behind her, across an unknown country.

When they arrived at their journey's end, wonders did not by any means cease, but rather assumed a concentrated form. Their hostess, Mrs Kinsella, lived with an only daughter at the back gate of Sir Francis Denroche's demesne, that used to be a fine place entirely; and though the family's fortune had for some time past fallen into disrepair, the lodge was still what appeared to the girls a spacious and

splendid residence. Stacey was immediately impressed by the convenience of the hearth-fire that
glowed to greet them through polished bars, with
grand wide hobs to be standing your saucepans or
kettles on, and a great little oven at one side that
you could slip a cake of bread or anything into
very handy. For Mrs Dan's cooking had to be
done mainly in a pot hung from a hook dangling
among the smoke, and on the lid inverted to serve
as a makeshift griddle. Peg's attention, on the other
hand, was at once caught by a young woman seated
in the sunset-lit window, working with a needle and
thread, a thing not very commonly done up at
Lisconnel. A rather small slender person she was,
with a clear brunette complexion, and hazel eyes,
and black hair, dressed in such wonderful ways that
at a first glance it might seem doubtful whether all
those frizzes and puffs were the result of extreme ·
untidiness or supreme art. Her dress was of plain
grey linen, with a little bow of rose-coloured ribbon
at the throat, so deftly tied that its loops and ends
looked as precisely in their right places as the
petals of a flower. The Kinsellas spoke of her as
Miss Jacket, explaining that she was the sister of
her ladyship's French maid, and at present their
lodger.

Something about Miss Jacket interested and
attracted Peg from the first; and they became
better acquainted somewhat quickly during the next
few days. For the visit of these pilgrims from
Lisconnel was not to be so brief as they had at the
outset proposed. It appeared that the grand doings

at Saint Bridget's Well would not take place until the following Sunday, and nothing would their hostess hear of but that they should stay over it, Ody Rafferty fetching them home the next evening : " And plenty soon enough," she remarked, hospitably sugaring a moistened crust to propitiate the baby, who was criticising his new surroundings in no friendly spirit.

So Peg had two whole days to pass at the lodge, and spent them mostly *tête-a-tête* with the "furrin" girl, who would not accompany the Kinsellas and Stacey to the Pattern up at the Donoghues, on the ground that walking in such a desert was less supportable than the lace-making, though that might be dull to desolation. "And I must one day finish Julie's flounce," she added. It was a puzzle to Peg how anybody could look as listlessly as Miss Jacket did upon the work of her own hands, when it took such a fascinating shape as the strip of fairy-fine tracery, wherein snowy shadows of leaves and tendrils and blossoms seemed to be twined and tangled in the meshes of an elfin net. As Peg sat intently watching its growth, Miss Jacket thought there was a wistfulness in the admiring gaze.

"You shall yourself attempt it, Meess Pècque," she said, handing her a gossamer-threaded needle.

"Ah, but sure, I could never be makin' a right offer at it at all," Peg protested, taking it cautiously. "Why, the finest spriggin' ever I seen is a joke to it. A spider that was any size 'ud scarce consait he could be workin' wid that terrible thin thread— There, it's broke on me, sure enough."

"You must commence with a grosser number," Miss Jacket said, searching among her reels and bobbins.

"Somethin' coorser might be better," said Peg.

"But certainly, coorser," said Miss Jacket, adopting the correction; "that was what I intended."

Thus Peg began her first lesson in lace-making, at which her sunburnt fingers showed a dexterity which surprised both teacher and pupil. And as Miss Jacket was of a communicative disposition, Peg, although failing often to understand, and still oftener to make herself understood, picked up along with her new stitches sundry facts about her new acquaintance. It seemed evident that Miss Jacket was dissatisfied with her present situation, and thinking home-sickly of her distant native land—a state of feeling which Peg could but too easily imagine. Probably, however, she went widely astray in the details of the picture which she supposed to be occupying the stranger's memory. Her own mind was full of a wide-sweeping brown bogland, with its far-away blue hills, and little fleck of thatches huddling together on the solitude; accordingly, when Miss Jacket said, "Do you not find this Toubèrbride a very sad place?" she replied, "Well, thruth to say, it does seem to me a thrifle gathered-up like, wid all them big trees standin' thick, and them unnathural high walls round about; you can't git a look at anythin'. It's as if one was on'y lettin' on to be steppin' outside. And the power of walkin' an' dhrivin' there does be goin' by on this road has me head moidhered, if I sit in the window."

As the traffic along Tubberbride road scarcely
exceeds on an average a couple of donkey-carts and
half-a-dozen pedestrians in an hour, Peg's complaint
would have much perplexed Miss Jacket had its
purport been intelligible to her, which it was not.

"Ah, but it was pleasant, Meess Pècque," she said,
"in the Rue La Marck. My brother Charles and
I had a great comfort in his little chocolate shop,
before my half-sister, the widow Delande, came with
her two children. They are what you call bozzer-
ing brats, all both of them, particularly Adolphe, a
detested infant—and a glutton, *ma foi!* However,
the end was that we dispute—we quarrel—I give
her impidence, as you say. I abused her much,
but very much," Miss Jacket said, meditatively. "So
my sister Julie, who is with a family here, got for
me a post of lace-teacher at the Convent in Water-
strand. I can make this fine lace to admiration, but
it is tedious. Far more joyfully would I tie up the
packets of *confitures*. Yes, that is a good try at a
bride; you are adroit, Meess Pècque. But the Convent
was horrible, with the poor girls sitting there every
morning in rows on the benches in the whitewashed
class; and as for distraction or diversion—perhaps
one time or two times of a month, some lady comes
to see our samples in the glass-case, and says, *Ooh,
exquisite*, and *Oo-oh, too expensive a price*, and goes away.
Well, my dear, after a while I give very great abuse
to Sister Marie Evangelista, who speaks the French.
So my sister Julie has procured me this lodging
here. But you agree with me that it is *triste*, and
dull inconceivably? And as for a quarrel with

Madame Kinsella, I know but a few of your bad words: and ould baste—a great rogue—a black duffel—divel—how do you say it? But I must not think of such things yet," Miss Jacket said, regretfully, "for my sister Julie might not well be able to pay my expenses on another travel before I have the flounce finished. Then she can afford it easily. This piece is not less than two yards, and that should bring as much as five of your pounds— enough to keep one for half-a-year *ches* Madame Kinsella."

"Glory be to goodness, and would it be worth such a power of money?" Peg said, eyeing the filmy fabric with a little awe added to her admiration.

"Surely," said Miss Jacket, measuring off between two small brown thumbs about half-an-inch of whorls and fronds. "Should not that be too expensive a price for many cups of Madame Kinsella's tay? Bah, when shall I again taste veritable *café*? Do you know, Meess Pècque, I think that on Sunday I shall accompany you to the holy well, and wish a wish for myself of Saint Bridget, and that will be—— But no, that I must not tell, or it will not, they say, come to pass. Yours is, of course, no secret. I hope she will be very complaisant to you about the weak foot. But, without doubt, she will favour you; you are so *dévote*, Meess Pècque, with your book of hymns always at your side," Miss Jacket said, taking up Peg's old tattered song-book, which lay by her on the window-seat.

"It's not hymns, so to spake, accordin' to what I've heard read out of it," said Peg, looking a little mistrustfully at the nimble brown fingers as they turned over the ragged leaves, which she would fain have reserved for her own handling. Her statement was borne out by the fact that the page at which Miss Jacket had opened the volume contained the stanzas beginning—

> At Shamus Flynn's the cruiskeen lawn
> Drinks deep at dusk, tastes drought at dawn,
> For draughts as bright as Delia's glance,
> Or beams that dance from dew-springs drawn.

Yet on the important Sunday this volume, despite its secular contents, was in Peg's hand when Cornelius Dowling's car conveyed her to Saint Bridget's Well. Miss Jacket had insisted upon dressing her hair to such a height of fashion that she was thankful to hide her head beneath the heavy folds of her brown woollen shawl. And at the well she besought the good offices of its Patroness with a fervour which to Miss Jacket, who accompanied her, and duly presented a petition on her own account, seemed a presage of a gracious answer.

Stacey, who had been detained at the lodge by the indisposition of her little Felix, had felt equally sanguine, and was, indeed, somewhat disappointed at first when Peg came limping in no more agile than at setting out. She could only console herself with the expectation that the case would be one of those in which the cure, starting from the time of the pilgrimage, proceeds slowly and surely. However, Stacey's hopes and fears were presently diverted into another channel, for by next morning

the baby seemed so much worse that it was necessary to summon Dr Miller, who pronounced the
ailment to be scarlatina.   Happily, its form was
mild; still, as it involved risks of spreading in-
fection, it had the effect of quartering Mrs Kinsella's
guests upon her for several weeks longer. "And
bedad, now," she said to them at parting, "it's
kindly welcome yous are to anythin' yous got in
it, barrin' the ugly sickness come on the little
crathur; and sure, he's finely betther of that, glory
be to God."

Peg Sheridan used this extension of her visit as
an opportunity for taking more lessons in the
fascinating lace-work. So eagerly, in fact, did she
grasp the chance of learning, that Miss Jacket, who
was at the outset only amused by her enthusiasm,
ended by catching some of it herself, and stitched
away so diligently that Julie's flounce began to
approach completion. She enlivened their industry
with much vivacious chatter, from which Peg, growing accustomed to the queer foreign accent and
phrases, gathered various particulars about the defective qualities of the Widow Delande and her
children. "It seemed an incomprehensible thing
how Charles could suffer the constant ravening of
that pig Adolphe among the assorted caramels and
creams. The loss must be ruinous. However, if
Saint Bridget——"   In the course of these conversations Miss Jacket often narrowly escaped revealing
the purport of her prayer, and a very little curiosity
on the part of her companion would have elicited
it. But it was more to Peg's purpose that she

acquired a thorough grounding in the technique of
the art which had charmed her. So proficient did
she become in the matter of " knots " and " brides,"
and veining and tracing, that before she left the
Kinsellas' her instructress pronounced her work to
be veritably excellent, and thereupon made over
to her a liberal supply of materials, folds of misty
white net, and reels and skeins of gossamer thread.
Peg eyed them somewhat as a greedy reader gloats
over a bundle of new books, and we may doubt that
she gave much heed to her friend, who was pointing
out to her that she could easily get three or four
francs a yard for the narrowest edging. For she
only observed dreamily, reverting fondly to the
strip on which she was putting the last touches to
a tiny spray of bell-flower, " There is a look of the
rael ones on them, but they 've a liker look of some
sort that I never seen yit."

" And, sure, how at all could you tell what that
sort *would* be lookin' like ?" objected Lizzie Kinsella,
whose views inclined to matter-of-fact. But Peg
lacked analytic gifts, and could only reply:

" It 's just the notion I have."

Soon after this, Peg and Stacey and the convalescent Felix turned their faces from Tubberbride
in the slant of mellow October sunbeams, Peg's
latest memory of Miss Jacket being her droll
grimace as she whispered with lifted eyebrows over
Mrs Kinsella's farewell cup of tea, " Oo-ooh, exquisite !" It was not, however, to be a final adieu.
One dapple-grey forenoon, when the air abroad on
the Lisconnel bogland had begun to rumour the

Y

spring, little Mick ran indoors to where Peg sat by the fire entertaining Stacey O'Beirne, and reported that "somebody quare and grand was afther drivin' up on a car, an' axin' where the Sheridans lived." This person proved to be Miss Jacket, who was standing a few yards from their dark cavernous door, looking perplexed and rather frightened, in her smart short cape hooded and lined with grey and scarlet silk, a small furry cap crowning her coils and fringes, and something wound about her neck, not unlike a magnified specimen of the flossy black caterpillars that Peg called woolly bears. Mick might well be amazed.

She explained, when the girls had established her by the hearth, that she was on her way home to the Rue La Marck and her brother's shop, where the obnoxious widow Delande and family interloped no longer. Miss Jacket's clear brown eyes danced as fast as the flame flickers that Peg hospitably stirred up among the embers, as she related the manner of the enemy's rout. "Terribly Charles, my brother, and she, Victorine, quarrelled—just as I beseeched of the good Saint Bridget that day at the well of Toubèrbride. It makes no harm now to tell my request. At about Christmas-time it happened. Nothing would content the detestable infant Adolphe but to devour the most superior *nougats* and *marrons* at three francs the pound, and because the little glutton had lately taken an attack of the influence—you call it? his mother would give him all that he desired. In consequence, my friends, there was a disagreement, and they leave,

and Charles sends for me to come. So you see me
voyaging back, and in passing I call to make my
adieux, and to give you my address, Meess Pècque,
that you may write for more of the net and thread,
should you require it. I have completed my flounce ;
but as for the price of it, my sister Julie cannot
expect to take it all in payment for the tay of
Madame Kinsella. She will rest satisfied with a
portion, and the remainder will be not much for
the renewal of my toilets. How goes it with your
lace-work, Meess Pècque? Ah, ah, you are still
lame of foot, I perceive. Saint Bridget has not
treated you so kindly."

"Bedad, no," Stacey said, mournfully. "Sorra
the hap'orth of good it done her at all. We'd
betther ha' sted at home." Stacey looked back upon
the Tubberbride expedition as a gloomy failure,
blotted with fears about Felix and disappointment
about Peg.

"Well, now, it wasn't, so to spake, her fau't,"
said Peg, who had limped across the uneven floor
with two turf-sods on a capacious shovel. "Truth
to say," she said, leaning on its handle, while their
outer fibres twinkled into golden threads, "that
time at the well there, the ould fut of me was gone
cliver and clean out of me head. Never a word I
thought to be sayin' to her about it whatsome'er.
So how was the crathur to know? But I'll tell you
what I was thinkin' of instead. There's them
couple of books Larry went and left behind for me
the black mornin' he took off out of this to be
gettin' his death away from us all. Many's the

time I would be callin' them ould thrash to him, because I was too ignorant meself to be spellin' them out the way he did. And more's the times ever since I 've been wishin' in me heart I could get to tell him that I wouldn't give them out of me hands, not for the full of them of silver and gould. So then, when we settled we 'd go to Tubberbride, I considhered to meself that I 'd have them along wid me, and it 's showin' them to Herself at the well I 'd be, an' axin' her could she be any manes make a shift to bring him word it was dymints and jewels worth I thought of them, or aught else ever he owned. And that 's what I done right enough; but if I did, I disremimbered everythin' else—and no great matter. So it 's small blame to Saint Bridget. But just the very minyit I was blessin' meself and comin' away, the notion caught a hould of me mind that if I could be conthrivin' some very super-iligant sort of cover for the two ould books, 'twould hinder them of fallin' into laves the way they was, and maybe—it *might* maybe—somehow show Larry that 'tis the great store intirely I 'm settin' be them, let alone callin' them thrash. And Miss Jacket's work was the purtiest thing ever I seen, and thinkin' it 'ud look delightful on them was the raison encouraged me to be larnin' it. 'Deed now, workin' at it I 've been all the winther, and makin' a botch more betoken of half me pieces of net, until I had the pattron right. It 's on'y the other day I got the girls to bring me up a grand bit of stuff from Mr Corr's—— But sure, I 'll fetch them out to yous."

Peg crossed the room to a commodious wall-cranny, and came triumphantly hobbling back, bearing her library, which was indeed gloriously transformed. For the stained and tattered pages were now clad in ample bindings of glowing scarlet, all frosted over with the most delicate white embroideries. " There's two folds of the glazy calico underneath the red flannen, for to stiffen it a bit," she explained, with pride, lifting each cover separately to show how the lace extended to the inner side.

" They're rael sumpchus," said Mrs Stacey. " I do declare you might think you had them rowled up in the end of Canon O'Hanlon's grandest vestments."

" And sorra a taste too good for them if they was," quoth Peg.

" The quantity of lace on them," Miss Jacket said, measuring off fingers on one of the covers, " would trim three fifty-franc *mouchoirs*; I could sell it for you without difficulty in Paris. You are extravagant, Meess Pècque."

" I'm thinkin' I'll make them another couple for fear of anythin' happenin' these ones," Peg said, smoothing out the creased margins of the song-book. " It's grand work, and I'd liefer be at it than not. On'y I do be wishin'," she added, half to herself, as she carried back her treasures to their hole in the wall,—" wishin' I do be that I was anyway sartin Larry knew a mortal thing about them these times at all. But it's just a chance; and sure, I'm thankful for that same to Saint Bridget, or whoever of Them it was put it into me head."

Thus, it appears that the library of Lisconnel can

hardly be termed extensive. A complete descriptive catalogue of it would run as follows :—

Ivanhoe, by Sir Walter Scott. Very cheap edition. London : Smith & Wilson ; no date.

A Song-book ; title-page and index missing.

But since Peg's visit to Tubberbride, it may at least be fairly described as unique in the matter of its bindings.

W. H. WHITE AND CO. LTD., RIVERSIDE PRESS, EDINBURGH.

A CATALOGUE OF BOOKS AND ANNOUNCEMENTS OF METHUEN AND COMPANY PUBLISHERS : LONDON 36 ESSEX STREET W.C.

CONTENTS

SEPTEMBER 1899

MESSRS. METHUEN'S
ANNOUNCEMENTS

---•◆•---

Travel and Adventure

THE HIGHEST ANDES. By E. A. FitzGerald. With 40 Illustrations, 10 of which are Photogravures, and a Large Map. *Royal 8vo.* 30s. *net.*

Also, a Small Edition on Handmade Paper, limited to 50 Copies, *4to.* £5, 5s.

A narrative of the highest climb yet accomplished. The illustrations have been reproduced with the greatest care, and the book, in addition to its adventurous interest, contains appendices of great scientific value. It also contains a very elaborate map, and a panorama.

THROUGH ASIA. By Sven Hedin. With 300 Illustrations from Photographs and Sketches by the Author, and 3 Maps. Second and cheaper Edition in 16 Fortnightly Parts at 1s. each net; or in two volumes. *Royal 8vo.* 20s. *net.*

Extracts from reviews of this great book, which *The Times* has called 'one of the best books of the century,' will be found on p. 15. The present form of issue places it within the reach of buyers of moderate means.

THE CAROLINE ISLANDS By F. W. Christian. With many Illustrations and Maps. *Large crown 8vo.* 12s. 6d. *net.*

This book contains a history and complete description of these islands—their physical features, fauna, flora; the habits, and religious beliefs of the inhabitants. It is the result of many years' residence among the natives, and is the only worthy work on the subject.

THREE YEARS IN SAVAGE AFRICA. By Lionel Decle. With 100 Illustrations and 5 Maps. Cheaper Edition. *Demy 8vo.* 10s. 6d. *net.*

A NEW RIDE TO KHIVA. By R. L. Jefferson. Illustrated. *Crown 8vo.* 6s.

The account of an adventurous ride on a bicycle through Russia and the deserts of Asia to Khiva.

Poetry
PRESENTATION EDITIONS

BARRACK-ROOM BALLADS. By Rudyard Kipling. *55th Thousand. Crown 8vo. Leather, gilt top,* 6s. *net.*

THE SEVEN SEAS. By Rudyard Kipling. *47th Thousand. Crown 8vo. Leather, gilt top,* 6s. *net.*

ENGLISH LYRICS. Selected and arranged by W. E.
HENLEY. Second and cheaper Edition. *Fcp. 8vo*, 2s. 6d. *Leather*,
3s. 6d. *net*.

LYRA FRIVOLA. By A. D. GODLEY, M.A., Fellow of Magdalen College, Oxford. *Pott 8vo.* 2s. 6d.

A little volume of occasional verse, chiefly academic.

The Works of Shakespeare.

General Editor, EDWARD DOWDEN, Litt. D.

MESSRS. METHUEN have in preparation an Edition of Shakespeare in
single Plays. Each play will be edited with a full Introduction, Textual
Notes, and a Commentary at the foot of the page.

The first volume will be :

HAMLET. Edited by EDWARD DOWDEN. *Demy 8vo.* 3s. 6d.

History and Biography

THE LETTERS OF ROBERT LOUIS STEVENSON.
Arranged and Edited with Notes by SIDNEY COLVIN. *Demy 8vo.*
2 vols. 25s. *net*.

These highly important and interesting volumes contain the correspondence of
Robert Louis Stevenson from his eighteenth year to almost the last day of his life,
selected and edited, with notes and introductions, by Mr. Sidney Colvin, his most
intimate friend. The letters are very various in subject and character, being
addressed partly to his family and private friends, and partly to such well known
living or lately deceased men of letters as Mr. Hamerton, Mr. J. A. Symonds,
Mr Henry James, Mr. James Payn, Dr. Conan Doyle, Mr. J. M. Barrie, Mr.
Edmund Gosse, Mr. F. Locker-Lampson, Mr. Cosmo Monkhouse, Mr. Andrew
Lang, Mr. W. E. Henley, and the Editor himself. They present a vivid and
brilliant autobiographical picture of the mind and character of the distinguished
author. It was originally intended that a separate volume containing a full
narrative and critical Life by the Editor should appear simultaneously with the
letters, and form part of the work: but the publication of this has for various
reasons been postponed.

THE LIFE AND LETTERS OF SIR JOHN EVERETT
MILLAIS, President of the Royal Academy. By his Son, J. G.
MILLAIS. With nearly 300 Illustrations, of which 9 are in photo-
gravure. *Two volumes. Royal 8vo.* 32s. *net*.

An edition limited to 350 copies will also be printed. This will
contain 22 of Millais' great paintings reproduced in photogravure,
with a case containing an extra set of these Photogravures pulled on
India paper. The price of this edition will be £4, 4s. *net*.

In these two magnificent volumes is contained the authoritative biography of the
most distinguished and popular painter of the last half of the century. They
contain the story of his extraordinary boyhood, of his early struggles and
triumphs, of the founding of the Pre-Raphaelite Brotherhood, now first given to
the world in authentic detail, of the painting of most of his famous pictures, of his
friendships with many of the most distinguished men of the day in art, letters,
and politics, of his home life, and of his sporting tastes. There are a large

number of letters to his wife describing the circumstances under which his pictures were painted, letters from Her Majesty the Queen, Lord Beaconsfield, Mr. Gladstone, Mr. Watts, Sir William Harcourt, Lord Rosebery, Lord Leighton, etc., etc. Among them are several illustrated letters from Landseer, Leech, Du Maurier, and Mike Halliday. The last letter that Lord Beaconsfield wrote before his death is reproduced in fac-simile. Mr. Val Prinsep contributes his reminiscences of Millais in a long and most interesting chapter.

Not the least attractive and remarkable feature of this book will be the magnificence of its illustrations. No more complete representation of the art of any painter has ever been produced on the same scale. The owners of Sir John Millais' most famous pictures and their copyrights have generously given their consent to their reproduction in his biography, and, in addition to those pictures with which the public is familiar, over two hundred pictures and sketches which have never been reproduced before, and which, in all probability, will never be seen again by the general public, will appear in these pages. The early chapters contain sketches made by Millais at the age of seven. There follow some exquisite drawings made by him during his Pre-Raphaelite period, a large number of sketches and studies made for his great pictures, water colour sketches, pen-and-ink sketches, and drawings, humorous and serious. There are ten portraits of Millais himself, including two by Mr. Watts and Sir Edward Burne Jones. There is a portrait of Dickens, taken after death, and a sketch of D. G. Rossetti. Thus the book will be not only a biography of high interest and an important contribution to the history of English art, but in the best sense of the word, a beautiful picture book.

THE EXPANSION OF EGYPT. A Political and Historical Survey. By A. SILVA WHITE. With four Special Maps. *Demy 8vo.* 15s. *net.*

This is an account of the political situation in Egypt, and an elaborate description of the Anglo-Egyptian Administration. It is a comprehensive treatment of the whole Egyptian problem by one who has studied every detail on the spot.

THE VICAR OF MORWENSTOW. A Biography. By S. BARING GOULD, M.A. A new and revised Edition. With Portrait. *Crown 8vo.* 3s. 6d.

This is a completely new edition of the well known biography of R. S. Hawker.

A CONSTITUTIONAL AND POLITICAL HISTORY OF ROME. By T. M. TAYLOR, M.A., Fellow of Gonville and Caius College, Cambridge, Senior Chancellor's Medallist for Classics, Porson University Scholar, etc., etc. *Crown 8vo.* 7s. 6d.

An account of the origin and growth of the Roman Institutions, and a discussion of the various political movements in Rome from the earliest times to the death of Augustus.

A HISTORY OF THE CHURCH OF CYPRUS. By JOHN HACKETT, M.A. With Maps and Illustrations. *Demy 8vo.* 12s. 6d. *net.*

A work which brings together all that is known on the subject from the introduction of Christianity to the commencement of the British occupation. A separate division deals with the local Latin Church during the period of the Western Supremacy.

BISHOP LATIMER. By A. J. CARLYLE, M.A. *Crown 8vo.* 3s. 6d.   [*Leaders of Religion Series.*

Theology

CHRISTIAN MYSTICISM. The Bampton Lectures for 1899. By W. R. INGE, M.A., Fellow and Tutor of Hertford College, Oxford. *Demy 8vo.* 12s. 6d. *net.*

A complete survey of the subject from St. John and St. Paul to modern times, covering the Christian Platonists, Augustine, the Devotional Mystics, the Mediæval Mystics, and the Nature Mystics and Symbolists, including Böhme and Wordsworth.

AN INTRODUCTION TO THE BOOKS OF THE BIBLE. By W. H. BENNETT, M.A., and W. F. ADENEY, M.A. *Crown 8vo.* 7s. 6d.

This volume furnishes students with the latest results in biblical criticism, arranged methodically. Each book is treated separately as to date, authorship, etc.

ST. PAUL, THE MASTER-BUILDER. By WALTER LOCK, D.D., Warden of Keble College. *Crown 8vo.* 3s. 6d.

An attempt to popularise the :ecent additions to our knowledge of St. Paul as a missionary, a statesman and an ethical teacher.

SUNDAY SCHOOL TEACHING. 6d. *net.*

The Churchman's Bible.

General Editor, J. H. BURN, B.D., Examining Chaplain to the Bishop of Aberdeen.

Messrs. METHUEN propose to issue a series of expositions upon most of the books of the Bible. The volumes will be practical and devotional rather than critical in their purpose, and the text of the authorised version will be explained in sections or paragraphs, which will correspond as far as possible with the divisions of the Church Lectionary.

The volumes will be produced in a very handy and tasteful form, and may be obtained in cloth or leather bindings.

The first volumes will be :

THE EPISTLE OF ST. PAUL TO THE GALATIANS. Explained by A. W. ROBINSON, B.D., Vicar of All Hallows, Barking. *Fcap. 8vo.* 1s. 6d. *net. Leather,* 2s. 6d. *net.*

ECCLESIASTES. Explained by W. A. STREANE, M.A. *Fcp. 8vo.* 1s. 6d. *net. Leather,* 2s. 6d. *net.*

The Churchman's Library.

Edited by J. H. BURN, B.D.

THE ENGLISH PRAYER BOOK : Its Literary Workmanship. By J. DOWDEN, D.D., Lord Bishop of Edinburgh. *Crown 8vo.* 3s. 6d.

This volume, avoiding questions of controversy, exhibits the liturgical aims and literary methods of the authors of the Prayer Book.

The Library of Devotion.

Pott 8vo.   Cloth 2s.; leather 2s. 6d. net.

NEW VOLUMES.

A SERIOUS CALL TO A DEVOUT AND HOLY LIFE. By WILLIAM LAW. Edited, with an Introduction by C. BIGG, D.D., late Student of Christ Church.

This is a reprint, word for word and line for line, of the *Editio Princeps*.

THE TEMPLE. By GEORGE HERBERT. Edited, with an Introduction and Notes, by E. C. S. GIBSON, D.D., Vicar of Leeds.

This edition contains Walton's Life of Herbert, and the text is that of the first edition.

Science.

THE SCIENTIFIC STUDY OF SCENERY. By J. E. MARR, Fellow of St John's College, Cambridge. Illustrated. *Crown 8vo.* 6s.

An elementary treatise on geomorphology—the study of the earth's outward forms. It is for the use of students of physical geography and geology, and will also be highly interesting to the general reader.

A HANDBOOK OF NURSING. By M. N. OXFORD, of Guy's Hospital. *Crown 8vo.* 3s. 6d.

This is a complete guide to the science and art of nursing, containing copious instruction both general and particular.

Classical.

THE NICOMACHEAN ETHICS OF ARISTOTLE. Edited, with an Introduction and Notes by JOHN BURNET, M.A., Professor of Greek at St. Andrews. *Demy 8vo.* 15s. net.

This edition contains parallel passages from the Eudemian Ethics, printed under the text, and there is a full commentary, the main object of which is to interpret difficulties in the light of Aristotle's own rules.

THE CAPTIVI OF PLAUTUS. Edited, with an Introduction, Textual Notes, and a Commentary, by W. M. LINDSAY, Fellow of Jesus College, Oxford. *Demy 8vo.* 10s. 6d. net.

For this edition all the important MSS. have been re-collated. An appendix deals with the accentual element in early Latin verse. The Commentary is very full.

ZACHARIAH OF MITYLENE. Translated into English by F. J. HAMILTON, D.D., and E. W. BROOKS. *Demy 8vo.* 12s. 6d. net.   [*Byzantine Texts.*

Sport.

The Library of Sport.

THE ART AND PRACTICE OF HAWKING. By E. B. MITCHELL. Illustrated by G. E. LODGE and others. *Demy 8vo.* 10s. 6d.

A complete description of the Hawks, Falcons, and Eagles used in ancient and modern times, with directions for their training and treatment. It is not only a historical account, but a complete practical guide.

THOUGHTS ON HUNTING. By PETER BECKFORD. Edited by J. OTHO PAGET, and Illustrated by G. H. JALLAND. *Demy 8vo.* 10s. 6d.

This edition of one of the most famous classics of sport contains an introduction and many footnotes by Mr. Paget, and is thus brought up to the standard of modern knowledge.

General Literature.

THE BOOK OF THE WEST. By S. BARING GOULD. With numerous Illustrations. *Two volumes.* Vol. I. Devon. Vol. II. Cornwall. *Crown 8vo.* 6s. each.

A description of the counties of Devon and Cornwall, in which the scenery, folk-lore, history, and antiquities of the two counties are treated with full knowledge and high interest.

PONS ASINORUM; OR, A GUIDE TO BRIDGE. By A. HULME BEAMAN. *Fcap. 8vo.* 2s.

A practical guide, with many specimen games, to the new game of Bridge.

The Little Guides.

Pott 8vo, cloth 3s. ; leather, 3s. 6d. net.

NEW VOLUME.

SHAKESPEARE'S COUNTRY. By B. C. WINDLE, F.R.S., M.A. Illustrated by E. H. NEW.

Uniform with Mr. Wells' 'Oxford' and Mr. Thomson's 'Cambridge.'

Methuen's Standard Library.

THE DECLINE AND FALL OF THE ROMAN EMPIRE. By EDWARD GIBBON. Edited by J. B. BURY, LL.D., Fellow of Trinity College, Dublin. *In Seven Volumes. Demy 8vo, gilt top.* 8s. 6d. each. *Crown 8vo.* 6s. each. *Vol. VII.*

The concluding Volume of this Edition.

THE DIARY OF THOMAS ELLWOOD. Edited by G. C. CRUMP, M.A. *Crown 8vo.* 6s.

This edition is the only one which contains the complete book as originally published. It contains a long introduction and many footnotes.

LA COMMEDIA DI DANTE ALIGHIERI. Edited by
PAGET TOYNBEE, M.A. *Crown 8vo.* 6s.

This edition of the Italian text of the Divine Comedy, founded on Witte's minor
edition, carefully revised, is issued in commemoration of the sixth century of
Dante's journey through the three kingdoms of the other world.

Illustrated and Gift Books.

THE LIVELY CITY OF LIGG. By GELLETT BURGESS.
With many Illustrations by the Author. *Small 4to.* 3s. 6d.

THE PHIL MAY ALBUM. *4to.* 7s. 6d. net.

This highly interesting volume contains 100 drawings by Mr. Phil May, and is
representative of his earliest and finest work.

ULYSSES ; OR, DE ROUGEMONT OF TROY. Described
and depicted by A. H. MILNE. *Small quarto.* 3s. 6d.

The adventures of Ulysses, told in humorous verse and pictures.

THE CROCK OF GOLD. Fairy Stories told by S. BARING
GOULD, and Illustrated by F. D. BEDFORD. *Crown 8vo.* 6s.

TOMMY SMITH'S ANIMALS. By EDMUND SELOUS.
Illustrated by G. W. ORD. *Fcp. 8vo.* 2s. 6d.

A little book designed to teach children respect and reverence for animals.

A BIRTHDAY BOOK. With a Photogravure Frontispiece.
Demy 8vo. 10s. 6d.

This is a birthday-book of exceptional dignity, and the extracts have been chosen
with particular care.
The three passages for each day bear a certain relation to each other, and form a
repertory of sententious wisdom from the best authors living or dead.

Educational.

PRACTICAL PHYSICS. By H. STROUD, D. Sc., M.A., Professor of Physics in the Durham College of Science, Newcastle-on-
Tyne. Fully illustrated. *Crown 8vo.* 3s. 6d.
                                    [*Handbooks of Technology.*

GENERAL ELEMENTARY SCIENCE. By J. T. DUNN,
D.Sc., and V. A. MUNDELLA. With many Illustrations. *Crown 8vo.*
3s. 6d.   [*Methuen's Science Primers.*

THE METRIC SYSTEM. By LEON DELBOS. *Crown 8vo.* 2s.

A theoretical and practical guide, for use in elementary schools and by the general reader.

A SOUTH AFRICAN ARITHMETIC. By HENRY HILL, B.A., Assistant Master at Worcester School, Cape Colony. *Crown 8vo.* 3s. 6d.

This book has been specially written for use in South African schools.

A KEY TO STEDMAN'S EASY LATIN EXERCISES. By C. G. BOTTING, M.A. *Crown 8vo.* 3s. net.

NEW TESTAMENT GREEK. A Course for Beginners. By G. RODWELL, B.A. With a Preface by WALTER LOCK, D.D., Warden of Keble College. *Crown 8vo.* 3s. 6d.

EXAMINATION PAPERS IN ENGLISH HISTORY. By J. TAIT WARDLAW, B.A., King's College, Cambridge. *Crown 8vo.* 2s. 6d. [*School Examination Series.*

A GREEK ANTHOLOGY. Selected by E. C. MARCHANT, M.A., Fellow of Peterhouse, Cambridge, and Assistant Master at St. Paul's School. *Crown 8vo.* 3s. 6d.

CICERO DE OFFICIIS. Translated by G. B. GARDINER, M.A. *Crown 8vo.* 2s. 6d. [*Classical Translations.*

The Novels of Charles Dickens.

Crown 8vo. Each Volume, cloth 3s., leather 4s. net.

Messrs. METHUEN have in preparation an edition of those novels of Charles Dickens which have now passed out of copyright. Mr. George Gissing, whose critical study of Dickens is both sympathetic and acute, has written an Introduction to each of the books, and a very attractive feature of this edition will be the illustrations of the old houses, inns, and buildings, which Dickens described, and which have now in many instances disappeared under the touch of modern civilisation. Another valuable feature will be a series of topographical and general notes to each book by Mr. F. G. Kitton. The books will be produced with the greatest care as to printing, paper and binding.

The first volumes will be :

THE PICKWICK PAPERS. With Illustrations by E. H. NEW. *Two Volumes.*

NICHOLAS NICKLEBY. With Illustrations by R. J. WILLIAMS. *Two Volumes.*

BLEAK HOUSE. With Illustrations by BEATRICE ALCOCK. *Two Volumes.*

OLIVER TWIST. With Illustrations by E. H. NEW. *Two Volumes.*

The Little Library.

Pott 8vo.   Each Volume, cloth 1s. 6d. net. ; leather 2s. 6d. net.

Messrs. METHUEN intend to produce a series of small books under the above title, containing some of the famous books in English and other literatures, in the domains of fiction, poetry, and belles lettres.   The series will also contain several volumes of selections in prose and verse.

The books will be edited with the most sympathetic and scholarly care. Each one will contain an Introduction which will give (1) a short biography of the author, (2) a critical estimate of the book.   Where they are neces- sary, short notes will be added at the foot of the page.

The Little Library will ultimately contain complete sets of the novels of W. M. Thackeray, Jane Austen, the sisters Brontë, Mrs. Gaskell and others.   It will also contain the best work of many other novelists whose names are household words.

Each book will have a portrait or frontispiece in photogravure, and the volumes will be produced with great care in a style uniform with that of ' The Library of Devotion.'

The first volumes will be :

A LITTLE BOOK OF ENGLISH LYRICS.   With Notes.

PRIDE AND PREJUDICE.   By JANE AUSTEN.   With an Introduction and Notes by E. V. LUCAS.   *Two Volumes.*

VANITY FAIR.   By W. M. THACKERAY.   With an Introduction by S. GWYNN.   *Three Volumes.*

PENDENNIS.   By W. M. THACKERAY.   With an Introduction by S. GWYNN.   *Three volumes.*

EOTHEN.   By A. W. KINGLAKE.   With an Introduction and Notes.

CRANFORD.   By Mrs. GASKELL.   With an Introduction and Notes by E. V. LUCAS.

THE INFERNO OF DANTE.   Translated by H. F. CARY. With an Introduction and Notes by PAGET TOYNBEE.

JOHN HALIFAX, GENTLEMAN.   By MRS. CRAIK.   With an Introduction by ANNIE MATHESON.   *Two volumes.*

THE EARLY POEMS OF ALFRED, LORD TENNYSON. Edited by J. C. COLLINS, M.A.

THE PRINCESS.   By ALFRED, LORD TENNYSON.   Edited by ELIZABETH WORDSWORTH.

MAUD, AND OTHER POEMS. By ALFRED, LORD TENNYSON. Edited by ELIZABETH WORDSWORTH.

IN MEMORIAM. By ALFRED, LORD TENNYSON. Edited by H. C. BEECHING, M.A.

A LITTLE BOOK OF SCOTTISH LYRICS. Arranged and Edited by T. F. HENDERSON.

Fiction

THE KING'S MIRROR. By ANTHONY HOPE. *Crown 8vo. 6s.*

THE CROWN OF LIFE. By GEORGE GISSING, Author of 'Demos,' 'The Town Traveller,' etc. *Crown 8vo. 6s.*

A NEW VOLUME OF WAR STORIES. By STEPHEN CRANE, Author of 'The Red Badge of Courage.' *Crown 8vo. 6s.*

THE STRONG ARM. By ROBERT BARR. *Crown 8vo. 6s.*

TO LONDON TOWN. By ARTHUR MORRISON, Author of 'Tales of Mean Streets,' 'A Child of the Jago,' etc. *Crown 8vo. 6s.*

ONE HOUR AND THE NEXT. By THE DUCHESS OF SUTHERLAND. *Crown 8vo. 6s.*

SIREN CITY. By BENJAMIN SWIFT, Author of 'Nancy Noon.' *Crown 8vo. 6s.*

VENGEANCE IS MINE. By ANDREW BALFOUR, Author of 'By Stroke of Sword.' Illustrated. *Crown 8vo. 6s.*

PRINCE RUPERT THE BUCCANEER. By C. J. CUTCLIFFE HYNE, Author of 'Captain Kettle,' etc. *Crown 8vo. 6s.*

PABO THE PRIEST. By S. BARING GOULD, Author of 'Mehalah,' etc. *Crown 8vo. 6s.*

GILES INGILBY. By W. E. NORRIS. Illustrated. *Crown 8vo. 6s.*

THE PATH OF A STAR. By SARA JEANETTE DUNCAN, Author of 'A Voyage of Consolation.' Illustrated. *Crown 8vo. 6s.*

THE HUMAN BOY. By EDEN PHILPOTTS, Author of 'Children of the Mist.' With a Frontispiece. *Crown 8vo. 6s.*
   A series of English schoolboy stories, the result of keen observation, and of a most engaging wit.

THE HUMAN INTEREST. By VIOLET HUNT, Author of 'A Hard Woman,' etc. *Crown 8vo. 6s.*

AN ENGLISHMAN. By MARY L. PENDERED. *Crown 8vo.* 6s.

A GENTLEMAN PLAYER. By R. N. STEPHENS, Author of 'An Enemy to the King.' *Crown 8vo.* 6s.

DANIEL WHYTE. By A. J. DAWSON, Author of 'Bismillah.' *Crown 8vo.* 6s.

A New Edition of the Novels of Marie Corelli.

This New Edition is in a more convenient form than the Library Edition, and is issued in a new and specially designed cover.

In Crown 8vo, Cloth, 6s.   *Leather,* 6s. *net.*

A ROMANCE OF TWO WORLDS.
VENDETTA.
THELMA.
ARDATH : THE STORY OF A DEAD SELF.

THE SOUL OF LILITH.
WORMWOOD.
BARABBAS : A DREAM OF THE WORLD'S TRAGEDY.
THE SORROWS OF SATAN.

The Novelist.

MESSRS. METHUEN are making an interesting experiment which constitutes a fresh departure in publishing. They are issuing under the above general title a Monthly Series of New Fiction by popular authors at the price of Sixpence. Each Number is as long as the average Six Shilling Novel. The first numbers of 'THE NOVELIST' are as follows :—

I. DEAD MEN TELL NO TALES.   E. W. HORNUNG.
[*Ready.*

II. JENNIE BAXTER, JOURNALIST.   ROBERT BARR.
[*Ready.*

III. THE INCA'S TREASURE.   ERNEST GLANVILLE.
[*Ready.*

IV. A SON OF THE STATE.   W. PETT RIDGE.
[*Ready.*

V. FURZE BLOOM.   S. BARING GOULD.
[*September.*

VI. BUNTER'S CRUISE.   C. GLEIG.
[*October.*

VII.
[*November.*

VIII. A NEW NOVEL.   MRS. MEADE.
[*December.*

A CATALOGUE OF
MESSRS. METHUEN'S
PUBLICATIONS

Poetry

Rudyard Kipling. BARRACK-ROOM BALLADS. By RUDYARD KIPLING. *55th Thousand. Crown 8vo. 6s.*

'Mr. Kipling's verse is strong, vivid, full of character. . . . Unmistakeable genius rings in every line.'—*Times.*

'The ballads teem with imagination, they palpitate with emotion. We read them with laughter and tears; the metres throb in our pulses, the cunningly ordered words tingle with life; and if this be not poetry, what is?'—*Pall Mall Gazette.*

Rudyard Kipling. THE SEVEN SEAS. By RUDYARD KIPLING. *47th Thousand. Cr. 8vo. Buckram, gilt top. 6s.*

'The new poems of Mr. Rudyard Kipling have all the spirit and swing of their predecessors. Patriotism is the solid concrete foundation on which Mr. Kipling has built the whole of his work.'—*Times.*

'The Empire has found a singer; it is no depreciation of the songs to say that statesmen may have, one way or other, to take account of them.'—*Manchester Guardian.*

'Animated through and through with indubitable genius.'—*Daily Telegraph.*

"Q." POEMS AND BALLADS. By "Q." *Crown 8vo. 3s. 6d.*

'This work has just the faint, ineffable touch and glow that make poetry.'—*Speaker.*

"Q." GREEN BAYS: Verses and Parodies. By "Q." *Second Edition. Crown 8vo. 3s. 6d.*

E. Mackay. A SONG OF THE SEA. By ERIC MACKAY. *Second Edition. Fcap. 8vo. 5s.*

'Everywhere Mr. Mackay displays himself the master of a style marked by all the characteristics of the best rhetoric.'—*Globe.*

H. Ibsen. BRAND. A Drama by HENRIK IBSEN. Translated by WILLIAM WILSON. *Third Edition. Crown 8vo. 3s. 6d.*

'The greatest world-poem of the nineteenth century next to "Faust." It is in the same set with "Agamemnon," with "Lear," with the literature that we now instinctively regard as high and holy.'—*Daily Chronicle.*

"A. G." VERSES TO ORDER. By "A. G." *Crown 8vo. 2s. 6d. net.*

'A capital specimen of light academic poetry.'—*St. James's Gazette.*

James Williams. VENTURES IN VERSE. By JAMES WILLIAMS, Fellow of Lincoln College, Oxford. *Crown 8vo. 3s. 6d.*

'In matter and manner the book is admirable.'—*Glasgow Herald.*

J. G. Cordery. THE ODYSSEY OF HOMER. A Translation by J. G. CORDERY. *Crown 8vo. 7s. 6d.*

'A spirited, accurate, and scholarly piece of work.'—*Glasgow Herald.*

Belles Lettres, Anthologies, etc.

R. L. Stevenson. VAILIMA LETTERS. By ROBERT LOUIS STEVENSON. With an Etched Portrait by WILLIAM STRANG. *Second Edition. Crown 8vo. Buckram.* 6s.

'A fascinating book.'—*Standard.*
'Full of charm and brightness.'—*Spectator.*
'A gift almost priceless.'—*Speaker.*
'Unique in Literature.'—*Daily Chronicle.*

G. Wyndham. THE POEMS OF WILLIAM SHAKESPEARE. Edited with an Introduction and Notes by GEORGE WYNDHAM, M.P. *Demy 8vo. Buckram, gilt top.* 10s. 6d.

This edition contains the 'Venus,' 'Lucrece,' and Sonnets, and is prefaced with an elaborate introduction of over 140 pp.
'One of the most serious contributions to Shakespearian criticism that have been published for some time.'—*Times.*
'We have no hesitation in describing Mr. George Wyndham's introduction as a masterly piece of criticism, and all who love our Elizabethan literature will find a very garden of delight in it.'—*Spectator.*
'Mr. Wyndham's notes are admirable, even indispensable.'—*Westminster Gazette.*

W. E. Henley. ENGLISH LYRICS. Selected and Edited by W. E. HENLEY. *Crown 8vo. Buckram, gilt top.* 6s.

'It is a body of choice and lovely poetry. — *Birmingham Gazette.*

Henley and Whibley. A BOOK OF ENGLISH PROSE. Collected by W. E. HENLEY and CHARLES WHIBLEY. *Crown 8vo. Buckram, gilt top.* 6s.

'Quite delightful. A greater treat for those not well acquainted with pre-Restoration prose could not be imagined.'—*Athenæum.*

H. C. Beeching. LYRA SACRA: An Anthology of Sacred Verse. Edited by H. C. BEECHING, M.A. *Crown 8vo. Buckram.* 6s.

'A charming selection, which maintains a lofty standard of excellence.'—*Times.*

"Q." THE GOLDEN POMP. A Procession of English Lyrics. Arranged by A. T. QUILLER COUCH. *Crown 8vo. Buckram.* 6s.

'A delightful volume: a really golden "Pomp."'—*Spectator.*

W. B. Yeats. AN ANTHOLOGY OF IRISH VERSE. Edited by W. B. YEATS. *Crown 8vo.* 3s. 6d.

'An attractive and catholic selection. — *Times.*

G. W. Steevens. MONOLOGUES OF THE DEAD. By G. W. STEEVENS. *Foolscap 8vo.* 3s. 6d.

'The effect is sometimes splendid, sometimes bizarre, but always amazingly clever.'—*Pall Mall Gazette.*

W. M. Dixon. A PRIMER OF TENNYSON. By W. M. DIXON, M.A. *Cr. 8vo.* 2s. 6d.

'Much sound and well-expressed criticism. The bibliography is a boon.'—*Speaker.*

W. A. Craigie. A PRIMER OF BURNS. By W. A. CRAIGIE. *Crown 8vo.* 2s. 6d.

'A valuable addition to the literature of the poet.'—*Times.*

L. Magnus. A PRIMER OF WORDSWORTH. By LAURIE MAGNUS. *Crown 8vo.* 2s. 6d.

'A valuable contribution to Wordsworthian literature.'—*Literature.*

Sterne. THE LIFE AND OPINIONS OF TRISTRAM SHANDY. By LAWRENCE STERNE. With an Introduction by CHARLES WHIBLEY, and a Portrait. 2 vols. 7s.

'Very dainty volumes are these: the paper, type, and light-green binding are all very agreeable to the eye.'—*Globe.*

Congreve. THE COMEDIES OF WILLIAM CONGREVE. With an Introduction by G. S. STREET, and a Portrait. 2 vols. 7s.

Morier. THE ADVENTURES OF HAJJI BABA OF ISPAHAN. By JAMES MORIER. With an Introduction by E. G. BROWNE, M.A., and a Portrait. 2 vols. 7s.

Walton. THE LIVES OF DONNE, WOTTON, HOOKER, HERBERT AND SANDERSON. By IZAAK WALTON. With an Introduction by VERNON BLACKBURN, and a Portrait. 3s. 6d.

Johnson. THE LIVES OF THE ENGLISH POETS. By SAMUEL JOHNSON, LL.D. With an Introduction by J. H. MILLAR, and a Portrait. 3 vols. 10s. 6d.

Burns. THE POEMS OF ROBERT BURNS. Edited by ANDREW LANG and W. A. CRAIGIE. With Portrait. *Second Edition. Demy 8vo, gilt top.* 6s.

This edition contains a carefully collated Text, numerous Notes, critical and textual, a critical and biographical Introduction, and a Glossary.

'Among editions in one volume, this will take the place of authority.'—*Times.*

F. Langbridge. BALLADS OF THE BRAVE; Poems of Chivalry, Enterprise, Courage, and Constancy. Edited by Rev. F. LANGBRIDGE. *Second Edition. Cr. 8vo. 3s. 6d. School Edition. 2s. 6d.*

'A very happy conception happily carried out. These "Ballads of the Brave" are intended to suit the real tastes of boys, and will suit the taste of the great majority.'—*Spectator.*

'The book is full of splendid things.'—*World.*

Illustrated Books

John Bunyan. THE PILGRIM'S PROGRESS. By JOHN BUNYAN. Edited, with an Introduction, by C. H. FIRTH, M.A. With 39 Illustrations by R. ANNING BELL. *Crown 8vo. 6s.* This book contains a long Introduction by Mr. Firth, whose knowledge of the period is unrivalled; and it is lavishly illustrated.

'The best "Pilgrim's Progress."'—*Educational Times.*

F. D. Bedford. NURSERY RHYMES. With many Coloured Pictures by F. D. BEDFORD. *Super Royal 8vo. 5s.*

'An excellent selection of the best known rhymes, with beautifully coloured pictures exquisitely printed.'—*Pall Mall Gazette.*

S. Baring Gould. A BOOK OF FAIRY TALES retold by S. BARING GOULD. With numerous Illustrations and Initial Letters by ARTHUR J. GASKIN. *Second Edition. Cr. 8vo. Buckram. 6s.*

'Mr. Baring Gould is deserving of gratitude, in re-writing in simple style the old stories that delighted our fathers and grandfathers.'—*Saturday Review.*

S. Baring Gould. OLD ENGLISH FAIRY TALES. Collected and edited by S. BARING GOULD. With Numerous Illustrations by F. D. BEDFORD. *Second Edition. Cr. 8vo. Buckram. 6s.*

'A charming volume.'—*Guardian.*

S. Baring Gould. A BOOK OF NURSERY SONGS AND RHYMES. Edited by S. BARING GOULD, and Illustrated by the Birmingham Art School. *Buckram, gilt top. Crown 8vo. 6s.*

H. C. Beeching. A BOOK OF CHRISTMAS VERSE. Edited by H. C. BEECHING, M.A., and Illustrated by WALTER CRANE. *Cr. 8vo, gilt top. 3s. 6d.*

An anthology which, from its unity of aim and high poetic excellence, has a better right to exist than most of its fellows.'—*Guardian.*

History

Gibbon. THE DECLINE AND FALL OF THE ROMAN EMPIRE. By EDWARD GIBBON. A New Edition, Edited with Notes, Appendices, and Maps, by J. B. BURY, LL.D., Fellow of Trinity College, Dublin. *In Seven Volumes. Demy 8vo. Gilt top. 8s. 6d. each. Also Cr. 8vo. 6s.*

each. *Vols. I., II., III., IV., V., and VI.*

'The time has certainly arrived for a new edition of Gibbon's great work. . . . Professor Bury is the right man to undertake this task. His learning is amazing, both in extent and accuracy. The book is issued in a handy form, and at a moderate price, and it is admirably printed.'—*Times.*

'The standard edition of our great historical classic.'—*Glasgow Herald.*

'At last there is an adequate modern edition of Gibbon. . . . The best edition the nineteenth century could produce.'—*Manchester Guardian.*

Flinders Petrie. A HISTORY OF EGYPT, FROM THE EARLIEST TIMES TO THE PRESENT DAY. Edited by W. M. FLINDERS PETRIE, D.C.L., LL.D., Professor of Egyptology at University College. *Fully Illustrated. In Six Volumes. Cr. 8vo. 6s. each.*

VOL. I. PREHISTORIC TIMES TO XVITH DYNASTY. W. M. F. Petrie. *Fourth Edition.*

VOL. II. THE XVIITH AND XVIIITH DYNASTIES. W. M. F. Petrie. *Third Edition.*

VOL. IV. THE EGYPT OF THE PTOLEMIES. J. P. Mahaffy.

VOL. V. ROMAN EGYPT. J. G. Milne.

'A history written in the spirit of scientific precision so worthily represented by Dr. Petrie and his school cannot but promote sound and accurate study, and supply a vacant place in the English literature of Egyptology.'—*Times.*

Flinders Petrie. RELIGION AND CONSCIENCE IN ANCIENT EGYPT. By W. M. FLINDERS PETRIE, D.C.L., LL.D. Fully Illustrated. *Crown 8vo. 2s. 6d.*

'The lectures will afford a fund of valuable information for students of ancient ethics.'—*Manchester Guardian.*

Flinders Petrie. SYRIA AND EGYPT, FROM THE TELL EL AMARNA TABLETS. By W. M. FLINDERS PETRIE, D.C.L., LL.D. *Crown 8vo. 2s. 6d.*

'A marvellous record. The addition made to our knowledge is nothing short of amazing.'—*Times.*

Flinders Petrie. EGYPTIAN TALES. Edited by W. M. FLINDERS PETRIE. Illustrated by TRISTRAM ELLIS. *In Two Volumes. Cr. 8vo. 3s. 6d. each.*

'Invaluable as a picture of life in Palestine and Egypt.'—*Daily News.*

Flinders Petrie. EGYPTIAN DECORATIVE ART. By W. M. FLINDERS PETRIE. With 120 Illustrations. *Cr. 8vo. 3s. 6d.*

'In these lectures he displays rare skill in elucidating the development of decorative art in Egypt.'—*Times.*

C. W. Oman. A HISTORY OF THE ART OF WAR. Vol. II.: The Middle Ages, from the Fourth to the Fourteenth Century. By C. W. OMAN, M.A., Fellow of All Souls', Oxford. Illustrated. *Demy 8vo. 21s.*

'The book is based throughout upon a thorough study of the original sources, and will be an indispensable aid to all students of mediæval history.'—*Athenæum.*

'The whole art of war in its historic evolution has never been treated on such an ample and comprehensive scale, and we question if any recent contribution to the exact history of the world has possessed more enduring value.'—*Daily Chronicle.*

S. Baring Gould. THE TRAGEDY OF THE CÆSARS. With numerous Illustrations from Busts, Gems, Cameos, etc. By S. BARING GOULD. *Fourth Edition. Royal 8vo. 15s.*

'A most splendid and fascinating book on a subject of undying interest. The great feature of the book is the use the author has made of the existing portraits of the Caesars and the admirable critical subtlety he has exhibited in dealing with this line of research. It is brilliantly written, and the illustrations are supplied on a scale of profuse magnificence.'—*Daily Chronicle.*

F. W. Maitland. CANON LAW IN ENGLAND. By F. W. MAITLAND, LL.D., Downing Professor of the Laws of England in the University of Cambridge. *Royal 8vo. 7s. 6d.*

'Professor Maitland has put students of English law under a fresh debt. These essays are landmarks in the study of the history of Canon Law.'—*Times.*

H. de B. Gibbins. INDUSTRY IN ENGLAND : HISTORICAL OUT-LINES. By H. DE B. GIBBINS, Litt.D., M.A. With 5 Maps. *Second Edition. Demy 8vo. 10s. 6d.*

H. E. Egerton. A HISTORY OF BRITISH COLONIAL POLICY. By H. E. EGERTON, M.A. *Demy 8vo. 12s. 6d.*

' It is a good book, distinguished by accuracy in detail, clear arrangement of facts, and a broad grasp of principles.'—*Manchester Guardian.*

' Able, impartial, clear. . . . A most valuable volume.'—*Athenæum.*

Albert Sorel. THE EASTERN QUESTION IN THE EIGH-TEENTH CENTURY. By ALBERT SOREL, of the French Academy. Translated by F. C. BRAMWELL, M.A. With a Map. *Cr. 8vo. 3s. 6d.*

C. H. Grinling. A HISTORY OF THE GREAT NORTHERN RAIL-WAY, 1845-95. By CHARLES H. GRINLING. With Maps and Illus-trations. *Demy 8vo. 10s. 6d.*

' Mr. Grinling has done for a Railway what Macaulay did for English History.'—*The Engineer.*

W. Sterry. ANNALS OF ETON COLLEGE. By W. STERRY, M.A. With numerous Illustrations. *Demy 8vo. 7s. 6d.*

' A treasury of quaint and interesting read-ing. Mr. Sterry has by his skill and vivacity given these records new life.'—*Academy.*

Fisher. ANNALS OF SHREWS-BURY SCHOOL. By G. W. FISHER, M.A., late Assistant Master. With numerous Illustrations. *Demy 8vo. 10s. 6d.*

' This careful, erudite book.'—*Daily Chronicle.*

' A book of which Old Salopians are sure to be proud.'—*Globe.*

J. Sargeaunt. ANNALS OF WEST-MINSTER SCHOOL. By J. SAR-GEAUNT, M.A., Assistant Master. With numerous Illustrations. *Demy 8vo. 7s. 6d.*

A. Clark. THE COLLEGES OF OXFORD : Their History and their Traditions. By Members of the University. Edited by A. CLARK, M.A., Fellow and Tutor of Lincoln College. *8vo. 12s. 6d.*

' A work which will be appealed to for many years as the standard book.'—*Athenæum.*

J. Wells. A SHORT HISTORY OF ROME. By J. WELLS, M.A., Fellow and Tutor of Wadham Coll., Oxford. *Second and Revised Edition.* With 3 Maps. *Crown 8vo. 3s. 6d.*

This book is intended for the Middle and Upper Forms of Public Schools and for Pass Students at the Universities. It contains copious Tables, etc.

' An original work written on an original plan, and with uncommon freshness and vigour.'—*Speaker.*

O. Browning. A SHORT HISTORY OF MEDIÆVAL ITALY, A.D. 1250-1530. By OSCAR BROWNING, Fellow and Tutor of King's College, Cambridge. *In Two Volumes. Cr. 8vo. 5s. each.*

VOL. I. 1250-1409.—Guelphs and Ghibellines.

VOL. II. 1409-1530.—The Age of the Condottieri.

O'Grady. THE STORY OF IRE-LAND. By STANDISH O'GRADY, Author of 'Finn and his Companions. *Crown 8vo. 2s. 6d.*

Byzantine Texts

Edited by J. B. BURY, M.A.

EVAGRIUS. Edited by Professor LÉON PARMENTIER of Liége and M. BIDEZ of Gand. *Demy 8vo. 10s. 6d.*

THE HISTORY OF PSELLUS. By C. SATHAS. *Demy 8vo. 15s. net.*

A 3

Biography

S. Baring Gould. THE LIFE OF NAPOLEON BONAPARTE. By S. BARING GOULD. With over 450 Illustrations in the Text and 12 Photogravure Plates. *Large quarto. Gilt top.* 36*s*.

'The best biography of Napoleon in our tongue, nor have the French as good a biographer of their hero. A book very nearly as good as Southey's " Life of Nelson."'—*Manchester Guardian.*

'The main feature of this gorgeous volume is its great wealth of beautiful photogravures and finely-executed wood engravings, constituting a complete pictorial chronicle of Napoleon I.'s personal history from the days of his early childhood at Ajaccio to the date of his second interment.'—*Daily Telegraph.*

P. H. Colomb. MEMOIRS OF ADMIRAL SIR A. COOPER KEY. By Admiral P. H. COLOMB. With a Portrait. *Demy 8vo.* 16*s*.

'An interesting and adequate biography. The whole book is one of the greatest interest.'—*Times.*

Morris Fuller. THE LIFE AND WRITINGS OF JOHN DAVENANT, D.D. (1571-1641), Bishop of Salisbury. By MORRIS FULLER, B.D. *Demy 8vo.* 10*s. 6d.*

J. M. Rigg. ST. ANSELM OF CANTERBURY: A CHAPTER IN THE HISTORY OF RELIGION. By J. M. RIGG. *Demy 8vo.* 7*s. 6d.*

F. W. Joyce. THE LIFE OF SIR FREDERICK GORE OUSELEY. By F. W. JOYCE, M.A. 7*s. 6d.*

'This book has been undertaken in quite

the right spirit, and written with sympathy, insight, and considerable skill.'—*Times.*

W. G. Collingwood. THE LIFE O. JOHN RUSKIN. By W. G COLLINGWOOD, M.A. With Portraits, and 13 Drawings by M: Ruskin. *Second Edition.* 2 *vols.* 8vo. 32*s*.

'No more magnificent volumes have published for a long time.'—*Times.*

'It is long since we had a biography such delights of substance and of for Such a book is a pleasure for the d and a joy for ever.'—*Daily Chronicle*

C. Waldstein. JOHN RUSKIN, CHARLES WALDSTEIN, M.A. With a Photogravure Portrait, *Post 8:* 5*s*.

'A thoughtful and well-written criticism Ruskin's teaching.'—*Daily Chronicle.*

A. M. F. Darmesteter, THE LI OF ERNEST RENAN. MADAME DARMESTETER. With Portrait. *Second Edition.* *Cr. 8:* 6*s*.

'A polished gem of biography, superior its kind to any attempt that has made of recent years in Eng Madame Darmesteter has indeed writt for English readers " *The* Life of Ern Renan."'—*Athenæum.*

W. H. Hutton. THE LIFE OF SI THOMAS MORE. By W. H HUTTON, M.A. With Portrait *Cr. 8vo.* 5*s*.

'The book lays good claim to high r among our biographies. It is excellentl even lovingly, written.'—*Scotsman.*

Travel, Adventure and Topography

Sven Hedin. THROUGH ASIA. By SVEN HEDIN, Gold Medallist of the Royal Geographical Society. With 300 Illustrations from Sketches and Photographs by the Author,

and Maps. 2 *vols. Royal 8vo.* 20*s. net.*

'One of the greatest books of the kin issued during the century. It is in possible to give an adequate idea of t richness of the contents of this book, nor of its abounding attractions as a story of travel unsurpassed in geographical and human interest. Much of it is a revelation. Altogether the work is one which in solidity, novelty, and interest must take a first rank among publications of its class.'—*Times.*

'In these magnificent volumes we have the most important contribution to Central Asian geography made for many years. Intensely interesting as a tale of travel. —*Spectator.*

'These volumes are of absorbing and fascinating interest, their matter is wonderful, and Dr. Hedin's style is surcharged with strong and alluring personality. No romance exceeds in its intense and enthralling interest this story.'—*Birmingham Post.*

R. E. Peary. NORTHWARD OVER THE GREAT ICE. By R. E. PEARY, Gold Medallist of the Royal Geographical Society. With over 800 Illustrations. 2 *vols. Royal 8vo. 32s. net.*

'The book is full of interesting matter—a tale of brave deeds simply told ; abundantly illustrated with prints and maps.' —*Standard.*

'His book will take its place among the permanent literature of Arctic exploration.' —*Times.*

'It yields neither in interest nor in ability to Nansen's "Farthest North," while its results are no less valuable.'—*Glasgow Herald.*

G. S. Robertson. CHITRAL: The Story of a Minor Siege. By Sir G. S. ROBERTSON, K.C.S.I. With numerous Illustrations, Map and Plans. *Second Edition. Demy 8vo.* 10s. 6d.

'It is difficult to imagine the kind of person who could read this brilliant book without emotion. The story remains immortal— a testimony imperishable. We are face to face with a great book.'—*Illustrated London News.*

'A book which the Elizabethans would have thought wonderful. More thrilling, more piquant, and more human than any novel.'—*Newcastle Chronicle.*

'One of the most stirring military narratives written in our time.'—*Times.*

'As fascinating as Sir Walter Scott's best fiction.'—*Daily Telegraph.*

'A noble story, nobly told.'—*Punch.*

H. H. Johnston. BRITISH CENTRAL AFRICA. By Sir H. H.

JOHNSTON, K.C.B. With nearly Two Hundred Illustrations, and Six Maps. *Second Edition. Crown 4to.* 18s. *net.*

'A fascinating book, written with equal skill and charm—the work at once of a literary artist and of a man of action who is singularly wise, brave, and experienced. It abounds in admirable sketches from pencil.' — *Westminster Gazette.*

L. Decle. THREE YEARS IN SAVAGE AFRICA. By LIONEL DECLE. With 100 Illustrations and 5 Maps. *Second Edition. Demy 8vo.* 10s. 6d. *net.*

'A fine, full book.'—*Pall Mall Gazette.*

'Its bright pages give a better general survey of Africa from the Cape to the Equator than any single volume that has yet been published.'—*Times.*

A. Hulme Beaman. TWENTY YEARS IN THE NEAR EAST. By A. HULME BEAMAN. *Demy 8vo.* With Portrait. 10s. 6d.

'One of the most entertaining books that we have had in our hands for a long time. It is unconventional in a high degree ; it is written with sagacious humour ; it is full of adventures and anecdotes.'—*Daily Chronicle.*

Henri of Orleans. FROM TONKIN TO INDIA. By PRINCE HENRI OF ORLEANS. Translated by HAMLEY BENT, M.A. With 100 Illustrations and a Map. *Cr. 4to, gilt top.* 25s.

R. S. S. Baden-Powell. THE DOWNFALL OF PREMPEH. A Diary of Life in Ashanti, 1895. By Colonel BADEN-POWELL. With 21 Illustrations and a Map. *Cheaper Edition. Large Crown 8vo.* 6s.

R. S. S. Baden-Powell. THE MATABELE CAMPAIGN, 1896. By Col. BADEN-POWELL. With nearly 100 Illustrations. *Cheaper Edition. Large Crown 8vo.* 6s.

S. L. Hinde. THE FALL OF THE CONGO ARABS. By S. L. HINDE. With Plans, etc. *Demy 8vo.* 12s. 6d.

A. St. H. Gibbons. EXPLORATION AND HUNTING IN CENTRAL

AFRICA. By Major A. St. H. GIBBONS. With full-page Illustrations by C. WHYMPER, and Maps. *Demy 8vo.* 15s.

'His book is a grand record of quiet, unassuming, tactful resolution. His adventures were as various as his sporting exploits were exciting.'—*Times.*

B. H. Alderson. WITH THE MASHONALAND FIELD FORCE, 1896. By Lieut.-Colonel ALDERSON. With numerous Illustrations and Plans. *Demy 8vo.* 10s. 6d.

'A clear, vigorous, and soldier-like narrative.'—*Scotsman.*

Fraser. ROUND THE WORLD ON A WHEEL. By JOHN FOSTER FRASER. With 100 Illustrations. *Crown 8vo.* 6s.

'A very entertaining book of travel.'—*Spectator.*
'The story is told with delightful gaiety, humour, and crispness. There has rarely appeared a more interesting tale of modern travel.'—*Scotsman.*
'A classic of cycling, graphic and witty.'—*Yorkshire Post.*

Seymour Vandeleur. CAMPAIGNING ON THE UPPER NILE AND NIGER. By Lieut. SEYMOUR VANDELEUR. With an Introduction by Sir G. GOLDIE, K.C.M.G. With 4 Maps, Illustrations, and Plans. *Large Crown 8vo.* 10s. 6d.

'Upon the African question there is no book procurable which contains so much of value as this one.'—*Guardian.*

Lord Fincastle. A FRONTIER CAMPAIGN. By Viscount FINCASTLE, V.C., and Lieut. P. C. ELLIOTT-LOCKHART. With a Map and 16 Illustrations. *Second Edition.* *Crown 8vo.* 6s.

'An admirable book, and a really valuable treatise on frontier war.'—*Athenæum.*

E. N. Bennett. THE DOWNFALL OF THE DERVISHES: A Sketch of the Sudan Campaign of 1898. By E. N. BENNETT, Fellow of Hertf College. With Four Maps and Photogravure Portrait of the Sirdar. *Third Edition.* *Crown 8vo.* 3s. 6d.

J. K. Trotter. THE NIGER SOURCES. By Colonel J. K. TROTTER, R.A. With a Map an Illustrations. *Crown 8vo.* 5s.

Michael Davitt. LIFE AND PROGRESS IN AUSTRALASIA. By MICHAEL DAVITT, M.P. 500 pp. With 2 Maps. *Crown 8vo.* 6s.

W. Crooke. THE NORTH-WESTERN PROVINCES OF INDIA: THEIR ETHNOLOGY AND ADMINISTRATION. By W. CROOKE. With Maps and Illustrations. *Demy 8vo.* 10s. 6d.

'A carefully and well-written account of one of the most important provinces of the Empire. Mr. Crooke deals with the land in its physical aspect, the province under Hindoo and Mussulman rule, under British rule, its ethnology and sociology, its religious and social life, the land and its settlement, and the native peasant.'—*Manchester Guardian.*

A. Boisragon. THE BENIN MASSACRE. By Captain BOISRAGON. *Second Edition.* *Cr. 8vo.* 3s. 6d.

'If the story had been written four hundred years ago it would be read to-day as an English classic.'—*Scotsman.*

H. S. Cowper. THE HILL OF THE GRACES: OR, THE GREAT STONE TEMPLES OF TRIPOLI. By H. S. COWPER, F.S.A. With Maps, Plans, and 75 Illustrations. *Demy 8vo.* 10s. 6d.

W. Kinnaird Rose. WITH THE GREEKS IN THESSALY. By W. KINNAIRD ROSE, Reuter's Correspondent. With Plans and 23 Illustrations. *Crown 8vo.* 6s.

W. B. Worsfold. SOUTH AFRICA. By W. B. WORSFOLD, M.A. With a Map. *Second Edition.* *Cr. 8vo.* 6s.

'A monumental work compressed into a very moderate compass.'—*World.*

Naval and Military

G. W. Steevens. NAVAL POLICY: By G. W. STEEVENS. *Demy 8vo.* 6s.

This book is a description of the British and other more important navies of the world, with a sketch of the lines on which our naval policy might possibly be developed. 'An extremely able and interesting work.' —*Daily Chronicle.*

D. Hannay. A SHORT HISTORY OF THE ROYAL NAVY, FROM EARLY TIMES TO THE PRESENT DAY. By DAVID HANNAY. Illustrated. 2 Vols. *Demy 8vo.* 7s. 6d. each. Vol. I., 1200-1688.

We read it from cover to cover at a sitting, and those who go to it for a lively and brisk picture of the past, with all its faults and its grandeur, will not be disappointed. The historian is endowed with literary skill and style.'—*Standard.*

'We can warmly recommend Mr. Hannay's volume to any intelligent student of naval history. Great as is the merit of Mr. Hannay's historical narrative, the merit of his strategic exposition is even greater.'—*Times.*

C. Cooper King. THE STORY OF THE BRITISH ARMY. By Colonel COOPER KING. Illustrated. *Demy 8vo.* 7s. 6d.

'An authoritative and accurate story of England's military progress.'—*Daily Mail.*

R. Southey. ENGLISH SEAMEN (Howard, Clifford, Hawkins, Drake, Cavendish). By ROBERT SOUTHEY. Edited, with an Introduction, by DAVID HANNAY. *Second Edition. Crown 8vo.* 6s.

'A brave, inspiriting book.'—*Black and White.*

W. Clark Russell. THE LIFE OF ADMIRAL LORD COLLINGWOOD. By W. CLARK RUSSELL. With Illustrations by F. BRANGWYN. *Third Edition. Crown 8vo.* 6s.

'A book which we should like to see in the hands of every boy in the country.'—*St. James's Gazette.*
'A really good book.'—*Saturday Review.*

E. L. S. Horsburgh. THE CAMPAIGN OF WATERLOO. By E. L. S. HORSBURGH, B.A. With Plans. *Crown 8vo.* 5s.

'A brilliant essay—simple, sound, and thorough.'—*Daily Chronicle.*

H. B. George. BATTLES OF ENGLISH HISTORY. By H. B. GEORGE, M.A., Fellow of New College, Oxford. With numerous Plans. *Third Edition. Cr. 8vo.* 6s.

'Mr. George has undertaken a very useful task—that of making military affairs intelligible and instructive to non-military readers—and has executed it with a large measure of success.'—*Times.*

General Literature

S. Baring Gould. OLD COUNTRY LIFE. By S. BARING GOULD. With Sixty-seven Illustrations. *Large Cr. 8vo. Fifth Edition.* 6s.

'"Old Country Life," as healthy wholesome reading, full of breezy life and movement, full of quaint stories vigorously told, will not be excelled by any book to be published throughout the year. Sound, hearty, and English to the core.' —*World.*

S. Baring Gould. AN OLD ENGLISH HOME. By S. BARING GOULD. With numerous Plans and Illustrations. *Crown 8vo.* 6s.

'The chapters are delightfully fresh, very informing, and lightened by many a good story. A delightful fireside companion.' —*St. James's Gazette.*

S. Baring Gould. HISTORIC ODDITIES AND STRANGE

EVENTS. By S. BARING GOULD. *Fourth Edition. Crown 8vo. 6s.*

S. Baring Gould. FREAKS OF FANATICISM. By S. BARING GOULD. *Third Edition. Cr. 8vo. 6s.*

S. Baring Gould. A GARLAND OF COUNTRY SONG: English Folk Songs with their Traditional Melodies. Collected and arranged by S. BARING GOULD and H. F. SHEPPARD. *Demy 4to. 6s.*

S. Baring Gould. SONGS OF THE WEST: Traditional Ballads and Songs of the West of England, with their Melodies. Collected by S. BARING GOULD, M.A., and H. F. SHEPPARD, M.A. In 4 Parts. *Parts I., II., III.,* 3s. *each. Part IV.,* 5s. *In one Vol., French morocco,* 15s.
'A rich collection of humour, pathos, grace, and poetic fancy.'—*Saturday Review.*

S. Baring Gould. YORKSHIRE ODDITIES AND STRANGE EVENTS. By S. BARING GOULD. *Fourth Edition. Crown 8vo. 6s.*

S. Baring Gould. STRANGE SUR-VIVALS AND SUPERSTITIONS. By S. BARING GOULD. *Cr. 8vo. Second Edition. 6s.*

S. Baring Gould. THE DESERTS OF SOUTHERN FRANCE. By S. BARING GOULD. *2 vols. Demy 8vo. 32s.*

Cotton Minchin. OLD HARROW DAYS. By J. G. COTTON MINCHIN. *Cr. 8vo. Second Edition. 5s.*
'This book is an admirable record.'—*Daily Chronicle.*

W. E. Gladstone. THE SPEECHES OF THE RT. HON. W. E. GLAD-STONE, M.P. Edited by A. W. HUTTON, M.A., and H. J. COHEN M.A. With Portraits, *Demy 8vo. Vols. IX. and X., 12s. 6d. each.*

E. V. Zenker. ANARCHISM. By E. V. ZENKER. *Demy 8vo. 7s. 6d.*
'Herr Zenker has succeeded in producing a careful and critical history of the growth of Anarchist theory.

H. G. Hutchinson. THE GOLFING PILGRIM. By HORACE G. HUTCHINSON. *Crown 8vo. 6s.*
'Full of useful information with plenty good stories.'—*Truth.*
'Without this book the golfer's library will be incomplete.'—*Pall Mall Gazette.*
'It will charm all golfers.'—*Times.*

J. Wells. OXFORD AND OXFOR LIFE. By Members of the Uni versity. Edited by J. WELLS, M.A. Fellow and Tutor of Wadham College *Third Edition. Cr. 8vo. 3s. 6d.*
'We congratulate Mr. Wells on the duction of a readable and intelligent account of Oxford as it is at the p time, written by persons who are possessed of a close acquaintance with the system and life of the University.'—*Athenæum.*

J. Wells. OXFORD AND ITS COLLEGES. By J. WELLS, M.A., Fellow and Tutor of Wadham College. Illustrated by E. H. NEW. *Third Edition. Fcap. 8vo. 3s. Leather. 3s 6d. net.*
'An admirable and accurate little treatise, attractively illustrated.'—*World.*
'A luminous and tasteful little volume.'—*Daily Chronicle.*
'Exactly what the intelligent visitor wants.'—*Glasgow Herald.*

A. H. Thompson. CAMBRIDGE AND ITS COLLEGES. By A. HAMILTON THOMPSON. With Illustrations by E. H. NEW. *Pott 8vo. 3s. Leather. 3s. 6d. net.*
This book is uniform with Mr. Wells' very successful book, 'Oxford and its Colleges.'
'It is brightly written and learned, and is just such a book as a cultured visitor needs.'—*Scotsman.*

C. G. Robertson. VOCES ACADE-MICÆ. By C. GRANT ROBERTSON, M.A., Fellow of All Souls', Oxford. *With a Frontispiece. Pott 8vo. 3s. 6d.*
'Decidedly clever and amusing.'—*Athenæum.*

Rosemary Cotes. DANTE'S GAR-DEN. By ROSEMARY COTES. With a Frontispiece. *Second Edition. Fcp. 8vo. 2s. 6d. Leather, 3s. 6d. net.*
'A charming collection of legends of the flowers mentioned by Dante.'—*Academy.*

Clifford Harrison. READING AND READERS. By CLIFFORD HARRISON. *Fcp. 8vo. 2s. 6d.*

'We recommend schoolmasters to examine its merits, for it is at school that readers are made.'—*Academy.*

'An extremely sensible little book.'—*Manchester Guardian.*

L. Whibley. GREEK OLIGARCHIES: THEIR ORGANISATION AND CHARACTER. By L. WHIBLEY, M.A., Fellow of Pembroke College, Cambridge. *Crown 8vo. 6s.*

'An exceedingly useful handbook : a careful and well-arranged study.'—*Times.*

L. L. Price. ECONOMIC SCIENCE AND PRACTICE. By L. L. PRICE, M.A., Fellow of Oriel College, Oxford. *Crown 8vo. 6s.*

J. S. Shedlock. THE PIANOFORTE SONATA : Its Origin and Development. By J. S. SHEDLOCK. *Crown 8vo. 5s.*

'This work should be in the possession of every musician and amateur. A concise and lucid history and a very valuable work for reference.'—*Athenæum.*

E. M. Bowden. THE EXAMPLE OF BUDDHA : Being Quotations from Buddhist Literature for each Day in the Year. Compiled by E. M. BOWDEN. *Third Edition. 16mo. 2s. 6d.*

Science and Technology

Freudenreich. DAIRY BACTERIOLOGY. A Short Manual for the Use of Students. By Dr. ED. VON FREUDENREICH, Translated by J. R. AINSWORTH DAVIS, M.A. *Crown 8vo. 2s. 6d.*

Chalmers Mitchell. OUTLINES OF BIOLOGY. By P. CHALMERS MITCHELL, M.A. *Illustrated. Cr. 8vo. 6s.*

A text-book designed to cover the new Schedule issued by the Royal College of Physicians and Surgeons.

G. Massee. A MONOGRAPH OF THE MYXOGASTRES. By GEORGE MASSEE. With 12 Coloured Plates. *Royal 8vo. 18s. net.*

'A work much in advance of any book in the language treating of this group of organisms. Indispensable to every student of the Myxogastres.'—*Nature.*

Stephenson and Suddards. ORNAMENTAL DESIGN FOR WOVEN FABRICS. By C. STEPHENSON, of The Technical College, Bradford, and F. SUDDARDS, of The Yorkshire College, Leeds. With 65 full-page plates. *Demy 8vo. 7s. 6d.*

'The book is very ably done, displaying an intimate knowledge of principles, good taste, and the faculty of clear exposition.'—*Yorkshire Post.*

TEXTBOOKS OF TECHNOLOGY.
Edited by PROFESSORS GARNETT and WERTHEIMER.

HOW TO MAKE A DRESS. By J. A. E. WOOD. *Illustrated. Cr. 8vo. 1s. 6d.*

'Though primarily intended for students, Miss Wood's dainty little manual may be consulted with advantage by any girls who want to make their own frocks. The directions are simple and clear, and the diagrams very helpful.'—*Literature.*

CARPENTRY AND JOINERY. By F. C. WEBBER. With many Illustrations. *Cr. 8vo. 3s. 6d.*

'An admirable elementary text-book on the subject.'—*Builder.*

PRACTICAL MECHANICS. By SIDNEY H. WELLS. With 75 Illustrations and Diagrams. *Crown 8vo. 3s. 6d.*

Philosophy

L. T. Hobhouse. THE THEORY OF KNOWLEDGE. By L. T. HOB-HOUSE, Fellow of C.C.C., Oxford. *Demy 8vo.* 21s.

'The most important contribution to English philosophy since the publication of Mr. Bradley's "Appearance and Reality."'—*Glasgow Herald.*

'A brilliantly written volume.'—*Times.*

W. H. Fairbrother. THE PHILO-SOPHY OF T. II. GREEN. By W. H. FAIRBROTHER, M.A. *Cr. 8vo.* 3s. 6d.

'In every way an admirable book.'—*Glasgow Herald.*

F. W. Bussell. THE SCHOOL OF PLATO. By F. W. BUSSELL, D.D., Fellow of Brasenose College, Oxford. *Demy 8vo.* 10s. 6d.

'A clever and stimulating book.'—*Manchester Guardian.*

F. S. Granger. THE WORSHIP OF THE ROMANS. By F. S. GRANGER, M.A., Litt.D. *Crown 8vo.* 6s.

'A scholarly analysis of the religious cere-monies, beliefs, and superstitions of ancient Rome, conducted in the new light of comparative anthropology.'—*Times.*

Theology

S. R. Driver. SERMONS ON SUB-JECTS CONNECTED WITH THE OLD TESTAMENT. By S. R. DRIVER, D.D., Canon of Christ Church, Regius Professor of Hebrew in the University of Oxford. *Cr. 8vo.* 6s.

'A welcome companion to the author's famous "Introduction."'—*Guardian.*

T. K. Cheyne. FOUNDERS OF OLD TESTAMENT CRITICISM. By T. K. CHEYNE, D.D., Oriel Pro-fessor at Oxford. *Large Crown 8vo.* 7s. 6d.

A historical sketch of O. T. Criticism.

'A very learned and instructive work.'—*Times.*

H. Rashdall. DOCTRINE AND DEVELOPMENT. By HASTINGS RASHDALL, M.A., Fellow and Tutor of New College, Oxford. *Cr. 8vo.* 6s.

'A very interesting attempt to restate some of the principal doctrines of Christianity. in which Mr. Rashdall appears to us to have achieved a high measure of success. He is often learned, almost always sym-pathetic, and always singularly lucid.'—*Manchester Guardian.*

H. H. Henson. APOSTOLIC CHRIS-TIANITY: As Illustrated by the Epistles of St. Paul to the Corinthians. By H. H. HENSON, M.A., Fellow of All Souls', Oxford. *Cr. 8vo.* 6s.

'A worthy contribution towards same solu-tion of the great religious problems of the present day.'—*Scotsman.*

H. H. Henson. DISCIPLINE AND LAW. By H. HENSLEY HENSON, B.D., Fellow of All Souls', Oxford. *Fcap. 8vo.* 2s. 6d.

H. H. Henson. LIGHT AND LEAVEN : HISTORICAL AND SOCIAL SERMONS. By H. H. HEN-SON, M.A. *Crown 8vo.* 6s.

W. H. Bennett. A PRIMER OF THE BIBLE. By W. H. BENNETT. *Second Edition. Cr. 8vo.* 2s. 6d.

'The work of an honest, fearless, and sound critic, and an excellent guide in a small compass to the books of the Bible.'—*Manchester Guardian.*

William Harrison. CLOVELLY SERMONS. By WILLIAM HARRI-SON, M.A., late Rector of Clovelly. With a Preface by 'LUCAS MALET.' *Cr. 8vo.* 3s. 6d.

Cecilia Robinson. THE MINISTRY OF DEACONESSES. By Deacon-

ness CECILIA ROBINSON. With an Introduction by the Lord Bishop of Winchester. *Cr. 8vo.* 3*s.* 6*d.*
'A learned and interesting book.'—*Scotsman.*

E. B. Layard. RELIGION IN BOY-HOOD. Notes on the Religious Training of Boys. By E. B. LAYARD, M.A. 18*mo.* 1*s.*

W. Yorke Fausset. THE *DE CATECHIZANDIS RUDIBUS* OF ST. AUGUSTINE. Edited, with Introduction, Notes, etc., by W. YORKE FAUSSET, M.A. *Cr. 8vo.* 3*s.* 6*d.*

F. Weston. THE HOLY SACRI-FICE. By F. WESTON, M.A., Curate of St. Matthew's, Westminster. *Pott 8vo.* 6*d. net.*
A small volume of devotions at the Holy Communion, especially adapted to the needs of servers and those who do not communicate.

À Kempis. THE IMITATION OF CHRIST. By THOMAS À KEMPIS. With an Introduction by DEAN FARRAR. Illustrated by C. M. GERE. *Second Edition. Fcap. 8vo.* 3*s.* 6*d. Padded morocco,* 5*s.*
'Amongst all the innumerable English editions of the "Imitation," there can have been few which were prettier than this one, printed in strong and handsome type, with all the glory of red initials.'—*Glasgow Herald.*

J. Keble. THE CHRISTIAN YEAR. By JOHN KEBLE. With an Introduction and Notes by W. LOCK, D.D., Warden of Keble College. Illustrated by R. ANNING BELL. *Second Edition. Fcap. 8vo.* 3*s.* 6*d. Padded morocco.* 5*s.*
'The present edition is annotated with all the care and insight to be expected from Mr. Lock.'—*Guardian.*

Oxford Commentaries.

General Editor, WALTER LOCK, D.D., Warden of Keble College, Dean Ireland's Professor of Exegesis in the University of Oxford.
THE BOOK OF JOB. Edited, with Introduction and Notes, by E. C. S. GIBSON, D.D., Vicar of Leeds. *Demy 8vo.* 6*s.*

Handbooks of Theology.

General Editor, A. ROBERTSON, D.D., Principal of King's College, London.
THE XXXIX. ARTICLES OF THE CHURCH OF ENGLAND. Edited with an Introduction by E. C. S. GIBSON, D.D., Vicar of Leeds, late Principal of Wells Theological College. *Second and Cheaper Edition in One Volume. Demy 8vo.* 12*s.* 6*d.*
'We welcome with the utmost satisfaction a new, cheaper, and more convenient edition of Dr. Gibson's book. It was greatly wanted. Dr. Gibson has given theological students just what they want, and we should like to think that it was in the hands of every candidate for orders.'—*Guardian.*

AN INTRODUCTION TO THE HISTORY OF RELIGION. By F. B. JEVONS, M.A., Litt.D., Principal of Bishop Hatfield's Hall. *Demy 8vo.* 10*s.* 6*d.*
'The merit of this book lies in the penetration, the singular acuteness and force of the author's judgment. He is at once critical and luminous, at once just and

suggestive. A comprehensive and thorough book.'—*Birmingham Post.*

THE DOCTRINE OF THE INCARNATION. By R. L. OTTLEY, M.A., late fellow of Magdalen College, Oxon., and Principal of Pusey House. *In Two Volumes. Demy 8vo.* 15*s.*
'A clear and remarkably full account of the main currents of speculation. Scholarly precision . . . genuine tolerance . . . intense interest in his subject—are Mr. Ottley's merits.'—*Guardian.*

AN INTRODUCTION TO THE HISTORY OF THE CREEDS. By A. E. BURNS, Examining Chaplain to the Bishop of Lichfield. *Demy 8vo.* 10*s.* 6*d.*
'This book may be expected to hold its place as an authority on its subject.'—*Spectator.*
'It is an able and learned treatise, and contains a mass of information which will be most useful to scholars.'—*Glasgow Herald.*

The Churchman's Library.

Edited by J. H. BURN, B.D.

THE BEGINNINGS OF ENGLISH CHRISTIANITY. By W. E. COLLINS, M.A. With Map. *Cr. 8vo.* 3s. 6d.

An investigation in detail, based upon original authorities, of the beginnings of the English Church, with a careful account of earlier Celtic Christianity.

'An excellent example of thorough and fresh historical work.'—*Guardian.*

SOME NEW TESTAMENT PRO-BLEMS. By ARTHUR WRIGHT, Fellow of Queen's College, Cambridge. *Crown 8vo.* 6s.

THE KINGDOM OF HEAVEN HERE AND HEREAFTER. By CANON WINTERBOTHAM, M.A., B.Sc., LL.B. *Cr. 8vo.* 3s. 6d.

'A most able book, at once exceedingly thoughtful and richly suggestive.'—*Glasgow Herald.*

The Library of Devotion

Pott 8vo, cloth, 2s.; leather, 2s. 6d. net.

'This series is excellent.'—THE BISHOP OF LONDON.
'A very delightful edition.'—THE BISHOP OF BATH AND WELLS.
'Well worth the attention of the Clergy.'—THE BISHOP OF LICHFIELD.
'The new "Library of Devotion" is excellent.'—THE BISHOP OF PETERBOROUGH.
'Charming.'—*Record.*
'Delightful.'—*Church Bells.*

THE CONFESSIONS OF ST. AUGUSTINE. Newly Translanted, with an Introduction and Notes, by C. BIGG, D.D., late Student of Christ Church. *Second Edition.*

'The translation is an excellent piece of English, and the introduction is a masterly exposition. We augur well of a series which begins so satisfactorily.'—*Times.*

THE CHRISTIAN YEAR. By JOHN KEBLE. With Introduction and Notes by WALTER LOCK, D.D., Warden of Keble College, Ireland Professor at Oxford.

'The volume is very prettily bound and printed, and may fairly claim to be an advance on any previous editions.'—*Guardian.*

THE IMITATION OF CHRIST. A Revised Translation, with an Introduction, by C. BIGG, D.D., late Student of Christ Church.

A practically new translation of this book, which the reader has, almost for the first time, exactly in the shape in which it left the hands of the author.

'A beautiful and scholarly production.'—*Speaker.*
'A nearer approach to the original than has yet existed in English.'—*Academy.*

A BOOK OF DEVOTIONS. By J. W. STANBRIDGE, M.A., Rector of Bainton, Canon of York, and sometime Fellow of St. John's College, Oxford.

It is probably the best book of its kind. It deserves high commendation.'—*Church Gazette.*

LYRA INNOCENTIUM. By JOHN KEBLE. Edited, with Introduction and Notes, by WALTER LOCK, D.D., Warden of Keble College, Oxford.

Leaders of Religion

Edited by H. C. BEECHING, M.A. *With Portraits, Crown 8vo.* 3s. 6d.

A series of short biographies of the most prominent leaders of religious life and thought of all ages and countries.

The following are ready—

CARDINAL NEWMAN. By R. H. HUTTON.

JOHN WESLEY. By J. H. OVERTON, M.A.

BISHOP WILBERFORCE. By G. W. DANIELL, M.A.

CARDINAL MANNING. By A. W. HUTTON, M.A.

CHARLES SIMEON. By H. C. G. MOULE, D.D.

JOHN KEBLE. By WALTER LOCK, D.D.

THOMAS CHALMERS. By Mrs. OLIPHANT.

LANCELOT ANDREWES. By R. L. OTTLEY, M.A.

AUGUSTINE OF CANTERBURY. By E. L. CUTTS, D.D.

WILLIAM LAUD. By W. H. HUTTON, B.D.

JOHN KNOX. By F. MacCUNN.

JOHN HOWE. By R. F. HORTON, D.D.

BISHOP KEN. By F. A. CLARKE, M.A.

GEORGE FOX, THE QUAKER. By T. HODGKIN, D.C.L.

JOHN DONNE. By AUGUSTUS JESSOPP, D.D.

THOMAS CRANMER. By. A. J. MASON.

Other volumes will be announced in due course.

Fiction

SIX SHILLING NOVELS
Marie Corelli's Novels
Large crown 8vo. 6s. each.

A ROMANCE OF TWO WORLDS. *Nineteenth Edition.*

VENDETTA. *Fourteenth Edition.*

THELMA. *Twentieth Edition.*

ARDATH: THE STORY OF A DEAD SELF. *Eleventh Edition.*

THE SOUL OF LILITH. *Ninth Edition.*

WORMWOOD. *Ninth Edition.*

BARABBAS: A DREAM OF THE WORLD'S TRAGEDY. *Thirty-third Edition.*

'The tender reverence of the treatment and the imaginative beauty of the writing have reconciled us to the daring of the conception, and the conviction is forced on us that even so exalted a subject cannot be made too familiar to us, provided it be presented in the true spirit of Christian faith. The amplifications of the Scripture narrative are often conceived with high poetic insight, and this "Dream of the World's Tragedy" is a lofty and not inadequate paraphrase of the supreme climax of the inspired narrative.'—*Dublin Review.*

THE SORROWS OF SATAN. *Fortieth Edition.*

'A very powerful piece of work. . . . The conception is magnificent, and is likely to win an abiding place within the memory of man. . . . The author has immense command of language, and a limitless audacity. . . . This interesting and remarkable romance will live long after much of the ephemeral literature of the day is forgotten. . . . A literary phenomenon . . . novel, and even sublime.'—W. T. STEAD in the *Review of Reviews.*

Anthony Hope's Novels
Crown 8vo. 6s. each.

THE GOD IN THE CAR. *Eighth Edition.*

'A very remarkable book, deserving of critical analysis impossible within our limit; brilliant, but not superficial; well considered, but not elaborated; constructed with the proverbial art that conceals, but yet allows itself to be enjoyed by readers to whom fine literary method is a keen pleasure.'—*The World.*

A CHANGE OF AIR. *Fifth Edition.*

'A graceful, vivacious comedy, true to human nature. The characters are traced with a masterly hand.'—*Times.*

A MAN OF MARK. *Fourth Edition.*

'Of all Mr. Hope's books, "A Man of Mark" is the one which best compares with "The Prisoner of Zenda."'—*National Observer.*

THE CHRONICLES OF COUNT ANTONIO. *Fourth Edition.*

'It is a perfectly enchanting story of love and chivalry, and pure romance. The Count is the most constant, desperate, and modest and tender of lovers, a peerless gentleman, an intrepid fighter, a faithful friend, and a magnanimous foe.'—*Guardian.*

PHROSO. Illustrated by H. R. MILLAR. *Fourth Edition.*

'The tale is thoroughly fresh, quick with vitality, stirring the blood.'—*St. James's Gazette.*

'A story of adventure, every page of which is palpitating with action.'—*Speaker*.

'From cover to cover "Phroso" not only engages the attention, but carries the reader in little whirls of delight from adventure to adventure.'—*Academy*.

SIMON DALE. Illustrated. *Third Edition*.

'"Simon Dale" is one of the best historical romances that have been written for a long while.'—*St. James's Gazette*.

'A brilliant novel. The story is rapid and most excellently told. As for the hero he is a perfect hero of romance'—*Athenæum*.

'There is searching analysis of human nature, with a most ingeniously constructed plot. Mr. Hope has drawn the contrasts of his women with marvellous subtlety and delicacy.'—*Times*.

Gilbert Parker's Novels
Crown 8vo. 6s. each.

PIERRE AND HIS PEOPLE. *Fifth Edition*.

'Stories happily conceived and finely executed. There is strength and genius in Mr. Parker's style.'—*Daily Telegraph*.

MRS. FALCHION. *Fourth Edition*.

'A splendid study of character.'— *Athenæum*.

'A very striking and admirable novel.'— *St. James's Gazette*.

THE TRANSLATION OF A SAVAGE.

'The plot is original and one difficult to work out; but Mr. Parker has done it with great skill and delicacy. The reader who is not interested in this original, fresh, and well-told tale must be a dull person indeed.'— *Daily Chronicle*.

THE TRAIL OF THE SWORD. Illustrated. *Sixth Edition*.

'A rousing and dramatic tale. A book like this, in which swords flash, great surprises are undertaken, and daring deeds done, in which men and women live and love in the old passionate way, is a joy inexpressible.'—*Daily Chronicle*.

WHEN VALMOND CAME TO PONTIAC: The Story of a Lost Napoleon. *Fourth Edition*.

'Here we find romance—real, breathing, living romance. The character of Valmond is drawn unerringly. The book must be read, we may say re-read, for any one thoroughly to appreciate Mr. Parker's delicate touch and innate sympathy with humanity.' — *Pall Mall Gazette*.

AN ADVENTURER OF THE NORTH: The Last Adventures of 'Pretty Pierre.' *Second Edition*.

'The present book is full of fine and moving stories of the great North, and it will add to Mr. Parker's already high reputation.'—*Glasgow Herald*.

THE SEATS OF THE MIGHTY. Illustrated. *Ninth Edition*.

'The best thing he has done; one of the best things that any one has done lately. —*St. James's Gazette*.

'Mr. Parker seems to become stronger and easier with every serious novel that he attempts. He shows the matured power which his former novels have led us to expect, and has produced a really fine historical novel.'—*Athenæum*.

'A great book.'—*Black and White*.

THE POMP OF THE LAVILETTES. *Second Edition*. 3s. 6d.

'Living, breathing romance, genuine and unforced pathos, and a deeper and more subtle knowledge of human nature than Mr. Parker has ever displayed before. It is, in a word, the work of a true artist.' —*Pall Mall Gazette*.

THE BATTLE OF THE STRONG: a Romance of Two Kingdoms. Illustrated. *Fourth Edition*.

'Such a splendid story, so splendidly told, will be read with avidity, and will add new honour even to Mr. Parker's reputation.'—*St. James's Gazette*.

'No one who takes a pleasure in literature but will read Mr. Gilbert Parker's latest romance with keen enjoyment. The writing is so good as to be a delight itself, apart altogether from the interest of the tale.'—*Pall Mall Gazette*.

'Nothing more vigorous or more human come from Mr. Gilbert Parker than novel. It has all the graphic power his last book, with truer feeling for the romance, both of human life and wild nature. There is no character without i unique and picturesque interest. M Parker's style, especially his descripti style, has in this book, perhaps even more than elsewhere, aptness and vitality.' *Literature*.

S. Baring Gould's Novels

Crown 8vo. 6s. each.

'To say that a book is by the author of "Mehalah" is to imply that it contains a story cast on strong lines, containing dramatic possibilities, vivid and sympathetic descriptions of Nature, and a wealth of ingenious imagery.'—*Speaker.*

'That whatever Mr. Baring Gould writes is well worth reading, is a conclusion that may be very generally accepted. His views of life are fresh and vigorous, his language pointed and characteristic, the incidents of which he makes use are striking and original, his characters are life-like, and though somewhat exceptional people, are drawn and coloured with artistic force. Add to this that his descriptions of scenes and scenery are painted with the loving eyes and skilled hands of a master of his art, that he is always fresh and never dull, and it is no wonder that readers have gained confidence in his power of amusing and satisfying them, and that year by year his popularity widens.'—*Court Circular.*

ARMINELL. *Fourth Edition.*

URITH. *Fifth Edition.*

IN THE ROAR OF THE SEA. *Sixth Edition.*

MRS. CURGENVEN OF CURGEN-VEN. *Fourth Edition.*

CHEAP JACK ZITA. *Fourth Edition.*

THE QUEEN OF LOVE. *Fourth Edition.*

MARGERY OF QUETHER. *Third Edition.*

JACQUETTA. *Third Edition.*

KITTY ALONE. *Fifth Edition.*

NOÉMI. Illustrated. *Fourth Edition.*

THE BROOM-SQUIRE. Illustrated. *Fourth Edition.*

THE PENNYCOMEQUICKS. *Third Edition.*

DARTMOOR IDYLLS.

GUAVAS THE TINNER. Illustrated. *Second Edition.*

BLADYS. Illustrated. *Second Edition.*

DOMITIA. Illustrated. *Second Edition.*

Conan Doyle. ROUND THE RED LAMP. By A. CONAN DOYLE. *Sixth Edition. Crown 8vo. 6s.*

'The book is far and away the best view that has been vouchsafed us behind the scenes of the consulting-room.'—*Illustrated London News.*

Stanley Weyman. UNDER THE RED ROBE. By STANLEY WEYMAN, Author of 'A Gentleman of France.' With Illustrations by R. C. WOODVILLE. *Fourteenth Edition. Crown 8vo. 6s.*

'Every one who reads books at all must read this thrilling romance, from the first page of which to the last the breathless reader is haled along. An inspiration of manliness and courage.'—*Daily Chronicle.*

Lucas Malet. THE WAGES OF SIN. By LUCAS MALET. *Thirteenth Edition. Crown 8vo. 6s.*

Lucas Malet. THE CARISSIMA. By LUCAS MALET, Author of 'The Wages of Sin,' etc. *Third Edition. Crown 8vo. 6s.*

George Gissing. THE TOWN TRAVELLER. By GEORGE GISSING, Author of 'Demos,' 'In the Year of Jubilee,' etc. *Second Edition. Cr. 8vo. 6s.*

'It is a bright and witty book above all things. Polly Sparkes is a splendid bit of work.'—*Pall Mall Gazette.*

'The spirit of Dickens is in it.'—*Bookman.*

S. R. Crockett. LOCHINVAR. By S. R. CROCKETT, Author of 'The Raiders,' etc. Illustrated. *Second Edition. Crown 8vo. 6s.*

'Full of gallantry and pathos, of the clash of arms, and brightened by episodes of humour and love. . . .'—*Westminster Gazette.*

S. R. Crockett. THE STANDARD BEARER. By S. R. CROCKETT. *Crown 8vo. 6s.*

'A delightful tale in his best style.'— *Speaker.*

'Mr. Crockett at his best.'—*Literature.*

Arthur Morrison. TALES OF MEAN STREETS. By ARTHUR MORRISON. *Fifth Edition. Cr. 8vo. 6s.*

'Told with consummate art and extraordinary detail. In the true humanity
of the book lies its justification, the
permanence of its interest, and its indubitable triumph.'—*Athenæum.*
'A great book. The author's method is
amazingly effective, and produces a
thrilling sense of reality. The writer
lays upon us a master hand. The book
is simply appalling and irresistible in
its interest. It is humorous also ; without humour it would not make the mark
it is certain to make.'—*World.*

Arthur Morrison. A CHILD OF
THE JAGO. By ARTHUR MORRI-
SON. *Third Edition. Cr. 8vo. 6s.*
'The book is a masterpiece.'—*Pall Mall
Gazette.*
'Told with great vigour and powerful sim-
plicity.'—*Athenæum.*

Mrs. Clifford. A FLASH OF
SUMMER. By Mrs. W. K. CLIF-
FORD, Author of 'Aunt Anne,' etc.
Second Edition. Crown 8vo. 6s.
'The story is a very beautiful one, exquis-
itely told.'—*Speaker.*

Emily Lawless. HURRISH. By the
Honble. EMILY LAWLESS, Author of
'Maelcho,' etc. *Fifth Edition. Cr.
8vo. 6s.*

Emily Lawless. MAELCHO : a Sixteenth Century Romance. By the
Honble. EMILY LAWLESS. *Second
Edition. Crown 8vo. 6s.*
'A really great book.'—*Spectator.*
'There is no keener pleasure in life than
the recognition of genius. A piece of
work of the first order, which we do not
hesitate to describe as one of the most
remarkable literary achievements of this
generation.'—*Manchester Guardian.*

Emily Lawless. TRAITS AND
CONFIDENCES. By the Honble.
EMILY LAWLESS. *Crown 8vo. 6s.*

E. W. Hornung. THE AMATEUR
CRACKSMAN. By E. W. HOR-
NUNG. *Crown 8vo. 6s.*
'An audaciously entertaining volume.'—
Spectator.
'Fascinating and entertaining in a supreme
degree.'—*Daily Mail.*
'We are fascinated by the individuality,
the daring, and the wonderful coolness
of Raffles the resourceful, and follow
him breathlessly in his career.'—*World.*

Jane Barlow. A CREEL OF IRISH
STORIES. By JANE BARLOW,

Author of 'Irish Idylls.' *S
Edition. Crown 8vo. 6s.*
'Vivid and singularly real.'—*Scotsma*

Jane Barlow. FROM THE
UNTO THE WEST. By J
BARLOW. *Crown 8vo. 6s.*
'The genial humour and never-failing
pathy recommend the book to those wi
like healthy fiction.'—*Scotsman.*

Mrs. Caffyn. ANNE MAULEVEREI
By Mrs. CAFFYN (Iota), Author
'The Yellow Aster.' *Second Edition
Crown 8vo. 6s.*
'The author leaves with us a most delec:
able addition to the heroines in moder
fiction, and she has established herse
as one of the leading women novelists o
the day.'—*Daily Chronicle.*
'A fine conception and absorbingly interesting.'—*Athenæum.*

Dorothea Gerard. THINGS THAT
HAVE HAPPENED. By DORO-
THEA GERARD, Author of 'Lady
Baby.' *Crown 8vo. 6s.*
'All the stories are delightful.'—*Scotsman.*

J. H. Findlater. THE GREEN
GRAVES OF BALGOWRIE. By
JANE H. FINDLATER. *Fourth
Edition. Crown 8vo. 6s.*
'A powerful and vivid story.'—*Standard.*
'A beautiful story, sad and strange as truth
itself.'—*Vanity Fair.*
'A very charming and pathetic tale.'—*Pall
Mall Gazette.*
'A singularly original, clever, and beautiful
story.'—*Guardian.*
'Reveals to us a new writer of undoubted
faculty and reserve force.'—*Spectator.*
'An exquisite idyll, delicate, affecting, and
beautiful.'—*Black and White.*

J. H. Findlater. A DAUGHTER
OF STRIFE. By JANE HELEN
FINDLATER. *Crown 8vo. 6s.*
'A story of strong human interest.'—*Scots-
man.*

J. H. Findlater. RACHEL. By
JANE H. FINDLATER. *Second
Edition. Crown 8vo. 6s.*
'Powerful and sympathetic.'—*Glasgow
Herald.*
'A not unworthy successor to "The Green
Graves of Balgowrie."'—*Critic.*

Mary Findlater. OVER THE
HILLS. By MARY FINDLATER.
Second Edition. Cr. 8vo. 6s.
'A strong and fascinating piece of work.'—
Scotsman.

'A charming romance, and full of incident. The book is fresh and strong.'—*Speaker.*

'A strong and wise book of deep insight and unflinching truth.'—*Birmingham Post.*

Mary Findlater. BETTY MUSGRAVE. By MARY FINDLATER. *Second Edition. Crown 8vo. 6s.*

'Handled with dignity and delicacy. . . . A most touching story.'—*Spectator.*

'Told with great skill, and the pathos of it rings true and unforced throughout.'—*Glasgow Herald.*

Alfred Ollivant. OWD BOB, THE GREY DOG OF KENMUIR. By ALFRED OLLIVANT. *Second Edition. Cr. 8vo. 6s.*

'Weird, thrilling, strikingly graphic.'—*Punch.*

'We admire this book. . . . It is one to read with admiration and to praise with enthusiasm.'—*Bookman.*

'It is a fine, open-air, blood-stirring book, to be enjoyed by every man and woman to whom a dog is dear.'—*Literature.*

B. M. Croker. PEGGY OF THE BARTONS. By B. M. CROKER, Author of 'Diana Barrington.' *Fourth Edition. Crown 8vo. 6s.*

Mrs. Croker excels in the admirably simple, easy, and direct flow of her narrative, the briskness of her dialogue, and the geniality of her portraiture.'—*Spectator.*

'All the characters, indeed, are drawn with clearness and certainty; and it would be hard to name any quality essential to first-class work which is lacking from this book.'—*Saturday Review.*

H. G. Wells. THE STOLEN BACILLUS, and other Stories. By H. G. WELLS. *Second Edition. Crown 8vo. 6s.*

'They are the impressions of a very striking imagination, which, it would seem, has a great deal within its reach.'—*Saturday Review.*

H. G. Wells. THE PLATTNER STORY AND OTHERS. By H. G. WELLS. *Second Edition. Cr. 8vo. 6s.*

'Weird and mysterious, they seem to hold the reader as by a magic spell.'—*Scotsman.*

Sara Jeanette Duncan. A VOYAGE OF CONSOLATION. By SARA JEANETTE DUNCAN, Author of 'An American Girl in London.' Illustrated. *Third Edition. Cr. 8vo. 6s.*

'A most delightfully bright book.'—*Daily Telegraph.*

'The dialogue is full of wit.'—*Globe.*

'Laughter lurks in every page.'—*Daily News.*

C. F. Keary. THE JOURNALIST. By C. F. KEARY. *Cr. 8vo. 6s.*

'It is rare indeed to find such poetical sympathy with Nature joined to close study of character and singularly truthful dialogue: but then "The Journalist" is altogether a rare book.'—*Athenæum.*

E. F. Benson. DODO: A DETAIL OF THE DAY. By E. F. BENSON. *Sixteenth Edition. Cr. 8vo. 6s.*

'A perpetual feast of epigram and paradox.'—*Speaker.*

E. F. Benson. THE VINTAGE. By E. F. BENSON. Author of 'Dodo.' Illustrated by G. P. JACOMB-HOOD. *Third Edition. Crown 8vo. 6s.*

'Full of fire, earnestness, and beauty.'—*The World.*

E. F. Benson. THE CAPSINA. By E. F. BENSON, Author of 'Dodo.' With Illustrations by G. P. JACOMB-HOOD. *Second Edition. Cr. 8vo. 6s.*

'The story moves through an atmosphere of heroism and adventure.'—*Manchester Guardian.*

Mrs. Oliphant. SIR ROBERT'S FORTUNE. By. Mrs. OLIPHANT. *Crown 8vo. 6s.*

Mrs. Oliphant. THE TWO MARYS. By Mrs. OLIPHANT. *Second Edition. Crown 8vo. 6s.*

Mrs. Oliphant. THE LADY'S WALK. By Mrs. OLIPHANT. *Second Edition. Crown 8vo. 6s.*

W. E. Norris. MATTHEW AUSTIN. By W. E. NORRIS, Author of 'Mademoiselle de Mersac,' etc. *Fourth Edition. Crown 8vo. 6s.*

'An intellectually satisfactory and morally bracing novel.'—*Daily Telegraph.*

W. E. Norris. HIS GRACE. By W. E. NORRIS. *Third Edition. Crown 8vo. 6s.*

'Mr. Norris has drawn a really fine character in the Duke.'—*Athenæum.*

W. E. Norris. THE DESPOTIC LADY AND OTHERS. By W. E. NORRIS. *Crown 8vo. 6s.*

'A budget of good fiction of which no one will tire.'—*Scotsman.*

W. E. Norris. CLARISSA FURIOSA. By W. E. NORRIS. *Cr. 8vo. 6s.*
'As a story it is admirable, as a *jeu d'esprit* it is capital, as a lay sermon studded with gems of wit and wisdom it is a model.'—*The World.*

W. Clark Russell. MY DANISH SWEETHEART. By W. CLARK RUSSELL. *Illustrated. Fourth Edition. Crown 8vo. 6s.*

Robert Barr. IN THE MIDST OF ALARMS. By ROBERT BARR. *Third Edition. Cr. 8vo. 6s.*
'A book which has abundantly satisfied us by its capital humour.'—*Daily Chronicle.* Mr. Barr has achieved a triumph.'—*Pall Mall Gazette.*

Robert Barr. THE MUTABLE MANY. By ROBERT BARR. *Second Edition. Crown 8vo. 6s.*
'Very much the best novel that Mr. Barr has yet given us. There is much insight in it, and much excellent humour.'—*Daily Chronicle.*

Robert Barr. THE COUNTESS TEKLA. By ROBERT BARR. *Second Edition. Crown 8vo. 6s.*
'Thrilling and brilliant.'—*Critic.*
'Such a tale as Mr. Barr's would ever receive a hearty welcome. Of these mediæval romances, which are now gaining ground, "The Countess Tekla" is the very best we have seen. The story is written in clear English, and a picturesque, moving style.'—*Pall Mall Gazette.*

Andrew Balfour. BY STROKE OF SWORD. By ANDREW BALFOUR. Illustrated. *Fourth Edition. Cr. 8vo. 6s.*
A banquet of good things.'—*Academy.*
'A recital of thrilling interest, told with unflagging vigour.'—*Globe.*
An unusually excellent example of a semi-historic romance.'—*World.*

Andrew Balfour. TO ARMS! By ANDREW BALFOUR. Illustrated. *Second Edition. Crown 8vo. 6s.*
'The marvellous perils through which Allan passes are told in powerful and lively fashion.'—*Pall Mall Gazette.*

R. B. Townshend. LONE PINE: A Romance of Mexican Life. By R. B. TOWNSHEND. *Crown 8vo. 6s.*
'It is full of incident and adventure. The great fight is as thrilling a bit of fighting as we have read for many a day.'—*Speaker.*

'The volume is evidently the work of a clever writer and of an educated and experienced traveller.'—*Athenæum.*

J. Maclaren Cobban. THE KING OF ANDAMAN: A Saviour of Society. By J. MACLAREN COBBAN. *Crown 8vo. 6s*
'An unquestionably interesting book. It contains one character, at least, who has in him the root of immortality.'—*Pall Mall Gazette.*

J. Maclaren Cobban. WILT THOU HAVE THIS WOMAN? By J. MACLAREN COBBAN. *Cr. 8vo. 6s.*

J. Maclaren Cobban. THE ANGEL OF THE COVENANT. By J. MACLAREN COBBAN. *Cr. 8vo. 6s.*
'Mr. Cobban has achieved a work of such rare distinction that there is nothing comparable with it in recent Scottish romance. It is a great historical picture, in which fact and fancy are welded together in a fine realisation of the spirit of the times.'—*Pall Mall Gazette.*

Marshall Saunders. ROSE À CHARLITTE: A Romantic Story of Acadie. By MARSHALL SAUNDERS. *Crown 8vo. 6s.*
'Graceful and well written.'—*Saturday Review.*
'Charmingly told.'—*Manchester Guardian.*

R. N. Stephens. AN ENEMY TO THE KING. By R. N. STEPHENS. *Second Edition. Cr. 8vo. 6s.*
'It is full of movement, and the movement is always buoyant.'—*Scotsman.*
'A stirring story with plenty of movement.'—*Black and White.*

Robert Hichens. BYEWAYS. By ROBERT HITCHINS. Author of 'Flames, etc.' *Second Edition. Cr. 8vo. 6s.*
'The work is undeniably that of a man of striking imagination.'—*Daily News.*

Percy White. A PASSIONATE PILGRIM. By PERCY WHITE, Author of 'Mr. Bailey-Martin.' *Cr. 8vo. 6s.*

W. Pett Ridge. SECRETARY TO BAYNE, M.P. By W. PETT RIDGE. *Crown 8vo. 6s.*

E. Dawson and A. Moore. ADRIAN ROME. By E. DAWSON and A. MOORE, Authors of 'A Comedy of Masks.' *Crown 8vo. 6s.*
'A clever novel dealing with youth and genius.'—*Academy.*

J. S. Fletcher. THE BUILDERS. By J. S. FLETCHER. Author of 'When Charles I. was King.' *Second Edition. Cr. 8vo. 6s.*

J. S. Fletcher. THE PATHS OF THE PRUDENT. By J. S. FLETCHER. *Crown 8vo. 6s.*
'The story has a curious fascination for the reader, and the theme and character are handled with rare ability.'—*Scotsman.*
'Dorinthia is charming. The story is told with great humour.'—*Pall Mall Gazette.*

J. B. Burton. IN THE DAY OF ADVERSITY. By J. BLOUNDELLE-BURTON. *Second Edition. Cr. 8vo. 6s.*
'Unusually interesting and full of highly dramatic situations. —*Guardian.*

J. B. Burton. DENOUNCED. By J. BLOUNDELLE-BURTON. *Second Edition. Crown 8vo. 6s.*
'A fine, manly, spirited piece of work.'—*World.*

J. B. Burton. THE CLASH OF ARMS. By J. BLOUNDELLE-BURTON. *Second Edition. Cr. 8vo. 6s.*
'A brave story—brave in deed, brave in word, brave in thought.'—*St. James's Gazette.*

J. B. Burton. ACROSS THE SALT SEAS. By J. BLOUNDELLE-BURTON. *Second Edition. Crown 8vo. 6s.*
'The very essence of the true romantic spirit.'—*Truth.*

R. Murray Gilchrist. WILLOW-BRAKE. By R. MURRAY GIL-CHRIST. *Crown 8vo. 6s.*
'It is a singularly pleasing and eminently wholesome volume, with a decidedly charming note of pathos at various points.'—*Athenæum.*

W. C. Scully. THE WHITE HECATOMB. By W. C. SCULLY, Author of 'Kafir Stories.' *Cr. 8vo. 6s.*
'Reveals a marvellously intimate understanding of the Kaffir mind.'—*African Critic.*

W. C. Scully. BETWEEN SUN AND SAND. By W. C. SCULLY, Author of 'The White Hecatomb.' *Cr. 8vo. 6s.*
'The reader passes at once into the very atmosphere of the African desert: the inexpressible space and stillness swallow him up, and there is no world for him but that immeasurable waste.'—*Athenæum.*

M. M. Dowie. GALLIA. By MÉNIE MURIEL DOWIE, Author of 'A Girl in the Karpathians.' *Third Edition. Cr. 8vo. 6s.*

M. M. Dowie. THE CROOK OF THE BOUGH. By MÉNIE MURIEL DOWIE. *Cr. 8vo. 6s.*

Julian Corbett. A BUSINESS IN GREAT WATERS. By JULIAN CORBETT. *Second Edition. Cr. 8vo. 6s.*

OTHER SIX-SHILLING NOVELS
Crown 8vo.

MISS ERIN. By M. E. FRANCIS.

ANANIAS. By the Hon. Mrs. ALAN BRODRICK.

CORRAGEEN IN '98. By Mrs. ORPEN.

THE PLUNDER PIT. By J. KEIGHLEY SNOWDEN.

CROSS TRAILS. By VICTOR WAITE.

SUCCESSORS TO THE TITLE. By Mrs. WALFORD.

KIRKHAM'S FIND. By MARY GAUNT.

DEADMAN'S. By MARY GAUNT.

CAPTAIN JACOBUS: A ROMANCE OF THE ROAD. By L. COPE CORNFORD.

SONS OF ADVERSITY. By L. COPE CORNFORD.

THE KING OF ALBERIA. By LAURA DAINTREY.

THE DAUGHTER OF ALOUETTE. By MARY A. OWEN.

CHILDREN OF THIS WORLD. By ELLEN F. PINSENT.

AN ELECTRIC SPARK. By G. MANVILLE FENN.

UNDER SHADOW OF THE MISSION. By L. S. McCHESNEY.

THE SPECULATORS. By J. F. BREWER.

THE SPIRIT OF STORM. By RONALD ROSS.

THE QUEENSBERRY CUP. By CLIVE P. WOLLEY.

A HOME IN INVERESK. By T. L. PATON.

MISS ARMSTRONG'S AND OTHER CIRCUMSTANCES. By JOHN DAVIDSON.

DR. CONGALTON'S LEGACY. By HENRY JOHNSTON.

TIME AND THE WOMAN. By RICHARD PRYCE.

THIS MAN'S DOMINION. By the Author of 'A High Little World.'

DIOGENES OF LONDON. By H. B. MARRIOTT WATSON.

THE STONE DRAGON. By MURRAY GILCHRIST.

A VICAR'S WIFE. By EVELYN DICKINSON.

ELSA. By E. M'QUEEN GRAY.

THE SINGER OF MARLY. By L HOOPER.

THE FALL OF THE SPARROW. By M. C. BALFOUR.

A SERIOUS COMEDY. By HERBERT MORRAH.

THE FAITHFUL CITY. By HERBERT MORRAH.

IN THE GREAT DEEP. By J. A. BARRY.

BIJLI, THE DANCER. By JAMES BLYTHE PATTON.

JOSIAH'S WIFE. By NORMA LORIMER.

THE PHILANTHROPIST. By LUCY MAYNARD.

VAUSSORE. By FRANCIS BRUNE.

THREE-AND-SIXPENNY NOVELS

Crown 8vo.

DERRICK VAUGHAN, NOVELIST. 42nd thousand. By EDNA LYALL.

THE KLOOF BRIDE. By ERNEST GLANVILLE.

A VENDETTA OF THE DESERT. By W. C. SCULLY.

SUBJECT TO VANITY. By MARGARET BENSON.

THE SIGN OF THE SPIDER. By BERTRAM MITFORD.

THE MOVING FINGER. By MARY GAUNT.

JACO TRELOAR. By J. H. PEARCE.

THE DANCE OF THE HOURS. By 'VERA.'

A WOMAN OF FORTY. By ESMÉ STUART.

A CUMBERER OF THE GROUND. By CONSTANCE SMITH.

THE SIN OF ANGELS. By EVELYN DICKINSON.

AUT DIABOLUS AUT NIHIL. By X. L.

THE COMING OF CUCULAIN. By STANDISH O'GRADY.

THE GODS GIVE MY DONKEY WINGS. By ANGUS EVAN ABBOTT.

THE STAR GAZERS. By G. MANVILLE FENN.

THE POISON OF ASPS. By R. ORTON PROWSE.

THE QUIET MRS. FLEMING. By R. PRYCE.

DISENCHANTMENT. By F. MABEL ROBINSON.

THE SQUIRE OF WANDALES. By A. SHIELD.

A REVEREND GENTLEMAN. By J. M. COBBAN.

A DEPLORABLE AFFAIR. By W. E. NORRIS.

A CAVALIER'S LADYE. By Mrs. DICKER.

THE PRODIGALS. By Mrs. OLIPHANT.

THE SUPPLANTER. By P. NEUMANN.

A MAN WITH BLACK EYELASHES. By H. A. KENNEDY.

A HANDFUL OF EXOTICS. By S. GORDON.

AN ODD EXPERIMENT. By HANNAH LYNCH.

TALES OF NORTHUMBRIA. By HOWARD PEASE.

HALF-CROWN NOVELS
Crown 8vo.

HOVENDEN, V.C. By F. MABEL ROBINSON.

THE PLAN OF CAMPAIGN. By F. MABEL ROBINSON.

MR. BUTLER'S WARD. By F. MABEL ROBINSON.

ELI'S CHILDREN. By G. MANVILLE FENN.

A DOUBLE KNOT. By G. MANVILLE FENN.

DISARMED. By M. BETHAM EDWARDS.

A MARRIAGE AT SEA. By W. CLARK RUSSELL.

IN TENT AND BUNGALOW. By the Author of 'Indian Idylls.'

MY STEWARDSHIP. By E. M'QUEEN GRAY.

JACK'S FATHER. By W. E. NORRIS.

A LOST ILLUSION. By LESLIE KEITH.

THE TRUE HISTORY OF JOSHUA DAVIDSON, Christian and Communist. By E. LYNN LYNTON. *Eleventh Edition. Post 8vo. 1s.*

Books for Boys and Girls

A Series of Books by well-known Authors, well illustrated.

THREE-AND-SIXPENCE EACH

THE ICELANDER'S SWORD. By S. BARING GOULD.

TWO LITTLE CHILDREN AND CHING. By EDITH E. CUTHELL.

TODDLEBEN'S HERO. By M. M. BLAKE.

ONLY A GUARD-ROOM DOG. By EDITH E. CUTHELL.

THE DOCTOR OF THE JULIET. By HARRY COLLINGWOOD.

MASTER ROCKAFELLAR'S VOYAGE. By W. CLARK RUSSELL.

SYD BELTON: Or, The Boy who would not go to Sea. By G. MANVILLE FENN.

THE WALLYPUG IN LONDON. By G. E. FARROW.

ADVENTURES IN WALLYPUG LAND. By G. E. FARROW. 5s.

The Peacock Library

A Series of Books for Girls by well-known Authors, handsomely bound, and well illustrated.

THREE-AND-SIXPENCE EACH

A PINCH OF EXPERIENCE. By L. B. WALFORD.

THE RED GRANGE. By Mrs. MOLESWORTH.

THE SECRET OF MADAME DE MONLUC. By the Author of 'Mdle. Mori.'

OUT OF THE FASHION. B L. T. MEADE.

DUMPS. By Mrs. PARR.

A GIRL OF THE PEOPLE. By L. T. MEADE.

HEPSY GIPSY. By L. T. MEADE. 2s. 6d.

THE HONOURABLE MISS. By L. T. MEADE.

MY LAND OF BEULAH. By Mrs. LEITH ADAMS.

University Extension Series

A series of books on historical, literary, and scientific subjects, suitable for extension students and home-reading circles. Each volume is complete in itself, and the subjects are treated by competent writers in a broad and philosophic spirit.

Edited by J. E. SYMES, M.A.,
Principal of University College, Nottingham.

Crown 8vo.   Price (with some exceptions) 2s. 6d.

The following volumes are ready :—

THE INDUSTRIAL HISTORY OF ENGLAND. By H. DE B. GIBBINS, Litt. D., M.A., late Scholar of Wadham College, Oxon., Cobden Prizeman. *Sixth Edition, Revised. With Maps and Plans.* 3s.

A HISTORY OF ENGLISH POLITICAL ECONOMY. By L. L. PRICE, M.A., Fellow of Oriel College, Oxon. *Second Edition.*

PROBLEMS OF POVERTY : An Inquiry into the Industrial Conditions of the Poor. By J. A. HOBSON, M.A. *Fourth Edition.*

VICTORIAN POETS. By A. SHARP.

THE FRENCH REVOLUTION. By J. E. SYMES, M.A.

PSYCHOLOGY. By F. S. GRANGER, M.A. *Second Edition.*

THE EVOLUTION OF PLANT LIFE : Lower Forms. By G. MASSEE. *With Illustrations.*

AIR AND WATER. By V. B. LEWES, M.A. *Illustrated.*

THE CHEMISTRY OF LIFE AND HEALTH. By C. W. KIMMINS, M.A. *Illustrated.*

THE MECHANICS OF DAILY LIFE. By V. P. SELLS, M.A. *Illustrated.*

ENGLISH SOCIAL REFORMERS. By H. DE B. GIBBINS, D. Litt., M.A.

ENGLISH TRADE AND FINANCE IN THE SEVENTEENTH CENTURY. By W. A. S. HEWINS, B.A.

THE CHEMISTRY OF FIRE. The Elementary Principles of Chemistry. By M. M. PATTISON MUIR, M.A. *Illustrated.*

A TEXT-BOOK OF AGRICULTURAL BOTANY. By M. C. POTTER, M.A., F.L.S. *Illustrated.* 3s. 6d.

THE VAULT OF HEAVEN. A Popular Introduction to Astronomy. By R. A. GREGORY. *With numerous Illustrations.*

METEOROLOGY. The Elements of Weather and Climate. By H. N. DICKSON, F.R.S.E., F.R. Met. Soc. *Illustrated.*

A MANUAL OF ELECTRICAL SCIENCE. By GEORGE J. BURCH, M.A. *With numerous Illustrations.* 3s.

THE EARTH. An Introduction to Physiography. By EVAN SMALL, M.A. *Illustrated.*

INSECT LIFE. By F. W. THEOBALD, M.A. *Illustrated.*

ENGLISH POETRY FROM BLAKE TO BROWNING. By W. M. DIXON, M.A.

ENGLISH LOCAL GOVERNMENT. By E. JENKS, M.A., Professor of Law at University College, Liverpool.

THE GREEK VIEW OF LIFE. By G. L. DICKINSON, Fellow of King's College, Cambridge. *Second Edition.*

Social Questions of To-day

Edited by H. DE B. GIBBINS, Litt. D., M.A.

Crown 8vo.   2s. 6d.

A series of volumes upon those topics of social, economic, and industrial interest that are at the present moment foremost in the public mind. Each volume of the series is written by an author who is an acknowledged authority upon the subject with which he deals.

The following Volumes of the Series are ready :—

TRADE UNIONISM—NEW AND OLD. By G. HOWELL. *Second Edition.*

THE CO-OPERATIVE MOVEMENT TO-DAY. By G. J. HOLYOAKE. *Second Edition.*

MUTUAL THRIFT. By Rev. J. FROME WILKINSON, M.A.

PROBLEMS OF POVERTY. By J. A. HOBSON, M.A. *Fourth Edition.*

THE COMMERCE OF NATIONS. By C. F. BASTABLE, M.A., Professor of Economics at Trinity College, Dublin. *Second Edition.*

THE ALIEN INVASION. By W. H. WILKINS, B.A.

THE RURAL EXODUS. By P. ANDERSON GRAHAM.

LAND NATIONALIZATION. By HAROLD COX, B.A.

A SHORTER WORKING DAY. By H. DE B. GIBBINS, D. Litt., M.A., and R. A. HADFIELD, of the Hecla Works, Sheffield.

BACK TO THE LAND: An Inquiry into the Cure for Rural Depopulation. By H. E. MOORE.

TRUSTS, POOLS AND CORNERS. By J. STEPHEN JEANS.

THE FACTORY SYSTEM. By R. W. COOKE-TAYLOR.

THE STATE AND ITS CHILDREN. By GERTRUDE TUCKWELL.

WOMEN'S WORK. By LADY DILKE, Miss BULLEY, and Miss WHITLEY.

MUNICIPALITIES AT WORK. The Municipal Policy of Six Great Towns, and its Influence on their Social Welfare. By FREDERICK DOLMAN.

SOCIALISM AND MODERN THOUGHT. By M. KAUFMANN.

THE HOUSING OF THE WORKING CLASSES. By E. BOWMAKER.

MODERN CIVILIZATION IN SOME OF ITS ECONOMIC ASPECTS. By W. CUNNINGHAM, D.D., Fellow of Trinity College, Cambridge.

THE PROBLEM OF THE UNEMPLOYED. By J. A. HOBSON, B.A.

LIFE IN WEST LONDON. By ARTHUR SHERWELL, M.A. *Second Edition.*

RAILWAY NATIONALIZATION. By CLEMENT EDWARDS.

WORKHOUSES AND PAUPERISM. By LOUISA TWINING.

UNIVERSITY AND SOCIAL SETTLEMENTS. By W. REASON, M.A.

Classical Translations

Edited by H. F. FOX, M.A., Fellow and Tutor of Brasenose College, Oxford.

ÆSCHYLUS — Agamemnon, Chöephoroe, Eumenides. Translated by LEWIS CAMPBELL, LL.D., late Professor of Greek at St. Andrews. 5s.

CICERO—De Oratore I. Translated by E. N. P. MOOR, M.A. 3s. 6d.

CICERO—Select Orations (Pro Milone, Pro Murena, Philippic II., In Catilinam). Translated by H. E. D.

BLAKISTON, M.A., Fellow and Tutor of Trinity College, Oxford. 5s.

CICERO—De Natura Deorum. Translated by F. BROOKS, M.A., late Scholar of Balliol College, Oxford. 3s. 6d.

HORACE: THE ODES AND EPODES. Translated by A.

GODLEY, M.A., Fellow of Magdalen College, Oxford. 2s.

LUCIAN—Six Dialogues (Nigrinus, Icaro - Menippus, The Cock, The Ship, The Parasite, The Lover of Falsehood). Translated by S. T. IRWIN, M.A., Assistant Master at Clifton; late Scholar of Exeter College, Oxford. 3s. 6d.

SOPHOCLES — Electra and Ajax. Translated by E. D. A. MORSHEAD, M.A., Assistant Master at Winchester. 2s. 6d.

TACITUS—Agricola and Germania. Translated by R. B. TOWNSHEND, late Scholar of Trinity College, Cambridge. 2s. 6d.

Educational Books

CLASSICAL

PLAUTI BACCHIDES. Edited with Introduction, Commentary, and Critical Notes by J. M'COSH, M.A. Fcap. 4to. 12s. 6d.

PASSAGES FOR UNSEEN TRANSLATION. By E. C. MARCHANT, M.A., Fellow of Peterhouse, Cambridge; and A. M. COOK, M.A., late Scholar of Wadham College, Oxford; Assistant Masters at St. Paul's School. Crown 8vo. 3s. 6d.

' We know no book of this class better fitted for use in the higher forms of schools.'— Guardian.

TACITI AGRICOLA. With Introduction, Notes, Map, etc. By R. F. DAVIS, M.A., Assistant Master at Weymouth College. Crown 8vo. 2s.

TACITI GERMANIA. By the same Editor. Crown 8vo. 2s.

HERODOTUS: EASY SELECTIONS. With Vocabulary. By A. C. LIDDELL, M.A. Fcap. 8vo. 1s. 6d.

SELECTIONS FROM THE ODYSSEY. By E. D. STONE, M.A., late

Assistant Master at Eton. Fcap. 8vo. 1s. 6d.

PLAUTUS: THE CAPTIVI. Adapted for Lower Forms by J. H. FREESE, M.A., late Fellow of St. John's, Cambridge. 1s. 6d.

DEMOSTHENES AGAINST CONON AND CALLICLES. Edited with Notes and Vocabulary, by F. DARWIN SWIFT, M.A. Fcap. 8vo. 2s.

EXERCISES IN LATIN ACCIDENCE. By S. E. WINBOLT, Assistant Master in Christ's Hospital. Crown 8vo. 1s. 6d.

An elementary book adapted for Lower Forms to accompany the shorter Latin Primer.

NOTES ON GREEK AND LATIN SYNTAX. By G. BUCKLAND GREEN, M.A., Assistant Master at Edinburgh Academy, late Fellow of St. John's College, Oxon. Crown 8vo. 3s. 6d.

Notes and explanations on the chief difficulties of Greek and Latin Syntax, with numerous passages for exercise.

GERMAN

A COMPANION GERMAN GRAMMAR. By H. DE B. GIBBINS, D.Litt., M.A., Assistant Master at Nottingham High School. Crown 8vo. 1s. 6d.

GERMAN PASSAGES FOR UNSEEN TRANSLATION. By E. M'QUEEN GRAY. Crown 8vo. 2s. 6d.

SCIENCE

THE WORLD OF SCIENCE. Including Chemistry, Heat, Light, Sound, Magnetism, Electricity, Botany, Zoology, Physiology, Astronomy, and Geology. By R. ELLIOTT STEEL, M.A., F.C.S. 147 Illustrations. Second Edition. Cr. 8vo. 2s. 6d.

ELEMENTARY LIGHT. By R. E.

STEEL. With numerous Illustrations. Crown 8vo. 4s. 6d.

VOLUMETRIC ANALYSIS. By J. B. RUSSELL, B.Sc., Science Master at Burnley Grammar School. Cr. 8vo. 1s. 6d.

' A collection of useful, well-arranged notes.' —School Guardian.

ENGLISH

ENGLISH RECORDS. A Companion to the History of England. By H. E. MALDEN, M.A. *Crown 8vo.* 3s. 6d.
A book which aims at concentrating information upon dates, genealogy officials, constitutional documents, etc., which is usually found scattered in different volumes.

THE ENGLISH CITIZEN: HIS RIGHTS AND DUTIES. By H. E. MALDEN, M.A. 1s. 6d.

A DIGEST OF DEDUCTIVE LOGIC. By JOHNSON BARKER, B.A. *Crown 8vo.* 2s. 6d.

A CLASS-BOOK OF DICTATION PASSAGES. By W. WILLIAMSON, M.A. *Second Edition, Crown 8vo.* 1s. 6d.

TEST CARDS IN EUCLID AND ALGEBRA. By D. S. CALDERWOOD, Headmaster of the Normal School, Edinburgh. In three packets of 40, with Answers. 1s.

METHUEN'S COMMERCIAL SERIES

Edited by H. DE B. GIBBINS, Litt. D., M.A.

BRITISH COMMERCE AND COLONIES FROM ELIZABETH TO VICTORIA. By H. DE B. GIBBINS, Litt.D., M.A. *Third Edition.* 2s.

COMMERCIAL EXAMINATION PAPERS. By H. DE B. GIBBINS, Litt.D., M.A. 1s. 6d.

THE ECONOMICS OF COMMERCE. By H. DE B. GIBBINS, Litt.D., M.A. 1s. 6d.

FRENCH COMMERCIAL CORRESPONDENCE. By S. E. BALLY, Master at the Manchester Grammar School. *Second Edition.* 2s.

GERMAN COMMERCIAL CORRESPONDENCE. By S. E. BALLY. 2s. 6d.

A FRENCH COMMERCIAL READER. By S. E. BALLY. 2s.

COMMERCIAL GEOGRAPHY, with special reference to the British Empire. By L. W. LYDE, M.A. *Second Edition.* 2s.

A PRIMER OF BUSINESS. By S. JACKSON, M.A. *Second Edition.* 1s. 6d.

COMMERCIAL ARITHMETIC. By F. G. TAYLOR, M.A. *Second Edition.* 1s, 6d.

PRÉCIS WRITING AND OFFICE CORRESPONDENCE. By E. E. WHITFIELD, M.A. 2s.

A GUIDE TO PROFESSIONS AND BUSINESS. By HENRY JONES. 1s. 6d.

WORKS BY A. M. M. STEDMAN, M.A.

INITIA LATINA: Easy Lessons on Elementary Accidence. *Third Edition. Fcap. 8vo.* 1s.

FIRST LATIN LESSONS. *Fifth Edition. Crown 8vo.* 2s.

FIRST LATIN READER. With Notes adapted to the Shorter Latin Primer and Vocabulary. *Fourth Edition revised.* 18mo. 1s. 6d.

EASY SELECTIONS FROM CÆSAR. Part I. The Helvetian War. *Second Edition.* 18mo. 1s.

EASY SELECTIONS FROM LIVY. Part 1. The Kings of Rome. 18mo. 1s. 6d.

EASY LATIN PASSAGES FOR UNSEEN TRANSLATION. *Sixth Edition. Fcap. 8vo.* 1s. 6d.

EXEMPLA LATINA. First Lessons in Latin Accidence. With Vocabulary. *Crown 8vo.* 1s.

EASY LATIN EXERCISES ON THE SYNTAX OF THE SHORTER AND REVISED LATIN PRIMER. With Vocabulary. *Seventh and cheaper Edition, re-written. Crown 8vo.* 1s. 6d. Issued with the consent of Dr. Kennedy.

THE LATIN COMPOUND SENTENCE: Rules and Exercises.

Crown 8vo. 1s. 6d. With Vocabulary. *2s.*

NOTANDA QUAEDAM : Miscellaneous Latin Exercises on Common Rules and Idioms. *Third Edition. Fcap. 8vo. 1s. 6d.* With Vocabulary. *2s.*

LATIN VOCABULARIES FOR REPETITION : Arranged according to Subjects. *Eighth Edition. Fcap. 8vo. 1s. 6d.*

A VOCABULARY OF LATIN IDIOMS. *18mo. Second Edition. 1s.*

STEPS TO GREEK. *18mo. 1s.*

A SHORTER GREEK PRIMER. *Crown 8vo. 1s. 6d.*

EASY GREEK PASSAGES FOR UNSEEN TRANSLATION. *Third Edition Revised. Fcap. 8vo. 1s. 6d.*

GREEK VOCABULARIES FOR REPETITION. Arranged according to Subjects. *Second Edition. Fcap. 8vo. 1s. 6d.*

GREEK TESTAMENT SELECTIONS. For the use of Schools. *Third Edition.* With Introduction, Notes, and Vocabulary. *Fcap. 8vo. 2s. 6d.*

STEPS TO FRENCH. *Fourth Edition. 18mo. 8d.*

FIRST FRENCH LESSONS. *Fourth Edition Revised. Crown 8vo. 1s.*

EASY FRENCH PASSAGES FOR UNSEEN TRANSLATION. *Third Edition revised. Fcap. 8vo. 1s. 6d.*

EASY FRENCH EXERCISES ON ELEMENTARY SYNTAX. With Vocabulary. *Second Edition. Crown 8vo. 2s. 6d.* KEY *3s. net.*

FRENCH VOCABULARIES FOR REPETITION : Arranged according to Subjects. *Seventh Edition. Fcap. 8vo. 1s.*

SCHOOL EXAMINATION SERIES

EDITED BY A. M. M. STEDMAN, M.A.   *Crown 8vo.   2s. 6d.*

FRENCH EXAMINATION PAPERS IN MISCELLANEOUS GRAMMAR AND IDIOMS. By A. M. M. STEDMAN, M.A. *Tenth Edition.*

A KEY, issued to Tutors and Private Students only, to be had on application to the Publishers. *Fourth Edition. Crown 8vo. 6s. net.*

LATIN EXAMINATION PAPERS IN MISCELLANEOUS GRAMMAR AND IDIOMS. By A. M. M. STEDMAN, M.A. *Ninth Edition.*

KEY (*Third Edition*) issued as above. *6s. net.*

GREEK EXAMINATION PAPERS IN MISCELLANEOUS GRAMMAR AND IDIOMS. By A. M. M. STEDMAN, M.A. *Fifth Edition.*

KEY (*Second Edition*) issued as above. *6s. net.*

GERMAN EXAMINATION PAPERS IN MISCELLANEOUS GRAMMAR AND IDIOMS. By R. J. MORICH, Manchester. *Fifth Edition.*

KEY (*Second Edition*) issued as above. *6s. net.*

HISTORY AND GEOGRAPHY EXAMINATION PAPERS. By C. H. SPENCE, M.A., Clifton College. *Second Edition.*

SCIENCE EXAMINATION PAPERS. By R. E. STEEL, M.A., F.C.S. *In two vols.*

Part I. Chemistry ; Part II. Physics.

GENERAL KNOWLEDGE EXAMINATION PAPERS. By A. M. M. STEDMAN, M.A. *Third Edition.*

KEY (*Second Edition*) issued as above. *7s. net.*

CPSIA information can be obtained
at www.ICGtesting.com
Printed in the USA
BVHW071708061118
532319BV00011B/701/P